Catalyst

Irene Wood

Published by Irene Wood, 2024.

This is a work of fiction. Similarities to real people, places, or events are entirely coincidental.

CATALYST

First edition. November 7, 2024.

Copyright © 2024 Irene Wood.

ISBN: 979-8227230898

Written by Irene Wood.

Chapter 1: Shadows in the Rain

The rain falls harder, fat droplets slicing through the air with a merciless precision, soaking into my clothes and making every breath feel heavy, damp, like breathing through fog. The streets gleam with slick cobblestone, reflecting the fractured neon signs from nearby clubs, where music pumps and laughter rises in bright, muffled snatches. But the alley I find myself in is darker, far from the careless joy of Bourbon Street revelers, and the shadows here are sharp-edged, lurking.

I grip the cold brick wall, pressing myself against it as I peer out from behind the corner. My heart pounds as the Enforcers sweep down the street, their dark uniforms stiff and immaculate despite the rain. I don't know what I expected, running like I did, but I know what'll happen if they catch me. They're relentless, the Enforcers, known to follow the scent of fear as bloodhounds do. A twitchy pulse of adrenaline fires through my veins, whispering, Run.

But just as I gather the nerve to slip out from my hiding place, a hand clamps onto my arm, yanking me back into the shadows. I stifle a cry, spinning around to face my assailant, fists raised, heart drumming an erratic beat. But the figure in front of me is no Enforcer, though he might as well be trouble incarnate.

Cole.

His familiar gaze—stormy, with flecks of gold that catch the light even in the dark—is locked on mine, and it takes every ounce of self-control not to lash out. This is the man who's had me pinned to the ground more times than I care to count, always a heartbeat away from a triumphant smirk, always outmaneuvering me in our endless rivalry. We're on opposite sides of a war with shifting loyalties and no clear winners, and I wouldn't trust him as far as I could throw him, but here we are.

"Quiet," he hisses, his voice a rough whisper that somehow finds its way under the pounding rain.

For a moment, I consider ignoring him, consider breaking free and taking my chances in the open, but then I catch a flicker of movement at the end of the alley. An Enforcer—red-slitted mask, unflinching in his stride—stops, scanning the area, and I know that one wrong move will have us both caught. I glance back at Cole, who's watching me, expression hard but somehow... patient. Like he's waiting for me to decide if I'm going to make this easy or difficult. Typical.

He doesn't release my arm, just eases back a little, keeping us both hidden in the folds of shadow. I can feel his breath, hot and steady, against my rain-chilled skin, and I almost laugh at the absurdity. We've faced off on rooftops, in abandoned warehouses, on crowded streets, each encounter charged with our refusal to back down. And now, with the thunder and the storm cloaking our voices, we're here, cornered together by fate or stupidity, maybe both.

"Are you planning to let me go anytime soon?" I murmur, though my voice betrays a note of irritation. I'm soaked to the bone, chilled, and frankly, exhausted from all this skulking about.

"Only if you promise not to run out there like a fool," he replies, his voice low but laced with a humor that grates on my nerves. "I'd hate to waste this moment of peace."

"Peace? Is that what we're calling it now?"

His lips twitch into something like a smirk, though he looks away, his focus shifting back to the Enforcers prowling the main road. We both know there's no peace between us, only a brittle truce in the face of something worse.

The rain begins to soften, though it still falls in lazy, unrelenting sheets. I take the chance to ease back, freeing my arm from his grasp, and feel an unexpected flash of loss when his fingers slip away.

Strange, how the briefest alliances can disarm you when you're not looking.

He catches my eye, his expression unreadable. "You didn't have to be here, you know. They're after you more than anyone."

"And yet here I am," I say, brushing a strand of wet hair from my face, as if I could sweep away the uncertainty that lingers between us. "Guess I have a penchant for risky decisions."

There's a flicker of something in his eyes, a glint that hints at understanding, or maybe even respect. It's an unsettling thought, that we might understand each other better than I'd care to admit. We've been circling each other like predators, each of us drawn to the danger the other represents, and somehow it feels like fate has pushed us together, daring us to see just how thin the line between enemy and ally really is.

"Let's say you manage to get out of here," he begins, shifting slightly to lean against the wall, arms crossed. "What then? Going to keep running until you're caught?"

I meet his gaze, refusing to let him see even a shred of hesitation. "If I have to," I reply, voice steadier than I feel. "Better than playing by their rules."

He chuckles, a low, rumbling sound that seems to vibrate through the damp air. "That stubborn streak will be the end of you, you know."

"Maybe." I shrug, feigning indifference, though I can't deny the gnawing truth of his words. The rain slows further, shifting to a mere drizzle, the storm's fury finally waning, as if it, too, is tired of this charade.

We linger in silence, the city's pulse echoing around us, louder now that the rain has eased. Somehow, without speaking, a truce forms between us, one that neither of us acknowledges but both of us feel. I realize that I don't want to slip away just yet, that there's something to be gained here in this quiet moment. The Enforcers drift down the street, their footsteps fading, leaving only Cole and me in our shadowed refuge.

The storm might be passing, but something in me senses that this is only the beginning, that fate has something in store I've yet to decipher. And as I stand there, shoulder to shoulder with a man I should despise, I feel a strange thrill—a glimmer of the unknown—that is somehow more frightening, and exhilarating, than anything I've faced before.

The rain has slowed to a whisper now, trailing down in thin rivulets that cling to the frayed edge of the awning above us, dripping onto the cobblestones below. Shadows flicker along the alley walls, shifting with every muted flash of distant lightning, and I realize I'm holding my breath, waiting for something to snap, to shift, to end this strange, quiet truce.

Cole shifts beside me, folding his arms, his gaze still fixed on the street beyond our hiding place. He doesn't say a word, and neither do I. It's almost comfortable, this silence, strange as that seems. But then, he breaks it, his voice low and edged with that dry humor that always leaves me guessing whether he's about to mock me or ask for a favor.

"You know," he says, his eyes drifting from the empty street back to me, "I could turn you in right now. Wouldn't even have to try that hard."

I roll my eyes, fighting the urge to shove him for the sheer satisfaction of it. "Funny, I was thinking the same thing about you."

He chuckles, a dark, rich sound that only makes me more irritated. "But you won't. And neither will I. So I guess that leaves us in a bit of a... predicament."

"A predicament," I echo, tasting the word like something bitter. "I'd call it more of an inconvenience."

He lets out a mock gasp, clutching a hand to his chest like I've wounded him. "An inconvenience? Here I thought I'd be the most thrilling thing you'd stumbled across tonight."

There's something dangerously charming in his voice, like a lure dipped just enough in humor to make it seem harmless. But I know better. Cole has never been harmless, not to me, and not to the city that pulses with life beyond our shelter. Still, there's a flicker of humor in his eyes that softens the usual edge of our rivalry, a warmth that makes me want to look away and keep watching, all at once.

"You're really going to make jokes right now?" I whisper, exasperated, but my tone is more resigned than angry. "The Enforcers aren't exactly known for their sense of humor. Or mercy."

"Ah, but that's why I have you," he murmurs, his gaze falling on me with something unsettlingly close to admiration. "Always so serious. You keep me grounded."

I stare at him, eyebrows raised, barely able to believe the audacity of this man. "We are not a team, Cole. This isn't some grand adventure where we go off into the night saving the world together."

He gives a small, almost imperceptible shrug, but his eyes remain locked on mine, unreadable. "Could've fooled me."

Before I can respond, a flicker of movement catches my eye—a shadow slipping along the rooftops above. Instinctively, I grab his arm, pulling him back, deeper into the alcove, and he doesn't resist. We both watch as another Enforcer rounds the corner, his heavy boots splashing through the lingering puddles, the scarlet slit in his mask pulsing faintly as he surveys the alleyway with robotic vigilance.

We're so close, I can feel Cole's breath on my neck, warm and steady, and despite everything, a strange calm settles over me. It's the silence before the storm, that single heartbeat of peace in a city that's forgotten what it means to rest. Cole's hand finds mine, his fingers curling around mine in an instinctive, protective gesture, and I'm not sure whether to pull away or hold on tighter.

The Enforcer stops, pausing just a few feet from where we're hidden, and I swear I can feel my heart hammering loud enough to betray us. For a split second, I wonder if he can hear it too. But then, just as quickly, he moves on, disappearing into the shadows as if he never existed. The moment passes, and I release the breath I hadn't realized I'd been holding.

"Well," Cole whispers, his voice low and taunting, "seems like we're in the clear. Unless, of course, you're planning on dragging me back here every time someone in black walks by."

I let out a huff of exasperation, releasing his hand and glaring at him. "Trust me, Cole, if I were going to drag you anywhere, it wouldn't be into an alley with the Enforcers on our heels."

He grins, that infuriating, too-charming grin that I've seen on the verge of victory one too many times. "Dare I ask where, then?"

"Oh, I don't know," I reply, sarcasm dripping from every word. "Perhaps straight into the swamp, where you belong?"

He raises an eyebrow, clearly unfazed. "I'll have you know I'm quite fond of swamps. Lots of character, you know? Can't say the same for some people around here."

I narrow my eyes at him, fully aware he's enjoying this far too much. "If you're implying that I lack character—"

"Me?" He laughs, a low, amused sound that grates at my patience. "I wouldn't dream of it. Besides, I think you've proven your... unique charm in abundance tonight."

Despite myself, I feel a reluctant smile tugging at the corner of my mouth, but I quickly suppress it. This is Cole, after all, my infuriating rival, my persistent thorn in the side. The fact that he's also somehow disarmingly charming in the middle of a rain-soaked alleyway doesn't change any of that.

"Look," I say, forcing the smile back into the depths of my frustration, "we both know we're stuck together for now, but once the Enforcers are gone, we go our separate ways. Agreed?"

He raises his hands in mock surrender, though his smirk betrays his amusement. "Agreed. But if you need a hand…"

I don't dignify that with a response, choosing instead to look back at the street. The rain has faded to a drizzle now, a soft patter that echoes in the quiet, abandoned alley. Part of me wants to slip away, to abandon this tenuous truce and leave him behind, but something about this strange encounter keeps me rooted to the spot, waiting.

Cole seems to feel it too, though he masks it with his usual bravado. "So," he says, glancing at me with a spark of mischief in his eyes, "what's next on your list of reckless decisions?"

"Probably one that doesn't involve you," I retort, folding my arms, but the jab lacks conviction. For some maddening reason, I can't shake the feeling that this isn't the last I'll see of him tonight. Or the last I'll want to.

He looks at me, his gaze softening, and for the briefest moment, I see something vulnerable in his expression, something that almost makes me believe we could be something other than enemies. But then, just as quickly, it's gone, replaced by that familiar smirk.

"Well, then," he says, stepping back into the street with a flourish, "I suppose this is where we part ways. Try not to get caught."

I watch him go, resisting the strange, inexplicable urge to call him back. Instead, I slip into the shadows, vanishing into the city's depths, a pulse of adrenaline and uncertainty beating with every step.

The rain-soaked streets melt into shadow as I make my way down the narrow, winding alleys of the French Quarter, each step echoing faintly against the damp cobblestones. The sounds of the city pulse around me, distant jazz notes weaving through the murmur of late-night revelers and the soft patter of rain as it fades to a mist.

I keep my pace steady, senses heightened, feeling every shift of air, every slight movement in the darkened corners of the city that feels more like home than I'd like to admit.

A sudden flash of lightning illuminates the alley, briefly throwing my surroundings into sharp relief. My breath catches as I spot a figure silhouetted against the light, tall and still, blocking my path with an air of effortless menace. I stop, pulse quickening as the shadows settle back around him. But even before I can fully make out his features, I know who it is. Cole, as infuriatingly calm as ever, leaning against the wall with a smirk I can feel more than see.

"Didn't think you'd be able to shake me that easily, did you?" he drawls, stepping out of the shadows and into the dim glow cast by a flickering streetlamp. His eyes gleam, dark and unreadable, and there's a challenge in his voice that sends a thrill of irritation through me.

"Honestly?" I fold my arms, raising an eyebrow. "I thought maybe I'd get five minutes of peace."

He chuckles, the sound low and rich, and takes a slow step toward me, his gaze never leaving mine. "Peace is overrated. Besides, I was curious."

"Curious," I echo, my voice flat. I don't bother hiding my skepticism. "About what, exactly?"

He tilts his head, studying me with that infuriating smirk. "Oh, I don't know. Why someone as... self-sufficient as you," he says, each word carefully measured, "seems to attract trouble like a magnet."

I let out a short laugh, crossing my arms tighter. "Maybe I just have terrible taste in company."

That earns me a glint of amusement from him, and he steps even closer, until there's barely a breath of space between us. The streetlamp above flickers, casting his face into sharp shadows, and for a moment, he looks almost dangerous. Almost.

"Is that so?" he murmurs, his voice dipping lower, softer, a hint of something unspoken lurking beneath his words.

I feel my pulse quicken despite myself, a reaction I instantly resent. It's maddening, the way he always manages to get under my skin with just a look, a smirk, a single word that could mean a hundred different things. But there's no way I'm going to let him know that.

"If you're done playing games," I say, forcing a cool tone, "maybe you could tell me why you're here. Because unless you have some grand plan to solve all of our problems, I really don't have time for whatever this is."

He raises an eyebrow, unimpressed, and his smirk deepens. "Who says I don't have a plan?"

I blink, taken aback for just a second, before I quickly regain my composure. "If you had a plan, you wouldn't be standing here, lurking in alleys, trying to look mysterious."

"Lurking?" He clutches his chest in mock offense, though the gleam in his eyes betrays his amusement. "I prefer to think of it as... waiting strategically."

I let out a frustrated sigh, shaking my head. "You're impossible."

"So I've been told," he says, unbothered, before his expression shifts, his gaze growing more serious. "But in all seriousness, I didn't come here just to annoy you."

"Oh, that's a relief," I say dryly, but something in his tone catches my attention, softening the edge of my sarcasm.

"There's something you need to know," he says, his voice so low it barely rises above a whisper. He glances around, his gaze sharp and alert, before he leans closer, lowering his voice even further. "You're not as safe as you think you are. The Enforcers aren't just after you for tonight. They're looking for something—someone—far more dangerous than either of us."

I stare at him, the words sinking in, heavy with unspoken meaning. "And you know this... how?"

He hesitates, just for a moment, his gaze flickering, as though weighing how much to tell me. It's a brief pause, almost imperceptible, but I catch it, and something in my gut tightens. He knows more than he's letting on—maybe even more than he should.

"I have... sources," he says finally, carefully avoiding my gaze. "Let's just say I have a vested interest in keeping certain information out of their hands."

A hundred questions burn on my tongue, but I hold them back. I've learned the hard way that Cole doesn't give anything away easily, and pushing him won't get me anywhere. Instead, I nod slowly, trying to make sense of his cryptic warning.

"So, what exactly do you expect me to do with this information?" I ask, trying to keep the frustration out of my voice.

He watches me for a moment, his gaze steady, unreadable. "Simple. You stay out of sight, out of trouble. Don't go looking for answers you don't need."

I narrow my eyes at him, not entirely convinced. "And what about you? Are you planning on following your own advice?"

A shadow of something—regret, maybe?—flickers across his face, gone almost before I can place it. "Let's just say I don't have the luxury of staying out of it."

Before I can respond, a sudden noise echoes down the alley, footsteps approaching, and we both freeze, instinctively stepping back into the shadows. My heart races as the footsteps draw closer, heavy and purposeful, and I feel Cole's hand grip my arm again, his fingers warm and steady against my chilled skin.

"Stay quiet," he whispers, his voice so close I can feel the warmth of his breath on my ear. I nod, swallowing hard, as we both press ourselves against the wall, barely daring to breathe.

The footsteps stop just a few feet away, and a chill runs down my spine as I recognize the familiar red-slit mask of an Enforcer, his gaze scanning the alley, lingering on every shadow, every corner. My heart thunders in my chest, the seconds stretching painfully as I wait, tense and motionless, praying he doesn't see us.

But then, without warning, the Enforcer steps forward, his gaze zeroing in on our hiding place. I feel Cole's hand tighten on my arm, his body tense, ready to move, and a surge of adrenaline floods my veins, hot and electric.

In a split second, he's pulling me forward, out of the alcove, our footsteps echoing as we dash down the narrow alley, the Enforcer's shout ringing out behind us. My pulse races as we sprint through the maze of streets, ducking around corners, slipping into the shadows wherever we can.

Finally, when we're far enough from the alley, we slow, both of us breathing hard, our faces flushed from the chase. I turn to Cole, heart pounding, eyes blazing with a mix of frustration and exhilaration.

"What... was that?" I manage to gasp, my breath coming in short, sharp bursts.

He meets my gaze, his own eyes glinting with a wild, reckless energy I've never seen before. "Consider it... my way of keeping things interesting."

Before I can respond, he grabs my hand, pulling me into another darkened alley, his grip firm and unyielding. I barely have time to protest before he presses me against the wall, his face inches from mine, his eyes blazing with an intensity that leaves me breathless.

"Listen to me," he says, his voice low and fierce. "They're not going to stop coming after you, not until they find what they're looking for. So if you want to survive, you're going to have to trust me."

I open my mouth to argue, to question, but his gaze holds mine, fierce and unrelenting, and for a moment, I feel the weight of his words settle over me, heavy and undeniable.

And then, before I can respond, the sound of footsteps echoes down the alley, closer this time, and Cole's expression hardens, his grip on my hand tightening as he pulls me back into the shadows, leaving me with a single, gut-twisting realization:

There's no turning back now.

Chapter 2: Dangerous Compromise

The café is damp, smelling faintly of burnt coffee grounds and something else, a cloying sweetness that sticks to the back of my throat. Cole picked the spot, naturally. I'm fairly certain he chose it specifically because it makes my skin itch, because it reminds me of places I swore I'd never return to. But here I am, fingers tapping on the scuffed tabletop, pretending not to care, pretending not to notice that I'm here with him, a man whose face I've cursed in more than one sleepless night. We're pretending a lot this morning, it seems.

He looks up, his eyes a shade too dark, studying me like he's weighing something he isn't quite ready to acknowledge. The file sits between us, thick and well-worn, its edges frayed from too many hands handling it. He catches me looking at it and arches an eyebrow.

"This is the part where you say thank you," he murmurs, voice low and laced with something that might have been humor if he weren't so damn insufferable.

I arch a brow back at him, trying to channel every ounce of my restraint into my tone. "Thank you for dragging me into a syndicate mess and putting a target on my back. I'm just thrilled to be here." I reach out, tugging the file toward me, feeling the weight of it, the promise of secrets trapped within the thin pages.

His smirk doesn't fade. He just leans back, crossing his arms, looking altogether too comfortable for a man who's supposedly as deep in this as I am. "Maybe you should be. You've been chasing the Enforcers for, what, two years now? And here I am, handing you the golden ticket."

The file lies open, but I don't flip through it yet. Instead, I study him, a sense of something that's both foreboding and strangely exhilarating winding tight in my stomach. Cole and I have always been on opposite sides of this twisted game—him, the Syndicate's slick, shadowy liaison, and me, the thorn in everyone's side, the one with just enough defiance and grit to make people in power uncomfortable. The thought that we're working together now feels as improbable as it is necessary, though every instinct in me screams that it's a dangerous compromise.

I finally look down at the file, the words blurring slightly in the dim light. But one name, one phrase, catches my eye immediately: Project Orion. Just seeing it in print makes my pulse stutter, and I feel a rush of adrenaline sharp as a blade.

"You're not serious." I lean back, crossing my arms in front of me, matching his casual posture with a tension that hums just beneath my skin. "Project Orion is a ghost story. A convenient fairy tale the Syndicate drags out to scare people like me off your scent."

Cole's expression hardens, the smirk wiped clean as he leans forward. "It's real. And it's far worse than any story you've heard." His voice drops, and for the first time, I catch a hint of something beneath his controlled veneer. Fear, maybe. "We both know the Enforcers don't just make mistakes—they erase them. Orion is their failsafe, and if you want any chance at taking them down, you're going to need every scrap of intel in that file. So, yes, I'm serious. Deadly serious."

The words settle over us, heavy and unyielding, and I feel the gravity of them pulling me under. My fingers tighten around the edge of the file as I imagine the data cache we're about to break into, the maze of corridors, the security systems. I see it in my mind's eye, layered and impossible, each step reminding me of everything I've lost to these people and everything I'm still fighting to regain.

And yet...Cole. He's still watching me, his gaze penetrating, waiting for a reaction, maybe some flicker of weakness he can exploit. It's a game he's good at, I'll give him that, but I'm not playing by his rules. Not today.

"What aren't you telling me?" I ask, keeping my voice measured. "You didn't drag me into this out of the goodness of your heart. So, what's the catch?"

He chuckles softly, but there's no warmth in it. "The catch, darling, is that if we get caught, the Syndicate won't even have to lift a finger to take you down. The Enforcers will do it for them. Orion's designed to weed out dissenters—troublemakers like you, like us. And let's just say they're very thorough."

A shiver runs down my spine, and I hate that he notices. He watches me too closely, like he's cataloging every flicker of doubt, every stray breath. It's unnerving, infuriating, and yet somehow, I can't look away.

"I don't need you, you know," I say, more for my own benefit than his. "I've gotten this far on my own."

"Oh, I know." His voice is a murmur, but it holds a strange sort of admiration. "But it's different this time. You can't take down an entire fortress without a little help."

There's a silence between us, a taut line neither of us wants to cross. And yet, it's clear there's only one way forward. My mind races through the options, the risks spiraling out like a web, each strand pulling me further into this mess. And for all my bravado, I can't deny the chill of fear curling in my chest.

He stands up suddenly, straightening his jacket and slipping his hands into his pockets. "We leave at midnight. Meet me by the docks. And, for what it's worth..." He hesitates, something unspoken hovering between us before he brushes it aside. "Don't trust anyone. Especially me."

He leaves the café with a casualness that's almost insulting, like he didn't just hand me a ticking time bomb wrapped in promises and lies. The door swings shut, leaving me alone with the file and a dozen questions that buzz in my mind like angry wasps.

As I sit there, staring at the flimsy pages that hold the answers I've been hunting for so long, a part of me knows I should walk away. I should leave the file on the table, walk out of the café, and disappear. I should run, but then, I never was very good at listening to reason.

The clock ticks toward midnight, and I find myself already planning, scheming, wondering what exactly lies in the shadows of that data cache—and just how much I'm willing to lose to find out.

Cole shows up at the docks, hands shoved deep in his coat pockets, the faint glow of a cigarette casting a ghostly halo around him in the mist. He's leaning against a rusted post, staring out over the water, the red light winking at intervals as he takes each slow, calculated drag. I could probably sneak up on him right now, knock him over the head, take the file, and disappear. But then I'd lose any edge he might have gained us by tonight. The truth is, as much as I hate to admit it, I need him. And he knows it.

He doesn't turn when I approach, only tilts his head slightly, acknowledging me without saying a word. The silence is heavy, stretching between us, weighted by a hundred things left unsaid. Finally, he tosses the cigarette into the water and straightens, giving me a once-over that feels far too familiar.

"Fashionably late," he says, lips curling in that infuriating smirk. "I was starting to think you might have bailed."

"Would've saved you the trouble," I shoot back, pulling my jacket tighter against the chill. "But I was curious. About you, mostly. What kind of idiot dives headfirst into a plan like this?"

"The kind with more to lose than he lets on," he murmurs, and for a moment, I catch a glimpse of something unguarded in his expression. But it's gone as quickly as it came, buried beneath that cool, inscrutable mask he wears so well.

We walk down the pier together, our footsteps echoing against the worn wood. The night is thick with fog, the kind that clings to your skin and seeps into your bones, making it hard to breathe. I can feel the tension radiating off him, a coiled spring ready to snap, and it makes me wonder just how much of this he's really prepared for.

"You sure you can handle this?" I ask, my voice low, probing.

He glances at me, a flicker of amusement in his eyes. "Worried about me already? We haven't even made it past the front door."

"You should be flattered. I don't usually waste my concern on people with shady allegiances."

"Then you're in luck. I'm only shady about fifty percent of the time." He holds out a hand, mockingly gallant, as though we're stepping into a grand ballroom rather than a syndicate stronghold where one wrong move could mean death.

I ignore the hand and step past him, my eyes already scanning the building looming ahead. It's exactly as imposing as I remember, a monolith of steel and concrete with a series of security cameras like dead eyes watching over the grounds. The front entrance is guarded, of course, by two men in black uniforms, their faces blank, expressions trained to give nothing away. And yet, as we slip into the shadows, I catch a flicker of something in their eyes—a hint of fear, perhaps. It's a comforting reminder that even the most loyal guard knows there are things in this world worth fearing.

Cole nudges me, his voice a whisper against my ear. "Our way in is through the service entrance around the back. Less security, and I've got the codes."

"Of course you do," I mutter, rolling my eyes. "How convenient."

"Convenience is my specialty," he says, and before I can stop him, he slips past me, disappearing into the shadows with a grace that's both infuriating and, annoyingly, impressive.

I follow him, moving quickly but carefully, my eyes darting around, searching for any sign of movement. The air is thick with the scent of wet metal and oil, the kind of stench that clings to everything in these industrial zones. The service entrance looms ahead, a single unassuming door tucked away in a corner, almost hidden by stacks of crates and barrels. Cole is already at the keypad, his fingers flying over the buttons with practiced ease. There's a soft click, and he pushes the door open, holding it for me with a smug smile.

"Ladies first."

I don't bother responding, slipping past him into the narrow corridor beyond. The walls are lined with pipes and wires, the air thick and stale, and every step echoes off the concrete floor, amplifying the sound until it feels like we're marching straight into the lion's den.

We move in silence, each of us hyper-aware of every sound, every shadow that could conceal a threat. The adrenaline is like a live wire in my veins, sharpening my senses, making every detail feel vivid and almost surreal. Cole's footsteps are barely audible behind me, a soft, steady rhythm that's oddly reassuring. It's strange, but in this moment, I feel an almost reluctant trust toward him, a bond forged not from loyalty but from the simple fact that he's the only one here with me in this madness.

We reach the end of the corridor, where another door waits, this one secured with a retinal scanner. Cole steps forward, his face illuminated briefly by the red glow as he presses his eye to the scanner. It beeps softly, the light turning green, and the door slides open with a low hiss. He gestures for me to follow, and as we step into the heart of the building, I can feel the weight of the place pressing down on me, a reminder of the power and ruthlessness the Syndicate wields.

The room is vast and cold, filled with rows of servers humming softly, their lights blinking in the darkness like a sea of stars. It's oddly beautiful, in a sterile, mechanical way, and for a moment, I almost forget where we are. But then Cole's voice snaps me back to reality, sharp and urgent.

"The data cache is in the central server. It's encrypted, but I've got the codes to bypass the first few layers of security." He glances at me, a glint of something like anticipation in his eyes. "Think you can handle the rest?"

I smirk, stepping forward to the console. "Just watch me."

My fingers move over the keyboard, the codes Cole provided flashing across the screen as I work, navigating through layer after layer of security. Each layer I break through feels like a small victory, a chink in the Syndicate's armor, and it sends a thrill through me, a reminder of why I do this, why I fight.

But just as I'm about to reach the final layer, an alarm blares, a harsh, shrill sound that slices through the air. My heart skips a beat, and I whirl around to see Cole's face, pale and tense, his eyes wide with alarm.

"Did you trip something?" I hiss, my voice barely audible over the blaring siren.

He shakes his head, his jaw clenched. "No. This isn't supposed to happen. Someone's onto us."

Panic flares in my chest, but I force it down, focusing on the console, on the last few keystrokes that will get us what we came for. I type faster, my fingers flying over the keys, racing against the clock, against the footsteps I can already hear pounding down the corridor.

With one final keystroke, the data cache opens, and I grab a flash drive from my pocket, plugging it into the console and downloading everything I can. The files transfer one by one, agonizingly slow, and I can feel Cole's tension behind me, his eyes darting to the door, waiting for the guards to burst in.

Just as the last file transfers, I yank the drive free, stuffing it into my pocket as Cole grabs my arm, pulling me toward the door. We sprint down the corridor, the alarms still blaring, the sound echoing off the walls, deafening in the confined space.

We burst out into the night, our breaths ragged, the fog thick around us.

Outside, the night is a swirl of mist and city lights, cold and sharp against our flushed skin. We dash through the maze of alleys, my legs burning, breath tearing from my chest as the sound of footsteps grows louder behind us. Cole's hand wraps around my arm, guiding me down a side street, the two of us blending into the shadows as a group of Enforcer guards rushes past, their flashlights cutting through the fog. I can feel the heat radiating off him, his grip firm and unyielding, and despite every instinct screaming that I shouldn't, I find myself leaning into his strength, trusting his pace, his silent, unspoken directions.

We duck into an abandoned warehouse, slipping through a broken door into darkness so complete I can't see an inch in front of me. Cole fumbles in his coat and pulls out a small flashlight, its narrow beam cutting a slice through the black, illuminating rows of old machinery covered in dust, a forgotten world hidden within the city's heart. The heavy, oily scent of metal hangs in the air, thick enough to taste, as if even the walls are hiding secrets.

"Nice place," I whisper, my voice barely carrying. "You take all your dates here?"

His laugh is soft, but it cuts through the tension like a knife. "Only the ones who can handle it," he murmurs, turning the light on me for the briefest moment, his gaze unreadable, before he sweeps it back toward the dark.

"Charming," I mutter, glancing around the shadowed interior. My pulse is still racing, the adrenaline refusing to fade, and I can feel a prickling sensation at the back of my neck, the familiar awareness that we're not out of danger yet. Not even close.

We weave through the maze of rusted equipment, our footsteps muffled by years of dust and grime. The silence presses down, making every creak and groan of the building feel amplified, like the ghosts of a thousand abandoned workers are watching us, waiting. Cole stops suddenly, holding up a hand, and I freeze, listening. A faint hum vibrates through the walls, barely audible, a steady, pulsing beat that makes the hairs on my arms stand on end.

"Generators," he mutters, his brow furrowing as he tilts his head, listening. "They shouldn't be on. This place has been closed for years."

"Fantastic," I whisper, the sarcasm laced with genuine unease. "What does that mean?"

He doesn't answer, just reaches for my hand, his fingers cold and unyielding around mine as he leads me deeper into the shadows. The pulsing grows louder, more insistent, each beat resonating like a countdown, and I can feel the panic building, an icy claw tightening around my chest. But I force myself to breathe, to focus on Cole's steady presence, the warmth of his hand a lifeline against the oppressive dark.

We reach the back of the warehouse, where a row of crates stands stacked against the wall, a makeshift barricade that looks suspiciously deliberate. Cole glances back at me, his expression shadowed and unreadable in the dim light.

"Help me," he murmurs, nodding toward the crates.

Together, we push them aside, revealing a narrow trapdoor embedded in the floor, almost invisible against the dark concrete. Cole kneels, prying it open, and a rush of cold air wafts up, tinged with the scent of damp earth and something metallic, something that sends a chill skittering down my spine.

"You've got to be kidding," I mutter, staring at the gaping hole. "A hidden passage? Seriously?"

He shoots me a wry look, one corner of his mouth lifting in a smirk. "What, you've never broken into an underground bunker before?"

I swallow back a retort, feeling the weight of the flash drive in my pocket, a reminder of why we're here, of the information we risked everything to steal. Without another word, I drop down into the darkness, my feet landing on cold, uneven stone. Cole follows, pulling the trapdoor shut above us, sealing us in a silence so thick I can almost feel it pressing against my skin.

The passage is narrow, lined with ancient brick that feels cold and damp under my fingers. Cole's flashlight casts eerie shadows along the walls, and I can hear the faint drip of water somewhere in the distance, echoing through the darkness. I focus on the rhythm of my footsteps, the steady beat grounding me, as we move deeper into the tunnel, the air growing colder, sharper with each step.

"Do you even know where we're going?" I ask, my voice barely above a whisper, half afraid to break the silence.

He glances back at me, his eyes catching the light in a way that makes him look almost... haunted. "More or less. Just... stay close."

I can't resist a small, bitter laugh. "Stay close, he says. Like I have anywhere else to go."

We walk in silence, the tension between us thick and unyielding, an unspoken acknowledgment of just how close we came to being caught, of the precariousness of this alliance. Every instinct in me screams that I shouldn't trust him, that the same man who just helped me escape could turn on me at any second. But as the passage winds deeper into the earth, I realize that, despite everything, I'm beginning to rely on him. And it terrifies me.

The tunnel opens into a cavernous room, the walls lined with old electrical panels and rows of dusty equipment that look like they haven't been touched in decades. I step forward, peering at the machinery, a strange sense of foreboding settling in my chest.

"What is this place?" I murmur, running a hand over a row of switches, their labels faded and worn.

Cole doesn't answer right away, just steps beside me, his gaze scanning the room with a mix of curiosity and something darker, something almost... nostalgic.

"This used to be one of the Syndicate's old hideouts," he says finally, his voice low. "Back in the day, before the Enforcers took over. It was abandoned years ago, but... I guess some things never really stay buried."

There's a quiet bitterness in his tone that I can't quite place, and for a moment, I feel the urge to ask, to dig deeper, to understand what it is he's not telling me. But before I can speak, a low rumble echoes through the room, a vibration that shakes the ground beneath our feet, sending dust cascading from the ceiling.

"Is that... normal?" I ask, heart pounding as the walls seem to shudder around us.

Cole's expression is grim, his gaze fixed on the far side of the room, where a set of heavy metal doors stands half-buried in rubble. "No. Not even a little bit."

As if in answer, the rumbling intensifies, a deafening roar that drowns out all other sound, and the ground beneath us gives a sudden, violent lurch. I stumble, catching myself against one of the panels as the room tilts, a massive crack splintering through the ceiling, sending a cascade of rocks and dust raining down.

"Move!" Cole's shout barely registers over the roar, but I push myself forward, sprinting toward the doors as the walls begin to collapse around us, the entire room trembling with the force of some unseen impact.

I reach the doors just as Cole throws them open, grabbing my arm and pulling me through as the ceiling caves in behind us, the air thick with dust and debris. We tumble into the darkness of another corridor, the sound of destruction echoing through the passageway as we scramble to our feet, breaths coming in short, panicked gasps.

And then, just as the dust begins to settle, a faint, metallic click echoes in the silence—a sound that sends a chill racing down my spine.

In the shadows ahead, a figure steps forward, their face obscured, a glint of steel catching the light as they raise a weapon, their voice cold and calm.

"Well, well," the voice drawls, a sinister edge lacing each word. "Didn't think I'd be welcoming guests tonight."

Chapter 3: Forbidden Territory

The mansion looms ahead of us, an ominous silhouette against the bruised evening sky, draped in a tangled mess of ivy and secrets. Each window glows faintly, golden halos that somehow seem more threatening than inviting. I cast a glance at Cole, his jaw clenched, eyes narrowing as he studies the mansion's formidable facade. He's looking at it the way a person might look at an old scar—resentment laced with an odd kind of familiarity. It's unsettling to think of all the things he might know about this place that I don't.

I keep my hand close to my side, a little wary every time our fingers brush as we inch closer. The touch, accidental or not, sends jolts through my veins, and I can't tell if it's adrenaline or something more dangerously addictive. He never turns, but I know he can feel it too, some invisible string stretching tighter between us every time we pass through another shadowed hallway.

"Stay close," he murmurs, barely a whisper, as if the mansion's walls might hear us.

"I wasn't planning on wandering off," I reply, trying to sound cavalier, but my voice is breathy. It betrays me, my attempt at sarcasm falling flat. He gives me a look, that half-amused, half-annoyed smirk that seems to say, You don't know what you've gotten yourself into. And he's right. But I'll be damned if I let him know that.

The interior is an opulent nightmare of glinting chandeliers and brooding portraits, capturing stern faces of long-dead patriarchs and matriarchs who seem to be watching us. We move past them, Cole's pace swift and deliberate, each step carrying us deeper into the labyrinthine corridors. He pauses only to take sudden, sharp turns or to pull me aside when the faint echo of footsteps draws near. A shiver creeps up my spine every time he yanks me into the shadows, our bodies pressed close, his breath warm and steady against my ear as we wait in silence. The guards pass, oblivious, and he lets go, his hand lingering a moment too long before he steps away.

"Are you sure you know where you're going?" I ask, my skepticism more of a defense mechanism than anything else.

"I'm sure," he replies, not even bothering to turn around. His confidence grates on me, but I follow anyway, like I always do. There's a history here, between him and this mansion, an intimacy in the way he avoids certain rooms and pushes open hidden doors that blend into the walls. And the questions multiply, twisting in my mind with every secret passage and every hushed movement.

Finally, we reach a room bathed in a strange amber light, and it's here that the nightmare takes on a new shape. A figure sits by the fireplace, their face cast in shadow, but the tension in the room makes it clear they've been expecting us. My stomach twists, my mind racing back through half-buried memories, ones I thought I'd left behind in a life I barely remember. But as soon as I see their profile catch the flickering light, recognition hits me like a punch to the chest.

It's someone I know, or at least, I once did. Someone I never thought I'd see again.

They turn slowly, their gaze sweeping over Cole, then landing on me. There's a flicker of something in their eyes—a glint that's both familiar and unnervingly foreign. Recognition, yes, but something sharper, something that makes my skin prickle.

"Well, well," they say, voice smooth and polished, as if we're sitting down for afternoon tea instead of sneaking through the belly of the beast. "I never thought you'd bring her here, Cole." Their words slither through the air, laced with a dark amusement that sets my nerves on edge.

Cole stiffens beside me, his easy confidence cracking for the first time since we set foot in this place. "This isn't what it looks like," he says, his voice strained.

"Oh, I know exactly what this is," the figure replies, leaning back with a languid grace that speaks of someone utterly in control. Their gaze shifts to me, appraising, dissecting. "You don't remember me, do you?"

The question cuts through the fog in my mind, stirring up fragments I thought I'd buried. Fleeting images of stolen moments, whispered conversations, and a trust that feels laughably naive now. I try to hold my ground, lifting my chin, refusing to let them see the fear coiling tight in my chest.

"I remember enough," I say, my voice coming out steadier than I feel.

They laugh, low and rich, as if I've just told the world's funniest joke. "Oh, darling, I doubt that. But you will. Soon enough."

Cole steps forward, his hand brushing against mine in a silent gesture of warning, or maybe reassurance—it's hard to tell. "This doesn't change anything," he says, his tone dangerously low. "We're leaving."

The figure raises an eyebrow, amusement still flickering in their eyes. "Leaving? Oh, no, I don't think you're quite done here yet. There's so much... unfinished business, wouldn't you say?" They lean in, voice dropping to a murmur meant only for me. "Especially you. You have no idea how much you left behind."

The words hit me like a slap, the weight of old mistakes and unspoken betrayals pressing down on my shoulders. My throat tightens, but I force myself to meet their gaze, to stand tall even as the foundations of my carefully constructed world begin to tremble.

Cole's hand wraps around mine, warm and solid, grounding me in the midst of this spiraling chaos. "We're done here," he says, his tone final, unyielding. "Come on."

I let him pull me away, our footsteps echoing in the quiet as we retreat from the room, but the figure's laughter follows us, a haunting reminder of what we've left behind. My mind races, questions spinning out of control, each one darker and more damning than the last.

"What was that?" I hiss once we're far enough away, my voice barely more than a whisper.

Cole doesn't answer right away, his expression closed off, guarded. "A complication," he says finally, his gaze flickering toward me with a glint of something unreadable. "One we'll have to deal with sooner or later."

I want to press him, to demand answers, but something in his expression stops me. There's a storm brewing beneath that calm facade, one I'm not sure I'm ready to face.

The silence between us is thick as we slip through another darkened corridor, lit only by the dim glow of wall sconces that cast our shadows long and sharp on the walls. Cole is leading us deeper into the mansion, his strides quick and purposeful, but I can feel the tension radiating from him, a barely restrained storm beneath the surface. My mind races with questions, but the weight of that figure's laughter still echoes in my ears, silencing my curiosity for now. It's unsettling, realizing that Cole might be holding back as much as I am.

We reach a narrow staircase hidden behind a tapestry—red velvet fraying at the edges, depicting some ancient battle scene where stoic knights face off against shadowy figures. It's ironic, really, how even the decor in this place seems to echo the battles being fought here, silently, in the corners and corridors. Cole pulls the tapestry aside and motions for me to follow, his expression unreadable as he watches me squeeze through the narrow entry.

The staircase winds down, tighter and steeper than I expected, leading us deeper underground. The air is colder here, laced with the faint, musty smell of stone and earth. Each step is an echo of the one before it, and I'm struck by how oddly familiar this feels, like a half-remembered dream. Maybe it's just the adrenaline, or maybe it's the shared understanding that we're venturing into something that can't be undone.

At the bottom, Cole pauses, his hand hovering over the worn iron handle of an unassuming door. He glances at me, a silent question in his eyes. I don't give him an answer, not verbally, but I raise my chin, daring him to open it. Whatever is on the other side, I'm ready.

The door swings open with a groan, revealing a small room lined with shelves packed full of ledgers and thick, leather-bound volumes. Papers are strewn across a heavy wooden desk, and a single candle flickers in the corner, casting a soft, trembling glow over everything. The sight is strangely anticlimactic, given the suspense of our journey here, but there's something about this room, some subtle undercurrent of danger, that makes me hesitate.

"This is where they keep the records," Cole says, his voice low as he steps inside, scanning the shelves with a practiced eye. He moves quickly, pulling down ledgers and flipping through them, his brow furrowing as he examines page after page. He's methodical, focused, every movement precise. It's impressive, I realize, how he knows exactly what he's looking for, exactly where to find it. And it's terrifying.

"Just how many times have you done this, Cole?" I can't help asking, my voice barely more than a whisper. The question slips out before I can stop myself, but once it's out there, I don't regret it. I need answers, and he knows it.

He pauses, glancing at me over his shoulder, his expression a strange mixture of reluctance and something that almost looks like regret. "More than I'd like to admit," he says finally, his voice flat. "But this is the last time. After tonight, we're done."

It sounds so simple, like he's making a promise he knows he'll keep. But I can't shake the feeling that it's not that easy, that whatever binds him to this place isn't something he can just walk away from.

He hands me a ledger, his fingers brushing mine as he does, sending an electric jolt up my arm. I focus on the book, flipping it open, trying to ignore the way my heart stutters. The pages are dense with rows of numbers and names, transactions documented in meticulous handwriting. It's a record of everything the Syndicate has ever done, every deal, every betrayal, laid out in cold, black ink. I scan the entries, my mind reeling as I piece together the enormity of it all. This isn't just a business; it's an empire built on secrets and lies, and we're standing right at its core.

And then, halfway down a page, I see something that makes my blood run cold.

My name.

Scrawled in delicate, looping script, surrounded by dates and figures that make no sense to me. But it's there, undeniable, staring back at me from the page like a ghost come to haunt me.

I feel Cole's presence at my side before I hear him speak. "They've been tracking you," he says, his voice a grim whisper. "For a long time."

"Why?" The word slips out, raw and desperate, laced with the fear I'm too tired to hide. I look at him, searching his face for answers, for some hint of the truth that's been kept from me.

But he doesn't look at me. His gaze is fixed on the ledger, his jaw clenched so tight I can see the muscles twitch. "Because you're more important to them than you realize," he says, finally meeting my eyes. There's something dark there, something almost protective, and it sends a chill through me.

I want to ask him more, to press him until he gives me something concrete, something that will make all of this make sense. But there's a sound from the corridor—a soft scrape, the unmistakable whisper of footsteps approaching. We both freeze, instincts kicking in as we move toward the shadows, pressing ourselves against the wall just as the door creaks open.

A figure steps inside, hooded and silent, moving with a fluid grace that sends alarm bells ringing in my head. Cole's hand tightens on my arm, a silent command to stay still, to stay quiet. But the figure pauses, tilting their head slightly as if sensing our presence.

"Come out, come out, wherever you are," the figure singsongs, their voice sickly sweet and dripping with menace. It's a voice I recognize, one that belongs to someone I'd hoped never to see again. My heart pounds, but I force myself to stay calm, to stay hidden, though every instinct screams at me to run.

Cole's hand slips down to his side, reaching for the knife I know he keeps hidden there. I grab his wrist, shaking my head, my heart hammering with the knowledge that if we make even the smallest sound, we're dead.

The figure takes another step into the room, glancing around, their eyes narrow and calculating. For a moment, they're close enough that I can see the scar running down the side of their face, a jagged line that splits their otherwise flawless skin. They scan the room one last time, muttering something under their breath, before finally turning and slipping back into the corridor.

I let out a breath I didn't realize I'd been holding, my body sagging against the wall in relief. But Cole doesn't relax; his gaze remains fixed on the door, his expression unreadable. I can feel the weight of what just happened settling between us, a silent acknowledgment that we've just crossed a line we can't come back from.

"What now?" I ask, my voice barely above a whisper.

He looks at me, his eyes dark, a storm gathering behind them. "Now we run."

We bolt from the records room, footsteps muffled by thick carpets as we retrace our path through the labyrinth of hallways. I clutch the ledger to my chest, the weight of it pressing against my ribs as if it's alive, a beast that breathes secrets and complications. Cole's face is a storm cloud, all shadows and fury, his jaw clenched in a way that tells me he's fighting to keep his temper on a leash. For once, I'm grateful for his anger. It's what's driving him, and right now, I need him focused.

The mansion feels even darker now, the air thicker with each step. Every creak of the floorboards, every distant whisper of a voice sounds like a warning, a reminder that we're trespassers in a place that belongs to ghosts and memories. I steal glances at Cole, hoping to catch some sign of what he's thinking, but his face is carved from stone, his eyes fixed forward. I want to ask him where we're going, but the tension in his body tells me to stay silent.

We reach a side door, almost invisible in the wall, and he pushes it open, leading us out into a narrow courtyard. A damp breeze hits my face, carrying the scent of wet earth and something metallic, a reminder of the past violence that lingers here. The sky is pitch-black, moonless, and the stars blink down at us like disapproving witnesses.

"Where now?" I finally whisper, glancing nervously at the shadows that stretch across the cobblestones. It feels like the walls have ears, like every word spoken here has a way of making its way back to the wrong people.

He doesn't answer, just nods toward a cluster of trees at the far end of the courtyard. We slip across the open space, every sense on high alert, my heart pounding loud enough that I'm convinced it'll give us away. I can feel his hand hovering near mine as we move, and there's a strange comfort in that, even now, with danger nipping at our heels.

As we reach the edge of the courtyard, a new sound reaches us—a low murmur of voices, laughter carried on the wind. Cole's hand tightens around mine, pulling me back into the shadows just as two figures appear from the opposite side of the courtyard. They're dressed in dark, tailored suits, faces obscured by the dim light, but there's no mistaking the relaxed confidence in their posture. These aren't just guards. They're higher up, the kind who would have access to the Syndicate's secrets. The kind who would recognize us.

Cole tenses beside me, and for a brief, insane moment, I wonder if he's considering taking them on, two against one. I give his hand a warning squeeze, and he glances down at me, his expression softening just a fraction. He knows better. We both do.

The men linger in the courtyard, their voices drifting toward us in fragments.

"...can't believe they actually brought her back here. After all this time?"

"Crazy, isn't it? After what happened last time..."

Their laughter fades as they move past us, disappearing into another wing of the mansion. I feel Cole's grip loosen, and I let out a shaky breath, my pulse thundering in my ears. His hand drops from mine, and he steps forward, leading us down a narrow path through the trees, away from the courtyard and the watchful eyes of the Syndicate.

We emerge onto a gravel path that stretches out into the darkness, lined with overgrown hedges and looming statues, stone figures frozen in expressions of horror and agony. I shiver, wrapping my arms around myself, and Cole glances back at me, his eyes softer now, less guarded.

"We're almost out," he says, his voice low but reassuring. "Just stay close."

I nod, following him as he picks up the pace, his footsteps crunching softly on the gravel. But before we can make it any farther, the sound of hurried footsteps catches up to us. I turn, my heart lurching as a figure emerges from the shadows, moving toward us with deliberate speed.

Cole swears under his breath, and for a split second, I think he's going to run. But then he stands his ground, his posture shifting, muscles tense, ready for a fight. The figure steps into the faint moonlight, and my stomach drops. It's the same person from the records room—the one who had looked at us with that sickeningly sweet smile, the one who had whispered those words that still echo in my mind.

"Well, isn't this a pleasant surprise," they say, their voice smooth as silk. "Trying to slip out without saying goodbye?"

Cole steps in front of me, his body a shield, and I can see his hand move to his side, where his knife is hidden. But the figure just laughs, a low, mocking sound that sets my teeth on edge.

"Do you really think that little blade of yours is going to make a difference here?" They shake their head, almost pitying. "Oh, Cole, you used to be smarter than this."

"Maybe," Cole replies, his voice steady, unwavering. "But I'm a quick learner."

Before I can fully register what's happening, he lunges, knife flashing in the dim light. The figure moves with a speed that's almost inhuman, sidestepping his attack and twisting his arm behind his back with a brutal efficiency that makes me wince. Cole grits his teeth, struggling against their hold, but it's no use. They've got him.

"Still so predictable," they murmur, tightening their grip until Cole hisses in pain. "I expected more from you."

I can feel the panic rising in my chest, every instinct screaming at me to do something, to help him. But I'm frozen, torn between the impulse to run and the realization that I can't leave him behind.

The figure's gaze shifts to me, a smirk spreading across their face. "And you... I have to admit, you're even more intriguing than I remembered." They tilt their head, studying me like I'm some rare artifact, something to be examined and dissected. "You don't even know what you are, do you?"

The words send a chill down my spine, twisting through me with a dread I can't fully explain. I open my mouth to respond, to demand answers, but my throat feels tight, my mind racing as I try to process what they're saying.

Cole twists in their grip, managing to break free just enough to stagger backward, his face pale but defiant. "Don't listen to them," he says, his voice rough but urgent. "They're just trying to mess with your head."

"Oh, but it's not a game, darling," the figure replies, their smile widening. "It's just the beginning."

With a sharp, almost theatrical motion, they reach into their coat, pulling out a small object wrapped in a dark cloth. They hold it up, unwrapping it with deliberate care, revealing a piece of smooth, polished metal that glints in the faint light. It looks like nothing special, just a small, unremarkable pendant. But the way they hold it, reverent and almost hungry, makes my skin crawl.

"This," they say, their voice dropping to a whisper, "is yours. Or, at least, it should be."

They hold it out toward me, and I feel an inexplicable pull, some strange, magnetic force drawing me toward it. I want to look away, to resist, but I can't. My feet take an involuntary step forward, and I feel the weight of Cole's gaze on me, warning, pleading.

"Don't," he says, his voice rough, barely more than a whisper. "You don't know what that is."

But I can't stop myself. My hand reaches out, fingers trembling as they close around the pendant, the cold metal biting into my skin. As soon as I touch it, a jolt of energy surges through me, sharp and electric, sending a shiver down my spine. The world blurs around me, and I can feel something shifting, something ancient and powerful, stirring deep within me.

The figure smiles, triumphant, and the last thing I see before everything goes dark is Cole's face, twisted in horror, as he whispers my name.

Chapter 4: The Game Unveiled

The air in our hideout felt thick as molasses, humid and clinging like it wanted to crawl into my lungs and never leave. Cole's fingers moved deftly over the laptop keys, the faint glow casting hard angles on his face. I'd grown used to watching him work, but tonight was different. There was something dangerous in the way he hunched over the screen, something in the set of his shoulders that whispered of secrets I wasn't supposed to know. It made me shiver, despite the warmth that clung to every corner of the dimly lit room.

When he finally looked up, his eyes were as dark as the Mississippi at midnight, churning with things I couldn't see but desperately wanted to understand. "This isn't a game, you know," he said, voice flat, all trace of his usual cocky smirk wiped clean. Cole was good at looking like he didn't care about anything, but I'd learned by now that he cared about this. Whatever "this" was.

I leaned forward, the creaky kitchen chair under me groaning in protest. "It's never been a game, Cole. But you know something, don't you? Something you haven't told me." My voice was sharp, more defiant than I felt, but I couldn't let him see that. Cole was the kind of guy who sensed weakness like a bloodhound, and he'd never let it go once he caught a whiff of it.

He clenched his jaw, lips pressed into a thin line. "Don't dig if you're not prepared to bury what you find," he said, his voice a soft, lethal whisper.

I rolled my eyes, masking the dread coiling in my stomach. "I've been digging since the day I met you. I think I can handle a little dirt."

"That so?" He leaned back, crossing his arms, his gaze never leaving mine. His eyes were hard, unreadable, and for a moment, I felt like I was staring into an abyss. But I couldn't look away. He was daring me, silently taunting me to challenge him.

I gave him a slow smile, the kind I knew made him nervous. "Try me."

With a flick of his wrist, he turned the laptop toward me, revealing the documents he'd painstakingly stolen from the Syndicate's database. My stomach dropped as I skimmed through lines of text and grainy photographs, piecing together the connections with each passing second. The Syndicate, the shadowy network of criminals that had us constantly looking over our shoulders, was more than a loose collection of underworld misfits. They were organized. Controlled. And worse, they had their claws in places I'd never dreamed of.

"I'll be damned," I muttered, my voice barely a whisper. The Syndicate wasn't just some under-the-radar crime family. They were in deep with the Enforcers, the same group that was supposed to be hunting them down. Suddenly, the twisted cat-and-mouse game we'd been playing felt even more sinister. And I felt like a pawn on a board far bigger than I'd ever imagined.

Cole watched me, a glint of something almost resembling pity flashing in his eyes. I hated it. "Now do you see why I've been cautious?"

"Cautious?" I scoffed, feeling a surge of anger burn away the dread. "You were holding out on me."

He smirked, but it didn't reach his eyes. "Wouldn't be the first time. Probably won't be the last."

I slammed the laptop shut, ignoring the pang of guilt that fluttered in my chest. "You don't get to decide how much I get to know, Cole. We're supposed to be in this together."

For a second, I thought I saw him flinch, but it was gone as quickly as it came. "If you think I'm hiding things because I don't trust you, you're wrong." His voice was low, carrying an edge that I'd never heard before.

I clenched my fists, feeling the grit under my fingernails from our last job. "Then tell me why. Give me one good reason why I shouldn't walk out that door and take my chances alone."

He took a step closer, his gaze so intense it felt like a physical force. "Because if you walk away, you're putting a target on your back. A big, red one." He paused, letting the words sink in. "And I won't be there to pull you out of the fire."

The weight of his words hit me like a freight train. For all his flaws, for all his secrets, Cole had been the one thing standing between me and a world that would chew me up and spit me out without a second thought. And I hated him for it.

I swallowed hard, keeping my voice steady. "I don't need saving."

A faint smile tugged at the corners of his mouth. "You don't think you do." He held my gaze, his face softer, almost... vulnerable. "But maybe, just maybe, we're both in over our heads here."

The silence between us was thick, stretching out like a live wire ready to snap. Finally, I took a shaky breath, feeling the fight drain out of me. "Fine. You win. For now."

He nodded, his expression unreadable. "Good. Now let's figure out what our next move is."

I rolled my eyes, feigning nonchalance. "Just another day in paradise."

Cole chuckled, the sound rough but oddly comforting. "Isn't it always?"

And just like that, the tension broke, and we were back to our usual dance—a dangerous, exhilarating game of secrets and lies, each of us pushing the other's buttons, testing the limits of trust. But as I glanced at the laptop, the weight of the new knowledge settled heavily in my chest. The Syndicate and the Enforcers—two sides of the same corrupt coin, and we were caught in the middle.

Cole shifted beside me, his shoulder brushing against mine, grounding me in the moment. "You ready for this?" he asked, a rare softness in his tone.

I looked up at him, feeling a spark of determination flare within me. "I was born ready."

He smirked, his eyes gleaming with that familiar glint of mischief. "That's my girl."

And as we dove back into the files, piecing together the puzzle that would either save us or destroy us, I couldn't help but wonder what twisted fate had led us here, tangled in a web of deceit with no way out. But one thing was clear: we were in this together, for better or worse, and I'd be damned if I let anyone—Syndicate, Enforcers, or even Cole himself—stand in my way.

The weight of his words lingered in the air, settling around us like a fine layer of dust. Outside, the city hummed and throbbed, a muffled melody of horns, laughter, and footsteps. New Orleans had a way of feeling like a fever dream—sticky and surreal, a place where shadows danced in the corner of your eye, where secrets slipped between the cracks in the pavement. It was both beautiful and brutal, a fitting backdrop for whatever this mess was between Cole and me.

He hadn't moved, his eyes still locked on me, waiting. Always waiting. He didn't break eye contact, didn't so much as blink. It felt like he was peeling me apart, layer by layer, trying to find the softest spot to poke, to see if I'd finally flinch. But I knew better than to show weakness. Not to him.

"Do you always give people ultimatums?" I asked, keeping my voice steady, folding my arms across my chest. I wanted to sound casual, disinterested, but the slight tremor in my fingers betrayed me. He noticed, of course. Cole noticed everything.

His mouth quirked into that infuriating half-smile, the kind that was more habit than humor. "Only when I'm not sure if I can trust them."

I rolled my eyes, forcing a laugh that felt too loud in the quiet room. "Trust? Really? That's what this is about? Last I checked, you don't exactly have the cleanest track record yourself, Cole." I leaned forward, fingers drumming against the table. "So maybe I should be the one questioning who I can trust."

He sighed, rubbing the back of his neck, and for a split second, I saw a flash of something raw, unguarded. But just as quickly, he blinked, and the mask slipped back into place. "You're not wrong," he admitted, and his voice was softer this time, as if he were confessing something he'd kept buried. "I don't have the best track record. But believe me when I say this—if I'm not telling you everything, it's because I'm trying to protect you."

"Oh, come on," I scoffed, hating how easily his words twisted the knife. "Don't do that. Don't play the martyr."

He leaned back, crossing his arms over his chest, mirroring my posture. "You think I enjoy keeping things from you?" His voice was sharp, clipped, his eyes sparking with a rare frustration. "Believe me, if I thought you'd be safe knowing everything, I'd spill my guts right here, right now. But this? This goes deeper than you realize."

"And you're the only one who gets to decide what I can handle?"

Silence stretched between us, taut as a wire. His gaze flickered, just briefly, to the files on the table. "Maybe I am," he said, almost to himself.

Something inside me snapped. Maybe it was the lack of sleep, maybe it was the claustrophobia of this dingy apartment, or maybe it was just Cole himself, with all his secrets and walls and that maddening smirk he wore like armor. Whatever it was, I was done being in the dark.

"Fine. You want to protect me? Then give me the truth. All of it. Right now."

His jaw tightened, and for a moment, I thought he'd refuse. But then he exhaled, long and slow, as if he were letting go of something heavy. "Alright," he murmured, his voice barely above a whisper. He picked up the file, flipping through the pages with a strange reverence, like he was handling something sacred and dangerous all at once. "If you want the truth, here it is."

He spread the documents out on the table, each piece of paper a jagged piece of a puzzle that I wasn't sure I wanted to solve. The Syndicate's logo was stamped in the corner of each page—a twisted, looping insignia that I'd come to associate with sleepless nights and adrenaline-fueled escapes. But now, alongside the Syndicate's emblem, there were names. Names I recognized.

And then there was mine.

I stared at the paper, my breath catching in my throat. "This... this can't be right." My voice sounded hollow, foreign to my own ears. "Why am I on this list?"

Cole didn't answer. He just watched me, his gaze steady, unwavering, and I realized that he had known. He'd known all along, and he hadn't told me.

My fingers trembled as I traced the outline of my own name, scrawled in that familiar, sterile font. "You knew. You knew I was on their radar, and you didn't say a word."

His expression darkened, shadows flickering across his face. "You think I wanted you to find out like this?"

"Then how was I supposed to find out, Cole?" I was yelling now, the words spilling out in a tangled mess of anger and hurt. "Were you just planning to keep me in the dark until it was too late? Or were you going to wait until they were knocking down the door?"

He flinched, just slightly, but enough for me to see it. "I was trying to buy us time," he said quietly. "Time to figure out how deep this goes. Time to figure out a way to get you off that list."

"And you thought I'd just go along with it? Blindly follow your lead?" I shook my head, feeling the familiar surge of defiance rise up in me. "You should know by now that I don't take orders."

A faint smile tugged at his lips, the kind that was more resigned than amused. "I know. Believe me, I know."

We stood there, the silence between us heavy and charged, each of us locked in our own tangled web of frustration and fear. I wanted to hate him for keeping this from me, for making decisions on my behalf, but the truth was, part of me understood why he'd done it. And that was almost worse.

"So what now?" I asked finally, my voice barely a whisper.

He looked at me, his eyes dark and unreadable. "Now, we make a choice. We can either keep running, keep hiding, and hope that they don't find us." He paused, glancing down at the papers, his expression hardening. "Or we can take the fight to them. End this before they have a chance to come after you."

A shiver ran down my spine. The thought of going head-to-head with the Syndicate, of facing the Enforcers and whatever twisted alliance they'd built, was terrifying. But the alternative—living in constant fear, always looking over my shoulder—felt worse.

I met his gaze, my heart pounding. "I'm done running."

He smiled, a real, genuine smile that lit up his face in a way I hadn't seen before. "That's what I thought."

And just like that, the tension between us shifted, morphing into something else—something fierce and unbreakable. We were in this together, for better or worse, bound by a shared determination to fight back, to reclaim our lives from the shadows that had hunted us for far too long.

Cole reached out, his hand brushing against mine, a silent promise. And in that moment, standing in our dingy little hideout, surrounded by files and secrets and the lingering scent of stale coffee, I felt something I hadn't felt in a long time.

Hope.

As we sifted through the last of the files, Cole stood up abruptly, crossing the room in a few long strides to the narrow window. He pulled back the tattered curtain and peered out, his expression tense. The light from the streetlamps cast sharp shadows across his face, adding an almost sinister edge to his profile. I couldn't tell if he was looking for someone or just getting a moment to clear his head, but something about the way he scanned the street made me uneasy.

"We need to move," he murmured, barely loud enough for me to hear. His gaze lingered outside as if he could see whatever danger lay just around the corner. Then he turned back to me, eyes dark and serious. "Tonight."

I arched an eyebrow, resisting the impulse to laugh. "Oh, so we're just supposed to pack up and run again? Where exactly are we going to go, Cole? It's not like they don't know who we are now. Or didn't you notice my name on that list?"

He clenched his jaw, but didn't look away. "I noticed, alright. I noticed, and I didn't sleep for two days after that." His voice softened, just a fraction. "But you're right. Running isn't going to fix this. They'll find us wherever we go. That's why we can't just slip away quietly this time."

I raised my eyebrows, arms crossing as I leaned back in the creaky kitchen chair. "Oh, really? And what exactly do you suggest? Because I'm not sure if you've noticed, but we don't exactly have an army waiting to go to battle for us."

"An army would just slow us down." He moved away from the window, crouching beside me, his voice lowering to a conspiratorial murmur. "We don't need an army. We need a plan. And if I'm right, we're sitting on more than enough to flip this game around."

I blinked at him, half-expecting that familiar, cocky grin to break through his serious expression. But he wasn't kidding. Cole was more collected than I'd ever seen him, his eyes filled with a determined focus that bordered on terrifying. I felt a thrill of fear and excitement shiver down my spine.

"You're actually serious," I said, my voice softer now, hardly daring to believe him.

He smirked, but there was no humor in it. "When have you known me not to be?"

I rolled my eyes, ignoring the way my heart quickened. "Please. Do you want the short list or the long one?"

"Funny." He tilted his head, and for a second, the barest hint of a smile tugged at his mouth. "Listen, the Syndicate and the Enforcers—they're not as untouchable as they think. They've been able to get away with this because no one's ever called them out. But we have their dirty laundry right here." He tapped a finger on the stack of documents between us. "This is leverage. And leverage, my dear, is exactly what we need."

The way he said "we" made my heart flip, but I forced myself to focus. "So what are you suggesting, Cole? Blackmail them into leaving us alone?"

He leaned closer, and his voice dropped to a whisper. "Something like that. But we need to make it count. They've got eyes and ears all over this city, and one slip-up would be the end of us. So we've got to play this smart."

His words hung heavy in the air, filling the small, dim apartment with a sense of urgency. I couldn't shake the feeling that we were standing on the edge of something huge, something dangerous and thrilling that could either destroy us or set us free.

"What do we need?" I asked finally, feeling a reluctant thrill of adrenaline. My heart raced, knowing that I was crossing a line I could never uncross, but somehow, I didn't care.

"Contacts," he said. "People who aren't afraid to get their hands dirty. We need eyes on every corner of the city, people we can trust to cover our tracks. And," he paused, glancing down, "we need a place to hide once this blows up in their faces."

"And where, exactly, are we supposed to find all of that?" I asked, folding my arms across my chest.

Cole smiled, the kind of slow, dangerous smile that made my stomach flip. "I might know a guy."

"Of course you do," I muttered, but I couldn't help the grin that tugged at the corner of my mouth. That was the thing about Cole—he was always one step ahead, always prepared, always ready with some reckless plan that seemed impossible until he pulled it off.

Without another word, he pulled out his phone and started dialing. I watched, curiosity mingling with trepidation as he muttered a few clipped sentences into the phone, his voice tense and urgent. After a minute, he hung up, shoving the phone back into his pocket.

"He's in," Cole said simply. "But we need to go now."

"Now?" I sputtered, glancing around at the scattered papers, the cluttered remnants of our hideout. "You don't think they'll be suspicious if we leave in the dead of night?"

"They're always suspicious," he said, voice grim. "But if we wait any longer, they'll be more than suspicious. They'll be on our doorstep. Now let's go."

There was no more time to argue. I grabbed my bag, shoving in a few essentials—a flashlight, some spare cash, the well-worn pocketknife I'd carried since high school. Every instinct screamed at me to be careful, to think this through, but there was no time for that now. I could feel the walls closing in around us, the danger tightening like a noose. We had no choice but to leap.

Outside, the streets were quiet, the usual hustle and bustle of the French Quarter reduced to a few stragglers stumbling out of bars. Cole led the way, his movements quick and sure, every step echoing against the silent buildings around us. He didn't say a word, his eyes darting around as if expecting a shadow to lunge from every alley. I kept my head down, matching his pace, my heart pounding in my chest.

After what felt like an eternity, we ducked into a narrow side street, hidden from the main drag by a tangle of old buildings and overgrown ivy. Cole stopped, glancing over his shoulder, his gaze sharp and searching. I barely had time to catch my breath before he grabbed my arm, pulling me into a dark, cramped basement stairwell.

"This is it?" I whispered, trying to keep the nerves out of my voice.

He gave a quick nod, glancing up the stairs behind us. "For now. We lay low here, wait for the call, and see what they know."

"But what if—"

He cut me off with a finger to his lips, his gaze locking onto mine with an intensity that stole the words from my mouth. "No what-ifs," he said, his voice barely a breath. "Not tonight."

We stood there in silence, pressed close in the shadowed stairwell, our breaths mingling in the narrow space. My heart hammered in my chest, but I forced myself to stay still, to trust him even though every instinct screamed that we were cornered.

Suddenly, a faint noise echoed from above, the sound of footsteps approaching. Cole's hand tightened on mine, his eyes wide with alarm. The footsteps grew louder, closer, until they stopped just outside the door, and I could hear the faintest whisper of voices.

Then the door creaked open, and a shadow fell over us.

Chapter 5: In the Heart of the Labyrinth

The air is thick, damp, heavy with the scent of decay and the cold bite of stone. Each breath feels stolen, as though the tunnels are hoarding the oxygen for themselves. I press myself against the uneven wall, a jagged outcrop digging into my shoulder, grounding me in the darkness. I'm hyper-aware of the slightest sound—the shuffle of boots, the faint clink of metal—and, even more unsettling, Cole's steady breath beside me. In the years we've worked together, we've developed an almost wordless language, a system of nods, glances, and signals. And yet, right now, with his chest a scant inch from mine, words feel heavy on my tongue, unspoken but insistent.

Our task here is straightforward, at least on paper: find the artifact buried somewhere in the labyrinthine underbelly of the city and get out before the Syndicate's guards catch so much as a glimpse of us. But straightforward doesn't account for the guards prowling these twisting, ancient corridors with deadly weapons and colder intentions, nor does it consider the artifact's rumored power—a power that has sent more seasoned operatives than us to early graves. Cole raises his hand, palm open toward me, signaling for silence as heavy footsteps echo down the passageway ahead.

It's impossible to know how long the guard will stay, so we stand still, the only movement the pulse pounding in my ears, loud and persistent. My eyes adjust to the shadows, tracing the sharp lines of Cole's profile, his jaw clenched in concentration. His face is all hard angles, a stubborn set to his mouth, and that constant, aggravating smirk that hovers just beneath his stoic mask. For all his flaws—and they are numerous—he's infuriatingly competent. The kind of person who never flinches, who stands unyielding even when the world is falling apart. And right now, his attention is locked on the sounds ahead, his focus unbreakable.

After what feels like an eternity, the footsteps recede, swallowed by the twisting paths and stone walls. Cole exhales, just a subtle shift in his posture, but it releases some of the tension coiling in my own muscles. He turns to me, his mouth quirking up in that infuriating, half-amused way that makes me want to simultaneously punch him and, embarrassingly, kiss him. But I bury the thought, crush it under the weight of a hundred justifications. It's not the first time I've felt the tension humming between us like a taut string ready to snap, and it likely won't be the last. In this line of work, distraction is a fatal flaw.

We creep forward, Cole taking the lead, his movements smooth and calculated. He doesn't say anything, but I feel him watching over his shoulder, making sure I keep pace. The Syndicate has done everything to make this labyrinth their own, twisting it to suit their cruel whims. Symbols etched in the stone flicker with unnatural light, faint and blue, casting eerie shadows that dance on the walls. I try not to look at them too long; there are stories about those who do, who are drawn in and lose themselves in the sinister maze forever.

The path splits ahead, and Cole's hand reaches back, catching my wrist before I can make a choice. His grip is firm, grounding, the roughness of his fingers somehow reassuring. He glances at me, a question flickering in his eyes before he releases my arm. I'm supposed to lead this time. My instinct says left, something I can't explain but trust enough to follow. The left passage slopes downward, deeper into the bowels of the city. Cold seeps up through the stone, wrapping around my ankles and working its way up, as if the very walls are alive and reaching for us.

We press on, the silence almost oppressive, filled with everything we won't say out loud. Just ahead, faint glimmers catch my eye, small tokens scattered on the floor. Coins, bits of jewelry—offerings, maybe, or things dropped by those who came before us and never made it out. The air grows colder, staler, and for a moment I feel as if the tunnel itself is pressing in, watching, waiting for one wrong move.

I freeze, one foot in the air, and gesture for Cole to stop. In the dim light, something glimmers across the floor: a thin wire, almost invisible against the dark stones, stretched taut across the narrow passage. One step more, and it would've sliced my ankle clean through. Cole's expression shifts, his mask slipping just enough for me to see a flicker of something—fear, maybe? Or is it something more complicated? He doesn't look at me, but he's not moving either, his muscles taut, every line of his body alert and on edge.

He kneels, fingers reaching carefully toward the wire, his focus sharp. I hold my breath, watching the practiced precision in his hands as he disarms the trap with a steady, almost careless ease. But I know him well enough to see the strain. For all his skill, he's as human as I am, as vulnerable to the Syndicate's tricks. As he rises, he doesn't immediately let go of my hand. It's just for a second—a heartbeat, no more. But there's something there, something that makes my pulse stutter, an echo of things unspoken and untouchable.

The silence thickens, charged, and I know I should look away, should focus on the mission. But I don't. Not immediately. Instead, I meet his gaze, hold it, my thoughts a mix of frustration, admiration, and something dangerously close to affection. In this unforgiving world of shadows and secrets, letting myself feel anything for Cole is a weakness, a crack in the armor I've built so carefully. And yet, in this moment, under the flickering light and the hum of unspoken words, the walls around my heart seem fragile, thin enough to shatter at a single touch.

He steps back, finally releasing me, his eyes unreadable as he nods toward the path ahead. I take a steadying breath, gripping my weapon tighter, trying to shake the strange, electric tension lingering in the air. There's no room for mistakes, no room for soft, foolish feelings. Yet, as we move forward, his presence at my back feels like a safety net I never asked for but can't deny wanting.

The silence is a living, breathing thing down here, thick and filled with the weight of all the secrets these walls have swallowed. Every step forward feels like a gamble, a silent prayer that our next move won't be the one that gets us caught. The cold sears against my skin like ice, numbing my hands where they grip the rough hilt of my knife. Cole is just ahead of me, his silhouette outlined by a faint blue glow filtering through cracks in the stone. He moves with such ease, barely a sound, his focus unbreakable, his confidence maddening.

I move forward, matching his pace as best I can, though the hairs on my arms prickle with a nagging sense of being watched. It's not just the guards, or the way shadows stretch and shift like they're alive. No, there's something else in the air, an energy pulsing through these tunnels, watching, listening. I don't know if Cole feels it too, but he hasn't shown any sign of it. He's all business, and that irks me more than I'd like to admit.

Just as I'm thinking I can't take much more of this silence, Cole stops short, his hand raised to signal danger. I halt in my tracks, every sense flaring to life. From somewhere close by, there's the unmistakable scrape of a metal boot against stone. A guard, too near for comfort. Cole glances back at me, his expression unreadable but intense. In a flash, he's pressed against the wall, motioning for me to do the same. I can hear his breath, steady and measured, while mine feels like it's trying to climb out of my throat.

The guard's footsteps grow louder, echoing off the stone in a slow, deliberate rhythm. I hold my breath, willing myself to disappear, to blend into the shadows like Cole does so effortlessly. The footsteps stop, and for a heartbeat, it feels like time itself has halted with them. I can feel Cole's gaze on me, assessing, reassuring in a strange way. The moment stretches, painfully taut, until finally, the footsteps retreat, fading into the labyrinth once more. I exhale, a small, shaky sigh of relief, though Cole's eyes stay on me a beat longer.

"You breathe any louder, and the whole city'll hear you," he murmurs, a glint of mischief flickering in his eyes.

"Maybe I'm just giving them a head start," I whisper back, the words spilling out before I can stop myself. His lips twitch into that infuriating, lopsided smirk. It's the smallest thing, a brief crack in his otherwise impenetrable facade, but somehow it feels like a win.

We continue down the twisting passage, the silence settling back over us like a heavy cloak. I can feel Cole's presence at my side, a steady and grounding force, though his nearness only complicates things. I can't afford to let myself get distracted, not here, not with the Syndicate's eyes lurking around every corner. But there's something undeniably magnetic about him, something that pulls at me in ways I can't explain. It's infuriating, really. And yet, here I am, following him deeper into the heart of this deadly labyrinth, like a moth to a particularly dangerous flame.

The path narrows, forcing us closer together, the space barely wide enough to allow us through side by side. I can feel the warmth radiating off him, a stark contrast to the icy chill of the tunnels. His hand brushes mine as we navigate a tight corner, and I pull back, the contact brief but electric. He glances at me, a question in his eyes, but I look away, focusing on the path ahead. No distractions, I remind myself. Not now.

We reach a fork in the path, and Cole pauses, his brow furrowing in thought. He takes a step forward, squinting at the faint symbols carved into the stone walls. They're crude, worn down by time, but they have an ominous energy, as if they're alive, pulsing faintly in the darkness. He mutters something under his breath, tracing a finger over the markings.

"Any ideas?" I whisper, though my voice comes out more breathless than I'd like.

He shrugs, the movement almost careless. "Well, if you have a better sense of direction, feel free to lead the way."

I roll my eyes, my irritation flickering back to life. "Maybe if you'd stop glaring at the walls like they insulted your mother, we'd make some actual progress."

He huffs a laugh, quiet and unexpected. "Trust me, if these walls had the guts to talk, I'd have a few words of my own for them."

His humor is dry, sharp, and for a moment, it slices through the tension that clings to us. He chooses the left path, gesturing for me to follow, and I do, though not without a muttered curse about his unfounded sense of direction. He pretends not to hear, though I catch the faintest hint of a smile in his profile.

As we move deeper into the labyrinth, I feel an unshakable sense of dread building in my chest. The walls seem to press in closer, and a strange, eerie hum fills the air, vibrating through the stone. It's faint, almost imperceptible, but it sends a chill down my spine. I don't know if Cole senses it too, but his shoulders tense, his movements slower, more cautious.

Out of nowhere, a loud, shuddering crash echoes through the tunnel behind us, the ground shaking beneath our feet. My heart lurches, my hand instinctively reaching for Cole's arm. He pulls me close, steadying us both as the sound reverberates through the stone walls. When the echo finally fades, he releases me, his expression hardening.

"That wasn't an accident," he says, his voice low, eyes scanning the shadows.

"No kidding," I manage, though my voice is shaky. The crash has set my nerves on edge, every muscle in my body primed for whatever's coming. Cole moves forward, his stance guarded, his hand hovering over his weapon. I follow, my heart pounding in my chest, every instinct screaming at me to turn and run. But running isn't an option, not here, not now.

We press on, the tunnel twisting and narrowing until we reach a dead end. Cole curses under his breath, his eyes narrowing as he scans the walls, searching for something—anything—that might get us out. There's a small, jagged opening near the floor, barely big enough to crawl through. He glances back at me, his expression a mix of exasperation and resolve.

"Well," he says, crouching down and examining the gap, "looks like we're not getting a choice on this one."

I sigh, dropping to my knees beside him. The thought of squeezing through that tiny space sends a wave of claustrophobia crashing over me, but I shove it down, focusing on the task at hand. "Guess we'd better hope whatever's on the other side isn't worse than what's behind us."

He meets my gaze, a glint of determination in his eyes. "Only one way to find out."

I brace myself and crawl through the narrow opening, gravel biting into my palms as I squeeze through. The tunnel feels like it's closing in around me, pressing against my shoulders and ribs, forcing the breath from my lungs. There's no light here, only the damp chill and the gritty stone beneath me. I inch forward, ignoring the way my pulse pounds in my ears, the way every scrape and shuffle echoes through the silence like a taunt. I feel Cole's presence close behind, his own quiet breaths a steady anchor in the dark.

"Comfy?" he mutters, his voice low and dry, even here, even now.

"Oh, like I'm lounging on a beach," I hiss back, but the words come out strained, caught somewhere between panic and bravado.

I keep moving, one arm in front of the other, feeling my way along the uneven ground until the space begins to widen. Finally, mercifully, the tunnel opens up enough for me to sit up and draw in a full breath. The relief is short-lived, though, as I glance around and realize where we are. We're in some kind of chamber, but this isn't a place of safety. No, it's a room filled with relics of the Syndicate's dark history.

Artifacts line the stone walls, each one encased in glass and pulsing faintly with that eerie blue light. The objects range from weapons to strange, twisted sculptures, and each one seems to hum with a sinister energy, as if they're watching us, waiting. I feel Cole's hand on my shoulder, grounding me, reminding me that we're not alone in this eerie place.

"Don't touch anything," he says, his tone as sharp as the edge of his knife. "These aren't souvenirs."

"You think I want a keepsake from this nightmare?" I mutter, but there's a tension coiled inside me that even I can't brush off. Something about this room feels wrong, like it's a trap set just for us, waiting to spring.

Cole moves forward, studying the artifacts with a wary eye. He pauses in front of a particularly gruesome-looking dagger, its blade curved and wickedly sharp, and I can't help but wonder what horrors it's seen. He doesn't touch it—none of us are that reckless—but his fingers hover near it, as if he's drawn to its dark allure.

"You'd think the Syndicate would have better taste in decor," I whisper, trying to shake off the unease prickling at the back of my neck.

He snorts softly, glancing over his shoulder at me. "Maybe they were aiming for something more 'haunted dungeon chic.'"

Before I can respond, there's a sound—a low, grinding noise like stone on stone. We both freeze, eyes snapping to the source. A hidden door, camouflaged by shadows, is slowly sliding open on the far side of the chamber. I feel a jolt of fear as I realize what this means: we're not alone down here. And whoever—or whatever—is behind that door isn't likely to be friendly.

Cole's hand goes to his weapon, his posture shifting into a stance I know all too well. It's the look he gets when he's ready for a fight, all coiled energy and ruthless focus. He glances at me, his expression a mixture of determination and something darker, something that tells me he's ready for whatever comes next, even if it means going down swinging.

"Stay behind me," he says, his voice a low growl that leaves no room for argument.

I bite back a retort—now's not the time for stubborn pride—and slip into the shadows beside him, my own weapon at the ready. The door finally grinds to a halt, revealing a figure shrouded in darkness, their silhouette sharp and foreboding. They step into the chamber, and for a moment, I can't breathe. They're cloaked in black, a hood casting their face into shadow, but the aura around them is unmistakable. Power, cold and suffocating, radiates from them, filling the room with a palpable menace.

"Well, well," the figure says, their voice smooth and unsettling, like silk stretched too thin. "What do we have here? Trespassers in my domain."

Their words are laced with amusement, but there's an undercurrent of threat that chills me to the bone. Cole shifts beside me, his gaze locked on the figure, assessing, waiting for the right moment to strike. But I can feel his hesitation too, a tension in the air that tells me even he isn't sure of our chances here.

"Just passing through," he says, his tone calm, even flippant. "Didn't realize the Syndicate was running a museum down here."

The figure chuckles, a low, unsettling sound. "You have a sharp tongue, Mr. Cole. But I suggest you choose your words carefully. One wrong move, and you may find this visit far more... permanent than you intended."

I stiffen, the weight of the situation pressing down on me. Whoever this is, they know us—know Cole by name, at least, and that's more information than I'm comfortable with them having. I tighten my grip on my weapon, forcing myself to breathe, to stay focused. Fear is a luxury we can't afford right now.

Cole glances at me, his eyes flicking over my face in a silent question. I give a barely perceptible nod, my muscles tensing as I prepare for whatever comes next. The figure watches us, their expression unreadable beneath the hood, but there's a flicker of something in their stance, a momentary lapse in their icy demeanor. And in that split second, Cole moves.

He lunges forward, swift and silent, his blade flashing in the dim light. But the figure is faster, sidestepping his attack with an eerie grace. They raise one hand, a dark energy crackling at their fingertips, and I feel a rush of panic as I realize the danger we're in. This isn't just another guard. This is someone—or something—far more dangerous.

I react on instinct, throwing myself into the fray, my weapon swinging toward the figure in a desperate attempt to distract them. But they anticipate my move, deflecting my attack with a flick of their wrist. The force of it sends me stumbling back, my vision swimming as I struggle to regain my balance. Cole is by my side in an instant, his hand steadying me, but his expression is grim.

"You two are amusing," the figure says, their voice dripping with disdain. "But I have no time for games."

They lift their hand, and I feel a strange, suffocating pressure building around us, as if the very air is turning against us. Cole's grip on my arm tightens, his eyes darting around the room, searching for an escape. But there's nowhere to go. The walls feel like they're closing in, the darkness thickening, swallowing us whole.

And then, just as the pressure becomes unbearable, the figure speaks a single word, low and venomous. It reverberates through the chamber, a command that thrums in my bones, leaving me frozen in place. Cole's hand slips from my arm, and I watch in horror as he crumples to the ground, his eyes wide with shock and pain.

"Cole!" I scream, reaching for him, but the figure steps between us, blocking my path with an infuriatingly calm expression.

"You've both been meddling in things you don't understand," they say, their voice icy and final. "And now, it's time for you to pay the price."

The room plunges into total darkness, and I feel the ground shift beneath me, a sickening drop that sends my stomach lurching. I reach out, blindly grasping for something, anything to hold onto, but there's nothing. Only the void, swallowing me whole.

Chapter 6: Ghosts of the Past

The safe house smells of damp wood and forgotten memories, a thick musty scent that clings to the walls and lingers in the air like a bad secret. Dust rises in little clouds as we step inside, my boot scuffing the floor just enough to unsettle it. My eyes take in the room, which has the unpracticed air of a place someone once called home but has since tried to forget. Broken furniture is pushed against the walls, abandoned by time, and the only light filters in from a narrow window on the far wall, casting pale shadows across the floor.

I feel him watching me, Cole's gaze sharp as a knife's edge. For the past few hours, he's been nothing but distant, the silence between us thick and heavy, and I'm not sure whether to be relieved or worried. It's the first time I've ever seen him rattled. For all his stoic composure, something has shifted. The confident, icy demeanor he wore like armor has cracked, and through it, I catch glimmers of a man he's tried hard to bury.

My gaze drifts to a wall lined with faded photographs, each one a fragment of someone's life. Some are of strangers, unfamiliar faces that smile in frozen moments of forgotten joy. But a few... a few seem achingly familiar. I squint, trying to place them, a strange sense of déjà vu pulling at my thoughts. It's like staring into a broken mirror, catching glimpses of memories that aren't my own.

"Don't look too closely," he says softly, and there's an edge to his tone, a warning. But it's too late. My curiosity has already dug in deep, prying at the cracks.

"You knew these people?" I ask, keeping my voice even. It's a casual question, but the look he gives me is anything but. His jaw tightens, a flash of something raw crossing his face before he shutters it again, closing himself off. Cole, ever the enigma.

"They were my family," he says, the words so quiet I almost don't catch them. My breath hitches, and I fight the urge to press him for more, sensing this is a rare glimpse behind the mask. His gaze flickers to one of the photos, a candid shot of a young woman laughing, her head thrown back, a spark of life captured in a single frame. The look in his eyes is almost reverent, haunted. I realize then that whoever she was, she meant something to him. Maybe everything.

"What happened to her?" The words slip out before I can stop them, a thoughtless intrusion. His face hardens, and I regret asking, but he answers anyway, his voice carrying a weight that feels ancient and unyielding.

"She died." His voice is flat, as if he's rehearsed this line a hundred times, practiced it until it became a fact rather than a wound. But the bitterness in his eyes gives him away, a glint of grief he can't quite conceal.

"Sorry," I say, though the word feels hollow, insufficient. We stand there in the dim light, silence stretching between us. Part of me wants to reach out, to offer something, anything, to bridge the gulf of loss that yawns wide in the space between us. But the look on his face warns me off, a silent plea to leave well enough alone.

Turning away, I let my eyes wander the room, landing on a stack of books piled precariously on a nearby table. They're old, worn from use, the pages yellowed and brittle. I run my fingers over one of them, tracing the faded spine, and I can't help but wonder if he left them here deliberately, tokens of a life he's tried so hard to escape.

"You don't strike me as the sentimental type," I say, trying to lighten the mood, though my voice comes out more somber than I intended. Cole huffs a quiet laugh, and it's the closest thing to warmth I've seen from him all day.

"Sentimentality doesn't suit me," he replies, but there's something in his tone that suggests otherwise. His gaze flickers to the wall of photos again, lingering for just a heartbeat too long before he turns away. "Sometimes, though, the past has a way of sticking around."

I don't push further, sensing the conversation has veered into dangerous territory. Instead, I settle onto an old, sagging couch, letting the silence fill the room again. My mind races, piecing together fragments of what little I know about him. Cole, the man of mystery. Cole, who's spent the better part of our journey treating me like an annoyance he can't quite shake off, and yet here he is, revealing slivers of himself in ways that make him human. And, annoyingly, it makes me want to understand him more.

He moves to the window, staring out into the night. The city beyond the glass is quiet, a ghost town of memories and half-forgotten dreams, and his reflection in the glass is like a shadow, haunting and detached.

"Why are you still here, then?" I ask softly. "If this place hurts so much, why come back?"

For a moment, I think he won't answer. His posture is rigid, his shoulders tense, and I can almost feel the battle waging inside him, a tug-of-war between holding on and letting go. Finally, he turns, his expression unreadable.

"Sometimes we don't get to choose what we leave behind," he says, each word measured, carrying a heaviness that settles over the room. He's looking at me like he's daring me to understand, to peel back the layers he's built up around himself. But there's also a glimmer of fear in his eyes, a flicker of vulnerability he can't quite hide.

I swallow, feeling the weight of his gaze. Whatever he's carrying, it's something that's scarred him deep, something he's kept locked away for so long that I doubt even he remembers what it's like to let someone else see it.

In that moment, I want to tell him he doesn't have to carry it alone. I want to reach out, to break through the walls he's built and show him he's not as alone as he thinks. But I don't. Instead, I offer him a quiet smile, a silent promise that I'm here, even if he doesn't want me to be.

"Suit yourself, then," I say, settling back, and his lips quirk in the faintest hint of a smile. It's a fragile truce, a hesitant acceptance, and I know it won't last. But for now, in the quiet of the safe house, with the ghosts of his past surrounding us, it's enough.

The air in the room feels thick, weighed down by the presence of things left unsaid and unresolved. I let my eyes wander, drifting from the photos on the wall to the sparse, battered furniture, imagining a version of Cole who might've once sat here, laughing with those people in the pictures. It's hard to reconcile that image with the man standing a few feet away, arms folded tightly across his chest, his jaw clenched as if he's bracing himself against something invisible.

"I didn't know you were... sentimental," I say, my voice softer than intended, the words floating between us like an olive branch. It's half a taunt, half a plea, hoping he'll fill the silence with something real, something that lets me in.

"Sentimental," he repeats, and the way he says it sounds like he's tasting the word for the first time. "Is that what you think this is?" He gestures vaguely to the room, his mouth twisting in a half-smile that doesn't reach his eyes. "Sentimentality is a luxury I can't afford."

The words hang in the air, cold and clipped, but I don't miss the edge of bitterness beneath them. It's strange to think that, somewhere beneath all that steel and stone, there's a heart that remembers, even if it doesn't want to. I step closer to him, studying his profile, watching how his gaze flickers between the photos and the window, as if he's caught between past and present.

"It must be nice," I say, barely a whisper, and he turns, his expression quizzical. "Having a place to remember. A place where you can see their faces."

His eyes narrow, and for a moment, I think I've crossed some line, pushed him too far. But then he exhales, the tension in his shoulders easing ever so slightly. "You're assuming that remembering is a good thing," he replies, his voice low, barely more than a murmur. "Sometimes, it's just... a wound that won't heal."

The vulnerability in his words catches me off guard, and before I can stop myself, I reach out, resting a hand on his arm. It's a bold move, a reckless one, but there's something in his eyes that makes me want to bridge the distance between us. His gaze drops to my hand, and for a moment, I think he might shake me off. But he doesn't. Instead, he lets out a breath, a small sigh that seems to carry the weight of the world.

"I didn't mean to pry," I say, my voice barely above a whisper. "I just... I know what it's like to lose people. To carry them with you, even when you wish you could let them go."

His eyes meet mine, and for a heartbeat, the walls between us seem to crumble. "Then you know," he says, his voice rough. "You know it never really goes away. It just... settles. Becomes part of you, like a scar you forget about until one day it starts to ache again."

I nod, understanding more than I care to admit. The silence that follows is thick, but it's not uncomfortable. It's the kind of silence that comes when two people share something raw, something real. And maybe it's foolish, maybe it's reckless, but in that moment, I don't feel so alone.

He shifts, breaking the spell, and I let my hand drop, feeling a strange sense of loss as I step back. "We should get some rest," he says, his voice steady again, the mask slipping back into place. "It's not safe here, but it's better than nothing."

I nod, casting a wary glance at the sagging couch. "I guess I'll take the luxury suite, then?" I joke, trying to lighten the mood, but my voice comes out more brittle than I intended.

Cole's lips quirk in the faintest hint of a smile. "Just try not to fall through it," he says, a glimmer of his usual sarcasm peeking through. "I don't think I can haul you out of another disaster tonight."

There it is—that familiar snark, the shield he wears so well. But I can't shake the feeling that, for just a moment, I saw something underneath. Something that makes me want to stay, to dig deeper, even if I know it's a terrible idea.

I sink onto the couch, wincing as the springs groan beneath me. Cole takes the chair by the window, his gaze fixed on the shadows outside, one hand resting on his knee, his fingers tapping a silent rhythm. I study him from across the room, wondering what he's thinking, what ghosts he's fighting. It's strange, but there's a part of me that wants to reach out again, to tell him he doesn't have to face them alone. But the look on his face tells me he wouldn't accept the offer, even if I made it.

The hours stretch on, and the city outside falls silent, a hush settling over the old quarter. I close my eyes, trying to quiet my racing thoughts, but sleep doesn't come easily. My mind keeps drifting back to the photos on the wall, the fragments of a life that Cole has tried so hard to leave behind. I wonder who he was before all of this—before the walls, the silence, the pain. I wonder if there was ever a time when he laughed easily, loved openly, without fear of what he might lose.

Eventually, exhaustion pulls me under, and I drift into a restless sleep, haunted by images of faces I don't recognize and memories that aren't mine. I dream of shadows and whispers, of voices calling my name, pulling me back into the dark. And through it all, there's a constant presence, a steady warmth that grounds me, anchoring me to the present. Even in sleep, I know it's him.

When I wake, the room is bathed in the faint gray light of dawn, casting long shadows across the floor. Cole is still by the window, his gaze distant, lost in thought. He looks so different in the morning light—softer, almost human. There's a weariness in his posture, a vulnerability that I haven't seen before. For a moment, I'm tempted to reach out, to bridge the gap between us, but I know better.

Whatever connection we shared last night, it's fragile, and I don't want to break it.

Instead, I clear my throat, breaking the silence. "I'd say good morning, but that feels a little optimistic, considering." My voice is rough, laced with a humor that feels too forced, too hollow.

Cole glances at me, his expression unreadable. "You get used to it," he says simply, as if he's resigned himself to a lifetime of bleak mornings and half-hearted attempts at optimism.

But I'm not ready to let the moment slip away, not yet. "You know, you don't have to do this alone," I say, my voice steady. "Whatever you're running from, whoever you're carrying... you don't have to carry it by yourself."

He looks at me then, really looks, and for a moment, I see something in his eyes that makes my heart stutter—a glimmer of hope, or maybe fear, or maybe something else entirely. But just as quickly, it's gone, and he turns away, his gaze fixed on the horizon.

"Maybe," he says quietly, the word barely more than a whisper. And for now, it's enough.

The quiet between us stretches out, but this time, it feels different—thicker somehow, loaded with all the words neither of us knows how to say. I feel the tension simmering beneath the surface, a tension that doesn't just come from the city around us or the dangers that lurk beyond these walls. No, this is something else entirely. It's the weight of secrets, of lives abandoned and memories that refuse to stay buried.

Cole breaks the silence first, his voice low and almost reluctant, as if he's fighting the urge to speak even as the words spill out. "There was a time," he begins, his gaze distant, fixed on some unseen point beyond the window, "when I thought I could just... start over. Walk away from everything and leave it all behind. But the past has a way of following you, no matter how fast you run."

His words hang in the air, and I feel a pang of empathy so sharp it almost hurts. "Yeah," I murmur, not trusting myself to say much more. I know all about running. It's practically a hobby of mine.

He turns to look at me, his eyes dark, unreadable. "And yet, here you are," he says, his voice laced with something I can't quite place. Amusement? Resignation? "You could have left any time, but you didn't."

A part of me wants to argue, to tell him that it's not as simple as he's making it sound. But there's another part, a louder, braver part, that knows he's right. Whatever this strange partnership is, it's tied me to him, for better or worse.

"What can I say? I have a thing for lost causes," I reply, injecting just enough sarcasm to keep things light, though my heart isn't in it. His mouth twitches in what might almost be a smile, but it's gone before I can be sure.

He studies me for a moment, a curious intensity in his gaze. "Is that what you think this is?" he asks, his tone softer, almost challenging. "A lost cause?"

I shrug, feigning nonchalance. "I don't know what it is," I admit, and for once, I'm not being flippant. "But I know I'm not ready to walk away yet."

Something shifts in his expression, a crack in the stoic facade he's worn like armor since the moment I met him. He looks almost... uncertain, as if he's caught off guard by my honesty. And for a second, I think he might actually open up, might give me a glimpse of the person beneath all the layers of cynicism and control.

But then, as quickly as it appeared, the vulnerability vanishes, replaced by a cool detachment that feels like a slap in the face. "Well, then, I suppose you'll just have to live with the consequences," he says, his tone turning cold.

I stare at him, feeling a mix of frustration and something else, something I don't want to admit, stirring in my chest. "You know,"

I say, my voice sharper than I intended, "for someone who's supposedly running from the past, you sure do a lot to keep it close. Maybe you like the weight of it."

The words are out before I can stop them, and the moment they hit the air, I regret it. I expect him to snap back, to retaliate with some cutting remark, but instead, he just looks at me, a mixture of anger and something that looks suspiciously like hurt flickering across his face.

"You don't know the first thing about my past," he says quietly, and there's a hardness in his voice that makes my chest ache. "And you have no idea what I'd give to let it go."

There's a part of me that wants to apologize, to tell him that I didn't mean to dig so deep. But another part, a stronger part, refuses to back down. "Then show me," I say, my voice barely a whisper. "Show me what it is you're so afraid of."

The challenge hangs between us, and I see the flicker of indecision in his eyes, the brief moment of vulnerability that he's trying so hard to hide. He opens his mouth, as if he's about to say something, but then he stops, his gaze shifting to the door, his body tensing like a coiled spring.

Before I can ask what's wrong, he's already moving, crossing the room in three long strides and pressing his ear to the wall. I feel my pulse quicken, a sense of dread creeping up my spine.

"What is it?" I whisper, though I'm not sure I want to know the answer.

"Someone's here," he says, his voice barely audible, his gaze fixed on the door with a focus so intense it sends a chill down my spine.

I feel a surge of panic, my mind racing through the possibilities. We're alone, vulnerable, with only the memories on the walls as witnesses. And whoever's on the other side of that door isn't here for a friendly visit.

Cole motions for me to stay quiet, his hand reaching for the knife strapped to his belt. I watch as his fingers curl around the hilt, his body tense and ready. It's like watching a predator preparing to strike, and for a moment, I'm struck by the sheer ferocity in his gaze.

The footsteps outside grow louder, the faint creak of old wood straining under weight, and my heart pounds in time with each step. I press myself against the wall, barely daring to breathe, my own hand reaching instinctively for the small knife tucked into my boot. It's a flimsy weapon at best, but it's better than nothing.

The door rattles, a low creak echoing through the room, and I feel my pulse quicken, every nerve on edge. Cole glances at me, a silent warning in his eyes, and I nod, understanding without words that whatever happens next, we're in this together.

The door swings open slowly, the creak piercing the silence like a scream. A figure steps into the room, shrouded in shadow, their face obscured by the dim light. My grip tightens on the knife, my breath catching as I prepare for the worst.

And then, in a voice that's both familiar and chilling, the figure speaks.

"Hello, Cole. It's been a long time."

The words hang in the air, dripping with menace, and I feel a cold dread settle in my stomach. Cole's face goes pale, his jaw clenched, and for the first time since I met him, I see real fear in his eyes.

He doesn't respond, his gaze locked on the figure, his body rigid with tension. I can feel the weight of whatever history exists between them, a history that suddenly feels all too real, all too dangerous.

The figure takes a step closer, and I catch a glimpse of a cruel smile, a smile that promises nothing but pain.

"I thought you'd learned by now," the figure says, their voice a low, mocking whisper. "You can't outrun the past."

And with those words, everything we thought we knew shatters, plunging us into a nightmare that neither of us is prepared to face.

Chapter 7: Secrets Under Moonlight

The night was cool and still, a rare and welcome relief from the ceaseless chase we'd been running for weeks. The stars spread across the sky like spilled sugar, casting a faint glow over the city beneath us, twinkling almost as if they were trying to offer some glimmer of hope. Cole sat a few feet away, his silhouette carved in moonlight, shoulders hunched as he stared off into the distance, his gaze unreadable. I'd never seen him so quiet, so still. It was strange, almost unsettling, to see him stripped of his usual armor of sarcasm and swagger. We were both battle-worn, weary, and somehow that quiet between us felt sharper than any of the close calls we'd faced.

I didn't dare break it. Not yet. I figured if he wanted to fill the silence, he would, and it would be better that way. He was the kind of person who needed to circle a thing a dozen times before he got close enough to touch it. And whatever weighed on him tonight felt immense, like an anchor chained around his chest. I waited, counting the stars one by one, letting the cool breeze prickle my skin. I almost didn't notice when he finally spoke, his voice just a whisper, caught on the edge of the wind.

"I used to come out here a lot, back when—" He stopped, clenching his fists on his knees, knuckles pale in the moonlight. I leaned in, not wanting to miss a word, sensing he was about to let me in on one of the mysteries that clung to him like a second skin.

"Back when?" I prompted gently, careful not to push too hard. The night was delicate enough without my usual blundering curiosity.

His jaw clenched, and he glanced at me, eyes shadowed but piercing. "Back when my brother was still around. This was our spot. We'd sit up here, talk about everything we were gonna do. He was younger. Always had these big dreams, you know? But when he got... when the Syndicate took him, that stopped. The world stopped."

His voice trembled, and I could feel the rawness there, like he was bleeding in a place that hadn't healed.

My breath hitched as his words sank in. I'd known he had a vendetta against the Syndicate—who didn't, these days? They took everything they touched, snatched away the brightest and best people for their own twisted schemes. But knowing that loss was buried this close to his heart added a whole new layer to Cole. For the first time, I could see the vulnerable, broken part he'd buried deep under his smirks and brash confidence.

"He was the good one," Cole continued, a bitter laugh escaping his lips, as if the irony was too much to hold back. "The kind who saw hope everywhere, even in a place like this. The kind who'd probably laugh at me for still coming up here."

Without thinking, I reached out, my hand brushing his arm, trying to offer some small bit of comfort. He stiffened, glancing down at my hand as if it were something foreign, something he didn't quite know how to accept. But he didn't pull away, not right away. I held my breath, letting the silence wrap around us, my hand a lifeline, a reminder that he wasn't alone in this.

But just as I felt him soften, his walls came crashing back, and he pulled his arm away, turning his face back to the stars. "It's in the past," he muttered, voice harsh again, clipped, as if that confession had been a slip he regretted immediately.

I bit back the urge to argue, to tell him that pushing it away wouldn't make it hurt less. But I knew better than to try and peel back his defenses. I had my own armor, after all. We all did. Instead, I kept my voice soft, steady. "You don't have to fight alone, you know. Not all of us are afraid of the Syndicate."

He gave me a sidelong glance, a trace of his usual cocky smirk playing on his lips, but it didn't reach his eyes. "Pretty sure you should be afraid. They don't exactly leave a good Yelp review after they're done with someone."

I snorted, unable to hold back a smile. "Yeah, well, maybe I'm just stupid. But last I checked, you weren't running away from them either. Unless I'm mistaken and the tough guy act is just for show?"

He rolled his eyes, leaning back against the cold metal of the rooftop railing. "It's not an act. And if I didn't know better, I'd say you were just as foolish as I am. I mean, sitting here with me? You must be crazy." He gave me a once-over, trying to sound detached, but I caught the flicker of something in his gaze, a crack in the carefully constructed façade.

"Maybe I am," I replied, shrugging. "But maybe that's exactly why you need someone like me around. To remind you that not everything has to be a one-man mission."

He didn't answer right away, just stared out over the city, jaw clenched, as if considering my words and rejecting them all in one breath. But I saw the hesitation, the doubt, and for a moment, I thought maybe, just maybe, he'd let his guard down.

But then he rose, brushing himself off as if the conversation were nothing more than a speck of dust. "Don't get too comfortable," he muttered. "The Syndicate doesn't take long to catch up with people who think they're invincible."

I watched him go, feeling the strange ache he always left behind. Part of me wanted to shout after him, demand he let someone in. But I knew he'd only turn back with that familiar, infuriating smirk and tell me to worry about myself.

As I sat there, alone under the stars, I realized that maybe I was in over my head. But for the first time, the fear didn't outweigh the pull. I'd seen something in Cole tonight, a glimpse of his humanity, of the raw pain he carried, and I knew I couldn't walk away from that—not yet. Maybe that made me foolish. Or maybe it made me just crazy enough to stay.

The chill of the rooftop settled deeper as the night stretched on, settling into the spaces between us, filling in where conversation should have been. I could hear Cole's breath, steady and measured, but I knew he was anything but calm. He sat close enough that I could see the faint lines etched in his face, lines I hadn't noticed before. He looked older, worn down in a way that had nothing to do with the years. Maybe it was the weight he carried, or the scars the world had left on him that I couldn't see.

Just when I thought the silence would consume us both, he exhaled, a quiet surrender. "You ever have one of those nights where you can't stop thinking about all the things you'd undo if you had the chance?" He spoke so softly that for a second, I wondered if he was talking to himself. His voice sounded different, stripped of the bravado he wore so easily.

I tilted my head, studying him. "You think I don't?" I asked, trying to keep my tone light, but he caught it—the crack, the weight I couldn't hide.

He glanced at me, something like surprise flickering in his eyes, and for a second, I wanted to tell him. I wanted to spill every regret, every mistake, every ghost I carried around. But there was something about Cole that made me hold back, something about his silence that made it feel like an intrusion. He was someone who was used to his own company, used to holding his secrets close. I wasn't sure he'd welcome mine.

Instead, I shrugged, keeping my voice even. "I think everybody's got their own load of regrets. Some of us just carry them better than others."

A faint smile tugged at his lips, barely there, but enough to give me a glimpse of something I hadn't seen before—maybe gratitude, or just relief that I wasn't going to pry. "I used to think if I could just get to them—if I could just make them pay for what they did—it'd be enough," he said, his voice tight with the kind of anger that simmered, the kind you could never quite let go of. "But it doesn't feel like enough. Not anymore."

I could feel the heat of his words, the way they wrapped around me, pulled me in. Part of me wanted to press him, to ask what he meant, but I held back, sensing the delicacy of the moment. Instead, I let the silence sit, heavy but strangely comforting.

He looked at me, something raw in his gaze, and for a moment, I thought he might say more. But then he laughed, a short, sharp sound that cut through the stillness. "Look at me, getting all sentimental up here. Must be the altitude," he said, flashing me that familiar crooked grin, but it was missing its usual spark. I could see the mask slipping back into place, piece by piece.

I rolled my eyes, leaning back on my hands. "Sure, blame it on the altitude. Just admit you're human like the rest of us," I teased, but my voice was softer than usual, my words laced with something I couldn't quite name.

"Human?" he scoffed, a bit of the usual Cole shining through, though it felt like he was trying too hard to lighten the mood. "I thought I was a little more mysterious than that."

"Oh, absolutely. You're an enigma wrapped in a puzzle, shrouded in darkness and brooding in existential angst," I said, mockingly dramatic, hoping to draw out that smirk of his that made everything feel a little less heavy. "And here I was, thinking I'd cracked the code."

He snorted, shaking his head. "You think you've cracked me, huh? That's bold." He leaned in, close enough that I could feel the warmth of him, his eyes gleaming in the low light. "So, tell me, Sherlock—what do you think you've figured out?"

My heart thudded, caught off guard by the sudden intensity in his gaze. I wanted to look away, make some joke to break the tension, but I couldn't. His eyes held me there, locked in place, and for once, I felt like I was the one being read.

I took a breath, gathering my thoughts, not entirely sure if I should say what was on my mind. But something in his gaze told me he was listening, really listening, in a way he rarely did. "I think you're carrying around a lot more than you let on," I said quietly, my voice barely a whisper. "And I think sometimes, you want someone to help you carry it."

He held my gaze, his expression unreadable, but I saw a flicker of something—pain, maybe, or recognition. For a heartbeat, I thought he might let me in, let me see past the walls he kept so firmly in place. But then he shook his head, his expression hardening.

"Maybe," he said, his voice flat, dismissive. "But that's not your job."

I wanted to argue, to tell him that sometimes, people needed others, that it didn't make him weak. But I knew better. Cole was the kind of person who had to come to things on his own terms. Pushing him would only make him retreat further. So instead, I just gave a small nod, letting him know I'd heard him, even if I didn't agree.

We sat there for a while, the silence stretching between us again, but this time, it felt different. It was a comfortable sort of quiet, the kind you didn't need to fill. I watched the stars, feeling their light wash over me, and for a moment, I felt a strange sense of peace. Maybe we didn't have all the answers, and maybe Cole was still a mystery I hadn't fully unraveled. But for now, this was enough.

After a while, he sighed, running a hand through his hair, his expression softening just a bit. "You're stubborn, you know that?" he muttered, a hint of amusement in his voice.

I grinned, leaning back, the tension between us easing. "That's funny, coming from you. You're basically the human embodiment of a brick wall."

He chuckled, the sound low and warm, and for the first time that night, it felt like we were just two people, sitting under the stars, forgetting for a moment all the darkness waiting for us down below. It was a rare thing, this quiet connection, and I held onto it, hoping that maybe, just maybe, it was a step toward something real.

Just as I was starting to relax, he shifted, his gaze turning serious again, catching me off guard. "But hey," he said, his tone softer now, almost vulnerable. "Thanks. For sticking around, I mean. Even when it would probably be smarter to leave."

I looked at him, my heart doing that annoying thing where it sped up at the slightest hint of sincerity from him. "What can I say? I'm as stubborn as they come."

And just like that, the barrier between us softened, if only a little. We sat in silence once more, and I couldn't help but feel like maybe, despite everything, we were both exactly where we were supposed to be.

The breeze picked up, a cool shiver that ran down my spine, though I didn't know if it was from the chill of the night or the weight of everything left unsaid between us. Cole was quiet again, his profile etched against the city's distant lights, and I wondered if he even realized how tightly he held himself, like one wrong move and he'd shatter.

I nudged his shoulder with mine, a gentle nudge meant to break the tension without words. "You know," I said, my voice playful, though my heart was pounding, "for someone who seems allergic to sharing, you're surprisingly good at it when you want to be."

He huffed, the barest hint of a smile tugging at the corner of his mouth. "Don't get used to it," he muttered. "I'm pretty sure I've met my yearly quota of heartfelt confessions."

I smirked, leaning back on my hands. "Noted. But hey, for the record, I think you've got one or two more in you. Somewhere, buried under all that grit and scowl, there's a heart."

"Oh, don't start that," he warned, but there was warmth in his voice, a softness that had nothing to do with the words. "I'm still dangerous, you know. That's the whole reason you're supposed to be keeping your distance."

I rolled my eyes. "Yes, yes, dangerous and brooding and just so tragically misunderstood," I teased, tipping my head back to look at the stars. "It's a wonder I'm not shaking in my boots."

He raised a brow, a spark of challenge in his eyes. "You should be."

"Oh, please." I laughed, louder than I'd intended, but it felt good, releasing some of the tension that had built up. "Cole, you couldn't scare me if you tried. You're too... human." I knew it was risky to say, to pull back the layers he'd so carefully crafted, but I couldn't stop myself. "You try to be this untouchable, impenetrable guy, but you care. Whether you like it or not, you care about the people you've lost. And that makes you... not scary."

For a moment, I saw something crack in his expression, a flash of vulnerability so quick I might have imagined it. He looked away, jaw tight, and when he spoke, his voice was low. "Maybe that's what makes me dangerous," he said. "Because caring? It's a liability. You get people involved, and you put a target on their back. And if something happens to them... that's on you." His words were hard, but there was an ache beneath them, one he couldn't hide.

I felt a pang in my chest, an instinct to reach out, to reassure him. But I held back, knowing it wouldn't be welcome, that he'd pull away the second I got too close. Instead, I kept my tone light, even as my heart twisted. "Well, maybe some of us are okay with a target. Ever think of that?" I said, keeping my voice steady. "Maybe some of us don't need protecting."

He gave me a long, measured look, his eyes dark and searching, as if he were seeing me for the first time. "You say that now," he replied, his voice quiet, "but you don't know what you're asking for."

"Maybe I do." I crossed my arms, meeting his gaze with a stubborn tilt of my chin. "Or maybe I'm just reckless. Either way, you're stuck with me, so you might as well accept it."

His lips quirked, and for a second, I thought he'd relax, let his guard down, even if just a little. But then a flicker of something caught his attention, a shadow moving in the alley below us. Instantly, he was on alert, every line of his body tense, his gaze sharp and focused.

"Stay down," he whispered, his hand moving to his side where his weapon was hidden. His entire demeanor shifted, any hint of humor or warmth gone in an instant, replaced by the cold, calculating person I'd first met.

I flattened myself against the rooftop, my heart hammering. I followed his gaze, squinting into the darkness below, trying to make out what had caught his attention. Shadows danced in the narrow alley, but I couldn't tell if it was just the wind, or something... or someone.

"What is it?" I whispered, the words barely escaping my lips.

"Not sure yet," he murmured, his eyes narrowed, tracking something just out of sight. "Could be nothing. But around here, you can never be too careful."

He edged closer to the ledge, and I couldn't help the way my stomach knotted, the unease spreading like wildfire. I wanted to reach out, pull him back, but I knew he'd never listen. He lived for this, the thrill, the danger. But there was something else in his stance, a tension I hadn't seen before. It was as if he was torn between charging in and holding back.

"Stay here," he said, his voice like steel.

I gritted my teeth. "And if I don't?"

He gave me a sharp look, but there was a flicker of something else in his eyes—worry, maybe, or a warning. "Just do it, okay? Please."

It was the "please" that got me. I swallowed, nodding, my mind racing as he slipped toward the edge, blending into the shadows with practiced ease. I watched him go, my chest tight with a fear I couldn't shake.

Minutes passed, each one stretching longer than the last. The silence grew heavy, oppressive, and I strained to catch any sound, any sign of him. But there was nothing, just the soft murmur of the city below, oblivious to whatever danger lurked in the shadows.

And then, a flash—a sharp, bright light that cut through the darkness, followed by a muffled shout. My heart seized, and before I could think, before I could stop myself, I was on my feet, creeping toward the ledge.

Peering over, I saw him, barely, his figure outlined in the dim glow from a nearby streetlamp. He was crouched low, his back against the wall, breathing hard, his gaze flicking around as if he were cornered. And there, at the other end of the alley, was a figure cloaked in shadows, moving slowly, methodically, closing in.

I froze, my pulse pounding, my instincts screaming to get down, to hide. But I couldn't leave him there, couldn't just sit and watch while he faced whatever this was alone. My hand clenched around a loose brick, the only thing within reach, but I knew it was useless, a foolish weapon against whatever he was up against.

Then, without warning, the figure lunged, a blur of movement, and Cole sprang forward, meeting them head-on. They clashed in the darkness, a flurry of limbs and shadows, and I could barely make out who was winning, who was losing.

I bit back a shout, my nails digging into the rough surface of the rooftop. Everything in me screamed to jump down, to help, but I knew I'd only make things worse. And then, just as quickly as it had started, it was over.

Cole stood, panting, his figure slumped but still upright, his opponent sprawled on the ground, unmoving. Relief flooded through me, the tension in my shoulders loosening—until I saw it.

A second figure, lurking in the shadows, a gleam of silver in their hand.

Before I could scream, could warn him, the figure stepped forward, the blade catching the faint light. Cole's eyes flicked up, widening in recognition, but it was too late. The figure lunged, and in a heartbeat, everything went dark.

Chapter 8: Echoes in the Glass

Cole's hand on my waist feels more like a brand than an anchor, burning a path through the fabric of my dress. It's a calculated move, I remind myself, a ruse to keep us looking convincingly tangled in each other, just two strangers swept up in the fever of the dance floor. But as his fingers flex against my hip, I lose the thread of my own reminders. Just for a moment.

The music pounds in my chest, matching the quickening beat of my heart. Overhead, lights flash in erratic patterns, casting a kaleidoscope of colors across his face, highlighting the sharp angles of his jaw, the glint in his eyes that I can't quite read. He leans in, close enough that I can feel the warmth of him against my cheek, and his breath skates along my neck, so close it's almost a kiss.

"Try to look like you're enjoying this," he murmurs, low enough that only I can hear, though his tone has more of a taunt than an invitation.

"Oh, believe me," I shoot back, matching his smirk with one of my own, "I'm having the time of my life." I toss my head back, letting out a laugh that's all for show, even if there's a dangerous thrill stirring inside me. After all, we're playing a game here—one I know better than to lose.

His hand slides lower, and I realize we're getting close to the back room, the real reason we're here. The Syndicate keeps their secrets well-guarded, hidden beneath layers of luxury and indulgence, but we've managed to worm our way into their den. All we need now is access to their private quarters, where their leaders gather under the pretense of exclusivity, and if we're lucky, we might just walk away with the information that could bring them down.

Cole pulls me close, his mouth so near my ear that I can feel every syllable vibrate through me. "Keep it up," he says, voice laced with that familiar edge of mockery. "We're nearly there."

My heart thuds, both from the thrill of our proximity and the danger waiting behind that door. It's a strange mix, this cocktail of fear and exhilaration, but I can't let him see the nerves chipping away at my carefully built facade.

The doors to the VIP area are guarded by two hulking men in suits, their faces expressionless as they scan the crowd. But Cole, ever the actor, pulls me close, leaning down to brush his lips against my collarbone, all while slipping a folded hundred into the guard's hand. I barely have time to process the boldness of his gesture before the doors swing open, ushering us into a corridor lined with mirrors and dim, golden lights.

I can still feel the phantom warmth of his lips on my skin as we slip into the shadowed hallway. Our reflections trail alongside us in the mirrored walls, fractured and distorted by the low light, as if the glass itself is judging us. I catch glimpses of myself, a stranger in this expensive dress and smoky makeup, a mirage built solely for tonight. Cole's reflection hovers beside me, his face set in a determined mask, but I catch a flicker of something softer in his eyes—a vulnerability that I know he'd never admit to. I file it away, unsure what to make of it.

When we reach the end of the corridor, he glances down at me, his expression unreadable. "Ready?"

I lift my chin, meeting his gaze with a defiance I don't entirely feel. "I was born ready." It's a lie, but I'd rather die than let him see the truth—that my hands are trembling, that every nerve in my body is drumming with anticipation and fear.

We slip into the room, and the world changes. Gone is the vibrant chaos of the nightclub; here, the air is thick with a different kind of tension. The lighting is low, casting everything in a muted glow that speaks of secrets and whispered deals. A group of men sit around a sleek glass table, their faces half-hidden in shadow. They glance up as we enter, their expressions unreadable, but the flicker of suspicion in their eyes tells me they've already marked us as outsiders.

Cole's grip tightens on my hand, his body tense beside mine as he steps forward, his voice smooth as he introduces us under our carefully crafted aliases. I let him take the lead, weaving a story about connections and opportunities, painting a picture that's just believable enough to buy us a few minutes. The men listen, their eyes sharp and assessing, and I feel the weight of their scrutiny, each glance a silent question, each nod a small victory.

Just when I think we might have pulled it off, the tallest of them stands, his gaze locking onto mine with a sudden intensity. He steps forward, his voice low and deceptively soft. "Interesting," he says, his eyes flicking from me to Cole and back again. "But tell me... how does a couple like you find your way into a place like this?"

My stomach twists, but I force a smile, leaning into Cole as though he's my anchor, my safety. "We go where the fun is," I say, letting a lazy smile curve my lips, though my mind races for an exit plan. I can feel the weight of his hand on my hip, a silent reminder to keep it together.

The man's eyes narrow, his lips quirking into a humorless smile as he reaches into his coat pocket. "Funny," he murmurs, "I think you'll find we don't have room for uninvited guests."

Before I can react, he pulls out a sleek, black pistol, its barrel glinting in the dim light, aimed directly at us. My heart stutters, and for a moment, the world narrows to the cold metal in his hand, the lethal promise in his eyes. Cole's fingers press into my side, a silent command to stay calm, to not make any sudden moves.

Just as I'm calculating the odds of talking our way out of this, Cole's hand moves to his side, a barely perceptible flicker as he inches toward his own weapon. But the man catches the motion, his smile widening with a dark satisfaction that sends a chill down my spine.

The man's finger lingers just a little too long on the trigger, his gaze shifting between Cole and me, weighing his options, calculating. I can practically feel Cole's mind racing beside me, trying to gauge the timing, the angles. It would be easy to be afraid right now. That would be the most natural thing in the world. But instead, something sharper cuts through the fear—an indignant, simmering anger that we've been caught so soon, that the game might end before we've even had a real chance to play it.

"Well?" the man drawls, voice thick with a mocking lilt as he tilts the gun toward Cole. "Are you going to just stand there looking pretty, or are you going to explain why I shouldn't throw you both out on the street? Or worse." His brow arches, a smug little smile at the corner of his mouth, as if he thinks he's got us all figured out.

Cole glances at me, his eyes dark, a little wicked, and there's something fierce there—like he's just itching to knock this guy down a peg or two. But instead, he raises his hands slightly, a harmless, almost charming grin spreading across his face. I almost laugh at the sheer audacity of it, the ease with which he switches from threatening to suave, as though he'd planned this whole scenario down to the last detail.

"We were just looking for a good time," Cole says smoothly, his voice low, persuasive, laced with a dangerous allure that I know the man can't ignore. "Didn't realize we'd be so... unwelcome." He gestures to me, an exaggerated show of innocence, as if I'm the one who dragged him into this. I roll my eyes but play along, letting my expression soften, my body relax just a touch. If he wants to see us as harmless, I'm more than willing to play the part.

The man studies us, lips twisting as though he's weighing our excuses, deciding whether to believe our little charade. "Good time, huh?" he muses, a dark amusement flashing in his eyes. He lowers the gun a fraction, and I feel the tension in my spine loosen, just slightly.

"Funny, because I don't see many people like you down here. People with... ambitions."

I let out a soft laugh, letting my fingers trail up Cole's arm, a gentle, intimate gesture that feels foreign but necessary. "Ambitions?" I say, my voice smooth as silk, batting my lashes just a little. "Oh, honey, we just came to dance and maybe drink a little too much. This place is famous for its cocktails, after all. But if you're going to kick us out just because we like to mix things up..." I let the sentence trail off, leaving just enough room for him to wonder, to second-guess his assumptions about us.

The man's gaze lingers on me, clearly surprised by my boldness, my lack of fear—or maybe he's just deciding whether I'm genuinely foolish or expertly feigning innocence. But finally, he laughs, a sound that's as bitter as it is amused, and slides the gun back into his jacket with a small shrug. "Fine," he says, gesturing toward the door we came in through, as though it's all been a harmless misunderstanding. "But you'd better keep your noses clean. This isn't the place for nosy little dancers."

"Wouldn't dream of it," Cole replies, his voice dripping with mock sincerity, and he flashes the man a smile that's all teeth. He grips my arm, firmly guiding me back down the hallway, his posture deceptively calm, though I can feel the tightly coiled tension in every step.

We weave back through the crowded dance floor, slipping into the shadows, the music vibrating through my skin, a pounding reminder of just how close we'd come. As soon as we reach a quieter corner, Cole's mask drops, his expression darkening with frustration, his jaw clenched. "That was too close," he mutters, his voice barely audible over the beat of the music. "I thought I'd made it clear—"

"You made it clear?" I snap back, anger flaring up before I can stop myself. "If you'd just listened instead of charging in, maybe we wouldn't be dealing with bruised egos and empty hands right now."

He glances at me, one brow raised, a smirk tugging at the corner of his mouth despite the frustration simmering between us. "Oh, so now you're the authority on not charging in?"

"Yes," I hiss, crossing my arms, even though I know I'm being hypocritical. But he doesn't get to call me out on it, not when he'd practically shoved us right into the jaws of the Syndicate without a second thought. "And if you'd been just a little less reckless, we might have actually learned something useful in there."

Cole's smirk fades, his gaze hardening as he takes a step closer, lowering his voice so only I can hear. "You know what?" he murmurs, voice sharp as glass. "If you have a better plan, by all means, I'm all ears. But until then, maybe you could try trusting me just a little. Or is that too much to ask?"

I open my mouth to retort, but the words catch in my throat. Trust. It's a loaded word, one that digs its claws into old wounds, past betrayals. I want to tell him I don't trust easily, that I don't trust anyone—not anymore. But instead, I swallow the words, narrowing my eyes at him, letting the silence stretch taut between us.

Finally, he sighs, running a hand through his hair, his shoulders slumping just a fraction. "Look, let's just get out of here before we attract more attention," he mutters, glancing around as if expecting someone to leap out of the shadows. "We can regroup. Figure out a new approach."

I nod, unwilling to argue any further, but I can't help the way my heart clenches, the sting of our close call still fresh. We slip through the side exit, emerging into the cool night air, the sounds of the club fading into the background. The streets are quiet, deserted, and for a moment, we're just two people standing in the dark, breathing in the city's chill.

Cole glances at me, his expression softening as though he, too, is feeling the weight of our narrow escape. "Look," he says, breaking the silence, his voice unexpectedly gentle, "we'll get them next time. We just... need to be a little smarter about it."

I give a reluctant nod, unable to resist the faint smile tugging at my lips despite the tension still lingering between us. "Fine," I say, my tone playful, a teasing edge in my voice. "But next time, maybe don't get so handsy. People might start thinking we're... friends."

He laughs, a genuine sound that cuts through the darkness, and for a moment, I catch a glimpse of something raw and real in his eyes. He leans in close, his voice low and conspiratorial. "Trust me," he murmurs, his breath warm against my cheek, "that's the last thing I want people thinking." And yet, the flicker in his gaze suggests he's not entirely convinced of his own words.

The night air is sharp and cold, a stark contrast to the thick, throbbing warmth inside the club, and I'm grateful for it. I'm still reeling from the close call, from the heat of Cole's hand on my hip, from the way he'd played his role so perfectly, so convincingly, that I almost believed him. Almost. But as we stand in the alley, just out of the glow of the streetlight, reality crashes back in, and the stakes press against me like a physical weight.

Cole's posture is relaxed, too relaxed, as though we haven't just escaped a Syndicate enforcer by the skin of our teeth. His eyes scan the empty street, calculating, a faint smirk lingering on his lips as though he's still riding the high of our little charade. And despite everything, a small part of me hates that he can make it look so easy.

He glances over, catching me staring, and his smirk widens. "You know," he says, crossing his arms as he leans casually against the wall, "for someone who claims to have nerves of steel, you seemed a little... tense in there." His voice is light, teasing, but I can hear the edge beneath it, the challenge he can never seem to resist throwing my way.

I huff, crossing my own arms to mirror him. "Tense? Please. If anyone was tense, it was you, Mr. 'I-have-a-plan-but-let's-not-tell-anyone-until-the-last-possible-second.'" My voice drips with sarcasm, and I can't help but take satisfaction in the flicker of annoyance that crosses his face.

"Maybe if you could follow along without questioning everything, I wouldn't have to keep you in the dark," he shoots back, his tone sharper now, the playful edge fading.

"Oh, so it's my fault now?" I snap, my frustration bubbling over. "Forgive me for not blindly following your reckless, half-baked ideas. Some of us actually like having all the facts before we walk into a death trap."

He straightens, dropping the casual act, and for a moment, there's real anger in his eyes, a fire that matches my own. "You think I don't know what I'm doing?" he demands, his voice low, dangerous. "Because I hate to break it to you, but if it weren't for me, you'd still be fumbling your way through this city with a target on your back."

I open my mouth to fire back, but the words die on my lips. He's right, infuriatingly right, and we both know it. He's saved me more times than I care to admit, pulled me out of tight spots, kept me from making stupid, impulsive moves that would've gotten me killed. But I can't let him see that, can't let him know just how much I rely on him. Not when he already holds so much power over me, even if he doesn't realize it.

Instead, I take a steadying breath, forcing my voice to stay calm, measured. "Look," I say, trying to find some common ground, "we both want the same thing. We're on the same side, remember?"

For a moment, he just stares at me, the intensity in his gaze sending a shiver down my spine. Then, finally, he nods, his posture relaxing slightly, though the tension between us is still palpable, like a live wire. "Fine," he says, his tone softer, almost resigned. "But next time, try trusting me. Just a little."

I give a reluctant nod, though I can't shake the feeling that trusting Cole, of all people, is the last thing I should be doing. Still,

I don't argue. Not tonight. Not when we're both still coming down from the adrenaline of our close call.

We fall into a tense silence as we make our way down the empty street, each lost in our own thoughts. The city around us feels oddly quiet, the usual hum of nightlife muted, as though the whole world is holding its breath, waiting. I keep glancing over my shoulder, half-expecting the Syndicate enforcer to appear out of the shadows, to finish what he started. But the alley remains empty, the streetlights casting long, eerie shadows across the pavement.

As we round a corner, Cole suddenly stops, his hand shooting out to grab my arm, pulling me back into the shadows. I open my mouth to protest, but he silences me with a look, his eyes narrowed, focused on something just beyond the edge of the streetlight. I follow his gaze, and my heart skips a beat as I see them—two men, standing by a sleek, black car, their eyes scanning the street with a predatory intensity.

"Friends of yours?" I whisper, my voice barely audible, but I can't keep the edge of fear out of it.

Cole shakes his head, his jaw tight. "No. But they're definitely Syndicate. And they're looking for someone." He glances at me, his eyes dark, calculating. "Think we can lose them?"

I hesitate, the fear twisting in my gut, but I nod. "Yeah," I say, forcing a confidence I don't feel. "Let's go."

We slip back into the shadows, moving quickly but quietly, our footsteps muffled by the soft thrum of the city around us. My heart hammers in my chest, the familiar rush of adrenaline mingling with a sick sense of dread as we weave through narrow alleys and empty side streets, trying to put as much distance as possible between us and the Syndicate's men.

But it doesn't take long before I hear the sound of footsteps behind us, echoing off the brick walls, growing closer with each step. I glance over at Cole, my pulse racing, and I can see the same realization in his eyes. We're not going to outrun them.

Without a word, Cole grabs my hand, pulling me down a side alley, his grip firm, steady, and for a brief, absurd moment, I feel safe. As though as long as he's holding onto me, we'll be okay. But then we reach a dead end, a towering wall blocking our path, and the footsteps are getting closer, louder, until I can hear the low murmur of voices, cold and mocking, drawing nearer with each second.

Cole curses under his breath, his eyes darting around, looking for an escape, a way out. But there's nothing. Nowhere to go, nowhere to hide. And then, just as I feel the last shreds of hope slipping away, he turns to me, his expression hard, determined.

"Trust me," he says, his voice low, fierce, and before I can process what he's doing, he's pulling me toward him, his hands tangling in my hair, his lips crushing against mine in a kiss that's rough, desperate, a last-ditch attempt to keep us hidden in plain sight.

The footsteps slow, the voices hushed, and I can feel the men watching us, their gazes heavy, but I force myself to stay still, to play my part, my fingers clutching the fabric of Cole's jacket as though I'm lost in him, as though he's the only thing in the world that matters. And for one terrifying, thrilling moment, it almost feels real.

But then I hear a voice, cold and amused, slicing through the silence. "Well, well," the man says, his tone dripping with mockery. "What do we have here?"

Chapter 9: The Breaking Point

The night air outside the club is dense, clinging to my skin with that sticky kind of humidity that only the city in the throes of late summer can manage. Neon signs hum overhead, their pinks and blues casting strange, shifting shadows across the pavement, like some twisted impressionist painting that never quite settles. The plan was simple, executed clean, and yet, I can't shake the nagging feeling that we're leaving with a puzzle more tangled than before. We got what we came for, technically speaking—the encrypted drive now weighs down my jacket pocket, a heavy reminder of tonight's tangled mess. But there's something else, something gnawing at me, an unanswered question lurking behind his guarded stare.

He walks beside me, silent as a shadow, his hands stuffed into his coat pockets, shoulders drawn up like he's trying to make himself smaller. It's something he does when he's thinking, when he's wrestling with some inner monologue he's never going to share with me. A part of me wants to break the silence, to ask him what went wrong back there—because something did, I know it. But his face is all stone and iron, and I can already predict the chill in his response.

We reach the hideout—our hideout, I suppose, though I'm loath to call it home. It's nothing more than an abandoned loft, windows cracked and a layer of dust thick enough to write a manifesto in, if one were so inclined. The faint scent of dampness hangs in the air, but it's hidden behind the faint sweetness of the wildflowers I'd found in an alley a few days ago. I'd put them in an empty whiskey bottle and set them on the windowsill, and the absurdity of it makes me smile even now, despite the tension simmering between us.

He drops his coat over the back of a battered armchair and heads straight for the window, staring out like there's something out there he's forgotten. The silence stretches long, like he's testing it, waiting for me to crack. Fine. Two can play that game.

"So, are we just not going to talk about it?" My voice cuts through the stillness, sharper than I'd intended, but I don't care. He's been dancing around me for weeks now, and I'm done with his routine of brooding silence.

He doesn't turn around. "What's there to talk about?"

That calm, detached tone—it grates on my nerves, makes me want to grab his shoulders and shake him until something real, something human, spills out. "Oh, I don't know," I say, sarcasm lacing my words. "Maybe why you felt the need to sabotage every single lead we had in there. Or why you're acting like I'm the problem, when all I've done is try to figure out what the hell is going on in that head of yours."

Finally, he turns, and there's a flicker of something behind his eyes, a crack in the wall he's built around himself. But it's gone as quickly as it came, replaced by that icy calm that I've come to know far too well. "This is a job, nothing more. I don't need you overanalyzing every little thing, making it out to be some grand conspiracy. We get in, get what we need, get out. That's all it is."

I feel the words like a slap, and I know he sees it, knows that his indifference is cutting deeper than I'd ever admit. "Right," I say, forcing a laugh that comes out hollow. "Just a job. That's all this is to you."

The words echo in the room, hanging between us like a ghost neither of us wants to acknowledge. His face softens for a fraction of a second, something like regret flickering in his eyes, but he smothers it just as quickly, his gaze hardening again. I wonder if he's always been this way, or if he's just gotten better at hiding the parts of himself that might actually feel.

There's a long, weighty silence, broken only by the distant hum of traffic below. Then, to my surprise, he steps closer, his hand reaching out—hesitantly, like he's not quite sure what he's doing. His fingers brush my cheek, barely more than a whisper of a touch, but it's enough to make my breath hitch. He's close enough now that I can see the faint stubble on his jaw, the way his lips are pressed into a thin line, as if he's holding back words that he'll never let slip.

And then, as quickly as it began, the moment shatters. He pulls his hand back, retreating into himself, and the space between us feels colder, emptier than ever. I feel a pang of anger, a surge of something desperate and raw that I can't keep bottled up anymore.

"I don't get you," I say, my voice trembling with a frustration I can't hide. "One minute, you're pulling me close, acting like you actually care, and the next, you're pushing me away like I'm some kind of inconvenience. You don't get to play both sides, not with me."

He exhales sharply, like I've struck a nerve, but he doesn't respond, just stares at me with those unreadable eyes. And suddenly, I feel foolish, standing here, waiting for something that I'm not sure he's even capable of giving.

I take a step back, crossing my arms over my chest, more to shield myself than anything else. "Fine. If that's how it is, then that's how it is. But don't expect me to keep playing along with whatever game you think this is."

The words hang between us, brittle and jagged, and I feel a sudden urge to turn around, to leave before he can see how much this hurts. But I hold my ground, meeting his gaze with a defiance that I hope masks the hurt lurking beneath. And for a moment, just a moment, I think I see something shift in his eyes, a crack in the armor that he's spent so long building.

But he doesn't say anything, just watches me with that same guarded expression, as if he's waiting for me to be the one to walk away. So I do, heading toward the window, staring out into the night, my heart pounding like a war drum in my chest. It's only then, with my back to him, that I let my expression soften, let the weight of this impossible, infuriating, maddening thing between us sink in.

But whatever happens next, I know one thing for certain: he might think he can keep me at arm's length, but I'm done letting him dictate the rules of this game.

The quiet stretches between us, thick with words unspoken and emotions neither of us is brave enough to admit to, though they hover just under the surface, itching to spill out. He's retreated again, folding back into himself like he's mastered the art of disappearing in plain sight. I lean against the cracked window, the faint city lights outside flickering in and out through the grimy glass. The night air is cool against my skin, but it does nothing to calm the heat simmering under my ribs, the mix of anger and something I dare not name. The silence is unbearable.

I turn, feeling my frustration rise. "You know, you could at least pretend to care about something beyond this 'mission' you keep going on about." I say, barely able to mask the bitterness in my voice. He doesn't look at me, but I see his jaw tighten, the tiniest flicker of something slipping through the mask he wears so religiously.

"Why should I?" he replies, his voice low, a quiet intensity threading through his words. "Getting attached is a weakness. You, of all people, should understand that."

I let out a short, bitter laugh. "Right. So, I'm just supposed to shut down, keep everything neat and tidy in little boxes, never let anything or anyone in? That's how you want me to be?"

He finally looks at me, and there's a flicker of frustration in his eyes, a hint that maybe, just maybe, he's as tired of this as I am. "You don't know what you're asking for," he says, his voice a razor's edge away from a warning. "This isn't the kind of life that leaves room for—" He stops himself, biting off the rest of his words like he's afraid they might betray him.

"For what?" I push, stepping closer, unable to help myself. I want to know what he's holding back, why he's so intent on keeping everything at arm's length, even me. Especially me.

His eyes flicker away, and I almost think he's going to retreat again, to disappear into that iron fortress he's built around himself. But instead, he lets out a long, weary sigh, his shoulders slumping just enough that I know I've hit a nerve.

"For anything real," he says finally, so quietly I almost miss it. "The moment you let something become real, it's a liability. It becomes something they can use against you."

There it is, the truth hidden in those few, carefully chosen words. It's not that he doesn't feel anything—he does. He's just terrified of it, of what it might mean, of what it might cost him. I want to tell him that I understand, that I've spent most of my life guarding myself just as carefully, building walls around every vulnerable piece of me so that no one could ever reach them. But somehow, he's slipped past my defenses, and I don't know how to make him see that I'm not afraid of that. Or maybe I am, but I'm willing to face it, for him. And that realization terrifies me more than anything else.

Before I can respond, he shakes his head, as if he's already regretting letting anything slip. "This isn't a conversation we should be having," he mutters, turning his back to me. "It's pointless."

"Pointless?" I repeat, incredulous. "So, that's it, then? You're just going to pretend like none of this matters, like you don't feel anything?"

He's silent for a long moment, and then, without turning around, he says, "Maybe it's better that way."

The words hit me like a punch to the gut. I know he's trying to protect himself, that this is his way of keeping everything safe and predictable, but it doesn't make it hurt any less. For a brief, wild moment, I consider storming out, leaving him to his brooding silence and his carefully constructed walls. But something in me won't let me. I'm not done yet—not by a long shot.

"Fine," I say, crossing my arms over my chest, refusing to let him see how much this is getting to me. "If that's how you want to play it, then go ahead. Keep pushing everyone away, keep pretending like nothing matters. But don't expect me to just sit here and watch you tear yourself apart."

He turns then, his eyes blazing with something raw and fierce, something I've never seen before. "You think I don't know what I'm doing?" he says, his voice barely more than a whisper, laced with an edge of something dangerously close to desperation. "You think I don't know exactly what this is costing me?"

For the first time, I see past his defenses, past the carefully crafted facade he hides behind. There's fear there, yes, but there's also something else, something vulnerable and achingly human that he's spent so long trying to bury. And in that moment, I realize that he's just as trapped as I am, just as caught up in this web of secrets and lies that we've built around ourselves.

I take a step closer, reaching out before I can stop myself, my fingers brushing against his arm. "You don't have to do this alone," I say softly, my voice barely more than a whisper. "You don't have to keep shutting everyone out."

For a moment, he just stands there, frozen, like he's not sure what to do with the gesture. And then, slowly, almost reluctantly, he reaches up, his hand covering mine. It's a small, tentative gesture, but it's enough to make my heart pound, to make me feel like maybe, just maybe, there's hope for something beyond this endless cycle of pain and self-destruction.

But then, just as quickly, he pulls away, his expression hardening once again. "This is a mistake," he says, his voice cold and detached. "Getting close to people... it only leads to pain. You should know that better than anyone."

The words sting, but I refuse to back down. "Maybe it does," I reply, my voice steady, even though I can feel my heart breaking. "But maybe some things are worth the risk."

He looks at me then, really looks at me, and for a brief, fleeting moment, I think he's going to let his walls come down, that he's going to let me in. But then he shakes his head, his gaze turning distant, like he's already a million miles away.

"This isn't one of those things," he says quietly, and I can hear the finality in his voice, the unspoken promise that he's not going to let me get any closer than this.

I bite back the frustration rising in my throat, the urge to scream at him, to make him see that he's not as alone as he thinks he is. But I know it won't do any good. He's made his choice, and as much as it hurts, I have to respect that. For now, at least.

Turning away, I head back toward the window, staring out into the dark, endless city below. It feels like we're both standing on the edge of a precipice, teetering on the brink of something we're too afraid to name. And as much as I want to take that leap, I know that he's not ready. Maybe he never will be.

But as I stand there, listening to the silence stretch out between us, I can't help but wonder if, someday, he'll find the courage to face whatever it is he's running from. And maybe, just maybe, I'll be there waiting for him when he does.

The room seems to close in around us, every inch of air between us charged with things we'll never say. He's pulled back into his shell, and I feel the cold absence of his touch on my cheek like a physical ache. It's maddening, this endless game of retreat and advance, and I'm not sure how much longer I can keep playing. But then, just as I'm about to let the silence swallow me whole, I catch a glimpse of something outside the window—a flicker of movement in the alley below, barely perceptible, but enough to snap me back to the moment.

I tense, scanning the darkness, every instinct honed from years of watching my back. His gaze sharpens as he follows my line of sight, his posture shifting, the guarded distance between us momentarily forgotten. He moves silently, slipping toward the window, his face set with that look he gets when he senses trouble. It's a reminder of why we're here, why we can't afford the luxuries of emotion or attachment. But even as I watch him, alert and focused, I can't shake the feeling that he's hiding more than just secrets from me.

He turns to me, a single look telling me all I need to know. I nod, reaching for the pistol strapped to my side, feeling the cold weight of it in my hand. We don't need words; we've done this enough times that instinct takes over, filling in the gaps where conversation would be too slow. Silently, we slip out of the room, moving through the abandoned building with the kind of practiced ease that comes from too many nights spent in places like this—places that reek of desperation and secrets better left buried.

Down in the alley, the sounds of the city are muted, wrapped in the thick silence of early morning, when even the rats have retreated to quieter shadows. My pulse quickens as I scan the shadows, every nerve alert, waiting for the slightest indication of who, or what, might be watching us. Beside me, he's just as tense, his gaze sweeping over the brick walls, the damp, glistening pavement, every dark corner where an ambush could be waiting. And then, like a whisper on the wind, there it is—a flicker of movement to our left, just beyond the reach of the streetlight.

I glance at him, my breath caught in my throat, and he gives a barely perceptible nod. We split, moving in opposite directions, our footsteps muffled against the grime-slick pavement. I feel the familiar rush of adrenaline, the way my senses sharpen, the weight of the pistol in my hand grounding me as I edge closer to the shadow.

And then, out of nowhere, a figure steps into the light, startlingly close. I freeze, and he does too, just long enough for me to take in the details—the hood pulled low over his face, the glint of something silver tucked into his waistband, the wary look in his eyes as they flicker between us. He's young, barely older than me, with the kind of lean, restless energy that speaks of too many sleepless nights and too much to hide. For a moment, I think he's going to bolt, and I feel the urge to call out, to tell him we're not here to hurt him, but something in his expression stops me cold.

"Who sent you?" he asks, his voice low, rough, like he's spent years swallowing secrets that have turned to rust inside him.

Beside me, my partner shifts, his face unreadable, but I can feel the tension rolling off him in waves. He doesn't respond, just watches the stranger with that quiet intensity that borders on unnerving. The silence stretches, taut and heavy, and I can see the young man's hand inching toward his waistband, toward whatever weapon he thinks will protect him.

I clear my throat, taking a careful step forward, my hands raised in a gesture of peace. "We're not here for a fight," I say, trying to keep my voice steady, calm. "We just want some answers."

His gaze snaps to me, sharp and assessing, and for a moment, I see a flicker of recognition in his eyes, as if he's sizing me up and finding something familiar. But then it's gone, replaced by a wary defensiveness that makes my skin prickle with unease.

"You're looking for something," he says, his voice barely above a whisper. "Something dangerous."

I swallow, glancing at my partner, whose face remains impassive, giving nothing away. But there's a shift in his stance, a subtle change that tells me he's as rattled as I am, even if he'd never admit it. "And how would you know that?" I ask, unable to keep the suspicion from my voice.

The young man's lips twist into a bitter smile. "Because I've been looking for it too."

He reaches into his pocket, and instinctively, I raise my pistol, my heart pounding. But instead of a weapon, he pulls out a small, worn notebook, its pages frayed and stained with something that looks alarmingly like blood. He holds it out, his gaze never leaving mine, and I hesitate, glancing at my partner for confirmation. He gives a slight nod, his eyes locked on the stranger, ready for any sudden moves.

I take the notebook, feeling the rough texture of the worn leather cover under my fingers. The pages are filled with cramped handwriting, strange symbols, notes scrawled in the margins. It's all a chaotic mess, but there's something familiar about the symbols, a faint echo of something I've seen before, though I can't quite place it.

The stranger watches me, his expression guarded, but there's a flicker of something else in his eyes—something like desperation. "They'll kill you for this, you know," he says softly, his gaze flicking between me and my partner. "They'll kill all of us."

I glance at my partner, a chill settling over me. He looks at the notebook, his face unreadable, but I can see the wheels turning in his mind, the same realization dawning on him that's creeping through my thoughts.

Before I can respond, the stranger steps back, his hand slipping into his pocket. "If you're smart, you'll leave this alone," he says, his voice barely more than a whisper. "But if you're as stubborn as I think you are, then... good luck."

And then he's gone, disappearing into the shadows with a swiftness that leaves us both frozen, caught in the gravity of what he's left behind. I glance at my partner, the unspoken question hanging between us, too heavy to ignore.

He meets my gaze, his expression hard, determined. "We can't walk away from this," he says, his voice firm, steady.

I nod, clutching the notebook, the weight of it pressing into my palm like a brand. Whatever secrets lie within these pages, they've become ours to uncover, whether we like it or not.

And just as we turn to head back, a low, rumbling sound echoes through the alley—a car engine, growing louder, closer, until it feels like the very walls are vibrating with its approach. I feel my heart stutter, the notebook clutched tighter in my hands, and I meet his gaze, a silent understanding passing between us.

Then, just as the headlights blaze around the corner, flooding the alley with a harsh, blinding light, I realize that this is no coincidence. We've been found.

Chapter 10: The Descent

The air was damp, thick with the scent of mildew and something faintly metallic, a smell that clung to the inside of my nostrils and coated my tongue. Cole moved just ahead of me, his shadow merging with mine, a flickering blur against the graffiti-streaked walls. Each of our steps on the cracked concrete floor echoed, a hollow sound that seemed to bounce back at us as if the darkness itself was alive, breathing, watching.

There was no light save for the single flashlight clutched in my hand, casting long, slender beams that only sharpened the shadows. The abandoned subway station stretched out around us, endless, with broken-down pillars and rusting tracks tangled like forgotten vines. A chill danced along my skin, the kind that prickles and itches as if someone's whispered something ominous just behind your ear.

"You sure this is the place?" I whispered, keeping my voice low, though I wasn't sure why. Even silence felt like it could crack under the weight of what lay beneath it.

Cole glanced back at me, one eyebrow raised, his jaw set in that ever-present mix of skepticism and amusement. "Only if you trust the intel," he replied, his tone dripping with sarcasm that might've annoyed me on a better day. But down here, in this half-light, with his face partially hidden, he looked like he belonged to this world, to the mystery and shadows. It unnerved me more than I'd admit.

We pressed on, and the station seemed to breathe around us. The farther we went, the thicker the shadows grew, swallowing the remnants of light that managed to slip down from the fractured ceiling. I could almost feel the weight of the city above us, a pulsing, distant reminder of the world that still went on, oblivious to the secrets festering below.

Cole stopped suddenly, and I nearly collided into him. His arm was warm and solid as I braced myself, and for a heartbeat, I stayed there, fingers brushing against the fabric of his sleeve. He looked down, the smirk gone, replaced by something far more intent, and I could swear his gaze softened, just for a moment.

"Look," he murmured, gesturing toward an archway partially obscured by debris and rusted metal shards. Symbols—crude, jagged symbols—had been scratched into the stone. They were dark, inky stains on the dull gray wall, like bruises that never healed. Symbols I didn't understand, but that sent a prickle of something—fear, or excitement, or both—down my spine.

"The Syndicate's mark," I whispered, reaching out without thinking, my fingertips brushing over the rough etchings. They were strange and twisted, spiraling into each other with a chaotic, almost dizzying pattern. "So this is it. We're in their lair."

He nodded, but there was an edge to his expression, a tightening of his mouth that told me he was as uneasy as I was. "Don't get too excited. They don't leave these kinds of clues just lying around. This could be bait, you know."

"I thought you liked taking risks," I replied, a half-smile tugging at my lips.

His eyes flickered, catching the light in a way that made them almost glint. "With risks, sure. With traps? Not so much."

I rolled my eyes, but I could feel the heat of his gaze as he stepped closer, his voice low. "Besides, I need you alive for this." His breath was warm against my ear, stirring the fine hairs on my neck, and I swallowed, hoping he didn't notice. Whatever was between us—this tension, this push and pull of attraction and suspicion—was almost tangible. It hung in the air, sharper than any of the rusty metal strewn around us.

The room we stepped into next was unlike anything I'd seen, and it made even the Syndicate's symbols outside look like child's play. The walls were lined with shelves, sagging and crumbling, but still filled with strange relics—twisted masks, rusted knives, pieces of what looked like ancient maps scribbled over with spidery handwriting. My gaze traveled over each item, feeling like I was looking at fragments of a dark, tangled story I couldn't quite unravel.

A faint flicker of movement caught my eye, and I stiffened, reaching for my weapon, only to realize it was a curtain swaying, blown by some hidden draft. Cole noticed it too, his shoulders relaxing just slightly, but the look he gave me was one of wary amusement. "Jumping at curtains now, huh?"

"Just because you don't scare doesn't mean the rest of us are robots," I muttered, gripping the hilt of my blade tighter.

His mouth curved into that cocky, infuriating grin that somehow still managed to make me feel warm. "Scared? You?"

I shot him a glare, but he just chuckled softly, the sound low and surprisingly intimate in the close quarters. Then, his expression shifted, and his gaze turned serious, his eyes locking onto mine. He was so close now, the lines of his face softened by the dim, flickering light from my flashlight. For a split second, it felt like there was no abandoned subway, no Syndicate—just the two of us in the thick, electric quiet.

But then, he pulled away, as if remembering himself, and the moment shattered like glass. "Keep your guard up," he said, his voice rougher than before, and I wondered if he'd felt it too—that strange, dizzying pull. Or if this was just part of his game, the same game he'd been playing since the day we met.

Shaking it off, I moved past him, determined not to let him see just how rattled I was. The room stretched on, with more strange objects scattered across the floor, symbols carved into nearly every surface. There was something unsettlingly deliberate about it all, as if it was left here to be found. A warning. Or a trap. Either way, it was hard to shake the feeling that we were being watched.

Cole seemed to sense it too, his posture shifting, his movements more calculated as he scanned the shadows. We were nearly to the far side of the room when I heard it—a faint sound, like footsteps, barely a whisper against the silence.

I froze, my pulse hammering, and turned to look at Cole, whose expression was deadly serious. He gave me a nod, his gaze hardening, and together we slipped back toward the shadows, hearts pounding, nerves alight, bracing ourselves for whatever waited in the depths of the darkened subway station.

A low creak echoed from somewhere behind us, the sound slipping through the silence like a knife. Cole stiffened beside me, his eyes narrowing as he scanned the darkness. My fingers twitched around the flashlight, and for a moment, I found myself holding my breath, the air thick with the sense that something—or someone—was lurking just out of reach, concealed in the shadows. I swallowed hard, hoping the noise was just the old station settling, but in a place like this, hope was a fragile thing.

"Did you hear that?" I whispered, my voice barely more than a breath.

Cole gave a tight nod, his expression unreadable, but I caught the glint of determination in his eyes. "Stay close. If this goes south, don't try to play hero," he muttered, his voice barely audible. "I'm not dragging you out of here if you get yourself into trouble."

I rolled my eyes, even as my heart hammered. "Noted," I said, more confidently than I felt.

We pressed on, slipping past decaying columns and skirting around piles of debris that had accumulated over the years. With each step, the air grew colder, a biting chill that seemed to wrap around me, tightening like an invisible grip. My breath puffed out in small clouds, visible even in the faint light. I tried to focus, tried to ignore the fact that Cole's arm brushed against mine as we walked, the warmth of him startlingly noticeable in this frozen, shadowy underworld.

Then we came to a stop, abruptly, as if pulled by some invisible force. Cole held up a hand, signaling for silence, though the tension in his jaw made it clear that he wasn't exactly at ease himself. I followed his gaze to a darkened corner of the room, where an ancient, weathered door stood ajar, its surface etched with more of the Syndicate's eerie symbols. Beyond it, a narrow stairwell twisted down into an even deeper layer of darkness, as if inviting us to leave every shred of reason and caution behind.

"You first," I whispered, nudging him with a smirk I didn't quite feel.

He shot me a look, one eyebrow arched, but he didn't argue. Without a word, he stepped forward, his hand brushing mine for a moment, sending an unexpected jolt through me that I pretended not to notice. We moved slowly, the rickety stairs creaking beneath us with each step, the sound amplified by the oppressive quiet. Down here, every noise felt like a betrayal, like it was giving away our presence to something lurking in the shadows, something waiting for us to slip.

At the bottom of the stairs, we found ourselves in another corridor, narrower and darker than before. This one was different, though—fresher. The walls here were devoid of dust, the floors free of debris, as though this section of the station hadn't been abandoned at all. The symbols on the walls glistened in the light, freshly carved and still slick with paint. Whoever had done this had been here recently, and they had taken care to leave a message.

Cole shot me a warning glance, his mouth set in a grim line. "Stay sharp. We're not alone."

He didn't have to tell me twice. I could feel it, too—a heavy, almost suffocating awareness that pressed down on me, making my skin prickle with unease. Every shadow seemed to shift, every echo seemed to carry a hidden threat. We moved forward, and with each step, I couldn't shake the feeling that we were being watched, that unseen eyes were tracking our movements, waiting for the perfect moment to strike.

Then, without warning, a figure stepped out of the shadows, blocking our path. Tall, draped in dark clothing, his face obscured by a hood, he stood there silently, his presence menacing in its stillness.

My pulse quickened, and I instinctively tightened my grip on my flashlight, feeling the small, reassuring weight of my knife hidden in my jacket pocket.

Cole took a step forward, his stance calm but alert, his gaze fixed on the stranger. "Nice night for a stroll, isn't it?" he drawled, his tone light but edged with warning.

The stranger didn't respond, just tilted his head slightly, as if studying us, his gaze moving from Cole to me with a chilling intensity. I could see the glint of something metallic in his hand—a knife, thin and deadly sharp, catching the faint light with a gleam that sent a shiver down my spine.

"Not one for small talk, are we?" Cole continued, his voice casual, though I could see the tension in his shoulders, the readiness to strike if it came to that. "Fine by me. We're just here for a look around."

The stranger's lips curved into a thin smile, a gesture devoid of warmth. "You don't belong here," he said, his voice low and smooth, each word sliding through the silence like oil over glass. "Turn back now, while you still have the chance."

Cole's eyes flashed, a spark of challenge in his gaze. "Thanks for the advice," he replied, his tone mocking. "But I'm afraid we're already invested. Isn't that right?" He glanced over at me, the corner of his mouth twitching up in that infuriating half-smile that I somehow found myself matching.

The stranger's eyes narrowed, his expression darkening, and for a split second, I thought he might lunge at us, knife in hand. My muscles tensed, ready to react, but instead, he took a step back, melting into the shadows as silently as he had appeared. His final words echoed down the corridor, a whisper that chilled me to the core.

"Remember, you were warned."

The silence that followed was suffocating, heavy with unspoken threats and promises of things we couldn't yet understand. Cole and I exchanged a glance, and for the first time, I saw real concern flicker across his face, a rare glimpse past the armor he wore so well. It was oddly reassuring, seeing him unnerved, as if it validated my own racing heart and the tight, anxious knot in my stomach.

"Still feel like taking risks?" I murmured, my voice barely above a whisper.

His smirk returned, though it didn't quite reach his eyes. "If you're worried, you can always wait at the top of the stairs," he shot back, his tone light but strained.

I rolled my eyes, shoving down the surge of nerves that his words had stirred. "Not a chance," I replied, forcing confidence into my voice. I stepped forward, brushing past him, ignoring the way his gaze lingered on me, as though trying to gauge whether I meant it or if I'd bolt at the first sign of trouble.

As we continued down the corridor, the walls seemed to close in around us, narrowing, darkening, until it felt like the weight of the entire city was pressing down. Every step felt heavier, every shadow seemed to stretch longer, and in the distance, I could hear something—a faint, rhythmic sound, like the beating of a heart, pulsing in time with my own.

We reached the end of the corridor, a heavy metal door looming before us. Cole stepped forward, pressing his ear to it, his eyes narrowing as he listened. I held my breath, every nerve in my body on high alert, waiting for whatever lay on the other side.

The door before us loomed like the last gate to something forbidden. It was solid metal, dented and scratched in places, and looked thick enough to block out the sound of anything that might be happening on the other side. I could almost feel a hum of energy behind it, like whatever was concealed within was so powerful it pressed against the walls, struggling to break free.

Cole tilted his head, listening, his brow furrowed in concentration. I watched him, the line of his jaw tight, his entire body tensed. It was like he was calculating something, gauging if we should turn back or step deeper into the belly of this underground labyrinth.

I barely dared to breathe, the stillness between us so taut it felt like even a whisper might set off an avalanche. Just when I thought he'd finally decided to move, he straightened, his gaze locking onto mine. "Ready?" His voice was low, almost a murmur, but there was a challenge in his eyes, a glint that dared me to back out.

I didn't give him the satisfaction. Instead, I nodded, hoping my face didn't betray the nervous jolt in my chest. "Always."

He gave a faint smirk—just enough to be maddening—then reached out, gripping the rusted handle. The door resisted at first, as if it, too, didn't want to reveal what lay behind it, but with a hard pull, Cole forced it open, and a wave of cold air hit us, carrying a strange, pungent scent that turned my stomach. It was dark, pitch-black, and silent, like an animal lying in wait. I clicked on my flashlight, the beam cutting into the darkness and revealing a narrow, winding staircase spiraling downward.

"I'm starting to think they don't want visitors," I muttered, stepping carefully over the threshold and onto the stairs. The metal was cold under my feet, each step vibrating slightly, and it echoed down into the depths below. Cole followed close behind, his own flashlight casting shadows along the walls that seemed to move and sway with a life of their own.

We descended slowly, the walls tightening around us with each step, and the air grew thick with that same sickly-sweet smell. My eyes watered, and I covered my nose, glancing back at Cole, who looked equally disturbed. Whatever this was, it wasn't natural.

"Feels like a horror movie setup, doesn't it?" I whispered, hoping my attempt at humor would mask the tremor in my voice. "I mean, abandoned subway, creepy symbols, suspicious staircases—pretty sure this is the part where someone dies."

Cole didn't laugh. Instead, he looked at me with a seriousness that caught me off guard. "We don't know what's down here, but if you think it's too much, we can turn back. This isn't worth—"

"It's worth it," I cut him off, my voice firmer than I felt. "Besides, I'd hate to leave you here all alone. Who else would you annoy?"

For a brief second, something softened in his eyes, almost like he wanted to say something that was better left unsaid. But then he gave a brisk nod, and we continued down, his presence a quiet but steady reassurance.

At last, we reached the bottom, and I could tell immediately that we'd crossed into somewhere different. The room was cavernous, with high ceilings that seemed to stretch up into darkness, and strange, flickering lights mounted along the walls. The walls themselves were covered in more of those symbols, painted in blood-red lines that twisted and spiraled. A shiver ran down my spine as I scanned the space, taking in the eerie stillness that hung heavy, as if it was waiting for us to make the first move.

In the center of the room stood a long, stone table, its surface covered in what looked like an elaborate, ritualistic display—candles, dried flowers, and the remnants of what I prayed were just animal bones. A chill prickled along my skin, and I instinctively edged closer to Cole, my hand brushing his. He glanced down, a smirk tugging at his lips even in the middle of all this.

"Nervous?" he asked, his voice low, almost teasing.

"Let's just say this isn't my idea of a cozy night out," I shot back, pulling my hand away and hoping he didn't notice the way it shook.

But then I saw something that made my stomach drop. Just beyond the table, lying against the far wall, was a figure, half-hidden in shadow. I felt Cole stiffen beside me, and together, we moved closer, our footsteps slow, careful. My flashlight's beam landed on a face—a young man, his eyes half-open, staring blankly at the ceiling.

"Oh my god," I whispered, the words slipping out before I could stop them. His skin was pale, almost waxy, and there was a strange mark etched into his forehead, the same symbol that covered the walls around us.

Cole's hand tightened on my arm, and I looked up at him, finding his gaze fixed on the mark, his face grim. "Syndicate's work," he said, his voice barely more than a growl. "This isn't just a hideout. This is a...sacrifice."

I swallowed hard, the word making my skin crawl. "You think there's more of them?"

"We'd be lucky if there weren't," he muttered, scanning the room, his eyes sharp, focused. "This is bigger than we thought. Whatever they're planning, it's... dark."

Just then, a sound echoed through the room, faint but unmistakable—the scrape of metal on stone. I froze, the hairs on the back of my neck standing on end. Cole reached for his weapon, and I followed suit, my heart pounding. We waited, tense, listening, as the sound grew louder, more deliberate.

And then, from the far side of the room, a figure stepped out of the shadows. This one wasn't like the others. Dressed in long, dark robes, his face concealed by a hood, he exuded an air of authority, a presence that sent a wave of fear crashing over me. He moved with a calm, measured grace, as though he'd been expecting us.

"Curiosity, it seems, has brought you to my door," he said, his voice smooth, with an unsettling hint of amusement. "And now that you're here, I'm afraid I can't just let you leave."

Cole stepped in front of me, his stance protective, his gaze never wavering. "We're not here to cause trouble," he said, though his tone was a warning. "We just want answers."

The man's mouth curved into a slow, chilling smile. "Answers? Oh, I can give you answers." He raised a hand, and in an instant, the room seemed to darken, as though shadows themselves had gathered at his command. "But they'll cost you more than you're prepared to give."

I felt a pulse of dread deep in my chest, an instinctive, primal fear that screamed at me to run. Cole shifted beside me, his hand tightening around his weapon, but I could feel the tension radiating off him. He wasn't any more prepared for this than I was.

The man took a step closer, his gaze cold, predatory. "Tell me," he said, his voice barely more than a whisper, yet it echoed through the chamber. "Are you willing to pay the price?"

Before either of us could answer, he raised his hand, and a wave of force slammed into us, knocking us backward, the world tilting as shadows consumed everything. My last thought, as darkness swept over me, was that we had just crossed a line—one we could never uncross.

Chapter 11: Buried Truths

The floorboards creaked underfoot, the sound lost in the chorus of murmuring prayers that drifted through the high arches. This church had seen better days; the stone walls were cracked, a gentle draft filtered in through broken stained glass, and the pews bore a fine layer of dust as if no one had touched them in ages. It smelled of old books and frankincense, a scent that curled around me like an eerie lullaby, stirring memories I couldn't quite catch. Cole was a step ahead, silent but for the rhythmic tap of his boots, his face half in shadow, half lit by the flickering rows of candles lining the aisles. Each flame wobbled, casting strange shapes on the walls, breathing life into the stone saints and angels watching us with empty eyes.

As we found a spot near the altar to settle in, I noticed the way he was holding his wrist, almost absent-mindedly brushing his thumb over a thin, pale scar that cut across the skin there. The mark was faded, a ghost of something long past, but it held him captive, his gaze narrowing like he could see back through time if he stared hard enough. Curiosity gnawed at me, more than I wanted to admit. I shifted closer, tucking my legs beneath me as if settling in for an ordinary conversation—which, I suppose, for us, this was the closest thing we'd ever had to one.

"Where'd you get that?" I asked, letting my voice drop low, soft enough to keep from echoing in the hollow silence.

He blinked, startled, and for a moment his mask slipped. Vulnerability—a raw, jagged thing—flickered in his eyes before he caught himself, clearing his throat and looking away. "Nothing important," he murmured, his tone clipped, dismissive. But his fingers lingered on the scar, betraying him, and I couldn't let it go. Not this time.

"Cole." My voice held a note of insistence that surprised even me. It was an unspoken truce between us to keep our secrets close, only sharing enough to navigate this twisted path of mutual distrust and dependence. But that scar was a crack, and suddenly I wanted to see what lay behind it. He sighed, glancing at me like he wished I'd just drop it, but something in my face must have made him reconsider. I had a way of doing that, or maybe he was just exhausted from all the lies, just like me.

"It was a... test," he said finally, his voice barely more than a whisper. "A ritual, I guess you'd call it." He stared down at his wrist again, as though the details were inked there, waiting to be read. "To prove loyalty, to show I was serious about joining. I'd have done anything, at the time."

The words hung heavy in the air, settling over us like a cold weight. My stomach tightened, an uncomfortable twist of something I didn't want to name. This was the closest he'd come to an admission of just how deeply entangled he was in the Syndicate's web. The thought made my skin crawl, but at the same time, I found myself leaning in, almost as if I could share the weight of it. "Did it work?" I asked, though I wasn't entirely sure I wanted to know the answer.

He shrugged, a bitter twist to his mouth. "Depends on what you mean by 'work.' They trusted me, sure. But I lost things I'll never get back." He ran a hand through his hair, his gaze drifting back to the altar as if he could find some semblance of absolution among the flickering candlelight. "They make you believe it's a choice. But really, they just make you desperate enough that you forget you ever had one."

The words hit me harder than I wanted them to, a jagged edge scraping against whatever fragile sympathy I'd allowed myself to feel for him. Because I could see it, in his face, in the tight line of his jaw—he'd done terrible things. But here, in this crumbling church, surrounded by a thousand silent witnesses, he wasn't the villain he tried so hard to be. He was just... lost.

I glanced at his hand, still resting near mine on the wooden pew, fingers curled like he was holding onto something invisible and precious. Against my better judgment, I let my fingers brush his, a barely-there touch. His head jerked up, surprise flickering in his eyes, and for a second, neither of us breathed.

"I know what it's like to make choices you can't unmake," I murmured, feeling a strange warmth blossom in my chest. It was terrifying, this unexpected closeness, the way I could see pieces of myself mirrored in him, twisted and battered but undeniably there. And just like that, something shifted between us, an unspoken understanding threading through the silence.

The church was silent, save for the occasional creak of old wood and the whisper of candle flames. Outside, the city lay still, a sleeping giant unaware of the two shadows hiding within one of its oldest sanctuaries. But here, with Cole's hand a fraction of an inch from mine, it was as if the world had narrowed down to this moment, to this quiet confession shared in whispers and shadows. For the first time since we'd met, I wasn't sure where the line was anymore—between us, between right and wrong. And maybe, just maybe, I didn't want to know.

The night settled deeper, the shadows in the church growing long and sharp as the last remnants of daylight bled out through the broken stained glass. A chilly wind whispered through the cracked windows, ruffling the edges of the candle flames, which sputtered like they were trying to hold on for dear life. Cole had retreated a few feet away, a dark figure half-hidden in shadow, his head tilted down as he watched the flickering light. He was quiet, more so than usual, and something in his silence filled me with a mix of curiosity and dread.

I told myself to let it go, to be grateful for the reprieve from our usual tension, but a small, rebellious part of me couldn't leave him alone with whatever ghosts haunted him. I scooted a bit closer, my shoes scuffing against the stone floor, and immediately his eyes flicked up to meet mine, guarded as ever. There was something else there, too, something just under the surface—a weariness that made my chest tighten.

"Do you regret it?" I asked before I could stop myself. His brow furrowed, as if he couldn't quite decide what to make of the question. "The choices you made. The ones that led you here."

He let out a low, humorless chuckle, a sound that seemed to echo off the walls like an accusation. "Regret?" He said the word like it was foreign, testing its weight. "Sure. I regret things. But regret doesn't change anything, does it?"

"No," I agreed, feeling a pang of my own regrets rise to the surface, things I'd buried in places I didn't often visit. "But sometimes, it helps to say it out loud."

He tilted his head, studying me with an intensity that made me feel like he was peeling back layers I didn't want exposed. "And what about you? Any grand confessions waiting to spill out?"

I let out a breath, almost laughing. It was a game, this constant push and pull between us, daring each other to reveal things neither of us wanted to share. But this time, with the church silent and cloaked in the weight of secrets, I felt myself slipping, the tight grip I held on my own past loosening ever so slightly.

"Maybe," I said, the word slipping out in a whisper. I looked away, my gaze drifting to a small, dusty statue of an angel watching us from a high corner shelf. Its expression was soft, serene, but its eyes seemed to follow us with a solemn understanding. "I guess I'm no stranger to choices I'd rather not have made."

There was a pause, the kind that settled between people who understood each other a little too well. Then, out of nowhere, he laughed. A real laugh this time, rich and warm, and so unexpected that it felt like a shock to the system. I looked back at him, caught off guard, and found him grinning, an expression so rare on his face that I felt my heart stutter.

"What?" I demanded, crossing my arms in mock offense, though I could feel a smile tugging at the corner of my mouth.

"It's just..." He shook his head, still smiling. "Here we are, hiding out in a crumbling church, swapping regrets like we're two regular people with regular lives. It's almost... funny, isn't it?"

I laughed despite myself, a soft chuckle that echoed through the empty space, and suddenly, the tension between us seemed to crack, replaced by something lighter, something almost normal. It was absurd, yes, but there was a strange comfort in it, in the fleeting illusion of simplicity.

But as quickly as it had come, the moment passed, and the weight of everything we'd left unsaid settled back over us, heavy and undeniable. He cleared his throat, the humor in his expression fading as he looked down at his hands.

"I don't know if I can get out," he said, so quietly I almost missed it. "I thought I could. Thought I was smart enough, careful enough. But now..." He trailed off, his jaw tightening as if he'd said too much.

I wanted to reach for him, to bridge that invisible gap, but the words caught in my throat, tangled with doubts and fears I didn't want to admit. Because as much as I cared—and, God, did that realization terrify me—I knew better than to think I could save him from whatever shadows he'd willingly let consume him.

Instead, I forced a steady breath and let my voice come out as gently as I could manage. "You're not alone, you know." It wasn't a promise; it wasn't even a reassurance. It was just... a fact. A reminder that whatever happened, we were in this together, for better or worse.

He looked at me then, his gaze softer than I'd ever seen it, a mix of gratitude and something deeper, something that made my heart pound painfully in my chest. But before either of us could say anything else, a loud crash echoed from the far end of the church, shattering the fragile silence.

We both froze, our eyes meeting in an instant of shared understanding. Whatever brief moment of vulnerability we'd allowed ourselves vanished, replaced by the cold, hard reality that had driven us here in the first place. Without a word, we slipped back into the roles we knew best—cautious, guarded, and ready to fight if we had to.

Cole gestured for me to stay low, and I crouched behind a pew, my heart racing as the heavy footsteps grew closer. In the dim light, I could just make out the shape of a man moving through the shadows, his movements deliberate and measured. He paused, as if listening, and I held my breath, praying he hadn't heard us.

But luck wasn't on our side tonight. The man's gaze shifted, his eyes landing on our hiding spot, and I felt a surge of adrenaline as I realized we'd been found. Cole's hand shot out, grabbing my arm, and in a blur, we were up and moving, sprinting through the maze of pews, our footsteps echoing in the empty space.

The man's voice called out, sharp and taunting, but I didn't look back. I couldn't. All I could focus on was the frantic thud of my heartbeat and the feel of Cole's hand in mine, a lifeline in the chaos. The doors loomed ahead, a final barrier between us and the open night, and with a final burst of energy, we barreled through them, spilling out into the cold night air.

The city lay sprawled before us, dark and indifferent, its streets winding into the unknown. I glanced at Cole, his chest heaving, his face illuminated by the faint glow of the streetlights. For a moment, we stood there in silence, caught between what we'd left behind and the uncertainty of what lay ahead.

Then, with a wry smile, he nodded toward the street. "Shall we?"

And without waiting for an answer, he took off, leaving me no choice but to follow, our laughter trailing behind us like a whispered secret to the empty night.

The night air wrapped around us like a damp shroud, thick with fog that clung to the narrow streets and blurred the edges of everything in sight. Streetlights cast long, ghostly shadows, and each step echoed off the silent buildings, making the city feel both deserted and strangely alive. We kept to the shadows, instinctively moving as a unit, with Cole leading us through the labyrinthine alleys, his hand gripping mine with a silent urgency that told me we weren't out of danger yet.

He glanced back, his eyes scanning our surroundings, sharp and alert. "You good?" he asked, his voice barely louder than a breath.

I nodded, even though my lungs were burning and my feet ached from our breakneck sprint. "Just peachy," I managed, trying to ignore the flutter in my stomach whenever I caught him looking at me like that—protective, intense, as if I were something he was afraid to lose. I told myself it was just the adrenaline, that this didn't mean anything. But lying to myself was growing harder by the minute.

Ahead of us, the alley twisted sharply to the right, leading us deeper into a part of town I barely recognized. The buildings leaned close together here, their windows dark and unwelcoming, and an uneasy silence settled over us, making every scuffle and scrape of our shoes sound magnified.

"Where exactly are we headed?" I whispered, trying to sound casual but failing miserably. My voice came out a little too tight, a little too shaky, and Cole noticed, his mouth curving into that infuriating smirk of his.

"Trust me," he replied, his tone as infuriatingly smooth as ever. "This place is… off the grid, shall we say. And it's not on the Syndicate's radar. For now, anyway."

I wanted to roll my eyes, but something in his expression stopped me. There was a gleam of something almost mischievous in his gaze, a boyish spark I'd only seen a handful of times. It softened him, made him look a little less like the hardened man he pretended to be. Against my better judgment, I felt a flicker of curiosity.

"Lead on, then, fearless leader," I said, trying to keep my voice light even as my mind raced, wondering just where he was taking us—and why he seemed almost eager to get there.

We continued down the alley, finally stopping in front of a rundown door that looked like it hadn't been opened in years. Cole paused, pressing his ear to the wood, his body tense as he listened for any signs of movement. Satisfied, he shot me a quick glance, a hint of excitement in his eyes.

"Ready for a bit of adventure?" he asked, his voice barely containing his amusement.

"Oh, sure. Breaking and entering is my idea of a good time," I replied dryly. He just chuckled, clearly enjoying himself, and gave the door a quick push. It opened with a low groan, revealing a narrow stairwell that descended into darkness.

He didn't wait for me to protest, just grabbed my hand and tugged me forward, our footsteps echoing as we descended into the unknown. The air was thick with the scent of dust and damp, and I couldn't help but wrinkle my nose, glancing back to see the faint outline of the door we'd just left behind. The walls closed in around us, narrow and oppressive, and I had to force myself not to reach out and touch them, afraid of what I might find.

At the bottom, Cole stopped in front of another door, this one made of heavy metal. He pressed his hand against it, and for a moment, I thought he was going to turn back. But instead, he took a deep breath, squared his shoulders, and pushed it open, leading us into a large, dimly lit room.

The space was filled with rows of mismatched furniture—an odd assortment of chairs, couches, and tables that looked like they'd been scavenged from every corner of the city. A few people sat scattered around, their heads turning as we entered, eyes narrowing in suspicion. They looked like they belonged here in a way we didn't, their faces hard and wary, each one bearing the scars of lives lived on the fringes.

Cole gave them a brief nod, acknowledging their presence without really inviting any kind of interaction. He led me to a small table near the back, where we could sit with our backs to the wall and keep an eye on the room. I noticed the way his gaze flickered to each entrance and exit, cataloging every potential escape route. It was a habit I'd started to recognize in myself, too, the instinct to always know the way out.

As we settled in, a woman approached, setting two mismatched mugs in front of us without a word. She looked at Cole with a barely concealed glimmer of recognition, her lips twitching in what might have been the start of a smile before she moved away. I raised an eyebrow, watching her disappear into the shadows.

"Friends in low places, huh?" I murmured, taking a cautious sip from the mug. It tasted like some kind of spiced tea, rich and dark, warming me from the inside out. Cole just shrugged, a glint of mischief in his eyes.

"Friends in all sorts of places," he replied, his tone light but his gaze sharp, as if he were testing me, waiting to see how I'd react. "You never know who might be useful someday."

I snorted, setting my mug down with a soft clink. "Ever the pragmatist," I said, unable to hide the faint smile that tugged at my lips. But the truth was, I could see the appeal in his approach. Out here, trust was a luxury none of us could afford.

We sat in comfortable silence for a while, each of us lost in our thoughts, the weight of the night settling over us like a shared secret.

But then, just when I'd started to relax, I noticed a figure moving toward us—a tall man with a face half-hidden in the shadows, his gaze fixed on Cole with an intensity that set my nerves on edge.

Cole straightened, his body tensing as the man came closer, a silent warning in his eyes. I felt a shiver run down my spine, my instincts screaming that something was off.

"Cole," the man said, his voice low and rough, a barely contained edge of hostility in his tone. He didn't spare me a glance, his focus solely on the man sitting across from me. "You're a hard man to find."

Cole's jaw tightened, his hand slipping under the table, and I realized with a jolt that he was reaching for a weapon. My heart hammered, and I shot him a warning look, but he didn't seem to notice. His gaze was fixed on the stranger, his expression unreadable.

"What do you want?" he asked, his voice cold, controlled. The shift in his demeanor was almost startling—a reminder that the man sitting across from me wasn't just an ally or a reluctant confidant. He was dangerous.

The stranger smirked, a chilling smile that made my skin crawl. "A conversation," he said, his tone mocking. "And maybe a little payback for old times' sake."

Before I could react, the man reached into his coat, his movements too fast for me to track. I heard a sharp, metallic click, and then the cold press of a gun barrel against the back of my neck.

Cole's eyes went wide, a flash of panic breaking through his mask for the first time. And in that split second, as I felt the weight of the gun pressing into my skin, I realized just how far down this rabbit hole I'd fallen—and just how dangerous caring about someone like Cole could be.

Chapter 12: The Hollow Mask

My breath hitched when Cole's jaw tightened, his eyes gone dark and cold as the grave. We were in a dim, drafty corner of the abandoned warehouse, poring over stolen documents sprawled on a splintered table. Dust floated in the sparse light filtering through broken windows, and I could almost hear the paper crackle as Cole's knuckles went white. He was staring at a name scrawled in ink, his expression unreadable except for the slight tremor in his fingers.

"The Phantom," he whispered, barely loud enough for me to catch, but the weight of it hit me square in the chest. I didn't know who this Phantom was, but I knew what fear looked like on Cole—this was it, laid bare and raw.

I nudged him, trying to coax something out of the stone face he'd become. "Cole. Who is this? What did they do to you?"

He shot me a look that I could only describe as haunted, yet filled with fire, like he was reliving a battle no one else could see. "It's not what they did to me, Lou." His voice cracked like splintered ice. "It's what they did to everyone around me. They don't kill—they erase, bit by bit, until there's nothing left but a hollow shell. A mask."

I shivered, not from the chill in the warehouse but from the icy realization of what lay ahead. Cole, always cocky, always in control, looked like he'd just glimpsed a ghost. I swallowed the knot of fear forming in my throat. "Okay. So we know they're dangerous. But they're just one person, right? What can one person do against two stubborn rebels with a cause?"

His eyes met mine, the corners of his mouth tilting into a humorless smile. "You have no idea what you're talking about, Lou. This... person, if you can call them that, they've taken down entire factions on their own. And they don't leave survivors to tell tales."

The flicker of pain in his gaze made my stomach twist. I wanted to say something comforting, something strong and brave, but all that came out was a shaky whisper. "Then we don't give them the chance. We stick together."

He let out a harsh, humorless laugh. "You think it's that simple? Lou, you don't understand what the Phantom does. They find your weaknesses, peel back every layer until you're laid bare, helpless. They don't hunt. They dismantle."

Something fierce flared in me. I wasn't about to let him brush this off like I was some rookie he had to protect. "And you think I'm not strong enough to stand beside you, face whatever comes our way?"

He flinched, and I realized he wasn't just talking about the Phantom. He was talking about his own fears, fears he kept locked away. This wasn't about doubting me; it was about doubting himself. The silence stretched, a taut wire waiting to snap.

Finally, he sighed, his shoulders sagging. "It's not about being strong enough, Lou. It's about knowing when to run." He glanced at me with an almost pleading expression. "I need you to promise that if things go south, you'll go. You won't look back."

I scoffed, crossing my arms defiantly. "If you think I'm just going to leave you behind—"

He reached out, his hand warm and rough as he grasped mine. For a moment, the raw vulnerability in his eyes caught me off guard, made me forget the war outside, the Syndicate's looming threat. It was just us, two battered souls, leaning on each other in the middle of this madness.

"Promise me, Lou. This isn't about pride or bravery—it's survival. The Phantom won't hesitate to use me against you, to use you against me. If you have a chance to get out, take it. Live for both of us."

His words hung heavy in the air, and I couldn't bring myself to lie. I wanted to tell him I'd run if I had to, but something about the look in his eyes made me promise, silently, to stay. I wasn't going anywhere without him.

"Fine," I lied, squeezing his hand. "But don't expect me to go down without a fight. If the Phantom's looking for weaknesses, let them try to find mine. I'll take them down before they even get close."

Cole's mouth twitched, that hint of a smile easing some of the tension. "You always were too stubborn for your own good."

"Funny, I could say the same about you," I shot back, relishing the brief flicker of warmth between us, like a candle flickering against the wind. It felt fragile, our shared laughter, but in that moment, it was enough.

A distant clatter shattered the calm, and Cole's face turned sharp, alert, his hand releasing mine as he shifted into a defensive stance. Shadows moved in the darkness beyond the windows, just enough to remind us that we weren't safe here. Not now, maybe not ever.

Without a word, Cole motioned for me to follow, slipping silently through the maze of crates and shadows, his movements fluid and precise. I felt a thrill of fear and excitement, heart hammering as we crept towards an exit, scanning every corner for signs of movement. It was like some macabre dance, every step a delicate balance between fear and defiance.

As we edged closer to the door, I heard it—a low, chilling hum echoing through the empty warehouse, soft but piercing, as if the walls themselves were holding their breath.

Cole froze, his hand gripping my arm so hard I thought it would bruise. He mouthed one word, a single, breath-stealing syllable.

"Run."

Before I could process, before I could argue, he was pushing me towards the door, his expression grim and set. I stumbled, glancing back, but he shook his head, his gaze hard, urging me to go without him. My stomach twisted, every instinct screaming to stay, to fight.

But there, in the dim light, I saw the glint of porcelain—a pale, unblinking mask emerging from the shadows. The Phantom had arrived.

My feet hit the ground, adrenaline surging as I darted out into the night. The taste of fear and the thrill of defiance blurred together in my mouth as I ran, not for myself, but for the promise I couldn't keep. The promise that, against every logical reason, I would never leave him behind.

Cole was gone before I even made it out of the alley, the only trace of him a faint echo of his last whispered command: Run. I sprinted, my mind a tangle of fear and anger, every step pounding against the asphalt as if I could outrun the helplessness coiling in my chest. But I knew—there was no escaping the Phantom. Not here. Not tonight.

The city lights blurred as I turned corner after corner, ducking between shadows and abandoned storefronts, trying to shake the image of that mask, that unblinking, porcelain face. I couldn't stop seeing it, the eerie stillness, the way it seemed to float out of the darkness, haunting and silent. I couldn't understand why someone like the Phantom would want us dead with such obsessive precision. We were nothing more than thorns in the Syndicate's side, two ordinary rebels clinging to hope in a city that had long since surrendered to despair.

I was panting by the time I reached the edge of the warehouse district, a thin film of sweat sticking my hair to my forehead. Glancing back, I half-expected to see the Phantom gliding silently after me, but all I saw was darkness. Still, I felt their presence like a prickling under my skin, an itch I couldn't scratch.

As I slowed to a walk, I felt the faint hum of my comm link against my wrist vibrating softly. I slapped it on, hoping—no, praying—it was Cole.

"Lou?" His voice was barely a whisper, strained and low, but it filled me with relief so powerful I almost laughed out loud.

"Cole! Are you—where are you?"

A short, pained silence crackled through the line. "I'm fine. Just had to make sure you were clear. They're not following. For now."

There was something off in his voice, a tension he couldn't hide. I could practically feel him clenching his jaw. "I'm coming back to find you," I said, already turning on my heel.

"No. Stay put." His voice was sharp, the kind of tone he used when he was serious, the kind that usually made me stop and actually listen. "I need to handle this alone. It's... too risky. For both of us."

The urge to argue was immediate, a stubborn reflex, but something about the strain in his voice held me back. He was breathing heavily, each rasp making my stomach twist with worry. "You don't have to face them alone, Cole. You don't have to do this."

"Yes, I do," he replied, quieter this time, a finality in his words that made my chest ache. "Lou, this isn't just another Syndicate goon. This is the Phantom. You don't know what they're capable of."

"Maybe not," I countered, my voice fiercer than I felt, "but I know what we're capable of. Together."

A hollow laugh crackled through the comm, and I could almost picture him shaking his head, that sardonic smile tugging at the corner of his mouth. "Stubborn to the end, aren't you?"

"Look who's talking," I shot back, trying to inject some levity into the fear gnawing at me. "Now tell me where you are, or I swear I'll tear apart this city looking for you."

Silence stretched on the other end, taut and fraying, until he finally exhaled, resigned. "Fine. Meet me at the old clock tower. But stay sharp. If you see anything, anything out of place—"

"I know. Run."

A bitter smile curled my lips as I shut off the comm, steeling myself before heading toward the clock tower. The city was eerie at this hour, the usual hum of life reduced to an ominous quiet. Shadows stretched long and cold, twisting down empty streets, and every flickering streetlamp felt like it was hiding something sinister just out of sight.

By the time I reached the clock tower, a crumbling relic standing like a forgotten sentinel, Cole was already waiting. He was leaning against the stone, arms crossed, his silhouette rigid and tense under the fractured moonlight. Relief flooded me, and for a moment, I wanted to throw my arms around him, to hold onto something solid. But he was watching me with that guarded expression, his face half-hidden in shadow, and it stopped me cold.

"Don't look so surprised," he said, his voice low and wry. "I told you I could take care of myself."

I scoffed, crossing my arms. "Well, excuse me for not trusting a guy who's spent the last year diving headfirst into danger."

He smirked, but it didn't reach his eyes. "Fair point. Though I'd say you're not much better."

We stood there, the air thick with words unsaid, the weight of everything between us pressing down like the sky itself. I opened my mouth, but before I could speak, a soft sound—barely more than a breath of wind—echoed from the shadows.

Both of us froze, eyes locked, before Cole's hand shot out, pushing me behind him, shielding me instinctively. I tried to shove him back, tried to tell him that I wasn't some helpless bystander, but his grip was iron, his gaze sharp and searching the darkness.

"Stay close. Don't make a sound," he murmured, barely audible, his posture coiled and tense.

The shadows stirred, and I saw it—a flash of white, a gleam of porcelain in the moonlight. The Phantom moved with an eerie grace, almost gliding as they stepped into the light, the mask empty and expressionless, save for the faint, painted lips curved in a mockery of a smile. They stood, silent and still, watching us with an intensity that made my skin crawl.

"Ah," they murmured, voice muffled and strange through the mask. "So, the prodigal rebel and his devoted little accomplice. I was hoping for a challenge tonight."

Cole's muscles tensed, his fists clenched at his sides. "You've already caused enough damage. Why don't you crawl back to whatever hole you came from?"

The Phantom tilted their head, amused. "Such bravery, Cole. Though, given our history, I'd think you'd know better than to taunt me." Their gaze shifted to me, a slow, deliberate movement that made my blood run cold. "And you... I wonder what weakness he sees in you."

I took a step forward, forcing my voice to stay steady, meeting their masked gaze head-on. "Weakness? Maybe that's what you're looking for, but I'm not someone you can intimidate."

A slow, mocking clap echoed through the space, their head tilted as if they were sizing me up, dissecting every inch of bravado I had left. "Brave words. Let's see how long you can keep up that little fire of yours."

The tension in the air was so thick, it felt like a living thing, pressing down on us, filling every breath. I could feel Cole's hand inching toward his weapon, his eyes never leaving the Phantom.

But then the Phantom moved faster than I could blink, darting forward, their movements a deadly blur. Cole threw himself in front of me, the clash of their blows a brutal, silent symphony, the Phantom's mask glinting with every strike.

I couldn't just stand there. My heart pounded as I searched for something, anything, to help. My fingers closed around a shard of broken glass on the ground, sharp and cold in my hand, and without thinking, I lunged.

The shard sliced through the air, connecting with the Phantom's side just as they twisted to block Cole's blow. They staggered, a small crack splintering across the mask's surface, and for the first time, I thought I saw something behind it—a glint of wild, seething fury.

The mask crack shone like a thin fracture of light in the dark, a hairline weakness in that cold porcelain face. It was small, nearly invisible, but it was there. The Phantom jerked back, one gloved hand flying to the crack as if it were a wound that could bleed, and for a heartbeat, the air felt alive with possibility. My heart pounded with something wild and defiant, a rush of adrenaline that pushed me forward.

I didn't have time to think, didn't have time to weigh my next move or consider what Cole might do. All I knew was that the Phantom had a weakness now, one tiny fracture that felt like a door cracking open. Cole seemed to sense it too; his eyes flashed with a ferocity I hadn't seen in him before, something deep and unyielding.

The Phantom's masked face swiveled to Cole, and I could practically feel the rage simmering under that emotionless mask. "I see you've grown bold in my absence," the Phantom sneered, the words sharp and dripping with venom. "But you're still the same, aren't you? Reckless. Foolish."

Cole smirked, wiping a thin streak of blood from his brow where the Phantom's strike had just missed his eye. "Funny, I thought I'd improved with age."

I wanted to laugh, to shout encouragement, to throw myself headlong into the fight. But that glint of fury in the Phantom's eyes froze me. They were watching me now, gaze cutting like a blade. I felt the weight of that stare pressing down, as if they could peel me apart with sheer force of will. "And you," the Phantom said, each word laced with dark amusement. "So eager to play hero."

"Someone has to clean up your messes," I shot back, though my voice sounded braver than I felt. But I wasn't about to let the Phantom see that. Not now. Not ever.

The Phantom tilted their head, considering. "You think you're clever, don't you? Like a little mouse that's finally figured out how to nibble at the trap."

"Maybe," I said, clenching the shard of glass tighter, feeling its sharp edge bite into my palm. "Or maybe you're the one who's been caught." I raised the shard just a fraction, the promise of defiance clear.

But the Phantom merely laughed, a sound as cold and hollow as a winter wind. They lunged forward, faster than a blink, and I barely had time to brace myself before they were upon me, a blur of gloved hands and that merciless mask. I ducked and twisted, but the Phantom's movements were impossibly precise, calculating every turn and feint before I'd even thought of it.

And then Cole was there, stepping between us, intercepting the Phantom's strike with a brutal force that sent a jolt through the air. They grappled, each move a blur of controlled violence, and I could only watch, my breath tight in my chest, as Cole drove the Phantom back step by step.

It was almost like a dance, a dark, furious waltz, their bodies twisting and colliding with brutal elegance. I'd seen Cole fight before, but never like this. There was something raw in his movements, something almost desperate. I wanted to help, to leap in and join the fight, but I knew I'd be more of a hindrance than a help now. This was a battle they had started long before I'd even entered the picture.

The Phantom lashed out, their hand connecting with Cole's shoulder in a vicious blow that sent him stumbling back, and in that split second, they turned to me. I felt the weight of their gaze, the terrifying stillness of that mask, and I knew what they were going to do before they even moved. I threw myself to the side, but the Phantom was faster, grabbing me by the wrist, twisting until I could feel the bones grinding together, white-hot pain shooting up my arm.

"See, Cole," the Phantom murmured, their voice dark and low, "everyone has a weakness."

Cole's face went pale, his eyes widening as he took a step toward us. "Let her go," he said, his voice deadly quiet.

The Phantom tilted their head, feigning thoughtfulness, their grip on my wrist like iron. "Now, why would I do that?" They pulled me closer, a mocking smile barely visible through the crack in the mask. "After all, I was starting to think you cared about this one."

Cole's fists clenched, every line of his body tense, ready to spring. "If you hurt her..."

"Or what?" The Phantom's voice was thick with condescension, a predator toying with its prey. They jerked me forward again, forcing me between them and Cole, a human shield. "Will you throw yourself at me again? How many times do you have to fail before you understand, Cole? You. Can't. Win."

The words hung in the air, poisonous and smug, and I could see the struggle in Cole's face—the urge to charge in, to do anything to get me out of their grasp. But he hesitated, his gaze flickering between me and the Phantom, calculating, measuring his next move.

I grit my teeth, pain flaring up my arm as the Phantom twisted harder. "So what's your plan, huh?" I spat, glaring up at them. "To drag this out? Play games? Seems a little beneath you."

The Phantom's eyes narrowed behind the mask, and for a moment, I thought I saw a flash of irritation—a crack in their impenetrable calm. "You think you understand me, little girl? You're nothing more than a pawn."

"Funny," I retorted, biting back a wince. "I thought pawns were supposed to be expendable."

Their grip faltered just enough, and I seized the moment, twisting with every ounce of strength I had left, pulling free and stumbling back. Cole was on the Phantom in an instant, driving them back with a flurry of blows, each one more furious than the last. I scrambled away, breathless, watching as Cole pressed the Phantom to the edge, a relentless assault that left no room for them to counter.

But just as I thought he had the upper hand, the Phantom spun, ducking under his arm and delivering a sharp, calculated blow to his side. Cole gasped, staggering, and in that split second, the Phantom's gaze fell on me again, a cold, merciless glint in their eye.

I felt the floor tilt beneath me as they advanced, every step slow and deliberate, their mask a blank, expressionless canvas. I wanted to run, to shout, to do anything but stand there frozen, but my legs felt like lead, my body unwilling to obey.

"Goodbye, Lou," they whispered, the words chilling and final.

But before they could make another move, a loud crack echoed through the air—a shot, clear and sharp, ringing out like thunder. The Phantom jerked back, their hand flying to their side, blood seeping through the crack in the mask as they stumbled.

Cole lowered the pistol he'd somehow pulled from his jacket, his gaze steady, face grim. "You're done," he said, his voice a deadly calm that I'd never heard from him before.

The Phantom staggered, clutching their wound, but they didn't look defeated. Instead, a slow, eerie smile crept onto their face, eyes gleaming with something wild and unbroken.

"Done?" they murmured, laughter bubbling up through the pain. "Oh, Cole, this is just the beginning."

And with a sudden, violent motion, the Phantom threw a small, round device to the ground, smoke billowing up in thick clouds, swallowing them in a shroud of gray. I choked, stumbling backward, my vision blurring as the smoke filled my lungs. I could hear Cole coughing beside me, calling my name, but his voice sounded distant, muffled, like it was coming from miles away.

As the smoke thinned, I strained to see through the haze, my heart pounding, my head spinning. But by the time it cleared, the Phantom was gone.

Chapter 13: The Longing Beneath

The swamp breathes around us, alive with sounds that would unsettle anyone less accustomed to its odd symphony. Tree frogs chirp in time with the creaks of the old wood, and somewhere in the distance, a splash cuts through the quiet like a reminder that, out here, we're not alone. The humidity is thick, settling on our skin and making everything feel sticky and slow, as though the air itself wants us to be still, to let the quiet devour us.

Cole leans back against the tattered couch, his silhouette softened by the firelight. Shadows flicker across his face, highlighting the hard lines that have only deepened over the past weeks. Every time he meets my gaze, there's something unreadable in his eyes, a weight he keeps buried. He's both the sharp edge of a knife and the soothing balm that comes after the cut, an unlikely blend that has somehow tethered me to him with a bond I can't bring myself to sever.

I shift closer, not knowing if the pull is to warm myself by the fire or by his presence. "Do you think they're still out there?" I ask, voice barely above a whisper. The unspoken truth lingers between us: that the moment we let our guard down is the moment we lose everything. We've been running too long, watching our backs until the fear has morphed into something part of us, woven into our bones.

He gives a quiet, almost dismissive laugh, the kind that tells me he's spent too many nights in places like this, with shadows that linger long after you leave. "They're always out there. But we're ahead of them, for now." His words hang, weighted with the implication that our luck is running on borrowed time.

The firelight dances, and his thumb skims over the back of my hand, a touch so light it feels like it's made of secrets. My heart drums a little faster, as if it wants to betray me by beating loud enough for him to hear. I keep my eyes trained on the flames, their movement oddly hypnotic, like they're trying to pull my confession from me without a single word spoken.

"If we stop running…" I hesitate, feeling the question build in my chest, a question I don't want to give life to but can't seem to hold back. "What happens then?"

Cole's hand tightens around mine, a small squeeze that conveys more than words ever could. His gaze turns heavy, searching my face as though he's trying to find something in me he can't quite reach. "That depends on you." His voice is low, gravelly, full of an honesty that I'm not sure I want. "But it's risky, you know that."

I swallow hard, hating how vulnerable I feel, hating that he knows it too. But there's something about the darkness outside, pressing in on us, that makes this moment feel like it's both ours and borrowed, as if tomorrow might shatter everything. "Do you ever think about… stopping?" My voice is barely more than a breath.

He doesn't answer right away, his gaze flicking to the fire, then back to me. "More than I should. But if I did… what would we do? Go back to some semblance of a life?" The bitterness in his tone is tempered by something softer, a wistful hope that surprises me. "Maybe find a place where people don't know our names, or our faces."

It's a fantasy, and we both know it. But for that one moment, I let myself imagine it—a life free from the shadows, a life where I can laugh without looking over my shoulder. The idea is so foreign, it almost feels like a lie.

The wind picks up outside, rustling the branches of the cypress trees, and I can feel the tension snap back into place, like a taut string ready to break. Cole's hand pulls away, the warmth replaced by an uncomfortable chill that settles into my skin. We're on borrowed time, and every second ticks louder in the silence.

CATALYST 135

Then, the sharp crunch of footsteps outside the door shatters the fragile peace. My pulse leaps, adrenaline kicking in as instinct takes over. I scramble to my feet, barely catching my breath before Cole is by my side, his fingers brushing mine for the briefest moment, grounding me.

A voice calls out, muffled but distinct—a low drawl that sends a shiver down my spine. We've heard that voice before, though I hoped I'd never hear it again. "You think you can keep running?" It echoes, filling the cabin like an unwanted guest. "No one escapes me. Not for long."

Cole's jaw tightens, and I see the shift in him, a coiled readiness that reminds me why I trusted him to get me out of danger in the first place. He doesn't move, doesn't even blink, as if he's daring them to come closer.

"We can't stay here," I whisper, gripping his arm, feeling the tension in his muscles, the controlled calm that makes him so maddeningly unreadable. The safety of this place was always an illusion, and now the walls feel like they're closing in, trapping us.

Cole nods, his expression hardening into something unbreakable. "I know," he says, his voice a quiet promise. He pulls a knife from his belt, fingers steady as he holds it out to me. "If they come through that door, don't hesitate."

I take the blade, the weight of it cold and unfamiliar in my hand. For the first time, I realize what it means to have something to lose, something worth fighting for, and the fear I feel isn't for myself.

Outside, the footsteps grow louder, drawing closer. My heart pounds, each beat a countdown, each second slipping away too quickly. I glance at Cole, his eyes meeting mine with a steady intensity that roots me in place. I know that no matter what happens next, this moment is real, this connection forged in fire and fear.

And just as I brace for the door to burst open, a thought strikes me, sharper than the knife in my hand. Perhaps we've been running from more than just the people hunting us; perhaps, all this time, we've been running from each other.

The footsteps pause, sending a chill through me so sharp it cuts through the heat of the fire. I hold my breath, praying that whoever's out there will leave, disappear back into the dark, and let us cling to this last shiver of peace for just a little longer. But the silence that follows is almost worse than the steps. It's thick, pressing, full of unsaid things, like the quiet between Cole and me magnified a thousand times over and poisoned with dread.

I catch Cole's eye, and he gives me a look that's part challenge, part reassurance, as if daring me to show just one sliver of fear. Somehow, that tiny twist of his lips calms me, gives me the absurd, unexpected urge to laugh. Leave it to Cole to find humor even in the space between heartbeats, even in the darkest hour. But his hand is on the hilt of a knife now, his stance rigid, every line of his body ready, poised, deadly. My pulse hammers, and I wonder—not for the first time—who he really is.

The silence outside stretches, drawing tension taut between us. And then, just when I think the intruder might be gone, the faint scratch of fingers against the door makes the hair on the back of my neck stand up. I suck in a breath, hand gripping the knife Cole gave me earlier, feeling its cool, reassuring weight.

"Ready?" His voice is a soft murmur, but there's an edge to it, a glint in his eye that tells me he's almost looking forward to whatever's coming. He always has been drawn to danger, but this close, it makes me realize that maybe I am, too. Maybe that's what pulled me to him in the first place—a recklessness I could never indulge on my own, the thrill of it borrowed through his fearlessness.

I nod, my throat tight. "As I'll ever be."

And then it happens—a loud bang, the door splintering, and there's a rush of movement, shadows swirling in the dim firelight. Cole moves fast, a blur of strength and steel, and I follow his lead, my instincts kicking in. The chaos is immediate, disorienting, a brutal dance of limbs and knives and sharp, panicked breaths.

Somehow, I find myself pressed against the wall, my back cold against the rough wood as I struggle to keep a hold on my blade. One of the intruders—a large man, rough and unshaven—looms over me, his shadow cutting off the fire's glow. His grin is full of teeth, and his eyes are empty of any humanity. It's then that I realize he isn't here for any regular reason. He's here because he likes the thrill of the chase, the thrill of fear, and for one terrifying moment, I see myself as prey.

But I'm not helpless. I've been on the run long enough, learned enough to know how to fight, and before he can strike, I raise the knife, slashing forward. He yelps, stumbling back, and a surge of satisfaction floods through me as I see the thin line of blood welling on his forearm.

Behind me, Cole's voice rings out, sharp and commanding. "Stay down!" he barks, not at me but at someone else. I hear a body hit the ground, the sound followed by a groan. I can't resist a glance back, and I see him standing over another man, breath heavy but steady, his gaze flicking to me with a quick check that warms me more than I want to admit.

But there's no time for gratitude, not with another shadow creeping toward me, this one wiry and fast. He lunges, and I barely dodge, feeling his breath hot on my neck. Every instinct tells me to run, but I don't. Instead, I channel every ounce of courage, driving my knife forward, feeling it connect, feeling the slight resistance before he staggers back, clutching his side.

By the time the second attacker retreats, the air in the cabin is thick with smoke and the metallic tang of blood. Cole and I stand, backs against each other, chests heaving, the silence around us now an echo of what's just happened. Slowly, cautiously, he lowers his knife, and I do the same, my hand shaking as I let it fall to my side.

"That... was a bit too close for comfort," I manage, trying to keep my voice steady.

Cole glances at me, a flicker of a grin on his face. "What, didn't enjoy our cozy night in?"

His tone is so casual, so unaffected, that I can't help but laugh, though it sounds more like a choked gasp. But his grin fades as he looks around the cabin, his eyes darkening as he takes in the wreckage—the shattered door, the bloodstains on the floor, the now-empty, violated sanctuary that once offered us a flicker of peace.

"We need to leave," he says, his voice flat, practical. But there's a strain there, something worn and tired, like this fight is starting to wear him down. Like maybe it's finally catching up to him, too.

I nod, swallowing hard, feeling the familiar knot of fear and adrenaline settle into something more, something that lodges itself in my chest and refuses to let go. "Where will we go?"

"Anywhere but here." He glances back at me, and there's a flash of something raw in his eyes, something I can't name. "You trust me, don't you?"

I hesitate. There it is—the question that's been waiting, lingering between us all along. Do I trust him? Can I?

For reasons I can't explain, I do. Despite everything, despite the blood on his hands and the shadows in his past, there's a part of me that knows Cole is the only one I'd want by my side right now, the only one who could guide me through the dark and make me feel like I could survive it.

I give a small nod, and he exhales, the tension in his shoulders easing, if only slightly. Then, without another word, he grabs a bag from the corner, slinging it over his shoulder. He's already halfway to the door when he pauses, looking back at me, waiting. It's an invitation, a dare, a challenge wrapped in one look.

With one last glance at the remnants of the cabin, I follow him, stepping into the night with a heart pounding too hard and a mind that's a muddled mix of fear and thrill. I don't know where this road will lead or if we'll ever find safety, but with him, even in the uncertainty, there's a pull—a wild, reckless pull that I can't deny.

As we disappear into the darkness, I can't help but wonder if this journey will lead us out of the shadows or plunge us deeper into them. But right now, with Cole's figure moving just ahead, a part of me hopes, maybe even believes, that there might be something worth fighting for, somewhere down this path.

We move through the dense darkness, a thin line of trees guiding us along the edge of the swamp, where moonlight barely filters through the tangled canopy above. The air is thick, and I can feel it weighing on me, damp and almost suffocating, clinging to every exposed bit of skin like a reminder that we're somewhere we don't belong. Cole leads, silent and focused, his shoulders tense, his pace quickening with each step.

I keep close, stumbling once on a root that seems to come out of nowhere, my hand shooting out instinctively to grab his arm. His hand catches mine, steadying me, and for a second, he looks back, his face half-lit by the sliver of moonlight. His expression softens, just a flicker of something gentler than the steel he usually wears, and I feel my stomach twist in a way that has nothing to do with fear.

"You're going to have to keep up, or I'll be carrying you all the way," he murmurs, his voice just above a whisper but laced with that infuriating hint of amusement.

"Don't flatter yourself," I shoot back, letting go of his arm and trying to regain my footing, even as his grin flashes quick and wicked in the dark. It's like he knows that, despite everything, he's the one thing keeping me grounded, the one tether to something solid in this surreal, dangerous nightmare.

We walk for what feels like hours, the swamp around us echoing with strange calls and rustlings, each sound like a reminder of eyes that could be watching. But every time I feel my heartbeat spike,

Cole's presence beside me steadies it, a silent promise that he'll keep me safe, even when I'm not sure what safety looks like anymore.

Eventually, we break through the trees and find ourselves on a narrow dirt path that snakes through the marshes. It's barely wide enough for one person, with water on either side so dark it looks like ink. Cole hesitates, scanning the shadows before leading us along the edge, careful and deliberate.

"Where are we going?" I ask, trying to mask the nerves in my voice. He hasn't told me a thing about our destination, only that we had to get there by morning. It's unnerving, this blind trust I seem to have placed in him, and yet the thought of leaving him behind feels even worse.

"Somewhere no one can follow," he replies, his voice low, almost absent as he keeps his eyes on the path. "Not that you'll like it much. It's... rustic."

I let out a disbelieving laugh, the sound echoing off the water like a misplaced fragment of joy. "Oh, right, because that swamp palace back there was the height of luxury."

He gives me a sideways glance, his mouth curving slightly. "This place will make that cabin look like the Ritz. But it's hidden, and that's what matters."

There's something in the way he says it—a bitterness, maybe a trace of regret—that makes me pause. Cole has never been one to volunteer personal information, and I don't push; part of me suspects that whatever he's running from isn't a simple story, that it's layered and jagged, like the scars he tries to keep hidden. And as much as I want to ask, the words stick in my throat, afraid that if I dig too deep, I'll uncover something I won't be ready to face.

After a while, the path widens into a clearing, where an old fishing shack leans precariously over the water, half-collapsed and covered in vines. Cole stops, his eyes scanning the perimeter before he gestures for me to follow him inside.

The interior is exactly as I'd expected—dark, cramped, smelling faintly of mildew and something that might be fish or something that just died in here. I wrinkle my nose, but Cole barely reacts, his focus on the door and the small windows, checking them, securing them, his expression hard and unreadable.

"You're sure this is safer than the cabin?" I ask, doing my best not to sound ungrateful, though the words feel thin and unconvincing even to me.

"Safe enough," he replies, casting me a look that's almost apologetic. "It'll do for the night. Trust me, no one would think to look here."

A reluctant acceptance settles in my chest, and I nod, leaning against the wall, exhaustion finally catching up with me. But the silence between us feels too heavy, and before I can stop myself, the words spill out.

"Why did you do it?" I ask, my voice barely above a whisper. "Why did you get involved with… all of this?" My gaze doesn't leave his face, but he stiffens, his eyes narrowing, the familiar armor sliding back into place.

For a moment, I think he won't answer, that he'll dodge the question like he always does, but then he sighs, his shoulders slumping slightly. "Some things don't have simple answers. And some choices… they aren't really choices at all." He doesn't elaborate, his eyes distant, as though he's seeing something I can't, and a chill runs through me as I realize just how much of him is locked away, hidden behind layers I might never be able to reach.

But before I can respond, there's a faint sound outside, a scrape, so soft I almost miss it. Cole's head snaps up, his body tensing, and in an instant, he's by my side, pressing a finger to his lips, urging me to stay silent. We hold our breaths, listening as the noise grows closer, each footfall slow, deliberate, sending a new wave of dread through me.

Cole's hand grips my arm, pulling me back toward the rear of the shack, his eyes fierce, determined. "If I tell you to run, you run. Don't look back, don't wait for me. Just go." His voice is a barely controlled whisper, but it's the intensity in his gaze that unnerves me, as if he's already resigned to whatever might happen next.

But I can't imagine leaving him, can't stomach the thought of running while he stays behind. "I'm not going without you," I hiss, my voice fierce and unyielding, even as fear tightens in my chest.

He opens his mouth to argue, but before he can, the door creaks open, and a figure steps into the dim light—a figure I recognize instantly, though I'd hoped never to see him again. My blood turns cold as I take in the twisted grin, the familiar glint of malice in his eyes, and I feel my heart lurch, every instinct screaming for me to flee.

"Well, well," he drawls, his voice a sickly sweet mockery of warmth. "Fancy meeting you here." His gaze shifts to Cole, a slow, calculating sweep, and his smile widens. "And you brought a friend. How considerate."

Cole's stance shifts, a predator ready to pounce, his hand subtly inching toward his belt, where I know he keeps his knife. But there's something different in his expression now—something that goes beyond fear, beyond anger. It's determination, a wild glint that tells me he's willing to do whatever it takes to keep me safe.

I feel my own courage harden, my hand tightening around the handle of my own blade. The man's laughter echoes, taunting, filling the room, each sound a cruel reminder of the power he thinks he has over us.

But then, with a suddenness that takes me by surprise, Cole moves, fast and deadly, lunging forward just as the man reaches into his coat. The two collide, a brutal clash of limbs and fury, and I can only watch, heart pounding, hands trembling.

And then, just as I'm ready to jump in, to throw myself into the fray, something cold and metallic presses against the back of my neck.

Chapter 14: A Breath of Betrayal

The streetlights barely flickered in this part of town, casting a ghostly yellow glow that struggled to cut through the dense, soupy fog. My nose crinkled at the smell—stale air, mixed with a sharp, metallic scent that clung to every breath I took. I followed our contact, who was nothing more than a hunched silhouette weaving through narrow alleys with an ease that spoke of familiarity. Every instinct in me screamed caution, a sixth sense prickling at the back of my neck. I glanced at Cole beside me, his jaw set, his eyes scanning the shadows. He looked like he wanted to turn around, grab my arm, and pull me back to safety, but that was the thing about Cole—he'd follow me even if it meant marching into hell.

Our contact—a jittery, wiry man with a face that looked as if it had been left out in the sun too long—didn't even glance back as he ducked around another corner. I had the distinct feeling we were being led, not guided. The thought sat in my stomach like a bad meal, twisting and turning with each step. This wasn't the part of town you strolled into without a plan, and I felt exposed, like I was walking straight into the maw of something I couldn't see.

Then, just as we rounded the corner, I felt it—a shift in the air, the sort that made my skin prickle and my heart skip. Shadows moved, flitting from behind rusted metal dumpsters and cracked brick walls. I didn't even have a chance to draw my breath, let alone my weapon, before we were surrounded.

"Well," Cole muttered under his breath, his tone laced with a dark kind of humor. "Didn't take long, did it?"

A figure stepped forward, taller and bulkier than the rest, dressed in the unmistakable black gear of the Syndicate. They were a brutal lot, known for making examples out of people who crossed them. The one thing they didn't have was mercy, and I wasn't naive enough to expect any. Our contact had melted into the shadows, disappearing as easily as he'd appeared, leaving us standing in the midst of an ambush he'd likely orchestrated from the beginning.

"Fancy meeting you here," I said, managing to keep my voice steady, though my pulse was a rapid drumbeat in my ears. "Didn't realize the Syndicate did house calls."

The leader—a woman, from what I could tell beneath the helmet and visor—tilted her head, a mocking tilt that somehow cut deeper than any sneer could. "You've made quite a mess," she replied, voice smooth and icy, like the edge of a blade. "And unfortunately for you, we don't take kindly to loose ends."

I stole a glance at Cole. His jaw was clenched tight, his eyes narrowed in that calculating way that meant he was looking for an opening. The man could turn anything—a shard of glass, a broken-off pipe—into a weapon if he had to. But right now, it didn't look like we'd have much of a chance. There were at least a dozen operatives closing in, each one radiating the quiet, deadly confidence of someone who knew exactly how to dismantle another human.

The Syndicate woman raised her hand, and everything froze. The operatives halted, a wall of black armor and gleaming eyes trained on us. She gave a nod, and they moved forward in unison, every step synchronized like a pack of wolves closing in on a wounded deer. I swallowed, the taste of fear bitter on my tongue.

And then chaos erupted.

Cole lunged, quicker than a blink, his fist connecting with the nearest operative's jaw. I moved instinctively, ducking beneath a swinging arm and throwing my weight into a sharp jab to the side of another's ribs. It was all muscle memory now—fight or die, the stakes as high as they could go. I could hear the sounds of fists connecting, the grunts and curses, the sharp exhale of pain.

In the middle of it all, I caught a glimpse of Cole, blood trickling from a gash above his eyebrow, his eyes blazing. I barely had time to register it before an operative grabbed my arm, twisting it back with a cruel force that sent pain shooting through my shoulder. I bit back a scream, bringing my knee up sharply into his gut. He let go with a hiss, but another took his place, grabbing me by the collar and shoving me against the wall. My head hit brick, the rough surface scraping against my cheek, and stars exploded behind my eyes.

"Had enough yet?" the Syndicate woman asked, her voice a mocking whisper at my ear. I could feel her breath, cold and clinical, as she leaned close. "Or should I make this a bit more memorable for you?"

I gritted my teeth, forcing down the surge of anger. "You might want to rethink your tactics," I muttered, struggling against the grip that held me pinned. "Because you're about to find out that I don't go down that easily."

It was a bluff—mostly. But as Cole broke free from his own captor and threw himself at the operative holding me, I felt a flicker of hope ignite. He managed to knock them off balance, giving me just enough room to slip free. Blood streaked down his face, but he grinned at me, wild and reckless.

"We really need to stop getting into these situations," he panted, breathless but exhilarated. His eyes sparkled, the thrill of the fight lighting them up in a way that made him look a bit like a madman. "I don't think my health insurance covers Syndicate ambushes."

"Shut up and run," I shot back, grabbing his arm and pulling him away as the Syndicate regrouped behind us. We took off, tearing through the maze of alleys, our footsteps echoing through the narrow passages. My heart hammered in my chest, but I didn't look back.

Every twist and turn felt like an eternity, but finally, we burst into a slightly wider street, empty but blessedly open. I gasped for breath, my muscles screaming in protest, but we kept running, unwilling to slow down, unwilling to risk another ambush.

As we slipped into a quieter, hidden corner, I glanced over at Cole, who was breathing hard, blood smeared across his face but very much alive. Relief washed over me, so strong I nearly collapsed. I pressed a hand to his shoulder, grounding myself in the steady rise and fall of his breath.

"Next time," I said, barely able to get the words out through my own gasps, "we meet our contacts in a nice café, with coffee and croissants, and no homicidal Syndicate members."

Cole laughed, a low, rough sound that vibrated against my fingers. "You always have the best ideas."

We moved through the city like hunted animals, clinging to the narrowest alleys, our breath a ragged rhythm that echoed off the damp, crumbling walls. It was late, but in this part of town, time didn't matter. There was no relief in daylight here—just the perpetual grayness that hung like smoke, dimming everything it touched.

Cole kept up a few steps behind me, silent but for his breathing, steadying with every step we put between us and the Syndicate's grip. I could feel him there, his presence a solid reassurance against the twisting fear still lodged in my chest. My fingers throbbed where I'd clawed at the rough brick wall in the scuffle, but I couldn't afford to feel the pain now. Not yet.

When we rounded another corner, I slowed, trying to catch a breath and shake off the ache in my legs. Cole stopped beside me, still, watching the shadows with an intensity that made me realize he wasn't sure we were safe yet either.

"Think we lost them?" I asked, careful to keep my voice low. There was a metallic taste in my mouth from running, the raw burn of panic not quite dulled.

He looked back the way we'd come, his eyes narrowed. The thin slivers of light from the nearest streetlamp barely caught his face, but I could make out the lines of worry there. "Lost them?" he muttered, then shrugged, adding a half-smile as if to brush off the dread that hadn't quite left his eyes. "Sure. If by 'lost' you mean 'temporarily misplaced.'"

A laugh bubbled out of me, ragged and exhausted, but it helped. "I'll take temporarily misplaced. Better than the alternative."

He glanced down at his knuckles, still raw from the scuffle, and then tilted his head toward a series of tightly packed buildings a few blocks down. "Let's find somewhere to regroup. I'm not exactly eager for round two tonight."

I nodded, trying to shake off the lingering sensation of eyes on my back as we moved. The buildings here were old and tired, all jagged edges and shadows, a patchwork of worn red bricks and flickering neon signs that looked like they hadn't been updated since the last century. I wasn't exactly picky about aesthetics at the moment, but every doorway and window we passed felt like it could house someone watching us—someone waiting.

We finally ducked into an old bar that looked like it had seen better days, and not recently. The flickering sign above the door read Ernie's, though only half the letters were lit, casting an eerie green glow across the broken pavement. Inside, the place was mostly empty, save for a man nursing a beer at the far end of the counter and the bartender wiping glasses with a practiced boredom.

The bartender looked up as we entered, eyeing us with a raised eyebrow. His gaze lingered on the dried blood smeared across Cole's face, then flicked over to me with a mixture of suspicion and disinterest. I offered a faint, almost apologetic smile, trying to blend in with the dingy atmosphere, but he didn't seem convinced. The last thing I wanted was to attract attention, so I pulled Cole over to a table near the back, safely shrouded in shadows, and sank into a rickety chair that creaked beneath me.

Cole, ever vigilant, surveyed the room, eyes darting to every possible exit. "I hate bars like this," he said under his breath, a faint grimace tugging at his lips. "They always smell like stale beer and regret."

I smirked, leaning back in my chair and crossing my arms. "So, pretty much like your place, then?"

He shot me a look, feigning offense. "I don't smell like regret. If anything, I'm bottling my regret and using it to fuel my life choices."

"Must be potent stuff." I let out a quiet laugh, feeling the tension between my shoulders ease, if only by a fraction.

Cole's expression softened, and he settled back, his posture loosening a little as if he finally allowed himself to breathe. It was strange to see him like this, in this quiet moment, so far removed from the chaos of our usual encounters. He was all edges and sharp lines, and yet, sitting here, he looked almost...human.

We fell into a rare, comfortable silence. Outside, the rain began to patter against the window in a soft, rhythmic drumbeat. I could feel my heartbeat slowing, matching the pulse of the rain as it washed away the grime from the streets, even if it couldn't touch the weight of everything that clung to me.

Then, out of nowhere, he spoke, voice barely a murmur. "You know they're not going to stop, right?"

I looked up, caught off guard by the somber tone in his voice. His gaze was fixed on the table, his fingers tracing invisible patterns on the worn wood.

"Yeah," I replied, trying to keep my voice steady, though it was hard to ignore the pang that shot through my chest. "I know. But that doesn't mean we stop, either."

He gave a slight nod, something unreadable flickering in his eyes. "That's what I'm afraid of. This kind of life...it eats at you. Bit by bit, until there's nothing left but the fight." He looked away, almost embarrassed, as if he'd let a crack show in the armor he kept so carefully crafted.

I wanted to say something, to tell him that we'd figure it out, that maybe there was a way to break free of the endless loop we seemed to be trapped in. But I couldn't lie to him. The truth was, the Syndicate wasn't going to let us walk away that easily. We were their loose ends, dangling in the wind, a problem they needed to cut off before we unraveled anything else.

Instead, I reached out, resting a hand on his. His fingers were rough, scarred, hardened from years of fighting battles I could only guess at. But they were steady, grounded. For a second, he looked down at our hands, then back up at me, his expression softening, the corners of his mouth lifting in the faintest smile.

"Fine," he said, leaning back, the mask sliding back into place, though a little softer this time. "We'll keep going. Until we can't anymore."

It wasn't much, but it was enough.

We sat there for a while longer, nursing drinks neither of us wanted, savoring the quiet in a way I hadn't thought possible. The tension of the night was still there, a steady thrum beneath the surface, but for now, it felt bearable. Like maybe we'd outrun it, if only for a little while.

As we left the bar, stepping out into the freshly washed streets, I glanced at Cole, the rain trailing down his face, mixing with the dried blood and grime. His eyes met mine, and in that look, there was something almost fierce, a determination that mirrored my own. He reached out, and I let his hand find mine, his grip firm, a silent promise that whatever was coming, we'd face it together.

We walked into the night, shadows trailing behind us, but somehow, with his hand in mine, they didn't feel quite so heavy.

The rain picked up as we walked, the drizzle morphing into a steady downpour that soaked us in seconds. The air felt heavy, charged, like the city itself was in on the tension threading between us. Every step seemed louder in the quiet streets, echoing off the wet pavement, but even as the rain poured, a strange calm settled over me. Maybe it was the relief of being alive, or maybe just the numbness that follows a close call, but the fear was finally quieted, reduced to a steady thrum beneath the surface.

Cole kept his hand in mine as we moved, his thumb tracing absent patterns over my knuckles, grounding me. I tried to ignore the steady warmth of his grip, to shove down the familiarity of his touch, but it was hard. We'd been through a lot together, and every brush of his fingers reminded me of the countless times we'd dragged each other out of situations just as bad as this one. I knew better than to let the feelings sneak in. The moment you got attached, the world found a way to rip it all apart.

We ducked into a covered doorway to catch our breath, the overhang offering a moment's shelter from the deluge. Water trickled from my hair down my neck, a cold line that made me shiver, though I wasn't sure if it was from the rain or the reality we were still running from.

"You're thinking too hard," Cole murmured, his voice a warm rumble over the rain's constant patter. His eyes, shadowed and serious, softened as they met mine.

"I'm thinking exactly the right amount," I replied, trying for levity. "You know, about life, mortality, the likelihood of Syndicate operatives popping out of the nearest manhole to ambush us. The usual."

His mouth twisted into a smirk, and he let out a low chuckle, though it didn't reach his eyes. "If you're looking to play the odds, maybe don't bet on that last one. They're more the 'from behind a parked van' kind of people."

I laughed, the sound sharper than I intended, and it hung between us, brittle and raw. He watched me, and I could feel the weight of everything we weren't saying, all the things buried beneath the wisecracks and sideways glances.

"We can't keep running, you know." He said it softly, almost too quietly, as if voicing it out loud might make it real. "They're not going to give up, and I—" He stopped, shaking his head as if he could clear the thought away. "I don't want to see what they'd do to you if they got their hands on you."

I rolled my eyes, trying to ignore the way his concern sent a warm, unwanted flutter through me. "Lucky for you, I have no intention of finding out. I don't think they'd appreciate my sense of humor."

He gave me a long look, and I couldn't quite read it. "You laugh it off, but I know you're just as worried as I am."

For a moment, I opened my mouth to deny it, but the words dried up. He was right, and it was pointless to pretend otherwise. I wasn't some invincible action hero. I was as scared as anyone would be, if not more, because I knew just how ruthless the Syndicate could be when someone crossed them. And we'd done more than cross them—we'd thrown a wrench in their plans, unraveled secrets they couldn't afford to let out.

I swallowed, forcing down the sudden lump in my throat. "So what do we do?" I asked, my voice barely above a whisper. "Because we can't just keep looking over our shoulders forever."

Cole's eyes darkened, the familiar glint of determination replacing the worry in his gaze. "We stop running," he said, the words laced with a deadly calm. "We get the upper hand. If we find out what they're hiding, what they're protecting so fiercely, we might just have a chance to break free."

I felt a surge of something close to hope. He made it sound almost possible, like we weren't completely in over our heads. Like maybe there was a way out of this after all.

"Fine," I said, meeting his gaze head-on. "Let's find out what they're hiding. But if we're doing this, I'm not taking any half-measures. We play it smart, we play it safe. No more taking chances just to satisfy a whim." I raised an eyebrow, knowing full well his tendency to act first, think later.

He held up his hands in mock surrender, his lips curving into a grin. "Smart and safe—two of my favorite things."

I scoffed, giving him a light punch on the shoulder. "Right. I'll believe that when you start ordering salad instead of a double burger with extra fries."

He chuckled, a rich sound that seemed to warm the air around us. But the humor faded quickly, and he shifted closer, his expression hardening. "I'm serious, though. Whatever they're hiding, it's going to be heavily guarded. We're going to need more than just a rough plan and some luck."

I nodded, already calculating the risks. We'd need intel, allies, resources far beyond what we had. But it was better than running in circles, always one step from disaster.

Just as I opened my mouth to ask him about his next move, a strange sound echoed from down the alley, faint but distinct beneath the rain's steady rhythm. I froze, my hand instinctively going to my side, where my weapon was tucked.

Cole tensed beside me, his eyes narrowing as he scanned the darkness. "You hear that?"

I nodded, barely breathing as I strained to listen. It came again—a metallic scrape, like metal dragged over stone. My pulse sped up, a familiar dread prickling at the base of my spine. We'd barely escaped one ambush tonight, and now, just when I'd started to let my guard down...

He gestured for me to stay put, edging forward silently, his footsteps muffled by the rain-slicked pavement. I wanted to stop him, to insist that we stick together, but the tension in his shoulders told me he'd already made up his mind. He moved with the kind of controlled grace I envied, and as he slipped further into the shadows, he was almost invisible—a ghost slipping through the night.

The alley fell quiet, the rain softening to a whisper around me, and I felt a sick twist of anxiety in my gut. I clenched my fists, forcing myself to stay calm, to ignore the urge to follow him into the darkness.

And then, just as suddenly, the silence shattered.

There was a scuffle, a sharp, muffled curse, followed by a crash and the unmistakable ring of gunfire. My heart leapt to my throat, and before I could think, I was running, sprinting down the alley, my feet pounding against the wet pavement.

"Cole!" I yelled, my voice hoarse, drowned out by the rain. The sound of the struggle grew louder, punctuated by grunts and the brutal thud of fists connecting with flesh.

I skidded around the corner just in time to see Cole go down, one of the Syndicate operatives standing over him, a gun trained at his head. My breath caught, fear turning my blood to ice. I didn't think—I just acted, lifting my weapon and firing without hesitation.

The shot rang out, echoing down the alley, and the operative crumpled to the ground, lifeless. I rushed to Cole, dropping to my knees beside him, my hands shaking as I reached for his face.

"Cole," I whispered, barely able to keep the panic out of my voice. He was breathing, but his eyes were dazed, blood trickling down from a fresh wound at his temple.

"Hey," he muttered, trying for a smirk even as he winced. "Told you...two of my favorite things."

I laughed, though it sounded more like a sob. But before I could say anything else, another figure emerged from the shadows, gun aimed directly at me.

The world narrowed to a single point, my heart thudding painfully as I raised my hands in surrender, my own weapon out of reach.

Chapter 15: The Edge of Desire

The cabin creaked as if sharing some secret with the wind, its old bones settling into the quiet of the night. I'd barely had time to think about how lucky we were to have made it back here, to safety—if safety was even the right word anymore—before my gaze fell on Cole, propped against the faded wood-panel wall, his breathing labored.

I could barely stand to look at him, and not because he was battered and bruised. No, those scars were badges of honor; he wore them like some people wore expensive cologne—visible, unmistakable, and unforgettable. It was the intensity in his eyes that unnerved me, the way he looked at me like I was a puzzle he could solve if he just had a little more time, a little more patience. And we were fresh out of both.

With hands that trembled despite my best efforts, I grabbed the first aid kit, rummaging through antiseptic wipes and gauze as if I actually knew what I was doing. Cole, of course, smirked, his lips quirking up at the corners despite the cut that had sliced right across his cheek. Typical. Even half-destroyed, he found a way to make everything feel like a game.

"Am I amusing you, Cole?" I shot him a look that was all eyebrow and no mercy. The corners of his eyes crinkled, his laugh soft but mocking.

"Can't help it, sweetheart. You have that cute little wrinkle between your brows when you're trying to look mad."

I rolled my eyes, dabbing a particularly nasty gash on his forearm with a cloth that had seen better days. "Cute, right. That's exactly what I'm going for while cleaning up your blood."

"You're doing a hell of a job, though," he murmured, quieter now. His fingers grazed mine, just a brush of warmth amidst the cold sting of antiseptic and adrenaline. I froze, just for a second, feeling his heartbeat through that split-second connection, before he cleared his throat, pulling his hand away as if the touch had been an accident.

When I met his gaze again, something between us shifted, like a thread stretching and straining to hold under the weight of all the things we hadn't said. My breath caught, a fleeting moment of clarity in the chaos that had swallowed us whole these past few weeks. But clarity, as usual, came at a price, and this one had sharp edges, barbed and impossible to ignore.

"I know you don't trust me," he said, his voice barely more than a murmur.

"Who said I don't?" I shot back, a bit too quickly. His lips quirked up again, that maddening smirk returning.

"You're stubborn. It's one of the things I... admire about you." His voice softened on the last word, like he hadn't meant to let it slip out.

I could feel my face flush, the heat of embarrassment mixed with something much more dangerous—a simmering want that neither of us dared to name. I pressed the gauze a bit harder than necessary on his arm, earning a sharp inhale from him.

"Good to know you're entertained," I muttered, half-amused and half-terrified of what was happening between us. "Now, if you'd just hold still..."

The cabin walls closed in a little tighter, the flickering lantern casting our shadows like specters across the walls. Each movement felt electric, the air humming with the tension that lingered between us. If I'd had any sense left, I'd have put as much distance between us as I could, but something kept me rooted, unwilling to break the fragile truce we'd created here in the dim glow.

"Look, whatever you think this is, it's not... it's complicated, okay?" I heard myself saying, the words fumbling out without permission.

He laughed, the sound rough and dangerous, as if I'd just told him something he'd known all along. "Complicated is putting it mildly. But we're here, and that means something."

He was close now, close enough that I could smell the faint hint of gunpowder and something darker, more intoxicating, lingering on his skin. It was ridiculous, utterly foolish, but as his fingers traced along my jaw, I found myself leaning into the touch despite every warning bell blaring in my head.

Our lips met, not soft and sweet but wild, a clash of desperate, unspoken words. His hands tangled in my hair, and I found myself gripping his shoulders as if he were the last stable thing in a world that had spun off its axis. For a heartbeat, everything was clear, our bodies moving in a wordless understanding. His breath mingled with mine, a shared gasp in the stillness of the night. In that moment, it was as if nothing else existed—no threats, no danger, no pasts we'd tried and failed to outrun.

And then, just as quickly, it shattered. Reality hit like a cold slap, and I pulled back, the weight of what we'd just done crashing down like a wave. I took a step back, my pulse racing, trying to reclaim some semblance of control.

"This—this can't happen," I whispered, my voice shaking despite my best efforts.

Cole looked at me, his gaze steady, unwavering. "Why not?"

I didn't have an answer. Not one that didn't sound like a lie, anyway. So instead, I shook my head, turning away from the intensity in his eyes. "Because... because you're you. And I can't—"

He laughed again, softer this time, a bittersweet sound that seemed to echo in the silence. "You can't or you won't?"

I didn't answer. Couldn't. Instead, I picked up the remnants of the first aid supplies, trying to focus on anything but the feel of his lips on mine, the way his hands had lingered just a bit too long. But his words clung to me, stubborn and unyielding, just like the man himself.

When he finally spoke again, his voice was barely more than a whisper. "You're not as alone as you think, you know."

That did it. The walls I'd spent so long building came crashing down in a flood of emotions I couldn't control, couldn't contain. And for once, I let myself feel it all—the fear, the longing, the anger and heartbreak tangled up in this twisted connection between us.

But as I looked into his eyes, seeing that same tangle of emotions staring back at me, I couldn't help but wonder if maybe, just maybe, we could survive this together.

As I pulled back, my heart hammering louder than it had even in the midst of the firefight earlier, I tried to shake off the magnetic pull of his gaze. But Cole wasn't about to let me go so easily. His fingers lingered on my arm, thumb tracing small circles that sent shivers up my spine despite every good reason I had to resist. The cabin seemed to hold its breath around us, the silence heavy with a hundred unsaid things, all of them dangerous in ways that went far beyond the physical.

"Not running away already, are you?" he murmured, his voice thick with that infuriating confidence that bordered on reckless. A glint in his eye said he knew exactly what he was doing, pushing me, testing my limits the same way he tested his own with every impossible stunt he pulled.

I snatched my arm away, taking a step back for good measure. "Who says I'm running? Maybe I just don't like the idea of getting roped into something that has... complications."

Cole tilted his head, a half-smile tugging at his lips. "Complications. That's cute."

"Glad you're entertained," I shot back, trying to ignore the flush creeping up my neck. But my retort lacked conviction, and he knew it. Of course, he knew it. He always seemed to know exactly which buttons to press, and tonight, I was helpless to stop him.

A flash of amusement danced in his eyes as he straightened, wincing slightly from the movement but managing to look insufferably pleased with himself nonetheless. "If I didn't know any better, I'd say you were a little scared."

"Of you? Please," I scoffed, folding my arms across my chest. "I think you overestimate your own charm."

"Do I?" He took a step toward me, closing the distance I'd just tried to create, his gaze never wavering. His voice softened, low and dangerously close. "Because right now, I'm thinking you're fighting yourself more than me."

My throat tightened, words abandoning me as his nearness overwhelmed my senses. His hands settled at my waist, pulling me gently closer until I could feel the steady beat of his heart, so calm despite everything, as if he thrived on chaos. Maybe he did. Maybe that's what scared me most of all—that I could see myself falling for someone who'd never know how to stand still, who treated danger like a lover.

"Cole," I whispered, trying to sound resolute, though my voice betrayed me with a slight tremor. "We can't…"

He tilted his head, those sharp eyes narrowing with a dangerous glint. "Why not?"

I had a dozen reasons, a hundred, really, if I bothered to list them all, but with his fingers tracing slow, infuriating patterns against my hip, I couldn't think of a single one. And he knew that, too, curse him.

"We're both too…" I struggled for the right words, my brain scrambling for any coherent thought. "This isn't who I am. Or at least, it's not who I used to be."

His expression softened, and for a fleeting moment, I thought I caught a glimpse of vulnerability there, like a crack in his otherwise impenetrable armor. "Maybe that's the point, then. Maybe we're not the same people we were when this all started."

There was something terrifyingly honest in the way he said it, something that left me standing there, speechless, as if he'd just laid out a part of himself he didn't show to anyone else. And in that instant, I could feel the walls I'd so carefully built around my heart weakening, crumbling under the weight of his words.

But before I could respond, a sudden, sharp sound pierced the quiet—a branch snapping outside, followed by the unmistakable crunch of footsteps in the dead leaves surrounding the cabin. Every muscle in my body tensed, and Cole's expression shifted instantly, the softness vanishing, replaced by steely focus.

"Stay here," he whispered, his voice all business now. In one swift movement, he crossed to the door, pressing his ear to it and motioning for me to move back. I couldn't help the involuntary rush of fear that tightened my throat. We were too exposed, with no plan and nowhere to go if things turned south.

The footsteps drew closer, and I could hear low murmurs just beyond the door. Cole glanced back at me, his eyes flashing with a warning that I didn't need to be told twice to heed. I crouched low behind the old armchair in the corner, clutching the small knife I kept strapped to my boot as my last line of defense.

The door swung open, and three men stepped into the dim light of the cabin, their faces shadowed but their intentions unmistakable. They were here for Cole, and by association, they were here for me. One of them—a tall, broad-shouldered brute with a scar running down his jaw—sneered as he spotted Cole.

"Well, well, looks like we found our little fugitive," he drawled, his voice dripping with mockery. "Thought you could hide out here and we'd just forget about you?"

Cole didn't flinch, his stance calm but tense, like a coiled spring ready to strike. "Sorry to disappoint," he replied, his tone deceptively casual. "But I'm a hard man to forget."

I bit back a smirk despite the danger, the absurdity of his bravado almost laughable in the face of three armed men. But as much as I wanted to roll my eyes at him, I couldn't deny that his confidence was infectious, grounding me when panic threatened to take over.

The scarred man's gaze flicked around the cabin, his eyes narrowing as they landed on me. "And who's this? Got yourself a little partner in crime now, have you?"

Cole's jaw tightened, a flash of anger passing over his face. "She has nothing to do with this," he said, his voice colder than I'd ever heard it.

"Funny, because she looks plenty involved from where I'm standing," the man sneered, taking a step toward me. Instinctively, I tightened my grip on the knife, my heart pounding as he loomed over me.

But before he could make another move, Cole was in front of me, positioning himself between us with a defiant stance that left no room for argument. "Touch her, and you'll regret it," he growled, his voice low and dangerous.

The man's laugh was harsh, a grating sound that made my skin crawl. "Big words for someone outnumbered three to one," he taunted, but his confidence wavered, just slightly, as he looked at Cole. There was something in Cole's expression, a quiet, deadly certainty that seemed to give even the most hardened thug pause.

Without taking his eyes off the intruders, Cole reached back, his hand finding mine in a steadying grip. The warmth of his fingers laced through mine was an anchor, grounding me in the midst of the chaos. It was a small gesture, one I doubted he'd even thought twice about, but it spoke volumes—more than any words could.

"Get out," Cole said, his tone leaving no room for negotiation. "Or this ends here, and it won't be pretty."

For a tense moment, the room hung in silence, the men weighing their options, assessing the risks. And then, as if on some unspoken agreement, they backed away, shooting us one last glare before retreating into the night.

When the door clicked shut behind them, I exhaled a shaky breath, my heart still racing as I turned to Cole, who was watching me with that same inscrutable expression, unreadable yet somehow familiar. In the quiet that followed, I couldn't help but feel that something between us had shifted irrevocably, bound together by this harrowing moment.

The room felt small in the lingering silence, like the walls were pressing in, watching us, holding onto the heat of the moments we'd just shared. But any sense of safety was a temporary illusion, a thin veneer over the reality that waited for us just beyond the door. Cole's eyes hadn't left me, his expression a blend of relief, exhaustion, and something darker, something that told me he was weighing a dozen possibilities, none of them good.

I looked down, breaking his gaze as I tried to catch my breath. "You know," I murmured, aiming for a lightness I didn't feel, "this isn't exactly what I'd pictured when I thought of a quiet night in."

A small smile tugged at his lips, but there was a flicker of something in his eyes, something close to guilt. "Yeah? What were you picturing?"

"Oh, you know," I shrugged, feigning nonchalance as I gestured vaguely. "A little less gunpowder and bandages. Maybe even a candle or two if you'd been particularly thoughtful."

He chuckled, the sound low and almost bitter. "Romantic of you. Next time, I'll make sure we plan a little better."

His attempt at humor couldn't mask the tension radiating from him, though, and I felt a pang of worry—something I hadn't allowed myself to acknowledge until this moment. I'd seen Cole face down worse odds without flinching, but now, his shoulders seemed heavier, his gaze unfocused. A storm was building behind his eyes, a darkness that spoke to a past he never talked about, one he wore like armor but that seemed to be closing in on him tonight.

Without thinking, I reached out, touching his arm softly. "Cole, you know you don't have to carry all this alone, right?"

For a brief second, he let his guard down, his face softening in a way that made my heart ache. But just as quickly, he blinked, his expression hardening, and he pulled back, a small, almost invisible step, but enough to draw a line between us.

"It's better this way," he said quietly, his voice barely above a whisper. "Better if you don't know."

"Better for who?" I demanded, more frustrated than I'd intended. "You're not some martyr, Cole. You don't get to decide what I can or can't handle."

A muscle tightened in his jaw as he looked at me, that stubborn, infuriating glint back in his eyes. "If it keeps you safe, then yes, I do."

I opened my mouth to argue, but before I could get a word out, a loud, piercing ring cut through the silence—the burner phone we kept on the small table by the door. We both tensed, exchanging a wary glance. That phone only rang in emergencies, and I could tell by the way Cole's face drained of color that this wasn't one he'd anticipated.

He crossed the room in two strides, picking up the phone and pressing it to his ear. "Yeah?"

I couldn't hear the other side of the conversation, but the way his shoulders stiffened, his jaw clenching tighter with each passing second, told me everything I needed to know. His responses were clipped, his voice low and strained, a mix of frustration and something else—fear.

"Fine," he muttered at last, hanging up and tossing the phone onto the table with a look of barely contained rage. He rubbed a hand over his face, breathing hard as if he'd just run a mile, and when he looked at me, his expression was a mix of determination and resignation.

"What happened?" I asked, my voice hushed, bracing myself for whatever storm was about to hit.

"They found her," he said, his tone grim. "Marisol. They found her, and they're not alone."

I felt a chill wash over me, the name sinking like a stone in my stomach. Marisol had been in hiding for longer than I'd known Cole, a ghost with a price on her head and a knack for slipping through fingers like sand. She was one of the few people Cole trusted, one of the few who knew him before all of this. And if they'd found her, it meant that our enemies were closer than we'd thought, closer than was remotely safe.

"We have to go," he said, his tone leaving no room for argument. "If they've got her, they'll come here next. We're running out of time."

A part of me wanted to argue, to insist that we were already stretched too thin, that risking everything for someone we hadn't heard from in months was a fool's errand. But I saw the look in his eyes—the resolve, the loyalty, the guilt—and I knew that nothing I said would change his mind.

"Fine," I said, grabbing my bag and checking for our essentials, adrenaline surging through my veins. "But you'd better have a plan, because walking into this without one is suicide."

He didn't answer, but the look he gave me was both an apology and a promise, a silent vow that he'd protect me, even if it meant losing himself in the process. I wanted to believe him, to trust that he could keep us safe, but a gnawing feeling in my gut warned me that we were stepping into something far bigger than either of us could handle alone.

We slipped out into the night, moving as silently as shadows through the dense woods surrounding the cabin. The darkness was thick, oppressive, wrapping around us like a shroud as we navigated the narrow trails, every crack of a branch or rustle of leaves sending my heart into overdrive. The moon hung low and heavy in the sky, casting an eerie glow that made the shadows seem deeper, more treacherous.

"Where are we meeting her?" I asked, my voice barely a whisper.

"There's an old safe house a few miles out," he replied, his eyes scanning the trees around us. "If she's alive, that's where she'll be. If they're onto her trail, we'll be walking into an ambush."

"Perfect," I muttered, gripping my knife tighter. "And here I thought we'd just have a peaceful evening."

He shot me a wry smile, his teeth flashing in the moonlight. "Wouldn't want to bore you."

Despite the tension, I couldn't help but grin, shaking my head at the sheer absurdity of it all. But as we walked, the reality of the situation settled heavily around us, a silent reminder that every step forward brought us closer to danger.

We made it to the edge of the clearing where the safe house was supposed to be, and Cole held up a hand, motioning for me to stop. He crouched low, studying the area with a scrutinizing gaze, his entire body coiled like a spring. I held my breath, the forest eerily silent around us, as if even the animals were holding back, waiting for whatever came next.

And then, just as I was about to ask if he saw anything, a soft rustling to our left caught my attention. I turned, squinting into the shadows, and froze as I saw the faint glint of metal—a rifle, trained on Cole, held by a figure hidden among the trees.

"Cole!" I hissed, but before I could move, a voice rang out, sharp and cold.

"Drop your weapons. Both of you."

Cole didn't flinch, his expression as hard and unreadable as stone, but I could feel the tension radiating off him, a silent warning that we were out of options.

I slowly raised my hands, my heart racing as I met Cole's gaze, a shared understanding passing between us. We were trapped, outnumbered, and caught in a trap that had been waiting for us all along.

But as I looked into his eyes, I knew he wouldn't go down without a fight. And neither would I.

Chapter 16: Shadows of a Stranger

The night was thick and unyielding, the kind of darkness that swallows up every corner, leaving only the faint outlines of shapes to haunt the shadows. Draven's form was one of those shadows, a figure tall and looming, his coat dragging behind him like an extension of his own dark energy. I couldn't say if it was his face or his voice that set my nerves on edge, but something in his presence was as untrustworthy as it was magnetic. He shifted slightly, and the dim light caught the sharp line of his jaw, the glint in his eye that made me wonder if he knew exactly the effect he was having.

Cole's expression was all granite and steel beside me. He was wound tighter than a drum, arms folded across his chest, every line in his body practically screaming his mistrust. He had good instincts, I had to admit, but sometimes those instincts edged into something like stubborn pride. He wasn't letting Draven out of his sight, and though I could feel his protectiveness seeping into the tense air between us, I was strangely tempted to take a step forward, close enough to hear the gravel in Draven's voice when he spoke again.

"So, you're the ones after the Syndicate." Draven's voice was low, thick like smoke curling around a dying ember. He leaned back against the rough stone wall, the shadow of his hood casting his face into half-darkness. "I expected... more." He tilted his head, his gaze finally lifting from the cracked ground to meet mine, sharp and calculating. "I suppose appearances can be deceiving."

He was baiting me. I could feel it in the mocking curve of his mouth, the way his words dripped with barely concealed disdain. But something about him—maybe the quiet bitterness in his eyes or the ease with which he folded himself into the gloom—told me he had once been where I was, standing at the edge of some dangerous precipice, ready to throw himself in if it meant taking the Syndicate down with him. A shiver ran down my spine, unbidden.

"And you're the one who claims to have information that could bring them down?" I shot back, keeping my tone light, almost dismissive. I wouldn't give him the satisfaction of seeing my curiosity just yet. "Forgive me if I don't fall over myself to thank you."

Cole shot me a warning glance, and I could practically feel his thoughts brushing up against mine. Don't antagonize him. But the thrill of pressing just close enough to the edge, seeing if I could throw Draven off balance, was a temptation too sharp to resist.

Draven's mouth curled into something almost like a smile. "Good. A bit of skepticism will serve you well." He pushed off from the wall, closing the distance between us with an ease that suggested he was far more dangerous than he let on. "The Syndicate likes to root out any... unnecessary optimism. Consider that your first lesson."

Cole shifted beside me, and his hand grazed my shoulder as if reminding me he was there, watching, ready to step in if Draven so much as breathed wrong. There was a fierceness in Cole's gaze, an intensity I hadn't seen in him since that first mission we'd run together, when everything between us had been raw and untested. It was a reminder that he'd always have my back, even if he didn't like the risks I was willing to take.

Draven's eyes flicked between us, sharp and assessing, like he was cataloging our every move. "You want information," he continued, his voice dropping to a rough whisper, "but you might not like the price. The Syndicate doesn't leave loose ends, and they certainly don't forgive betrayal."

I let his words settle in, feeling the weight of them press against the walls of my resolve. The Syndicate had always been this looming presence, a constant shadow trailing my every step. If there was even a sliver of truth in what Draven was saying, if he really had something that could lead us straight to their heart... The thought of it was intoxicating, and terrifying.

"Why would you want to help us?" Cole's voice cut through the haze of my thoughts, sharp and direct. "You, of all people, must know that helping us would be suicide."

Draven's face was unreadable, his gaze steady and unblinking. "You assume I value my life." The words came out soft, almost lost in the stillness of the room, but the bitterness that colored them was unmistakable. "The Syndicate took everything from me. When you've got nothing left to lose, survival seems less... important."

His words struck a chord in me, resonating with that quiet, buried ache I never let surface. The Syndicate had taken plenty from me too, more than I could ever express with words, and yet there was something about Draven's bitterness that felt rawer, more recent. The kind of wound that hadn't quite scarred over yet. I wondered how much of it was still festering under that cold, impenetrable exterior of his.

The silence stretched between us, a delicate thread ready to snap, and then he leaned in, his voice low and filled with something darker than anger. "I could give you their names. The ones who pull the strings, the ones who would see you dead for even whispering the word 'betrayal.' But once you know them, there's no going back. You'd be signing your own death sentence."

His gaze was on me, not Cole, and I couldn't shake the feeling that he was daring me to back down, to admit I was afraid. Maybe he wanted to test me, to see if I was truly willing to go to the depths he had, or maybe he saw something in me that reminded him of himself—a reflection of someone who had lost too much and was ready to risk it all.

"Funny," I said, the words slipping out before I could stop them. "I thought I'd already signed that particular death sentence the day I started looking for the Syndicate."

A flicker of something—respect? Amusement?—passed through Draven's eyes, gone as quickly as it came. He straightened, taking a step back, as though satisfied with what he'd seen. "Then we may have more in common than I thought."

In that moment, with the shadows curling around us and his words hanging heavy in the air, I felt something shift. It wasn't trust—he was too dangerous for that—but there was an understanding between us, an unspoken acknowledgment that whatever lay ahead would require a darkness we both knew all too well.

Draven's eyes glinted, reflecting the dim light as he surveyed us, that strange smirk playing on his lips as though he was amused by a joke only he understood. He crossed his arms, and the leather of his coat creaked, a low, ominous sound in the silence that had fallen between us. The air seemed heavier, charged, and I could feel Cole bristling beside me, his tension unspoken but palpable. Draven's presence was like an unpredictable storm; you couldn't tell if it was about to unleash or simply drift on by, leaving only a lingering threat in its wake.

"So," Draven drawled, tilting his head as he looked me over with a laziness that felt somehow calculated, "you think you're ready for this?" His eyes, intense and unblinking, bore into mine, and I had the distinct impression he was measuring me, taking in every reaction, every flicker of emotion that might cross my face. "Because the Syndicate... they're not exactly forgiving, are they?"

I returned his gaze, refusing to blink first, determined to prove he wasn't the only one with a spine in this room. "I'm not looking for forgiveness," I replied coolly, though my heartbeat was thudding faster than I'd ever admit. "I'm looking for justice. And if that means doing things I can't come back from, well, I'm prepared."

He smiled, slow and sharp, and nodded. "Prepared. Sure." His tone was mocking, and I felt the sting of it as he let his gaze wander over me, settling for a fraction too long on my hands, clenched tight at my sides. "You talk a big game, but let's be real: everyone wants justice until they're staring down the price. Then it's 'please, let's negotiate,' or worse, 'maybe this was a bad idea.'"

Cole stepped forward, his voice tight. "She's not 'everyone,' Draven. And this isn't some game to us."

Draven didn't even flinch. He simply turned his head to Cole, giving him a look that was both amused and slightly pitying. "I know that, kid," he said, as if he were talking to a particularly naïve teenager. "That's exactly why I'm here. Because I'm betting she's just stubborn enough to actually go through with this madness. And maybe... maybe that's exactly what we need."

Cole's mouth was a thin line, his jaw clenched. I could feel the tension radiating off him, and it struck me, not for the first time, how protective he was. He'd probably deny it, pretend it was all about the mission, but I could see through the cracks in his armor. It was one of those things I both loved and hated about him—the way he cared so deeply, even when he tried to hide it behind that rough exterior.

Draven's eyes shifted back to me, and his gaze softened, just a fraction. "The Syndicate doesn't scare you, does it?" he asked, his voice low. It wasn't a question; it was more like a statement, a realization he'd come to on his own, as though he were seeing something in me he hadn't expected.

I shrugged, refusing to let him see the hint of nerves twisting in my stomach. "Maybe it should," I replied, "but fear doesn't get me where I need to go. And where I need to go... is right to the top of their hierarchy."

For a moment, something flickered in his expression—admiration, maybe, or perhaps just the ghost of something he'd lost a long time ago. "I used to think like that," he murmured, almost to himself. "Back when I thought I could change things."

"And what happened?" I asked, not even sure if I wanted to hear the answer.

His gaze went distant, his eyes unfocused as though he were staring through time itself. "Reality hit me, I guess. I realized that every bit of power comes with a price. A price I wasn't willing to pay." He gave a bitter laugh, one that echoed through the empty room, and I saw something raw and vulnerable in his face, something that didn't quite match the image of the shadowy, unshakable figure he projected. "Or maybe I was just too weak."

I swallowed, feeling the weight of his words. He wasn't telling me this to scare me, I realized. No, this was a warning, a glimpse into a path he thought I might be foolish enough to follow. A path he'd clearly stumbled down himself, only to find himself trapped on the other side with no way back.

But what he didn't understand—what he couldn't possibly understand—was that I didn't care about the cost. I'd already lost too much to turn back now. Whatever price I'd have to pay, I was willing to pay it if it meant finally, finally making a dent in the Syndicate's armor.

"Maybe you didn't have a reason strong enough," I replied, keeping my tone steady. "But I do."

He looked at me then, really looked, as though he were trying to read the story etched into my skin, the years of pain and loss that had led me to this moment. He seemed to come to some sort of decision because he nodded, almost imperceptibly, and something in his posture shifted, like he was no longer standing against us but with us.

"Fine," he said, his voice a low rumble. "If you're that determined, I'll help you. But make no mistake—once we start, there's no stopping, no turning back. And if you think the Syndicate's bad now, wait until you see them with their backs against the wall."

Cole's hand found mine, a silent gesture of solidarity, and I felt a wave of reassurance pass through me. I wasn't alone. Not entirely. Together, we could face whatever horrors the Syndicate would throw our way. I could feel the flicker of strength in Cole's touch, and I knew he was prepared to walk this path with me, no matter how dark it got.

Draven's eyes were still on us, his gaze unreadable, and I felt that strange kinship with him deepening, twisting in ways I hadn't expected. Maybe it was just the bitterness of shared loss, of knowing that we'd all been burned by the same flame, or maybe... maybe there was something more. Something he wasn't saying.

He took a deep breath, his jaw tightening as though steeling himself for what lay ahead. "There's someone you'll need to meet," he said finally, his voice flat. "A contact on the inside, someone who... well, let's just say they've been waiting for an opportunity to take a shot at the Syndicate."

I felt a surge of adrenaline, a spark of something that felt dangerously close to hope. "Who?"

Draven's smirk returned, sharper than ever, and he raised an eyebrow, clearly enjoying our anticipation. "You'll find out soon enough. Just... don't trust them any more than you trust me."

With that, he turned, disappearing back into the shadows from which he'd emerged, leaving us standing alone, the promise of a dangerous alliance hanging between us like a loaded weapon.

The air felt denser as Draven's presence faded into the shadows, the last remnants of his words hanging around us like a fog that refused to lift. I watched the dark corners, expecting him to slink back and throw some parting cryptic comment our way, but only silence filled the space. Cole was still by my side, unmoving, his fingers hovering near the small blade strapped to his hip. He was wound tight as a bowstring, the tension etched into his face making him look older, harder. I'd never seen him quite this on edge.

"You don't trust him," I murmured, breaking the silence. It wasn't a question, and we both knew it.

"Trust is earned," he replied flatly, his gaze still pinned on the spot where Draven had disappeared. "And the way I see it, he hasn't exactly made his case."

There was something unreadable in his eyes, a flicker of worry that he tried to hide but didn't quite manage. I reached out, placing a hand on his arm, and he looked at me, his expression softening just a little. "I know what I'm doing," I said quietly, trying to infuse my voice with more confidence than I felt. "And if Draven is the key to taking the Syndicate down, then I'll take the risk."

Cole's jaw clenched, but he gave a short nod. "Then we'll do it together. But don't think I'm letting you out of my sight with him. Not for a second."

There was a warmth in his words, a protectiveness that made something twist in my chest. But before I could respond, the sudden echo of footsteps filled the space, sharp and rhythmic, approaching from the opposite end of the room. Both Cole and I tensed, instinctively taking a step back, our hands moving toward our weapons.

A figure emerged, but it wasn't Draven. This one was leaner, almost wiry, with a sharp, angular face and an unsettlingly calm smile. He wore a tailored suit, black as ink, the edges pristine and without a single wrinkle. His hair was slicked back with a precision that seemed almost unnatural, and as he came closer, his gaze settled on me, piercing and unwavering.

"Apologies for the intrusion," he said smoothly, his voice carrying a lilt of amusement. "But I couldn't help overhearing your little conversation."

Cole's stance shifted, his body tensed, ready to lunge if necessary. "Who are you?" he demanded, his tone laced with suspicion.

The man didn't answer immediately. Instead, he took a measured step forward, his gaze flicking over me with an almost clinical curiosity. "Draven warned me you might be… cautious," he said, his tone mocking but polite. "He also mentioned you'd be expecting a contact."

Realization dawned, and I fought the urge to roll my eyes. Draven's cryptic departure had apparently come with a twist. "Let me guess," I said dryly. "You're the contact."

The man inclined his head with a smirk. "Elias," he introduced himself, extending a hand as though this was some sort of formal business arrangement. I ignored it, crossing my arms instead, and his smirk widened. "Straight to the point. I like that."

Cole's eyes narrowed, and I could feel the simmering tension radiating off him. Elias seemed to sense it too because he gave Cole a glance that bordered on disdain, a flick of his gaze as though sizing him up and finding him unimpressive. "Don't worry, I'm not here to hurt either of you," Elias said, a trace of boredom creeping into his tone. "In fact, I'm here to help."

"Funny," I replied, letting my voice drip with sarcasm. "Because that's exactly what Draven said. And look how trustworthy he turned out to be."

Elias raised a brow, clearly unfazed by my tone. "Draven has his own agenda. But then, don't we all?" His smile widened, cold and calculated. "The difference is, I have something you need. Something that'll make all this"—he gestured vaguely, as though our entire mission were some minor inconvenience—"worthwhile."

I didn't trust him. Not even a little. But the lure of information was too strong to ignore. "And what exactly is it that you have?" I asked, keeping my tone guarded.

Elias's eyes glinted, pleased by my interest. "The Syndicate's inner circle," he said, his voice softening to a whisper. "Their hideouts, their routines, their Achilles' heels. All neatly catalogued, ready for the taking. With this, you could dismantle their operations piece by piece. Cut them off at the knees."

His words hung in the air like a tantalizing promise, one that had the power to change everything. I could feel the weight of it settling over me, the enormity of what he was offering. But a warning pricked at the back of my mind, an instinctual resistance that urged me to question everything he said.

"And what's in it for you?" I asked, my tone sharp.

Elias chuckled, a sound so devoid of humor it sent a chill down my spine. "Let's just say... I have a personal interest in seeing the Syndicate fall. Call it a vendetta." He leaned closer, his voice dropping to a conspiratorial whisper. "I was once part of their circle. I know their secrets. And I know exactly how to hurt them."

There was something unsettling in his eyes, a darkness that seemed deeper than anything I'd seen in Draven. Elias's vendetta, whatever it was, didn't come from a place of justice or righteousness. It was pure, unfiltered vengeance, and it was dangerous.

Cole must have sensed it too because he stepped in front of me, a protective barrier between Elias and me. "You'll have to forgive us if we don't trust you blindly," he said, his voice as cold as steel. "We've been burned before."

Elias's smile faded, his expression hardening. "Then trust the results," he snapped, his voice laced with irritation. "I'm giving you the keys to their empire. Use them, don't use them—makes no difference to me. But don't waste my time with your distrust."

His gaze locked onto mine, intense and unyielding, as though daring me to refuse. And despite every warning bell in my head, every instinct that told me he was not to be trusted, I felt an undeniable pull. If what he was offering was real, it could be our chance to finally make a dent in the Syndicate's iron-clad grip.

After a long silence, I nodded slowly, my eyes never leaving his. "Fine," I said, the word feeling heavy on my tongue. "We'll take your information. But don't think for a second that we'll forget who you are or why you're doing this."

Elias's mouth curved into a sly smile. "I wouldn't expect anything less," he replied smoothly. "Now, let's get started, shall we?"

Without waiting for a response, he turned and gestured for us to follow, leading us down a narrow corridor that twisted and turned, growing darker with each step. Cole kept close to me, his presence solid and reassuring, a silent reminder that I wasn't alone in this. But as we moved deeper into the shadows, a strange, prickling sense of foreboding settled over me.

Elias stopped abruptly in front of a steel door, the kind that looked more suited to a high-security bank vault than an abandoned warehouse. He reached into his coat, producing a sleek metal key that caught the light, and inserted it into the lock with a deliberate twist. The door creaked open, revealing a darkened room beyond, the air thick with the scent of something old and metallic.

I felt a chill crawl up my spine as Elias gestured us inside, his smile widening in that unnerving way. "Welcome," he said, his voice a whisper that seemed to echo in the silence. "To the beginning of the end."

Before I could process his words, the door slammed shut behind us with a deafening clang, sealing us in the darkness. A single thought flared in my mind, sharp and undeniable: we'd just stepped into a trap.

Chapter 17: A Dance with Danger

The ballroom was a sea of opulence, every inch of it gilded in gold and glistening beneath chandeliers that seemed to drip with diamonds. The room thrummed with the soft chatter of the elite, every whisper coated in something dangerous and decadent, as if secrets were the true currency exchanged here. Masks shielded identities, disguising even the most familiar faces, and the thrill of hidden intentions simmered just below the surface. My own face was concealed behind an elaborate mask adorned with gold feathers that swept high and delicate filigree swirling over the edges. Beneath it, I could feel the weight of the night pressing down, heavy with unspoken threats and promises.

Cole's hand settled on my waist, firm but somehow gentle, as if he thought I might dissolve into the crowd if he didn't keep a steady grip on me. He looked dashing, his own mask a sleek black that turned his expression into something enigmatic and alluring. He was dangerous tonight—not just because of his skill and the way he wore power like it was stitched into his tuxedo, but because he knew me too well. He saw past my armor, understood the rhythm of my heart even as it raced.

"You don't have to look so serious," he murmured, voice low and a shade too close to my ear. I could feel his breath, warm and teasing, igniting a shiver I didn't dare acknowledge.

"Oh, I don't?" I replied, tilting my head to catch his gaze, arching a brow in playful defiance. "I thought serious was our mode tonight."

He chuckled, low and smooth, a sound that seemed to meld with the violins playing in the background. His fingers tightened slightly on my waist, pulling me infinitesimally closer. "There's serious, and then there's looking like you're going to fight everyone in this room."

"Maybe I am," I replied, refusing to give him the satisfaction of a smile, though my lips threatened to betray me. "Or maybe I'm just waiting for the moment someone decides to try and fight me."

"That's what I like about you," he said, with a glint of something both fierce and soft. "Always ready for a challenge."

Our feet moved in time with the music, the steps ingrained in us after weeks of practice, yet each movement tonight felt charged, like we were sparring as much as we were dancing. He spun me, and I let the room whirl around me, the colors and lights blurring into something fantastical and surreal. Yet even in this kaleidoscope of elegance, I kept my senses on high alert. I knew what tonight meant—knew that beneath the sparkle, the danger was real.

It wasn't until the third dance that I caught sight of him. The Phantom. The man who'd haunted our investigation from the beginning, his identity as elusive as the shifting shadows cast by the chandeliers. His mask was unmistakable: pure white, pristine and severe, covering his entire face. It was a chilling contrast against the extravagant colors around him, and in that instant, every instinct I possessed screamed in alarm.

Cole sensed it, too. His fingers tensed on my back as he followed my gaze, his own expression hardening beneath his mask. We both knew the gravity of the situation—this wasn't a man who made appearances without a purpose. And whatever that purpose was, it would come with consequences.

"We need to get closer," I whispered, my voice barely more than a breath, but he heard me.

His hand slipped down to grip mine, and he led me off the dance floor with a casual ease that belied the urgency thrumming between us. We moved through the throngs of guests, slipping between clusters of laughter and conversation, though my every nerve felt electrified, on edge. As we approached the edge of the ballroom, I spotted the Phantom lingering near a gilded column, his posture almost too casual, as if he were simply admiring the scene. But his eyes—dark and unreadable—flicked over the room with a precision that gave him away.

Cole's grip tightened, and we both froze, studying the way the Phantom's gaze skimmed over us, lingered just a fraction too long, then moved on. For a moment, I thought he hadn't recognized us, that maybe we'd succeeded in blending into the lavish crowd. But then his head tilted, and a faint smile—a twisted, mocking thing—curved under the mask. He knew.

There was a flicker of movement, a ripple of tension that moved like a shockwave through the room. The music faltered, then picked up again, but it was too late; the entire atmosphere had shifted. I could feel Cole's tension beside me, his posture coiled like a spring, ready to act, though he stayed rooted in place. We couldn't blow our cover now, not with half the Syndicate members within arm's reach.

"Are you thinking what I'm thinking?" I whispered, my voice barely audible, though I could hear the undercurrent of fear in it.

"I'm thinking we're in deep," he replied, lips barely moving, eyes locked on the Phantom as the man began to slip away, melting into the shadows along the perimeter of the ballroom. It was like watching a wraith disappear into smoke.

We followed, moving in silence, shadowing him as he slipped through a side door that led into one of the mansion's grand hallways. The opulence here was almost obscene—marble floors that seemed to stretch into eternity, walls adorned with ancient tapestries depicting grand battles and feasts. It was a fitting place for a man like the Phantom to dwell, a world removed from reality, untouched by anything as mundane as morality.

The door closed behind us, muffling the sounds of the party, and suddenly, the hallway felt colder, the air thicker. The shadows stretched longer here, swallowing the light. I could feel the adrenaline humming through my veins, every nerve alight, attuned to even the faintest sound.

Cole looked at me, his expression one of grim resolve. "We're in now. No turning back."

I nodded, steeling myself, but before I could speak, a quiet laugh echoed down the hall. It was a mocking sound, soft but unmistakable, and it made the hair on the back of my neck stand up.

"So predictable," the Phantom's voice purred from somewhere in the shadows, his words carrying an unsettling calm, like he had been expecting us all along.

Cole tensed beside me, his eyes narrowing as he searched for the source of the voice. I did the same, feeling the walls close in around us, the ornate fixtures and gilded decor suddenly turning sinister in the dim light.

"Do you really think," the Phantom continued, his voice slipping through the darkness like a serpent, "that you can stop what's already in motion?"

I felt a chill run through me, the kind that didn't just prickle the skin but sunk deeper, making my heart race in defiance. In the silence that followed, Cole's hand found mine, steady and grounding. And for the first time that night, I wasn't sure who was hunting whom.

Cole's grip on my hand was steady, but his jaw tightened as we prowled down the corridor, the silence stretching between us like taut piano wire. I tried to focus, tried to anticipate the Phantom's next move, but my pulse hammered with the weight of his final words still ringing in my ears. *Do you really think you can stop what's already in motion?* A trap was waiting here, hidden somewhere within the opulence, but backing down wasn't an option—not with the Phantom himself within reach.

Ahead, the corridor split in two directions, a perfect Y-shaped junction flanked by enormous marble columns and sinister shadows that crept along the walls. Cole paused, tilting his head just slightly, catching the faint echo of footsteps retreating to the right. He shot me a look that spoke volumes—a warning, a question, a reckless, undeniable challenge—and then we were off, veering right in pursuit.

The hallway narrowed, the ceilings rising impossibly high above us, as though designed to make anyone passing through feel insignificant. Portraits of men with hawkish noses and powdered wigs lined the walls, their gazes seeming to follow us as we moved. The Phantom's footsteps grew fainter, his figure vanishing behind yet another ornately carved door at the end of the hall. He wasn't running—no, he was luring, guiding us deeper into the heart of whatever twisted game he was playing.

Cole turned to me, his eyes sharp, dark and calculating even through his mask. "This feels too easy," he murmured, his voice low enough that only I could hear.

"I know," I replied, scanning our surroundings, my senses prickling. "But he's in there, and we're out here. And the longer we wait..."

"...the more advantage he has." He finished my sentence, flashing a wry smile, as if to say he already knew I wouldn't back down. He pressed his hand to the door, nudging it open just enough for us to slip inside.

The room was dim, but the glow from a single wall sconce revealed hints of dark wood paneling, leather-bound books, and a roaring fireplace at the far end. It had the feel of an old-world library—plush, comfortable, the sort of room that invited confidences and hidden agendas. But something else lingered in the air, a tension that crackled just beneath the surface.

And then, as if conjured by our very presence, he emerged from the shadows. The Phantom. He was exactly as I remembered: tall and elegant, his black tuxedo flawless, his porcelain mask giving him the eerie air of a puppet master. He watched us, silent and still, like we were pieces on a chessboard that he'd already positioned to his liking.

"I must admit," he drawled, voice smooth as silk, "you two are impressively persistent."

Cole and I exchanged a glance, our expressions tight. The Phantom's calm was maddening, his casual stance a reminder that he wasn't concerned in the slightest. Not about us, and certainly not about whatever trap he'd already laid out.

"Persistent's not the word I'd use," I replied, channeling a confidence I barely felt. "More like committed. You know, the kind of commitment that brings people to... unmasking old enemies."

The Phantom chuckled, a low, throaty sound that made my skin crawl. "And yet you're still dancing in circles, grasping at shadows. Surely you realize you're in far over your heads."

"Funny," Cole said, tilting his head with a mocking smile. "I was just thinking the same thing about you."

The Phantom's gaze flickered, barely a twitch, but it was enough to let me know we'd struck a nerve. For all his composure, he hadn't expected us to confront him here, not directly. I took a small, defiant step forward, feeling a strange surge of adrenaline as his eyes settled on me.

"So tell me," I said, my voice steady, "what's the point of all this? The masquerades, the elaborate games... Are you really so afraid of facing us head-on?"

For the first time, the Phantom's smooth facade cracked, a flicker of something—annoyance, perhaps—breaking through. But then it was gone, replaced by that unsettling, patient calm.

"Afraid?" He took a deliberate step toward us, and I had to resist the urge to retreat. "You misunderstand, my dear. I am simply... patient. I don't need to rush victory. It's already within my grasp."

Cole's eyes narrowed, his posture shifting, and I could feel the tension in him, a coiled spring waiting for the slightest provocation. "Victory isn't a given, not with us," he said, his tone hard.

The Phantom laughed again, but there was an edge to it now. "Ah, but you see, every choice you've made tonight—every step you've taken—has been guided by my hand. You think you're hunting me, but really, you're playing my game. And here we are, right where I wanted you."

A chill slid down my spine, his words coiling around me like a tightening noose. The fire crackled in the silence, casting flickering shadows across his mask, giving the impression of a face shifting, warping in the dim light.

Cole's hand brushed mine, grounding me, though his eyes never left the Phantom. "You know," he said, a dangerous glint in his gaze, "I've never been very good at playing by the rules."

In a flash, he moved, lunging forward with a precision that had caught even me off guard. The Phantom stepped back, narrowly dodging as Cole's fist grazed his side. But the Phantom was fast—faster than I'd anticipated, slipping into the shadows with a fluidity that defied logic.

I darted to the left, cutting off his escape route, blocking the door as Cole circled him. We had him cornered now, trapped between us, his back against a wall. And for a brief, intoxicating moment, I thought we had him.

But the Phantom only smiled, that eerie, twisted grin beneath his mask, as his hand flicked upward. I barely registered the movement before a sudden flash of light blinded me, an explosion of smoke filling the air. Coughing, I stumbled back, my vision blurred as the room swam around me.

"Cole!" I called, reaching out, trying to find him in the haze.

"I'm here," he replied, voice steady but strained, somewhere just beyond my reach. I heard him cough, the sound harsh and ragged, and my heart pounded as the smoke began to thin, revealing the room once more.

The Phantom was gone.

I bit back a curse, frustration boiling up as I scanned the room, knowing it was useless. He'd slipped away, vanished like the specter he'd named himself after, leaving nothing behind but the faint scent of smoke and a lingering sense of dread.

Cole stepped beside me, rubbing his eyes, his jaw set in a hard line. "I should have seen that coming," he muttered, anger simmering just beneath the surface.

"It wasn't your fault," I replied, though my own frustration was equally potent. We'd been so close. Inches away. And now he was gone, leaving us with nothing but more questions and the bitter taste of defeat.

The fire crackled in the silence, mocking us, the shadows deepening around us as we stood there, breathing in the emptiness he'd left behind. I could feel the weight of his final words echoing in my mind, heavy with promise and threat alike.

But one thing was clear—we weren't done with the Phantom. Not by a long shot.

The silence hung heavy between us, a dense, unspoken dread that clung to the edges of our confidence, eroding it like salt on steel. The Phantom's departure left a stillness so thick I felt like I could reach out and touch it, fingers grazing the faint shadow of his presence. Cole was the first to break the silence, a quiet sigh escaping his lips as he ran a hand through his hair, frustration edging into a rare glimpse of vulnerability.

He looked over at me, his gaze weary but sharp, as if the endless pursuit of our masked adversary had worn him down but hadn't quite managed to dull his spirit. "He's always one step ahead," he said, his tone more resigned than I'd ever heard it. "Always."

"Let's not give him too much credit," I replied, forcing a bit of defiance into my voice. "He's good, but he's not perfect. He leaves clues—breadcrumbs—even if he doesn't mean to."

"Is that so?" A faint smile tugged at the corner of Cole's mouth, a glimmer of the old spark resurfacing. "Because right now, all I see is smoke. Quite literally."

"Smoke is just the residue of something burning," I said, voice steady. "And something is burning, Cole. We just haven't figured out where the fire is yet."

His smile grew a little wider, and he shook his head, a touch of admiration in his eyes. "If anyone can find it, it's you. Even if you have to drag me through a blaze to do it."

I laughed despite myself, the sound a little raw. "Oh, I fully intend to drag you through it," I said, quirking a brow. "So brace yourself."

The silence that followed felt lighter, somehow. Even with the Phantom outmaneuvering us at every turn, the thought of facing him together lent me a confidence I hadn't realized I was missing. But as the quiet stretched, a faint sound—no louder than a whisper—caught my attention. A soft scuff against marble, just barely perceptible, but enough to make the fine hairs at the back of my neck prickle.

Cole went still beside me, his eyes narrowing as he, too, registered the sound. He shifted slightly, positioning himself protectively in front of me, his gaze darting to the corners of the room, where the flickering firelight barely held back the dark.

"Did you hear that?" he murmured, his voice barely a breath.

I nodded, my hand instinctively reaching toward the slender knife I kept hidden beneath the folds of my dress. My fingers brushed the cool metal, a comfort amid the uncertainty of the night. We listened, both of us straining to catch any hint of movement, any indication that we weren't as alone as we'd thought.

And then it came—a faint, rhythmic tapping, steady and deliberate. It echoed through the silence, each tap a calculated beat that grew louder, closer, until it filled the room, amplifying the tension between us. My grip tightened on the knife, my pulse quickening as I scanned the room, searching for the source of the sound.

Cole's expression darkened, a storm gathering in his eyes. "Show yourself," he called, his voice laced with authority, daring whoever—or whatever—was lurking in the shadows to reveal itself.

For a moment, the tapping ceased, leaving an oppressive silence in its wake. Then, slowly, a figure emerged from the shadows, stepping into the dim light cast by the fire. It wasn't the Phantom, but something about the man's presence carried that same unnerving stillness, that aura of someone accustomed to evading detection.

He was tall, dressed in a perfectly tailored suit, his face half-obscured by a mask similar to the Phantom's but less ornate, more functional. His eyes, dark and calculating, flicked between Cole and me, assessing us with a cold, detached interest.

"You're in over your heads," he said, his voice a low, even murmur. "The Phantom isn't the only one who's been watching."

Cole took a step forward, his posture rigid, controlled. "And who might you be? Another ghost haunting the shadows?"

The man tilted his head, a faint smirk touching his lips. "Let's just say I'm... an associate. Someone who knows when the game is nearly up."

"Nearly up?" I echoed, the words tasting bitter on my tongue. "If you think we're about to surrender, you've seriously underestimated us."

He chuckled, a sound that was more chilling than reassuring. "Oh, I have no doubt about your resolve. It's your odds I question. You're outnumbered, and the Syndicate is... well, let's just say they don't take kindly to disruptions."

Cole's jaw clenched, his hands flexing at his sides. "We're not here to debate our odds with you."

The man's smirk grew, his gaze settling on me with a disturbing intensity. "No, I suppose not. But consider this a warning. The Phantom doesn't play games he can't win. And neither do his... associates."

I held his gaze, refusing to let him see the flicker of unease his words had stirred in me. "I'd be more concerned if I thought any of you understood what winning really meant. But as far as I can tell, you're all just players in a game no one remembers the rules to."

His expression tightened, and for a brief moment, I thought I'd struck a nerve. But then he recovered, that cold amusement returning to his eyes.

"You think you're clever," he said, voice soft, deadly. "But clever won't save you when the Syndicate decides you've overstayed your welcome."

Cole moved again, positioning himself between me and the stranger. "We'll take our chances," he said, his tone firm, final. "But if you have something useful to tell us, now's the time."

The man watched us both, his gaze assessing, calculating. And then, with a shrug that bordered on dismissive, he reached into his jacket pocket and pulled out a small, black object. He tossed it to Cole, who caught it instinctively, his eyes narrowing as he examined it.

It was a sleek, unmarked USB drive.

"The contents of that drive are more than enough to tell you everything you need to know," the man said, his voice almost bored. "Consider it a... parting gift."

I didn't trust him, not for a second. But something about the way he held himself, that cool, detached confidence, told me he had no reason to lie. This was all part of the game, another piece of the

Phantom's plan, and I had the sinking feeling that by accepting it, we were playing directly into his hands.

But what choice did we have?

"Why are you giving this to us?" I asked, narrowing my eyes. "What's in it for you?"

The man's smirk returned, faint but unmistakable. "Call it a professional courtesy. Or maybe I just enjoy watching things unravel."

Before we could respond, he took a step back, retreating into the shadows with a fluid grace that made him seem more specter than human. He lingered just long enough to tip his head in a mock salute, his gaze fixed on me, a promise or a warning glinting in his eyes.

"Good luck," he said softly, his voice a whisper that seemed to echo in the stillness. "You'll need it."

And then he was gone, swallowed by the shadows as if he'd never been there at all.

Cole and I stood in silence, the weight of his words settling over us, cold and heavy. I looked down at the USB drive in Cole's hand, feeling a pulse of dread mixed with a twisted curiosity. Whatever it contained, it was the key to something—either the answers we'd been chasing, or a trap far more elaborate than anything we'd anticipated.

Cole met my gaze, his expression unreadable, and in that moment, I felt the weight of the path we'd chosen, the danger pressing in on all sides. I wanted to tell him we'd be fine, that we'd get through this unscathed, but the words stuck in my throat, swallowed by the cold certainty that nothing about this would end neatly.

Without another word, he reached for my hand, his touch warm and grounding, pulling me out of my thoughts. He held up the USB drive, his jaw set, his eyes dark and determined.

"We plug this in," he said, his voice low, steady. "And we see where it leads."

And then, in a single, gut-twisting instant, the fire behind us flared with a violent crack, the air filling with the acrid scent of smoke. We spun, staring at the doorway as flames began to lick up the walls, the shadows dancing wildly.

We were trapped.

Chapter 18: The Price of Truth

The air was thick with mildew and something sharper, something that made my throat scratch even as I tried to breathe shallowly through my mouth. It clung to everything in the abandoned factory, that scent of something rotten and metallic, layered with the hollow echo of past horrors. The place had been left to decay, skeletal machinery looming over us like silent sentries as Cole and I crept through the half-light. His face was taut, every line tense, his eyes narrowed to slits as he scanned each shadow with an almost feral intensity. Draven's tip had been vague—a muttered address, his gaze darting to the side like he'd rather bite off his tongue than tell us—but the implication had been clear: we'd find answers here. Answers, or perhaps the questions we hadn't dared to ask.

I found myself trailing my fingertips along the crumbling wall, the texture coarse under my skin, grounding me even as everything else spun wildly out of control. Evidence. I wanted something solid, something I could hold up like a shield to keep the dark at bay. We'd all heard the whispers about the Syndicate's experiments, but hearing was different from knowing, and knowing was different from seeing.

Cole was just a few feet ahead, his jaw clenched so tightly I could hear the faint grind of his teeth. It was strange, but I'd grown used to the way he carried himself, shoulders squared like he could physically take on every shadow in the world if it meant keeping us safe. But there was something else tonight, a tension coiled within him, a storm I could feel but couldn't read.

I barely recognized him in that moment, his eyes darkened, his face a mask I hadn't seen before. He wasn't my usual partner in crime with that easy, cocky grin; tonight, he was something else. And maybe I was too, because I didn't even flinch when I pried open a filing cabinet, the metal screeching like a wounded animal. It was empty, of course, because nothing here would make it that easy.

But then, as if summoned by my own bitterness, I saw it. A stack of dusty files lying on a desk, half-hidden under a pile of old rags. I reached for them, pulling the top one open, my stomach clenching as I skimmed the contents. Names, dates, strange annotations in a language I couldn't quite place. And then, underlined in thick, brutal strokes, the word "Subjects."

"Looks like Draven didn't exaggerate," Cole muttered, reading over my shoulder. His voice was hard, hollow. "They were experimenting on people."

I swallowed, my hands clammy against the brittle paper. The file was packed with horrific details—too many to absorb, and each one more twisted than the last. Whatever the Syndicate had been up to, it was dark enough to make even my reckless bravado stumble. A part of me wanted to throw the file across the room, let the scattered pages tell whatever story they wanted without me as witness.

"We should take these," I whispered, even though it felt pointless to whisper here. The whole place felt like a scream waiting to erupt.

Cole nodded, jaw still clenched. "Take what we can and burn the rest. They don't get to keep this."

But before either of us could make a move, a flicker of movement caught my eye. At the far end of the room, where shadows melted into shadows, three figures emerged. Silent, swift, each one dressed in dark clothes that seemed to swallow the light. Syndicate operatives, as sure as I could feel the blood draining from my face.

"Run," Cole hissed, low and fierce, but I was frozen, my pulse thundering in my ears as they closed in.

It was the sound that pulled me back—Cole's snarl, an animalistic sound that tore from him as he lunged forward, fists swinging with a brutality I hadn't known he possessed. He took down the first operative with a swift, crushing blow, moving with a ferocity that was equal parts precision and fury. And then he was gone, locked in combat, and I was alone, facing the remaining two.

I had no time to think, just react. I grabbed the nearest piece of debris—a rusted pipe—and swung, more out of desperation than skill. It connected, a solid thud that reverberated up my arm and left me dizzy, but I didn't stop. I couldn't stop. The files were still in my hand, clutched so tightly I thought the edges might slice into my palm, and all I could think was that I couldn't let them have it. Not after what I'd seen.

In a blur of movement, I was yanked backward, my back colliding with a metal post as one of the operatives pinned me, his hand a vise around my throat. The world began to darken, a tunnel closing in around me, but then suddenly the weight was gone, replaced by a crashing sound and a cry of pain. Cole stood over me, breathing hard, his face wild, his knuckles bloodied.

"You okay?" he asked, his voice rough, his gaze sweeping over me like he was afraid to look too close.

I nodded, trying to catch my breath, my pulse still racing. "I think so," I managed, though my voice shook. And then I looked at him, really looked at him, and saw the haunted expression in his eyes.

There was a darkness here that went beyond what we'd just faced, a darkness that seemed to wrap around him like a shadow. He held his hands out, stained with blood and dust, staring down at them with an expression I'd never seen before.

"We have to get out of here," I said, my voice barely above a whisper. I wasn't sure if I was talking to him or to myself.

Cole didn't respond at first, just stared at his hands as though they belonged to a stranger. And then, slowly, he nodded, reaching down to scoop up the files I'd dropped in the struggle. His hands trembled, just a little, as he tucked them into his jacket, but his face was set, his jaw firm.

I couldn't shake the feeling that something had shifted, like the ground had cracked open and we were teetering on the edge.

The silence hung between us as we stumbled back to the car, Cole's breathing still ragged, his jaw clenched like he was biting back words he wasn't ready to say. His hands were scraped and bruised, and every now and then, I caught him flexing his fingers, like he couldn't quite believe they were his. In the dim light of the factory's parking lot, he looked like a soldier returning from some invisible battlefield, shadows flickering in his eyes that even he seemed wary to acknowledge.

I threw myself into the passenger seat, half-expecting to feel safer with a door between us and that place, but the dread clung to me like smoke. The files sat between us, tainted artifacts from a nightmare we hadn't woken up from. I wanted to say something, anything that would cut through the darkness, but all I could think about was the look in Cole's eyes when he'd come for me, that fury, that raw, unrestrained wrath.

"You're bleeding," I said finally, motioning to his knuckles. It was a weak opening, but it was all I had.

He shrugged, a nonchalant gesture that was ruined by the wince he tried—and failed—to hide. "It's nothing," he muttered, pulling out a crumpled napkin from the glove compartment and pressing it to the worst of the cuts. "You should see the other guy."

I huffed out a shaky laugh, the absurdity of it hitting me square in the chest. "Cole, the other guy's probably halfway to calling in reinforcements by now. They don't exactly hand out gold stars for roughing up Syndicate operatives."

He smirked, but it was a thin, humorless thing, his gaze locked on the windshield, the light from the dashboard casting his face in harsh angles. "Wouldn't be the first time I got on their bad side."

The words hung heavy in the air, his tone too sharp, too bitter. It was one of those moments where I felt I'd caught a glimpse of him through a crack in his armor, just a sliver of vulnerability before he slammed the door shut again.

"Cole..." I started, but he cut me off, a hard edge in his voice.

"Don't," he said, his tone final. He glanced at me, his expression unreadable. "Let's just get this stuff back to Draven. Figure out our next move."

I bit back the dozen questions on the tip of my tongue and nodded, reaching over to start the car. The engine roared to life, and the factory faded in the rearview mirror, but the weight of it stayed with us, a silent third passenger we couldn't shake.

The drive back to Draven's was quiet, each of us locked in our own thoughts. I could feel the tension radiating off Cole, a storm brewing just under the surface. I wanted to reach out, to bridge the gap between us, but something held me back—a sense that whatever I found on the other side might be more than I was ready for.

Draven's place was tucked away at the edge of town, a rundown little house that looked like it had been abandoned to the elements decades ago. But inside, it was meticulously organized, every inch of space filled with books, maps, and an endless array of curiosities that spoke to a mind that missed nothing. He met us at the door, his sharp gaze flicking over us, taking in the disheveled state of our clothes, the bruises, the files clutched to Cole's chest.

"Rough night?" he asked, his tone dry, but there was a glint of worry in his eyes as he ushered us inside.

"You could say that," I replied, collapsing onto a worn-out armchair, the fabric sagging under me like it had seen its fair share of weary visitors. "Your lead was...accurate, Draven. Maybe too accurate."

Draven's lips twitched, and he gave me a look that was half-amused, half-concerned. "Did you get what we needed?"

Cole wordlessly handed him the files, his expression guarded, and for a moment, Draven just stared at them, a flicker of something dark and unreadable crossing his face. He sat down across from us, flipping through the pages with a grim efficiency, his brows knitting together as he scanned the contents.

After a while, he closed the file, his face unreadable. "I didn't expect it to be...quite this bad," he murmured, his gaze faraway.

I leaned forward, my voice sharp. "They're experimenting on people, Draven. Innocent people. Do you have any idea how deep this goes?"

He sighed, running a hand over his face. "I had my suspicions, but this confirms things I'd hoped weren't true." He looked at Cole, his gaze heavy. "This changes everything. We're dealing with something bigger than I realized."

Cole's face was a mask, but I saw the flicker of anger in his eyes. "Bigger? How much bigger does it get, Draven? They're taking people, experimenting on them like they're lab rats. This isn't just some underground operation. This is...organized. Structured."

Draven nodded, a grim determination settling over him. "And that's exactly why we need to be smart about this. We can't just charge in, guns blazing."

"Smart," I echoed, a bitter laugh slipping out. "Smart feels a little late right now. They already know we were there. They know we have the files. It's only a matter of time before they come looking for us."

Draven leaned forward, his gaze intense. "That's why we need to be ready. You two stumbled onto something big tonight, and that makes you both targets. They'll want to silence you, to keep this buried. But if we're careful, if we play this right, we can use this against them. We can expose them."

A chill ran down my spine, and I glanced at Cole, who was staring at Draven with a look I couldn't quite place. It was somewhere between anger and admiration, a simmering intensity that made my heart skip a beat.

"What do you need us to do?" Cole asked, his voice steady, but I could hear the tension beneath it.

Draven smiled, a sharp, knowing smile that made my stomach twist. "You're going to need to go underground, lay low for a while. I'll keep digging, find out who else might be involved. When the time is right, we'll make our move."

"Lay low?" I repeated, the words tasting bitter on my tongue. "You think they're just going to let us vanish?"

Draven shrugged, his gaze never wavering. "They won't have a choice if you're careful. Trust me, I've done this before. They can't hurt you if they don't know where to look."

The words should have been comforting, but they only deepened the dread pooling in my stomach.

The walls of the factory loom over us, casting shadows that are as thick as the memories they seem to hold. Every step echoes against the forgotten concrete, each sound amplifying the desolation that has settled here like dust. It's the kind of place you'd expect in nightmares, where light barely trickles in through broken windows covered in layers of grime. The smell of decay fills the air, but beneath it lingers a sharper scent, something metallic and unsettling. Cole's jaw is set tight, his eyes scanning every corner, as if he expects someone – or something – to leap from the darkness at any moment.

"This is it," he murmurs, voice low. "Draven wasn't exaggerating."

I nod, feeling a chill crawl up my spine. Draven had warned us that the Syndicate's operations were grim, but nothing could have prepared us for this. There's an unshakable heaviness in the air, as though the walls themselves are trying to suffocate us. Each room reveals more disturbing remnants, clues that hint at the horrors conducted here. Broken vials scattered across tables, streaks of something dark and unidentifiable staining the floors, crumpled notes scrawled with frantic, nearly illegible handwriting. It's like the worst of humanity has been locked in these walls, festering in silence.

Cole picks up a file from a rusting metal cabinet, his face hardening as he skims the contents. He hands it to me without a word, but his eyes say everything. I force myself to read, but the words blur as nausea twists in my stomach. Names of people who were once alive, with families, hopes, and dreams – now reduced to numbers in experiments that sound more like torture. "Subjects show increased physical durability post-infusion," one note says clinically, as if talking about lab rats instead of human lives.

"This... this is..." My voice trails off, unable to capture the horror. Cole places a steadying hand on my shoulder, his touch grounding.

"I know," he says, a quiet fury lacing his words. "We're going to make them pay for this."

We continue our search, every step revealing more evidence, more damning proof of the Syndicate's monstrous agenda. I can feel my anger bubbling up, the helplessness mixing with a fierce need to do something, anything to bring justice to those they've destroyed. But we're running out of time. The files we've found could be exactly what we need to dismantle the Syndicate, but it's a race against the clock. Somewhere above us, I hear the faintest scuff of a boot against concrete, and I freeze, motioning for Cole to listen.

"Did you hear that?" I whisper, barely moving my lips.

He nods, his expression shifting instantly from anger to caution. In a swift, fluid movement, he stashes the files into his backpack and pulls me into the shadows behind a row of rusted metal shelves. We hold our breath, our bodies tense as we wait, listening for any hint of movement. Moments later, three men in black uniforms enter the room, their faces hard, eyes cold. Syndicate operatives.

They move with the precision of soldiers, sweeping the area with practiced ease. My heartbeat pounds loud enough that I'm sure they'll hear it. One of them pauses near the shelves, his eyes scanning the room with suspicion. He inches closer, and I feel Cole's hand brush mine, a silent reassurance. My mind races, calculating our options. We're outnumbered and outgunned, but we can't afford to leave without the files.

Suddenly, one of the operatives says something into his radio, his voice low and tense. "We found the evidence room. Looks like someone's been here recently. Orders?"

A crackle of static answers him, followed by a curt response. "Neutralize any intruders. Don't leave a trace."

Cole's grip tightens, and I see his eyes flick toward the door. The message is clear: we have to get out, now. But as we inch backward, my foot catches on a metal pipe, sending it clattering to the ground with a resounding echo. The operatives' heads snap in our direction, and the moment stretches painfully, like the calm before a storm.

Then everything explodes into action.

Cole launches forward with a speed that's almost frightening, his fist connecting with the nearest operative's jaw before the man has a chance to raise his weapon. I duck as another lunges for me, barely dodging the swing of his baton. Adrenaline pulses through me, sharpening my senses, and I counter with a move Cole taught me, slamming my knee into his stomach. He staggers, but not for long. His recovery is swift, and he raises his baton again, a flash of rage in his eyes.

From the corner of my eye, I see Cole struggling with the third operative, a brute of a man with arms like tree trunks. Cole fights with a savagery that's both terrifying and mesmerizing, his movements precise and controlled, yet fueled by an intensity I hadn't known was in him. But the operative is strong, too strong, and he lands a crushing blow to Cole's ribs, making him stumble.

"Cole!" I shout, instinctively reaching for him, but my distraction costs me. The man I'd been fighting seizes the opportunity, grabbing my arm and twisting it behind my back. Pain shoots through my shoulder, sharp and blinding. I grit my teeth, refusing to cry out. The operative leans in close, his breath hot and sour against my ear.

"Thought you could outsmart the Syndicate?" he sneers. "You're in over your head, sweetheart."

Before I can respond, Cole breaks free from his opponent with a fierce growl, his eyes blazing. He tackles the man holding me, his fists a blur as he drives him to the ground. The brutality of it shocks me – this isn't the calm, level-headed Cole I know. This is someone else entirely, someone driven by a fury that seems to come from a place deep within. When it's over, he's breathing hard, his fists bloodied, and he looks at me with an expression I can't quite read.

"Are you okay?" he asks, his voice rough, as though he's just realized what he's done.

I nod, feeling a strange mix of fear and gratitude. This side of him is new, unexpected, and I'm not sure how to process it. But there's no time to dwell on it. Footsteps echo from down the hall – more Syndicate operatives. We're out of time.

"We have to go," I say, urgency overriding my confusion. We race through the factory, weaving through the maze of empty corridors. The sounds of pursuit grow closer, the footsteps thundering like a countdown.

Just as we reach the exit, a shadow appears in the doorway, blocking our path. My heart skips a beat as I recognize the figure, a face I never expected to see here. It's someone from our past, someone who shouldn't be with the Syndicate but stands there, weapon in hand, an unreadable expression on their face.

Chapter 19: Hearts Laid Bare

The room is thick with silence, a kind that feels alive, writhing in every corner. I can barely bring myself to look at Cole, though he's right next to me, the heat from his body seeping through the thin layers of my worn-out clothes. The air feels stagnant, a heaviness that's become as familiar as breathing since we ended up here, waiting and hiding like ghosts of ourselves. The concrete walls around us seem to close in, their cracked, gray faces dull and impassive, a far cry from the riotous, breathing life outside. I think I preferred it when things were loud and dangerous—at least then, there was something to fight against.

But it's Cole's voice, soft and fractured, that finally slices through the quiet. He doesn't look at me, instead staring ahead, his gaze fixed on some invisible point, something only he can see. "I used to think... I used to think I could save everyone," he begins, the words spilling out like he's been holding them back for years. His voice catches, and I watch his hands tremble slightly before he shoves them into his pockets, as if trying to keep himself from falling apart right here in front of me.

His confession is unexpected, like a stone dropped in still water, rippling out in ways neither of us can anticipate. My throat tightens, but I don't say anything. I just listen, letting his words wash over me. "You think it's hard to sleep when you're worried about yourself, about your own life," he continues, his voice rough, almost a whisper. "But it's a different kind of hell when you're awake every night thinking about all the people you couldn't save, all the people who..." He stops, shakes his head, and presses his lips together in a thin line. His eyes, always so sharp, look dull now, hollowed out by things I know he'll never fully share.

There's a small part of me that wants to touch him, maybe rest my hand on his shoulder or offer some comfort, but I can't. I'm not sure he'd accept it. I'm not sure I even know how to give it, not in a way that doesn't feel like I'm cheapening his grief, his guilt. Instead, I swallow and force myself to look at him, truly look at him, at the lines etched around his mouth, at the shadows lingering under his eyes. "You don't have to carry it alone, you know," I say quietly, not even sure if he'll believe me.

Cole laughs, a short, bitter sound that scrapes against the silence. "And who else would carry it? You?" His eyes finally meet mine, and there's something sharp there, something that cuts right through me. "You think you're some kind of savior, just like I did. But you can't... you can't always be the hero."

The words sting, but I keep my face calm, refusing to let him see how deeply they cut. He's not wrong, though. I've been clinging to this ridiculous notion that maybe, somehow, I could make a difference. That if I just fought hard enough, if I just did enough, it would mean something. But now, sitting here in this dim, claustrophobic room, I wonder if it was all a lie I told myself to keep going.

"You're right," I admit, my voice barely more than a whisper. "But that doesn't mean we stop trying."

He watches me for a long moment, his gaze unreadable. And then, slowly, he reaches out, his fingers brushing against mine. It's a simple touch, nothing more than a light graze, but it feels like a spark, a reminder that maybe, despite everything, we're still alive. That we're still here, still fighting, even if we don't know exactly what we're fighting for.

"I don't want to lose you," he says, so softly that I almost don't hear him. His voice is raw, stripped of the usual sarcasm and bravado he hides behind. It's just him, bare and vulnerable, and for a moment, I can see the fear he's been trying so hard to mask. It's not just the fear of losing the battle, of losing our cause—it's the fear of losing each other, of losing the one fragile connection that's kept us both tethered in this chaos.

The vulnerability in his voice sends a shiver down my spine, and I realize, with a clarity that's almost painful, that I don't want to lose him either. I've spent so long convincing myself that I didn't need anyone, that I was better off on my own, but here, now, with Cole's fingers tangled in mine, that lie shatters into a thousand pieces.

"I'm not going anywhere," I say, my voice steady, though my heart pounds wildly in my chest. "Not without you."

His gaze softens, and for a moment, he looks at me like I'm something precious, something worth holding onto. It's a look that makes my throat tighten, my heart lurch in a way that's both terrifying and exhilarating. And then, slowly, he leans in, his lips brushing against mine with a tenderness that steals my breath. The world fades away, and all that's left is him, his warmth, his steady presence grounding me in a way I never thought possible.

But even as I lose myself in him, a dark, nagging thought lingers at the edges of my mind. This path we're on is dangerous, and loving him—letting myself be this vulnerable—is the greatest risk I've ever taken. Because in a world like ours, attachments are weaknesses, vulnerabilities that can be exploited. And if anything were to happen to him, if I lost him... I don't know if I'd survive it.

Still, as his arms wrap around me, pulling me closer, I push those fears aside, letting myself live in this moment, just this once. Maybe it's foolish. Maybe it's reckless. But right now, with his heartbeat against mine, I don't care.

"Promise me," I whisper against his lips, my voice barely audible. "Promise me you'll stay."

He pulls back, just enough to look into my eyes, his expression fierce, determined. "I promise," he says, his voice a quiet vow. "As long as you're with me, I'm not going anywhere."

For the first time in a long while, I feel a glimmer of hope, a spark of something that feels like possibility. And as we sit there, wrapped in each other, I realize that maybe, just maybe, we can survive this.

Cole pulls back slightly, his breath warm against my cheek, and I feel his hesitation, as though he's bracing himself for whatever comes next. It's the briefest of pauses, but it's enough to remind me of all the things neither of us have said, all the truths hanging heavy between us. Outside, the world is a fractured mess, a constant grind of survival, but in here, with just the two of us, that chaos feels like a distant hum. For a moment, it's just his hand, rough and calloused, still wrapped around mine, anchoring me in a way I didn't think possible.

"You don't have to worry so much, you know," he says softly, as if trying to convince himself as much as me. His words are gentle, a startling contrast to the man I've known, the one who barks orders and throws himself into danger without a second thought. "I don't want you carrying all this... weight on your shoulders."

I bite back a retort, the instinctive sarcasm that's always been my armor. I could make a joke, brush it off, pretend that I haven't been lying awake every night, listening to his breathing beside me, wondering how long we can keep this up. But something about the rawness in his eyes stops me. So instead, I let out a sigh, glancing down at the cracks in the floor, the ones that spider out like tiny road maps, each one a reminder of how fragile this place—this world—really is.

"You think I can just turn it off?" I ask, a faint smile tugging at my lips. "Just... stop worrying? Because if you've figured that out, Cole, I'd love to know your secret."

He laughs, a real, genuine sound that rumbles up from somewhere deep inside him. It's been so long since I've heard him laugh like that, without the edge of bitterness or exhaustion. "If I knew how to stop worrying, you think I'd still be here, stuck in this godforsaken hideout with you?" He shakes his head, his grin softening. "I'd be lying on a beach somewhere, drinking something with a little umbrella in it. Maybe a book I'll pretend to read."

I raise an eyebrow, fighting the urge to laugh. "A beach? Really? You don't seem like the sand-between-your-toes type."

"Oh, and what type am I, then?" he challenges, his eyes narrowing in that playful way that makes him look younger, lighter, as if he could shed the burdens that weigh him down, even if only for a second.

"You're the type who thinks he can save everyone," I say, and the words come out sharper than I mean them to. It's not fair, I know that. But there's a part of me that wants to shake him, to make him see how dangerous that need is, how it's tearing him apart piece by piece.

Cole's smile fades, and he looks down, his jaw clenched. "Yeah, well," he murmurs, rubbing the back of his neck. "Guess that makes two of us."

There's a long silence, one that feels heavier than the walls around us. It's strange, this closeness, this intimacy born out of shared wounds and quiet confessions. I'm not used to it, and neither is he. We're both so used to fighting our battles alone, pushing everyone away before they can get too close. And yet, here we are, leaning on each other in a way that's as terrifying as it is comforting.

Finally, I break the silence, my voice barely a whisper. "What happens next, Cole?"

He looks up at me, and there's something fierce in his gaze, a determination that's both inspiring and heartbreaking. "We keep going," he says simply, as if it's the most obvious thing in the world. "We keep fighting. We don't give up."

I want to believe him, I really do. But there's a part of me that wonders how long we can keep this up, how long before the cracks in our resolve become too wide to ignore. Still, I nod, because I know that as long as he's by my side, I can keep going, even if it feels impossible.

"You're a stubborn fool, you know that?" I say, my voice tinged with affection I can't quite hide.

"Coming from you, I'll take that as a compliment," he replies, a hint of that familiar smirk returning to his face.

We lapse into a comfortable silence, the kind that feels as close to peace as we're ever going to get. Outside, I can hear the faint hum of machinery, the distant echoes of voices. It's a reminder that our little bubble won't last forever, that reality is waiting just beyond these walls, ready to pull us back into the fray.

"Do you ever think about... what it would be like?" I ask, surprising myself with the question. "If things were different?"

Cole looks at me, a flicker of something unreadable in his eyes. "What, like... if we had normal lives?"

I nod, feeling a strange mix of longing and sadness. "Yeah. If we didn't have to worry about missions and danger and... all of this."

He leans back, his expression thoughtful. "I think I'd be awful at normal," he admits, a wry smile tugging at his lips. "Can you imagine me, stuck behind a desk or doing something boring? I'd last about five minutes before I went completely insane."

"Maybe," I say, a smile breaking through despite myself. "But I think you'd be good at it. Better than you think."

He raises an eyebrow, clearly skeptical, but he doesn't argue. Instead, he reaches out, his fingers brushing against mine in a gesture that feels both familiar and brand new. "Maybe one day," he says, and there's a quiet hope in his voice that makes my chest ache.

It's a foolish dream, one that neither of us can afford. But in that moment, it feels real, tangible, like something we could reach out and grasp if we just held on tight enough. And maybe, just maybe, it's enough to keep us going, to remind us that there's still something worth fighting for, even if it's just a fragile hope.

As the moments stretch between us, I find myself leaning closer, my head resting on his shoulder. He doesn't pull away; instead, his arm wraps around me, holding me close in a way that feels both protective and vulnerable. We sit like that, in the quiet, listening to each other's breaths, finding solace in the silence. It's a small comfort, a stolen moment in a world that has taken so much from us. But it's ours, and for now, that's enough.

"I'm with you, you know," I whisper, my voice barely audible. "No matter what."

He doesn't respond right away, but his grip on me tightens, and I can feel the weight of his unspoken words, a silent promise that echoes my own.

The next morning, the cold light creeping through the boarded-up window reminds me that every brief comfort we'd found last night was just that—brief. Cole is already awake, moving quietly around the cramped space, his movements careful, almost reverent, like he's trying to hold onto the softness of the night before without breaking it. He glances at me, his gaze lingering for a beat longer than usual, and I can see the question in his eyes, the silent query he's too afraid to voice.

I offer him a small, tired smile, hoping it's enough to let him know that last night wasn't some impulsive mistake, that I'm here for whatever this is—whatever we're becoming. But there's no time to dwell on it, not with the danger pressing in on us from all sides, tightening its grip like an invisible hand at our throats.

As I sit up, rubbing the sleep from my eyes, I notice him slipping something into his jacket pocket. The way his shoulders tense, as if bracing himself for a fight, tells me everything I need to know. Whatever it is, it's something he didn't want me to see. And in a place where secrets are deadlier than bullets, that realization sends a chill down my spine.

"What's that?" I ask, keeping my voice as light as I can manage, though my heart hammers in my chest.

He freezes, his hand halfway to his side, and when he looks at me, there's a flicker of something dark in his eyes. "Nothing you need to worry about," he says, his tone almost too casual, like he's trying to sell me a lie he knows I'll never buy.

I raise an eyebrow, folding my arms across my chest. "You know that only makes me worry more, right?"

For a moment, he just stares at me, his jaw clenched, and I can practically see the wheels turning in his head, the internal debate raging behind those stormy eyes. Finally, he lets out a sigh, pulling a crumpled scrap of paper from his pocket and holding it out to me. "Here. Since you're so determined to know."

I take the paper from him, my fingers brushing his in a fleeting touch that sends a jolt of warmth through me, even as dread settles in my stomach. The writing is faint, scrawled in a shaky hand, but I recognize the name at the top instantly. A name we'd hoped never to see again.

"Are you kidding me?" I whisper, my eyes flicking up to meet his. "Cole, this... this isn't a good idea."

"Since when have any of our ideas been good ones?" he replies, a wry smile tugging at the corner of his mouth, but it doesn't reach his eyes. "We don't have a choice, and you know it."

He's right, of course. We never have a choice. That's the price of survival in a world like ours. But knowing it doesn't make it any easier, doesn't erase the fear gnawing at my insides as I imagine what it will mean to face the person whose name is scribbled on that paper. There's no way this ends well, for either of us.

"What's the plan, then?" I ask, folding the paper carefully and slipping it into my own pocket, as if hiding it will somehow lessen the weight it carries.

"We go in, get what we need, and get out," he says simply, his gaze unwavering. "Quick and clean. No unnecessary risks."

I snort, shaking my head. "Right. Because we're so good at avoiding those."

His lips twist into a smirk, a glint of something almost like mischief in his eyes. "Hey, I don't see you volunteering for a desk job. If you wanted safe and predictable, you're in the wrong line of work."

I roll my eyes, but the banter feels good, grounding us in a strange sort of normalcy, even as the tension coils tighter between us. "Trust me, I know exactly what I signed up for," I say, giving him a mock salute.

But beneath the playful words, an unease lingers, heavy and inescapable. We both know that this isn't like our usual missions, that there's a very real chance one or both of us won't make it out of this one. And as I follow him out of the hideout, my heart pounding in my chest, I can't shake the feeling that we're walking into something far more dangerous than either of us can handle.

The city stretches out before us, a sprawling mess of concrete and steel, scarred by years of conflict and decay. It's early enough that the streets are quiet, the usual clamor of voices and machinery dulled to a low hum. Shadows cling to the alleyways, winding between broken windows and crumbling facades, and the air is thick with the scent of smoke and rust.

Cole moves beside me, his steps measured and confident, but I can feel the tension radiating off him, a silent warning that sets my nerves on edge. We make our way through the labyrinth of backstreets, slipping through the city like ghosts, avoiding the main thoroughfares where watchful eyes and sharp ears might pick up on our presence.

When we finally reach the narrow, nondescript building at the edge of the city, Cole pauses, glancing over his shoulder to meet my gaze. "You ready for this?" he asks, his voice low, barely more than a whisper.

I nod, swallowing hard. "As ready as I'll ever be."

With a grim nod, he pushes open the door, and we slip inside, the shadows swallowing us whole. The interior is dimly lit, a maze of narrow hallways and peeling walls that seem to press in on us from all sides. My senses are on high alert, every creak and groan of the building sending a fresh jolt of adrenaline through me.

As we make our way deeper into the building, a low voice drifts through the hall, and I can feel Cole tense beside me. We exchange a glance, and without a word, he signals for me to follow him, his movements silent and deliberate. The voice grows louder, more distinct, and I recognize it instantly—a familiar cadence that sends a shiver down my spine.

We round a corner, and there he is, our target, standing with his back to us, oblivious to our presence. My pulse quickens, a rush of conflicting emotions surging through me. This is what we came for, what we've been planning for weeks. But as I raise my weapon, a strange sense of dread washes over me, an unshakable feeling that we're walking into a trap.

And then, as if sensing our presence, he turns, his gaze locking onto mine. A slow, knowing smile spreads across his face, and my blood runs cold. He's been expecting us.

"Hello, love," he says, his voice dripping with a sickening charm that makes my skin crawl. "I was wondering when you'd show up."

Beside me, Cole's jaw clenches, his fists balled at his sides. I can feel his anger, his frustration, but before either of us can react, a series of footsteps echoes through the hallway behind us. We're surrounded.

Panic flares in my chest, but I force myself to stay calm, to focus. There has to be a way out of this. There always is.

But as I glance at Cole, the look in his eyes tells me that he knows the truth just as well as I do. This time, we may not be so lucky.

The man in front of us chuckles, his eyes gleaming with a cold, twisted amusement. "Did you really think you could sneak in here unnoticed?" he asks, his voice laced with mockery. "You've gotten sloppy, both of you."

My hand tightens around my weapon, my mind racing, calculating every possible move, every chance at escape. But it's clear that he has the upper hand, that he's been waiting for this moment, savoring the anticipation of our downfall.

And as his gaze shifts to Cole, something dark and dangerous in his eyes, I realize, with a sickening certainty, that this was never about me.

Chapter 20: The Cracks Appear

We weave through the back alleys, the heavy fog clinging to the night, muffling every step and stifling every breath. Cole leads, his shadowed figure a few paces ahead, only just visible in the dim light cast by dying street lamps. The weight of the city's secrets presses against us, an oppressive force lurking in every corner. I can feel them—the Syndicate's enforcers—moving just beyond our vision, a constant, quiet threat stalking our every turn. The city feels alive in its malevolence, watching with narrowed eyes, waiting for us to slip.

My skin prickles, and I tighten my grip on the worn leather strap slung across my shoulder, the edge of a dagger hidden within reach. I never thought I'd be here, running through the underbelly of the city with a man whose loyalty I no longer trust. My mind spins with fragments of conversations, half-seen glances, the ghost of a hand reaching for something unsaid.

Cole slows, turning to glance back at me, his expression unreadable. His jaw clenches, a flicker of hesitation flashing across his face before he turns away, leading us down another darkened passage. It's that flicker—the tiniest crack in his confidence—that settles a new kind of dread in my stomach. Cole is the kind of man who never hesitates, never falters. The fact that he has now, even for a second, rattles me.

I swallow the lump in my throat, forcing myself to remember the way he looked at me when this all began, as if I were something worth risking it all for. But that was before. Before the shadows closed in, before the Syndicate turned their gaze on us, before whispers of betrayal started echoing in places I thought were safe.

The silence stretches between us, tense and brittle, until I can't take it anymore. "Cole," I say, my voice low, barely above a whisper. He stops, his shoulders rigid, and for a moment, I think he's not going to answer.

"Yes?" His tone is neutral, controlled, but there's an edge to it, a guardedness I've never heard before.

"We're being hunted," I say, taking a step closer, feeling the weight of every unsaid word between us. "And someone's given us up. You know that, don't you?"

A muscle in his jaw tightens, and he looks away, his eyes scanning the shadows. It's as if he's hoping they'll swallow my question, that he can pretend he didn't hear me. But I can't let it go; it festers inside me, a gnawing ache that demands answers.

"Who was it?" I press, my voice sharper than I intended. "Who betrayed us?"

He doesn't answer immediately, and that silence is worse than any denial. Finally, he turns to face me, his expression carefully blank. "You think it's me."

It's not a question, and the accusation hangs heavy in the cold night air. I meet his gaze, my heart pounding against my ribs, knowing that whatever I say next could break something between us that might never be mended.

"I don't know what to think," I admit, hating the crack in my voice, hating the vulnerability that slips through. "I want to trust you. But I can't shake the feeling that there's something you're not telling me."

His eyes narrow, and he steps closer, his voice dropping to a low, dangerous whisper. "You think I'd risk everything, put my life on the line, just to betray you?"

There's a flash of anger, hot and fierce, that sparks in my chest. "I don't know, Cole. I don't know who you are anymore."

The words cut deeper than I intend, and I see it in the way he flinches, a quick, almost imperceptible reaction. For a moment, something flickers in his gaze—hurt, maybe? Regret? But then it's gone, replaced by the same unreadable mask he's worn since the night this all began.

"You think you know everything," he says softly, almost to himself. "But you have no idea."

A chill races down my spine at his words, and suddenly, I'm not so sure if the man standing before me is the same one I thought I knew. The silence stretches again, thick and heavy, and I can feel the weight of a hundred unanswered questions pressing down on me. But before I can say anything more, a sound echoes down the alley—a low, ominous shuffle, too deliberate to be accidental.

In an instant, the tension between us shifts, replaced by the cold, hard reality of our situation. We don't have time for this, for accusations and secrets and lingering doubts. The Syndicate is closing in, and if we're going to survive, we have to keep moving.

"Let's go," he says, his voice flat, all traces of emotion wiped clean. He turns and starts down the alley again, and I follow, feeling a strange hollowness settle in my chest. There was a time when I would have trusted him with my life, when his presence would have been a comfort, a reassurance. But now, all I feel is the weight of doubt, an invisible wall that separates us even as we run side by side.

The city twists and shifts around us, its labyrinthine streets a maze of shadows and hidden dangers. We slip through side alleys and duck under low-hanging bridges, every sense on high alert. I can feel the Syndicate's enforcers closing in, their presence a dark, silent pressure at our backs. It's only a matter of time before they catch up, and I can't shake the feeling that, one way or another, this chase is going to end in blood.

The night stretches on, a relentless, unyielding darkness that swallows us whole. The silence between us grows heavier, thicker, an unspoken testament to the cracks that have begun to splinter our fragile alliance. And somewhere, deep in the pit of my stomach, a gnawing fear takes root—the fear that I might be running beside a man I no longer know.

The night unfurls around us, thick with fog and secrets. I don't know which weighs heavier—the persistent fear of the Syndicate closing in, or the silent rift stretching wider between me and Cole with every step. I want to believe that he's here, with me, all the way to the end, but there's something in his gaze now that makes me wary, something locked tight behind those steel-gray eyes.

We slip into an abandoned shop, its windows shattered, aisles dusty and forgotten, the stale scent of rotting wood in the air. Cole glances back at me, a flicker of urgency in his expression, and gestures for me to keep low. I follow, crouching behind a row of shelves, our breaths barely audible over the silence.

"Do you have a plan?" I murmur, leaning close enough to catch the faint scent of smoke on his clothes. It's familiar, almost comforting, and I hate that it is. A small part of me wants to shove him away, to put as much distance between us as this crumbling shop will allow.

He hesitates, and in that pause, the lingering suspicion that's been gnawing at me intensifies. "We need to get to the docks," he whispers finally, his voice low. "There's a contact there. Someone who can get us out."

"Someone else?" I let the words hang, dripping with accusation, and he flinches, just barely, but enough for me to notice. "Another friend I didn't know about? Another person you forgot to mention?"

He sighs, exasperated. "Would you rather I tell you everything, or would you prefer to keep us both alive?"

There's a flicker of anger in his eyes, and I can tell he's holding back, swallowing whatever biting words are on the tip of his tongue. The restraint is almost more insulting than anything he could have said.

"What I'd prefer," I reply, my voice sharp, "is a little honesty. Trust. Isn't that supposed to go both ways?"

He doesn't answer, just gives me that maddening look, as if he's weighing every word, deciding what to share, what to keep. And I realize then that he's made a habit of this, of deciding for both of us. Maybe he thinks it's protecting me, or maybe he just doesn't trust me enough to handle the truth.

Before I can press him further, there's a noise—a faint, shuffling sound coming from the back of the store. Cole stiffens, eyes narrowing, and in an instant, his hand is on my wrist, pulling me to the ground beside him. The air is suddenly too thick, too heavy, and I can feel my pulse racing, each beat a thunderous echo in the silence.

"Stay quiet," he breathes, his voice barely a whisper. We sit there, side by side, crouched in the shadows, listening as the footsteps grow louder, closer. Whoever's out there isn't trying to hide—they're moving with purpose, each step deliberate, the sound of it grating against my nerves.

I glance at Cole, his jaw set, his eyes focused, and despite everything, a part of me wants to believe in him. Wants to believe that he'd never lead me into a trap, that he'd never betray me. But that doubt lingers, coiled and poisonous, and it takes everything in me to keep it from spilling out.

The footsteps pause, just outside our hiding spot, and my heart stops. The silence is suffocating, and I can feel Cole's grip on my wrist tighten, grounding me, as if he knows I'm on the verge of bolting. We sit there, waiting, every muscle tensed, until finally, the footsteps recede, fading into the night.

Cole releases his hold, and I pull back, rubbing my wrist, the ghost of his touch lingering. I don't look at him, don't trust myself to meet his gaze without saying something I'll regret. Instead, I push myself to my feet, brushing the dust from my jeans, and start toward the exit.

He follows, silent, his presence a weight at my back, and for a moment, I consider running—disappearing into the city, leaving him and the Syndicate and all this mess behind. But the thought is fleeting, a flicker of impulse that fades as quickly as it came. Despite everything, despite the doubts and the silence, I'm still here. I hate myself a little for it.

We slip out of the shop, moving swiftly, sticking to the shadows, the city sprawling around us like a maze. The docks aren't far, but every step feels like a gamble, a risk that someone's watching, waiting for us to stumble. The buildings loom overhead, towering silhouettes against the night sky, and I can feel the city's heartbeat, steady and unyielding, a reminder that we're never truly alone here.

Cole's pace quickens, his movements precise, almost mechanical, as if he's done this a thousand times before. Maybe he has. Maybe there are a dozen versions of him, slipping through shadows in a dozen different cities, each one a stranger wearing his face. The thought makes me uneasy, and I push it aside, focusing on the path ahead.

We reach the edge of the docks, the water a dark expanse stretching out into oblivion. The air is sharp with salt and the faint, metallic tang of rust, the scent of it mingling with the murky smell of the harbor. Boats bob in the distance, their silhouettes barely visible against the night, and I can see a figure waiting, shrouded in shadow, standing near the edge of the pier.

Cole glances at me, a silent warning, and I nod, following him as we approach. The figure steps forward, a man with a scar running down his cheek, his eyes cold and calculating. He looks at Cole, then at me, and I can see the flicker of recognition there, the subtle shift as he sizes me up.

"This her?" the man asks, his voice rough, like gravel scraping against steel.

Cole nods, but he doesn't look at me. I can feel the tension between them, thick and heavy, and I know there's history here, something unspoken that lingers in the air.

The man's gaze settles on me, assessing, and I meet his stare, refusing to look away. I'm tired of being left in the dark, tired of the secrets and half-truths. If Cole won't give me answers, maybe this man will.

"She doesn't look like much," he says finally, a hint of amusement in his tone.

I arch an eyebrow, crossing my arms. "And you look like a bad decision I'll regret in the morning," I reply, my voice as steady as I can make it. "Guess we're all full of surprises."

There's a beat of silence, then the man laughs—a low, rough sound that seems out of place in the stillness. He glances at Cole, a smirk tugging at the corner of his mouth. "You didn't mention she had a mouth on her."

Cole's lips twitch, but he doesn't say anything, and the man shakes his head, chuckling softly. "Alright, let's get moving. Syndicate's got eyes everywhere tonight, and I'm not looking to get caught babysitting."

He turns, leading the way down the pier, and I follow, feeling Cole's presence beside me, solid and unyielding. For a moment, the doubts fade, replaced by a strange, fragile sense of trust—a fleeting belief that maybe, just maybe, we'll make it out of this mess alive.

The pier creaks beneath our feet, the boards loose and weathered from years of salt and neglect. The dark water slaps against the pylons, and for a moment, all I can hear is that rhythmic pulse, like a heartbeat in the depths. I keep my gaze fixed ahead, refusing to look at Cole, at the man with the scar, at anything that might remind me how dangerously close we are to the edge—both the literal one beneath my feet and the invisible one hovering between us.

Scar Man's steps are heavy, unhurried. He doesn't spare us a glance, though I can feel his wariness in the way his shoulders are set, like he's a spring, tightly coiled and waiting. Cole's been quiet since we left the shadows of the abandoned shop, and it bothers me how he's just trailing behind, the ghost of the man who used to take charge without a second thought. Now he's fading into the background, letting this stranger lead us, and every second of it grates against me.

Scar Man stops near the end of the pier, where a small, barely visible boat is tethered to a post. The vessel's low profile hugs the dark water like a shadow, and I wonder how many people it's ferried across these unforgiving waters under the cover of night. He turns, finally acknowledging us, his gaze sharp as a blade.

"We're cutting it close," he says, voice low, rough. "Syndicate's got patrols running through every dock in the city tonight."

Cole gives a single nod, his face expressionless. "We're not staying long."

Scar Man scoffs, leaning against the post with a look that suggests he's unimpressed, maybe even a little amused. "You think I'm here out of charity? That I enjoy the thrill of dodging Syndicate snipers?"

A sliver of irritation flashes across Cole's face, and he takes a step closer, his voice taut. "You're here because you owe me."

The man's smirk fades, and his gaze flicks over to me, lingering just long enough to set my nerves on edge. "Is that right?" He turns back to Cole, crossing his arms. "I don't recall owing you enough to risk my neck for two people."

I can feel Cole's tension from where I stand, a wire drawn too tight, and I wonder if he's about to snap. But he only tilts his head, his tone dropping to something close to a growl. "If you don't want to help, fine. But I think you know what happens if the Syndicate catches us here."

The man lets out a dry laugh, glancing at me with a glint of something in his eyes—curiosity, maybe, or something darker. "You're really willing to risk your life for this one?" He nods in my direction, his expression almost pitying. "Does she even know?"

"Know what?" I cut in, unable to keep silent any longer. "If you have something to say, say it to me."

Scar Man looks at me with a mixture of surprise and something close to respect. "She's got spirit, I'll give her that," he says to Cole, who stands there, silent as stone.

I wait, my patience fraying with every heartbeat, until finally, Cole glances at me, his gaze shadowed. "It doesn't matter."

"Doesn't matter?" I let out a bitter laugh, shaking my head. "So we're just supposed to keep walking blind, trusting whoever shows up with a boat and a bad attitude?"

His jaw tightens, but he doesn't respond, and that silence tells me everything I need to know. There's a gap between us now, wide and jagged, filled with things he won't say and truths he's determined to keep buried. I don't know if it's pride or fear that's holding him back, but either way, it feels like a betrayal.

I start to pull away, the ache in my chest growing with each second that passes, but then Scar Man steps forward, slipping something cold and metallic into my hand. I look down, surprised to see a thin, worn key resting in my palm, its edges rough and dull from use.

"You're going to need this," he says, his tone unexpectedly somber. "There's a place on the other side, tucked behind the docks. Look for the red door."

I glance up at him, confusion twisting in my mind. "What's behind the door?"

"Answers," he says, voice heavy, like he's carrying the weight of those answers himself. "But you may not like them."

Cole's expression shifts, almost imperceptibly, a flicker of something close to alarm, and he reaches for my arm. "We don't need—"

"I do," I interrupt, pulling my arm free. I don't know what's waiting for me on the other side, but I know that I can't keep walking through this nightmare with half the story, with shadows and lies twisting everything into something I barely recognize. "I'm going."

The man with the scar nods approvingly, and for the first time, I see a hint of understanding in his eyes, as if he's been here before, standing at the edge of something he couldn't fully see.

"Suit yourself," he mutters, gesturing to the boat. "But you'll have to make it quick. Syndicate's got ears everywhere, and they're not far."

Cole doesn't move, doesn't say a word as I climb into the boat, the key clutched tightly in my hand. Part of me expects him to stop me, to argue or give me a reason to stay. But he doesn't. He only watches, his face a mask, the flicker of something indefinable in his gaze, something that I can't quite interpret, and I realize with a jolt that maybe he wants me to go, that maybe he's just as ready for this distance as I am.

Scar Man takes his place at the helm, the engine a low, steady hum that vibrates through the silence. As we push off, the water splitting beneath us, I turn back, meeting Cole's gaze one last time. He stands alone on the pier, a solitary figure silhouetted against the darkness, and for a moment, I feel the strange weight of finality settle over us, as if this choice, this departure, is carving a line between us that can never be crossed again.

The city fades behind us, swallowed by the fog, and I turn my attention forward, to the open expanse of water stretching out ahead. The boat glides through the waves, and the tension in my chest loosens, just slightly, the cold air sharp and bracing against my skin.

"Where exactly is this door?" I ask, breaking the silence, my voice barely audible over the rumble of the engine.

He glances back at me, his face obscured by shadow, and points to a faint, distant glow on the shore. "Just beyond that light. You'll know it when you see it."

I nod, tucking the key into my pocket, feeling the weight of it pressing against me like a promise. Or maybe a threat. I don't know what I'll find behind that red door, but for the first time in a long time, I feel the stirrings of something close to hope—or maybe just the thrill of the unknown, of stepping into the darkness with only my wits to guide me.

The boat slows as we approach the shore, and Scar Man gives me a final nod, his expression unreadable. "Watch your back in there," he warns, his voice barely above a whisper. "Nothing is as it seems."

I step onto the damp sand, the boat pulling away behind me, and make my way toward the faint glow in the distance. The path twists and turns, narrow and winding, until I reach it—a tall, red door set into the stone, its surface chipped and weathered, like it's been waiting for me all along.

My hand hovers over the key, and I take a deep breath, steadying myself. Whatever lies beyond this door, it's my only way forward.

I slide the key into the lock and turn it, feeling the resistance as the tumblers click into place. The door swings open, revealing a narrow hallway lit by a single, flickering light, casting long shadows against the walls.

I take a step inside, my heart hammering, and as I move forward, the door slams shut behind me, echoing through the silence. The light flickers once, twice, then goes out, plunging me into darkness.

Chapter 21: Through the Fire

The warehouse blazed with a fervor that felt like it could consume the world. Every wall was a furnace, every step, a challenge, every breath stolen and replaced by smoke that clawed down my throat and tightened its grip around my lungs. I could barely see through the shifting layers of black and orange, the smoke writhing like living things, tendrils of dark magic trying to drag me down.

    I pressed a sleeve to my mouth, staggering forward with no real direction, just the instinct to survive, to keep moving. My boots scraped against the broken concrete floor, stumbling over debris, shards of glass, twisted metal that poked and slashed at my ankles. The Syndicate was nothing if not meticulous, leaving nothing behind but destruction and dead ends. And here I was, the last mouse left in the maze, corners closing in.

    My hand, slick with sweat, gripped the strap of my satchel tighter as I searched for a way out. My mind was a storm of calculations and half-formed plans. Every instinct told me I was alone; that was the way I'd trained myself to operate. Trust no one, believe in no one's rescue but your own. But survival seemed further away with each excruciating moment, each step into the thickening haze.

    And then, as though summoned by some defiant fragment of hope still rattling around in my head, I heard it—his voice. "Lena!" It was desperate and raw, the sort of sound you make when you're terrified it's too late. In the distance, I could just make out his silhouette through the undulating flames, cutting through the haze as if he'd come from another world. For a heartbeat, I thought he was a mirage. Surely, Cole wasn't here, wasn't risking himself to wade through this hellscape for me. And yet, here he was, shoulder braced against the splintering doorframe, eyes locked on mine. His face was streaked with soot and panic, and though he was trying for a controlled calm, I saw the truth, the fear flickering there in the shadows of his gaze.

"Cole," I coughed out, barely more than a whisper, but he heard it. His jaw tightened, a flash of relief softening the hard line of his mouth. Before I could blink, he was beside me, an arm around my shoulders, grounding me, keeping me upright as he pulled me toward the exit with a fierce determination that made my heart pound. We moved as one, his grip never faltering, his resolve bleeding into me, shoring up the last shreds of my strength.

The air outside hit me like a slap, crisp and cold, even under the haze of ash that still clung to it. I sucked in greedy breaths, coughing and gasping as the flames roared behind us, like the devil's applause for our miraculous escape. Cole didn't release his hold, his arm still wrapped around me, anchoring me as I tried to regain control of my own shaking body.

We stumbled down the alley, our footsteps echoing against the cracked pavement. The warehouse was now a smoldering behemoth behind us, embers floating like vengeful spirits in the air. Cole looked at me, his eyes searching, something unreadable flickering there. And in that moment, with the world quiet but for the crackle of the flames and the distant wail of sirens, I saw what he was trying to hide behind that iron mask of his. Desperation, yes, but something more—something deep and raw, something that left me breathless in a way no fire ever could.

For a heartbeat, we just stood there, face to face, close enough to feel the heat radiating off each other. I saw the way his gaze softened, the way his shoulders finally relaxed now that we were out of immediate danger. And I felt it too, that strange and terrifying pull that was always there, always lurking beneath the surface of our barbed conversations and wary glances. As much as I tried to fight it, as much as I wanted to keep that armor around my heart impenetrable, here in this moment, it was useless. Standing there, bathed in the eerie orange glow of the firelight, everything was stripped bare.

"Lena," he said softly, his voice like a prayer, his eyes catching mine and holding them, unwavering. There was a vulnerability there, a fragility he usually hid so well, and I felt a pang of something that could only be called tenderness, though I wasn't ready to admit it, not even to myself.

"I'm not sure why you came back," I murmured, trying for deflection, for distance, but my voice betrayed me. There was too much emotion tangled in it, too much honesty. He gave me a wry smile, something both sad and amused.

"Not sure I am either," he replied, his tone light but his eyes solemn, like he was confessing something he hadn't fully understood until this moment. He ran a hand through his hair, disheveling it even further, and for once, he looked less like the polished, impenetrable agent and more like a man who'd just walked through fire for a reason he couldn't explain.

For the first time, the weight of everything we'd been through—the betrayals, the lies, the dangers lurking around every corner—crashed over me like a wave. And somehow, in that brief silence between us, I knew it wasn't over. Whatever this was, it had dug its claws deep, leaving marks that wouldn't fade.

"Thank you," I whispered, a simple acknowledgment, but the words felt heavy, like they carried all the unspoken things neither of us could bring ourselves to say.

Cole's lips quirked up in a half-smile, but his gaze was still intense, focused. He stepped closer, brushing a strand of hair from my face, his fingers lingering for a fraction of a second too long. I felt a surge of warmth, unbidden and undeniable, and I knew he felt it too.

The silence was fragile, hanging between us like smoke, easily disrupted by the smallest misstep. I held my breath, the weight of what lingered unspoken almost heavier than the air I'd struggled to breathe inside the burning warehouse. Cole's hand was still on my shoulder, fingers rough and warm, grounding me even as I felt the world tilting in slow motion. His eyes searched mine, not for answers but for something quieter, something that maybe even he couldn't name.

I tried to shake off the tenderness, but my usual armor felt flimsy now, worn thin by the adrenaline and exhaustion. I forced a wry smile, hoping to inject some levity back into our exchange, some semblance of the prickly rapport we'd carefully built. "Well, if this was your idea of a rescue, you might need a little more practice."

He gave a low, soft chuckle, the sound cutting through the chill of the night. "Oh, I'm sure you'd have managed just fine without me. Maybe the walls would've caught fire a little faster, but you'd still have found a way to look smug about it."

I scoffed, rolling my eyes even as my pulse quickened. "You're confusing smug with resourceful. A common mistake."

"Resourceful, right," he replied, his tone just a shade too serious. "Like that time you tried to hotwire my car and ended up setting off the alarm instead."

I narrowed my eyes, but the playful spark in his gaze softened my glare. "Hey, that was an accident. Besides, I could've gotten it if I'd had just a few more minutes."

"You had forty-five seconds. I counted." His smile widened, and despite myself, I found it infectious. We shared a laugh, brief and bittersweet, like the echo of something we'd once had—or maybe never had but always wanted.

The street was deserted, every building casting long shadows in the dim streetlights. I felt a pang of dread as reality started to creep back in. Our situation hadn't magically improved just because we'd managed to escape one trap. The Syndicate was relentless, and we'd only just slipped through their grasp, bruised and battered, with no real plan.

But Cole didn't seem in any hurry to let go. His hand still rested on my shoulder, his thumb brushing an almost imperceptible circle, as though reassuring himself that I was still there. I wanted to lean into that touch, to let it promise something more, something safe and steady, but I couldn't quite bring myself to cross that line. Not with so many unspoken dangers lurking.

I cleared my throat, letting the tension ease as I stepped back, breaking the contact. His hand fell to his side, and for a brief second, I thought I saw disappointment flicker across his face, but it was gone in an instant. He hid it well, but I'd come to learn his subtle tells. "We should probably get moving before they figure out we made it out," I said, my voice steadier than I felt.

"Good idea," he said, slipping back into his composed, mission-focused demeanor. He gave a curt nod, already scanning our surroundings for any sign of threat. "But first, we need to get you checked out. You took in a lot of smoke back there."

"I'm fine," I replied, brushing off his concern with a wave of my hand. But even as I said it, I felt the scratchy burn in my throat, the ache deep in my chest that hadn't quite faded.

Cole raised an eyebrow, crossing his arms as he leaned against a nearby wall. "Really? Because you don't look fine. You look like you're two breaths away from collapsing."

"Thanks," I deadpanned. "Always good to hear how stunning I look after nearly dying."

His lips quirked into a smirk. "You always manage to make it work."

It was a strange compliment, backhanded but sincere, and I felt a blush creeping up my cheeks. "You know, for someone who prides himself on his steely resolve, you're shockingly sentimental tonight."

"Only when the occasion calls for it," he shot back, his voice softer now, the tease melting into something warmer. "And I think surviving a warehouse fire together warrants a little sentiment."

The words hung between us, heavier than I wanted to admit. I shifted my weight, glancing away from him, from the intensity in his eyes that felt far too close to the edges of what we'd never said aloud. I knew he wasn't saying it outright, but the sentiment was clear enough—that he wasn't just here out of obligation, that this wasn't merely a tactical partnership to him. And the thought left me feeling vulnerable, exposed in a way that all the Syndicate's threats and traps never could.

Finally, I forced myself to break the silence. "Look, I appreciate the whole knight-in-shining-armor thing, but I think it's time to figure out what our next move is." I tried to keep my voice steady, practical, but it was hard to ignore the way his gaze lingered, as if daring me to admit that maybe, just maybe, I felt the same pull he did.

He gave a slow nod, the spark in his eyes dimming just enough for him to slip back into his stoic, impenetrable mask. "Alright. There's a safehouse a few blocks from here, one that's not on any official records. If we're lucky, they won't know about it."

"'If we're lucky' is not exactly the most comforting plan I've ever heard," I muttered, trying to mask my nerves with a dose of sarcasm. But he just chuckled, unbothered, and I realized that even through all this, he hadn't lost his sense of humor—or his confidence.

We moved in silence, side by side, each step a silent pact that neither of us spoke of but both understood. It was strange, the way we navigated this fragile alliance, neither fully trusting but both unwilling to let go. I could feel the rhythm of his breathing, the warmth radiating from him, and despite everything, it felt reassuring.

We reached the safehouse, a nondescript building tucked away on a forgotten street, its windows dark and unwelcoming. Cole took a quick look around before unlocking the door with a set of keys I hadn't seen him use before. He nodded for me to follow him in, and I stepped over the threshold, feeling an odd blend of relief and apprehension.

The room was small, cluttered but clean, with a cot against one wall and a table scattered with old maps and files. It felt temporary, like the kind of place you'd pass through without ever leaving a trace, and that suited our purposes just fine. I sank onto the cot, exhaustion washing over me in a way that felt bone-deep, as though I'd been carrying the weight of a thousand near-misses and unsaid words.

Cole pulled up a chair, his gaze never leaving me as he watched for any sign of weakness. And for once, I didn't mind.

The low hum of the safehouse generator droned on as I sat on the cot, its thin mattress doing little to ease the ache that had settled into every muscle. The room was barely lit, a single, dim bulb swinging gently from a wire overhead, casting shadows that danced across the walls in a rhythm that felt almost hypnotic. Cole had taken his place across from me, leaning back against the door with his arms crossed, his sharp gaze flickering from me to the narrow, covered window, and back again.

I watched him watch me, an uneasy tension buzzing between us. The weight of unspoken words pressed down, though neither of us seemed willing to break the silence first. For a fleeting second, I wondered what he was thinking—if he was as aware as I was of the dangerous tightrope we walked. But the mask was back, his expression unreadable, the steady, composed look of a man who had trained himself to be unshakeable.

"So," I finally said, crossing my arms and tilting my head, "how did you find me back there?"

His lips twitched, a glimmer of that familiar wryness breaking through. "You didn't think I'd let you wander into a Syndicate trap alone, did you?"

I snorted, though it came out more like a strangled laugh. "Given how often we've double-crossed each other, yes, that's exactly what I thought."

"Touché," he said, his voice as dry as sandpaper. "But you're stuck with me for now. You should know by now that I have a soft spot for lost causes."

"Oh, so that's what this is?" I shot back, arching an eyebrow. "A mercy mission?"

He held my gaze, his expression turning serious. "You know it's more than that." His voice softened, but there was a hard edge underneath, a frustration he couldn't quite hide. "The Syndicate's coming after us because we're the only ones who've gotten close enough to their real operation. And whether we like it or not, we're in this together."

I wanted to argue, to push back against the implication that my choices were anything but my own, but I couldn't deny the truth in his words. We'd uncovered too many secrets, pulled too many loose threads for the Syndicate to let us walk away unscathed. My pulse quickened, a familiar restlessness building in my chest. I was trapped, bound to Cole by circumstance and the shadow of a war that loomed just out of sight.

"Well," I murmured, running a hand through my hair in a futile attempt to compose myself, "that's comforting."

"Comfort isn't exactly our style, is it?" He smiled, but there was no humor in it, just a grim acceptance that settled like a stone between us.

We fell silent again, the weight of our precarious alliance pressing down. I glanced around the room, searching for anything to distract me from the knot forming in my stomach. On the table in the corner, a set of blueprints lay scattered, the pages worn and creased, marked with red and black ink. I pushed myself up, crossing the room to get a better look, but before I could examine them, Cole was beside me, his presence a steady heat against my shoulder.

"They're for a warehouse on the other side of town," he said quietly, his breath warm against my neck. I shivered, refusing to let him see the effect he had on me. "We think it's one of their key locations. The Syndicate's been moving shipments in and out under the radar. If we can intercept one..."

"Then we might have a shot at shutting them down," I finished, my mind already racing with possibilities.

He nodded, his gaze intent on the blueprints, but I could feel the unspoken worry beneath the surface. This wasn't just another mission. If we went through with it, we'd be committing to a fight that had only two possible outcomes: victory or disaster. And the odds weren't exactly in our favor.

I traced a finger along the blueprint, noting the exits, the ventilation shafts, the narrow hallways where we could be cornered. "It's a death trap," I said bluntly.

"Probably," he replied, a small smile tugging at his lips. "But if we pull this off, it could be the last death trap we walk into."

I glanced up at him, searching his face for any sign of doubt, but he met my gaze with a calm determination that almost made me believe it was possible. Almost.

"Fine," I said, crossing my arms as I studied the blueprints with renewed focus. "But if we're doing this, we're doing it my way."

Cole chuckled, and the sound was like a spark in the darkness, brief but bright. "As if I'd expect anything else."

We spent the next few hours strategizing, mapping out every possible angle, every potential risk. The plan began to take shape, a fragile web of contingencies and half-formed ideas, held together by a thread of reckless optimism. By the time we'd exhausted every option, the sky outside had begun to lighten, the first hints of dawn seeping through the cracks in the boarded-up window.

I rubbed my eyes, feeling the exhaustion settle over me like a heavy blanket. Cole was quiet, his attention fixed on a small radio in the corner of the room. He'd insisted on bringing it, a habit he hadn't yet kicked, even after years of mistrusting anything that could be tracked. But this one was old, analog, impossible to trace. He switched it on, and a low, crackling hum filled the room.

And then, a voice—a voice we both knew far too well—filtered through the static. My stomach dropped as I recognized the clipped, calculating tone of the Syndicate's chief operator, a woman whose name I'd never learned but whose presence haunted every mission, every narrow escape. Her voice was cold, cutting through the static with a precision that sent a chill down my spine.

"We know you're listening, Lena. And you, too, Cole," she said, her tone calm and almost friendly, as if we were two old friends catching up. "You can keep running, but it's only a matter of time before we catch up. You've both crossed too many lines, left too many loose ends. This isn't a game you can win."

Cole's hand tightened on the radio, his jaw clenched, but he didn't respond. I could feel the tension radiating off him, the silent fury simmering just beneath the surface. I swallowed, fighting the urge to snap back, to let her know that we weren't afraid. But something held me back—a sense that she was baiting us, luring us into a trap we couldn't see.

"And just so you know," she continued, her voice dropping to a whisper, "we're closer than you think."

The transmission cut off abruptly, leaving only the empty static in its wake. I stared at the radio, my heart pounding, my mind racing with questions and half-formed fears. The room felt colder, the walls closing in as the implications settled over me like a dark cloud.

Cole looked at me, his expression unreadable, but I saw the resolve in his eyes, the determination that had kept him by my side despite every reason to walk away. He opened his mouth to speak, but before he could say a word, the door to the safehouse burst open, and a blinding light flooded the room, illuminating the shadows we'd tried so hard to hide in.

And for a split second, everything froze, the world narrowing down to the sharp, metallic click of a gun's safety being disengaged.

Chapter 22: The Dark Revelation

I could feel the weight of Draven's words settling over us like a storm cloud, thickening the air until it was hard to breathe. It was one thing to know the Syndicate was ruthless, an insidious organization that lived in the shadows, thriving on fear and loyalty bought through terror. But to hear that they were something older, something darker—a hidden order with a history as tangled as ancient roots—it was like trying to comprehend a nightmare while still awake. It was the kind of story told around dimly lit tables in forgotten pubs, or whispered between conspirators who looked over their shoulders for ghosts as much as they did for guards. And yet, here it was, laid bare before me, and it wasn't folklore or myth. It was my past, my family. Everything I'd ever known unraveled before me like a fraying thread, leaving me grasping at air.

I turned to Cole, hoping to find something, anything, to anchor me to reality. But his expression mirrored mine, a mixture of disbelief and betrayal. His jaw was set tight, but his eyes, usually sharp and unwavering, were lost. Draven's revelation had sliced through him too, leaving behind a raw wound that I could see even though he tried to hide it. He was good at that—burying his emotions under layers of grit and purpose. But this was too much, even for him.

"Centuries?" I finally managed to choke out, my voice sounding foreign in my own ears. "You're telling me they've been pulling strings for centuries? And my family—" The words tangled in my throat, too sharp, too real to fully form.

Draven nodded, his expression as unreadable as a stone. He was like that—impossible to decipher, with eyes that hinted at too many secrets to count. "They don't just pull strings, Evelyn. They weave the entire tapestry. Your family was a part of it, once. Deeply. Your father tried to sever that connection. He paid for it."

The room was quiet, a silence so thick it felt as though we were sinking into it. The dim, flickering light of the warehouse seemed suddenly oppressive, as if it too was caught in the gravity of Draven's revelation.

Cole cleared his throat, the sound breaking the spell for just a moment. "And you?" he asked, his voice laced with a hint of suspicion. "How do you know all this? Why come to us now?"

Draven's lips curved into something that might have been a smile if it didn't look so predatory. "I know because I was once a part of it. I escaped, or at least I thought I did. But no one truly leaves the Syndicate." His gaze flickered to me, a hint of something I couldn't place lingering in his expression. Pity, perhaps. Or maybe regret. "They have eyes and ears everywhere, Evelyn. Your father thought he could protect you, shield you from the truth. But the truth has a way of crawling out of the darkest places, doesn't it?"

A shiver ran through me. I wanted to recoil, to retreat to some place where this was all just a story, a terrible tale that happened to someone else. But there was no escape, not really. The weight of my family's legacy pressed down on me, suffocating and inescapable. I'd spent so long fighting the Syndicate, clawing at its edges, thinking that if I just pulled hard enough, I could tear down the whole rotten structure. But now, it felt like I'd been trying to tear down a mountain with my bare hands.

Cole's hand found mine, his grip firm and grounding. "We'll figure it out," he murmured, his voice barely more than a whisper, but enough to slice through the dread curling in my chest.

I wanted to believe him. Cole had always been a source of strength, a constant in a world that seemed to shift and shatter at every turn. But even he seemed shaken, his eyes dark with a haunted look that made me ache. He was as tangled in this as I was, his life as much a casualty of the Syndicate's games as mine. And yet, here he was, standing beside me, his thumb tracing gentle circles over my knuckles, offering me the only comfort he could in a world gone mad.

Draven shifted, breaking the fragile moment. "This isn't just about freedom anymore. This is about survival. The Syndicate won't stop until they have you back under their thumb, and they'll burn everything you love to do it."

The finality in his tone sent a chill down my spine. I looked up, meeting his gaze. "Why are you helping us, then? If they're so powerful, so ruthless, what's in it for you?"

Draven paused, something flickering in his eyes. "Let's just say I have my own score to settle," he replied, his voice barely concealing a bitterness that made me wonder just how deep his scars ran.

Cole's grip on my hand tightened, his voice cutting through the tension with a steel edge. "Whatever your reasons, Draven, remember this: if you're leading us into another trap, you'll regret it. I promise you that."

Draven didn't flinch, his gaze unwavering. "I'd expect nothing less from you, Cole." He inclined his head slightly, a gesture that was equal parts respect and challenge. "But be careful where you aim your threats. The Syndicate won't be so lenient."

With that, he turned, his footsteps echoing in the cavernous space of the warehouse. He paused at the door, looking back at us with a cold, calculating expression that sent a shiver through me.

"Good luck," he said, his voice almost mocking. "You'll need it."

And then he was gone, swallowed by the darkness.

For a long moment, Cole and I stood in silence, the weight of everything pressing down on us like a leaden blanket. I could feel my pulse pounding in my temples, a frenetic rhythm that matched the chaos swirling in my mind. There was so much I didn't understand, so much I hadn't known about my own family, my own past. It was as though someone had rewritten my entire life story while I wasn't looking, adding in secrets and betrayals that had always been there, lurking in the background, waiting for me to discover them.

Finally, Cole broke the silence. "We need a plan," he said, his voice steady, his gaze fierce. "They might have the power, the history. But we have something they don't."

I looked up at him, a spark of hope igniting in the midst of my despair. "What's that?"

Cole's lips twisted into a grim smile. "We have each other. And that, Evelyn, is more dangerous than any weapon in their arsenal."

Cole and I sat in the quiet aftermath of Draven's departure, the weight of his words pressing down on us like a tidal wave that refused to recede. It was a silence heavy with the unspoken, a shared disbelief as we pieced together fragments of what little we knew against the enormity of what we had just learned. And, as much as I wanted to rage or cry or simply scream into the hollow emptiness of the warehouse, I found myself unable to do anything at all. Instead, I sat in stunned, immobile silence, as if any sudden movement might shatter whatever illusion of stability remained.

Cole's hand was still in mine, his warmth a grounding presence even as my mind drifted. I looked over at him, catching the faint furrow of his brow, the faintest tremor in his jaw that belied the calm he was struggling to maintain.

"You alright?" I asked softly, surprised at the calmness in my own voice.

He let out a breath, one that sounded as though it had been held in for years. "Define 'alright,'" he replied, his lips twitching in a half-smile that did little to mask the turmoil in his eyes. "Considering we just found out our entire lives have been orchestrated by a criminal syndicate with a god complex, I'd say I'm a hair short of alright."

A laugh—dark, hollow, and entirely involuntary—escaped me. "Well, I guess that makes two of us," I said, shaking my head. "I don't know what I expected, but this? Definitely not this."

"Maybe we should have expected it," he muttered, running a hand through his hair with a mixture of frustration and exhaustion. "I mean, how many times did we wonder why they kept us close but never let us get too deep? We were raised on the edge of the circle, Evelyn. It wasn't an accident."

I wanted to argue, to tell him that we hadn't been raised by monsters lurking in shadows, that our families weren't the kind of people to manipulate and scheme on a scale like this. But the words felt hollow even in my mind. No, it was all too clear now, painfully clear. Our parents hadn't been raising us—they'd been grooming us, keeping us close enough to feel their warmth but far enough to shield us from whatever lay at the Syndicate's core. All those years of whispered conversations and veiled glances suddenly made sense in a way I desperately wished they didn't.

"Do you think... do you think they actually believed they could keep us safe from all of this?" I asked, my voice barely more than a whisper. I wasn't even sure who I was asking—Cole, the universe, maybe the ghosts of our parents, wherever they were.

"I don't know," he said, his voice low and uncharacteristically vulnerable. "Maybe they thought they could walk that line forever. Maybe they thought if we didn't ask, we wouldn't know, and that would be enough. But look where that's gotten us. We're left to clean up the mess they left behind."

A bitter laugh escaped me. "Lucky us."

For a moment, we simply sat there, letting the silence settle around us, allowing the enormity of everything to sink in. The truth was, I didn't know how to feel—angry, betrayed, terrified? Maybe all of it at once. The Syndicate wasn't just a monster lurking in the dark corners of my life; it was woven into the very fabric of who I was. And now, with Draven's revelation, it felt like every fiber was unraveling.

"Alright," I said finally, steeling myself. "We're not going to sit here and let them decide how this plays out. They might have been pulling the strings up until now, but that ends here. No more half-truths, no more secrets."

Cole looked at me, a hint of a spark lighting in his eyes. "That sounds like a declaration of war."

"Maybe it is," I replied, feeling a sense of resolve hardening within me. "If they want to see how far we're willing to go, they're in for a surprise."

He raised an eyebrow, a wry smile curving his lips. "Bold talk from someone who nearly hyperventilated two minutes ago."

"Oh, don't worry," I shot back, a grin tugging at my own lips despite everything. "I'm still barely keeping it together. But I'll be damned if I'm going to let them turn us into pawns in their twisted game."

Cole chuckled, the sound rough but genuine. "Alright, I'm in. Just don't start punching walls or anything. I'd rather not explain to the next random passerby why you have a broken hand."

"You underestimate me," I said, arching an eyebrow. "I can punch walls with style."

"Well, I can't argue with that," he replied, his tone light, though his gaze was still intense. "So, where do we start?"

I took a deep breath, feeling the weight of the decision settling over me. "We start by finding out everything we can about this... this hidden order Draven mentioned. If they're the ones pulling the strings, then they're the ones who need to be afraid. It's about time they knew what it feels like."

Cole's expression darkened, and I saw the same glint of determination in his eyes that I felt coursing through me. He nodded slowly, his grip tightening on my hand. "Then we get our lives back, one way or another."

The resolve between us was almost palpable, a current that sparked and crackled in the dimness of the warehouse. We didn't know what lay ahead, but for the first time, it felt like we were taking control. The Syndicate might have woven their web around us, but we were going to burn it down thread by thread.

He let go of my hand, rising to his feet and offering me his hand with a grin that held just a hint of danger. "Come on. Let's get out of this place. It reeks of stale conspiracies and bad decisions."

I took his hand, a laugh escaping me despite everything. "You're not wrong about that."

As we walked out of the warehouse and into the cool night air, I felt a strange sense of clarity settling over me. This battle wasn't just about vengeance or justice anymore. It was about reclaiming something that had been stolen from us before we even knew it was gone.

Cole glanced at me, his eyes reflecting the quiet determination I felt in my own heart. "You know," he said, a wry grin creeping onto his face, "if we're going to take on an ancient order, we're going to need more than good intentions."

"Good intentions?" I laughed. "No, Cole. We're going to need every ounce of ruthlessness we can muster. And maybe, just maybe, a little luck."

"Well, then," he replied, his grin matching mine. "Let's see if we can find some."

And as we stepped into the night, side by side, I felt something shift within me—a sense of purpose that burned brighter than any fear. They might have stolen our pasts, tangled us in lies and shadows, but they were about to learn that we weren't the kind of people who stayed trapped for long.

The moon hung heavy and low, casting a cold glow over the empty streets as we made our way through the labyrinthine back alleys that snaked around the city's hidden edges. Each step seemed to echo, amplifying the silence between us, thick with the weight of all we hadn't yet said. The air was crisp, and I could feel the chill biting through my jacket, but I welcomed it. Anything to ground me, to keep me present in this world that felt more surreal with each revelation.

Cole walked beside me, his expression unreadable, eyes focused straight ahead. There was something resolute, almost feral, in his stance—like he was bracing himself for whatever came next, ready to face it head-on. It was something I'd always admired about him, even envied. But tonight, I could feel that same fire smoldering within me, and it was both exhilarating and terrifying.

"So," I said, breaking the silence. "Where do we even start with all of this?"

He glanced over, a small, wry smile pulling at his lips. "I thought you had it all figured out. Weren't you the one declaring war back there?"

"Declaring war and actually waging it are two very different things, Cole. Don't tell me you're the one with all the plans now."

He chuckled, a low, dry sound that seemed to scrape the air around us. "Hardly. But I do know someone who might be able to help." He hesitated, the amusement fading from his eyes as they turned serious. "Though I can't promise he'll be thrilled to see me."

There was a story there, but I knew better than to pry. We were both carrying scars that didn't need to be prodded, at least not tonight.

"What's his name?"

"Arlo," Cole said, the name spoken with a mixture of familiarity and resentment. "He's... well, let's just say he's as close to an expert on the Syndicate as anyone outside their inner circle. He used to be one of their top analysts before he disappeared off the grid. If anyone can tell us where to find this hidden order, it's him."

I nodded, absorbing this new piece of information. "And how do you know he'll talk to us?"

Cole's gaze dropped to the ground, something dark flitting across his face. "I don't. But he owes me a favor. Let's hope he's in a charitable mood."

There was no time to dwell on the details. We needed answers, and Arlo seemed like the best chance we had. If he could offer us even a fragment of insight into the Syndicate's hidden workings, it would be worth it. I didn't want to admit how much I was counting on him, this stranger I'd never met, to provide us with a thread we could tug on, a thread that might eventually lead us out of this twisted web.

Cole led the way, guiding us through a maze of alleys and backstreets until we arrived at a decrepit, unmarked door tucked into the side of a crumbling building. He knocked, three slow taps followed by a quick double-tap, his movements sure and practiced. Clearly, he'd been here before.

We waited in tense silence, the moments stretching on as I glanced over my shoulder, every shadow feeling like it held a threat. Just as I was about to ask if we'd been ghosted, the door creaked open, revealing a narrow passage lit by a single bare bulb.

"Follow me," a voice grunted from the shadows.

We stepped inside, the door clicking shut behind us with a finality that made my stomach churn. The hallway was claustrophobic, lined with peeling wallpaper that seemed to hold the secrets of a thousand whispered conversations. I could feel my pulse quicken, my senses on high alert as we reached the end of the hall, where another door stood slightly ajar.

Inside, the room was dimly lit, cluttered with an assortment of gadgets, screens, and papers strewn across every available surface.

And there, sitting in the midst of the chaos, was a man whose presence seemed to fill the space with an intensity that bordered on volatile.

Arlo was tall and wiry, with sharp eyes that seemed to take in everything, missing nothing. He had a perpetual five o'clock shadow and an expression that hovered somewhere between distrustful and amused. He looked up as we entered, his gaze settling on Cole with a mixture of irritation and reluctant recognition.

"Cole," he said, his voice rough, like gravel being ground underfoot. "I thought I'd finally rid myself of you."

Cole offered a tight smile. "Trust me, Arlo, this isn't exactly a social call."

Arlo's gaze flicked to me, his eyes narrowing. "And you've brought company. How quaint. Don't suppose this is the same girl the Syndicate's been sniffing after?"

I felt a prickle of discomfort, but I met his gaze head-on. "Nice to meet you, too," I replied, injecting as much confidence into my voice as I could muster. "But we're not here to chat about me. We need your help."

Arlo snorted, crossing his arms over his chest. "You need my help. Now there's a line I haven't heard in a while." He leaned back, his gaze turning speculative as he studied us. "What makes you think I'd risk my neck for the likes of you two?"

Cole took a step forward, his expression hardening. "Because we both know you don't like the Syndicate any more than we do. And if I remember correctly, you have a few scores of your own to settle."

Arlo's eyes narrowed, but he didn't argue. "Maybe I do. Or maybe I'm quite happy staying out of their way."

"Funny," Cole said, a dangerous edge in his voice. "Because the Arlo I knew never stayed out of anyone's way."

The two of them locked eyes, a silent battle of wills stretching out between them, tension crackling in the air. Finally, Arlo let out a grudging sigh, his shoulders slumping slightly as he turned back to me.

"Fine," he said. "I'll help you. But don't think for a second that I'm doing it out of the goodness of my heart."

I nodded, grateful even as a new wave of nerves washed over me. "We'll take whatever you're willing to give."

He shook his head, muttering something under his breath as he began rifling through the mess of papers on his desk. "This hidden order you're after... it's not just some syndicate hierarchy. They're the architects of the Syndicate itself, a council of sorts, though 'council' makes them sound more diplomatic than they are. They're ruthless, ancient, and every bit as powerful as Draven made them out to be."

He pulled out a yellowed map, spreading it out over the desk with care. "Their vaults, if you're crazy enough to go looking, are hidden in an underground network beneath the city. A labyrinth, guarded and monitored twenty-four-seven."

I leaned forward, tracing my finger along the intricate lines of the map. "How do we get inside?"

Arlo laughed, the sound cold and sharp. "Getting in is easy. Staying alive once you're in there? That's another matter entirely."

I felt the weight of his warning settle in my chest, but I refused to let it deter me. "We'll take our chances."

Arlo raised an eyebrow, his gaze shifting between Cole and me. "Then you'd better be prepared for what you'll find. If you think the Syndicate's secrets are ugly, you're in for a shock."

There was a flicker of something in his eyes—a hint of fear, maybe regret. And that's when I realized just how dangerous this mission was. We were venturing into the heart of something darker and more twisted than we'd imagined.

With a final, heavy sigh, Arlo handed us the map. "God help you both," he said, his voice barely more than a whisper.

As we left his sanctuary, the weight of what lay ahead pressed down on us, every step feeling like a descent into the unknown.

Chapter 23: The Heart of Deception

The dim light from the cracked street lamp above cast long shadows over the alley, its feeble glow barely enough to illuminate Draven's face. The sharp angles of his jaw caught the light, the shadows painting him into something both alluring and dangerous. The kind of man you could never quite figure out but always found yourself inching toward, like a moth to a flame. And tonight, that fire felt hotter than ever, threatening to consume every last ounce of trust I'd placed in him.

"Start talking, Draven," I said, my voice steadier than I felt. "No more half-truths. No more games. I want to know everything."

He leaned against the brick wall, his arms crossed, and a faint, almost amused smile played at the corners of his mouth. It was maddening, that calm, calculating look in his eyes. The kind that told me he had known this moment would come and was savoring every second of it. "Careful what you wish for," he murmured, voice as smooth as silk, sliding under my skin in a way that left me unsettled.

I tightened my grip on Cole's hand. His palm was warm against mine, grounding me, and I could feel the pulse of his anger, a rhythm that matched my own. He was ready to jump in if things went south, a silent promise I could feel in every squeeze of his hand. But this was my fight—my need for answers.

"Enough of the riddles," I snapped, my patience unraveling with every second he let the silence stretch between us. "You've been pulling the strings, haven't you? All this time, guiding us where you wanted us to go, feeding us scraps of information just enough to keep us on your leash."

Draven tilted his head, considering me with a sort of detached curiosity. "And you're only just realizing this?" he replied, his tone so infuriatingly calm it made my fingers itch. "I'd expected more from you, honestly."

A flicker of doubt crept into my mind, but I shoved it aside. I couldn't afford to let him get under my skin. "You've been playing with our lives like pawns on a board. Do you even care what happens to any of us, or are we all just... expendable?"

The question hung in the air, thick and heavy. He didn't answer right away, his gaze shifting from me to the distant city lights, where the hum of life felt painfully normal in contrast to the madness we were wrapped up in. His silence was answer enough.

And that was the worst part—knowing that to him, we were nothing more than tools, replaceable. The weight of it pressed down on me, the realization sinking in with a cold finality. I felt a tightness in my chest, something fragile cracking under the surface.

Cole's hand squeezed mine again, and I found my voice, pushing down the anger enough to get my next words out. "So what's the plan, Draven? What twisted little game are we a part of now?"

A smirk tugged at his lips, though his eyes remained cold. "The plan, darling, is to survive. And if that means sacrificing a few—"

"A few?" My voice was a sharp edge now, the betrayal like acid on my tongue. "You lied to us. You knew exactly what the Syndicate was after, and you used us like bait."

He shrugged, as if it were a minor inconvenience. "Information doesn't come cheap, and sometimes, sacrifices have to be made." He took a step closer, his gaze shifting to Cole, his expression mocking. "You should be grateful, really. Without me, you wouldn't have made it this far."

Cole shifted beside me, his stance tense, ready to spring. But I held him back with a gentle touch. We were playing a dangerous game, and as much as I wanted to let Cole go off on Draven, we couldn't afford to lose control.

"Grateful," I echoed, tasting the bitterness in the word. "You know, Draven, there was a part of me that believed in you. I thought you were just... misunderstood. But now I see you're just another one of them, as twisted and ruthless as the rest."

His gaze flickered, just for a moment, a glimmer of something almost human. But it vanished as quickly as it appeared, replaced by that cold, detached expression that was all too familiar. "Believe what you want," he said. "But if you're going to survive, you'll need me."

I felt the weight of his words settle on me, as heavy and suffocating as the darkness around us. He wasn't wrong. As much as I hated to admit it, we needed him. Draven knew things—things that could tip the scales in this endless battle against the Syndicate. But the cost of that knowledge was a betrayal I wasn't sure I could forgive.

"You're no better than the Syndicate," I said, my voice trembling with a mix of anger and sorrow. "Using people, manipulating them for your own gain... You're just as corrupt as they are."

A hint of irritation creased his brow, the first sign that my words had hit a nerve. "Careful, darling. You're in over your head."

I held his gaze, refusing to let him intimidate me. "Maybe I am. But at least I know where I stand now." I took a step back, pulling Cole with me, needing to put distance between us and the man who'd spun a web of lies around us.

But Draven's voice followed, a soft, insidious whisper that sank into my bones. "You'll come back to me," he said, with a confidence that made my skin crawl. "You always do. Because deep down, you know I'm your only way out of this."

Cole's hand tightened in mine, his presence a reassuring anchor in the storm of emotions swirling inside me. But Draven's words lingered, a dark promise that left me feeling hollow.

As we turned and walked away, I could feel his gaze on my back, a cold reminder that, despite everything, he held a power over us we couldn't escape. And as much as I wanted to believe otherwise, a sliver of doubt gnawed at me, whispering that, perhaps, he was right.

And that, maybe, I'd already lost more of myself to him than I was willing to admit.

The tension between Draven and me hung thick in the air, a taut string pulled tighter with every second of silence that passed. It was unbearable, that chasm of betrayal and distrust widening with each quiet, unspoken truth that lay between us. I could feel Cole's eyes on me, steady and unblinking, like he was waiting for me to say something, to push back against Draven one last time. But all I could do was stare at the man in front of me, who I had once—stupidly—believed in. The realization stung more than I cared to admit.

"You know, Draven," I said, voice barely above a whisper, but sharp enough to cut through the silence, "for someone who seems to know so much, you don't know when to stop digging. You're going to end up burying yourself in your own lies."

A flicker of amusement lit his eyes, and he shrugged with that maddening nonchalance. "Lies are such an ugly word," he replied, crossing his arms, his posture a picture of insufferable ease. "I prefer to think of them as carefully crafted omissions. Details that, frankly, wouldn't do you any good to know."

"You don't get to decide that," I shot back, feeling the heat of anger rise in my cheeks. "We're in this mess because of you. If there's anyone who doesn't get a say anymore, it's you."

"Oh, sweetheart," he drawled, leaning in so close I could feel his breath against my cheek, low and mocking, "I think you'd be surprised at how little control you actually have here."

In that moment, I wanted nothing more than to slap that smirk off his face, to make him feel even an ounce of the betrayal simmering inside me. But I forced myself to stay still, my hands clenched at my sides, nails biting into my palms. Giving him that satisfaction would be exactly what he wanted, and I wasn't about to hand it over so easily.

Cole's voice broke through the tension, calm yet laced with steel. "So this is it? We just trust that whatever sick plan you're working on will somehow save us all? Because right now, Draven, it looks a hell of a lot like you're just saving yourself."

Draven's gaze shifted to Cole, his expression cool but with a glint of annoyance. "Believe it or not, I've been keeping you both alive longer than you would have managed on your own. You're not exactly swimming with the big fish here, Cole."

"Maybe not," Cole replied, his jaw set. "But we don't make a habit of throwing people into the fire and watching them burn. That's all you."

Draven's smirk wavered, just slightly, a sign that Cole had hit a nerve. "Morals are a luxury you can't afford in this world. Every step forward requires sacrifice—if you can't understand that, then you're already doomed."

I felt a pang of dread at his words, a darkness settling over me like a storm cloud. He was right, in a way—this was a world where innocence and trust were liabilities, where alliances were tenuous at best. But I wasn't ready to accept that his twisted, self-serving logic was the only way to survive.

"So that's it?" I said, my voice barely a whisper. "You're willing to throw us away, just like that? After everything?"

He let out a soft, almost pitying chuckle. "You think I'm doing this for fun, don't you?" His voice held a bitterness I hadn't heard before, and for a moment, it almost sounded like regret. Almost. "But if you want to believe I'm some monster, by all means. I've stopped caring about what anyone thinks of me a long time ago."

"Clearly," Cole muttered, casting me a look that said, *This guy is insufferable.*

Draven straightened, casting a glance at the alleyway behind us, his expression tightening. "You may hate me now, but you'll thank me later. Or maybe you won't. Either way, this is bigger than you, and the sooner you accept that, the better your chances of survival."

Before either of us could respond, he turned and began to walk away, disappearing into the shadows with a confidence that was both infuriating and unsettling. We watched him go, his silhouette swallowed by the darkness until there was nothing left but the faint sound of his footsteps fading into the night.

When he was gone, I let out a breath I hadn't realized I'd been holding. The cold air stung my lungs, grounding me, but the ache of betrayal lingered, a heavy weight I couldn't shake. Cole's hand found mine again, his touch warm and steady, and I clung to it, grateful for his presence.

"What do we do now?" I asked, my voice barely audible. The question hung between us, raw and uncertain, and for a moment, I felt as lost as I had the night this all began, when we'd first been drawn into Draven's web.

Cole's eyes met mine, filled with a determination I hadn't expected. "We figure it out. On our own terms. He's not the only one who knows how to play this game."

A small, reluctant smile tugged at my lips, a glimmer of hope in the darkness. It wasn't much, but it was enough—a spark, a reminder that no matter how twisted this world became, we still had each other. And maybe, just maybe, that would be enough to survive whatever was coming.

The two of us turned and headed down the empty street, our footsteps echoing in the quiet. We didn't speak, but I could feel the weight of Cole's resolve beside me, a silent promise that we would make it through this together, no matter the cost.

The streets around us were eerily quiet, an unsettling calm settling over the city as though it were holding its breath, waiting for the storm to break. I couldn't shake the feeling that we were being watched, that the darkness was hiding more than just secrets.

Cole's voice broke the silence. "Do you really think he meant it? That he's somehow helping us?"

I considered it, the memory of Draven's words still fresh in my mind, each one dripping with contempt and a twisted sense of righteousness. "I don't know. But one thing's for sure—he's in this for himself. Whatever he's doing, it's to further his own agenda."

Cole nodded, his jaw tight. "Then we do the same. We keep moving forward, and we don't stop until we know the truth. No matter what."

I felt a surge of resolve, bolstered by Cole's conviction. Draven might have led us into this nightmare, but he hadn't counted on us pushing back, fighting to take back control. And as the first sliver of dawn began to break over the horizon, casting a faint glow over the city, I knew that this wasn't the end. This was just the beginning.

The city unfolded before us as we walked, its sleeping streets humming with an eerie quiet that seemed to stretch on forever. Every shadow, every flicker of light felt like an omen, whispering threats I couldn't quite hear. Cole's hand in mine was the one constant, grounding me as we moved through the darkness with our backs straight and our jaws set, two people locked in a battle we hadn't chosen but were far too deep to escape from now.

We turned down a side street, one of those narrow alleys that stretched like a scar through the heart of the city, and I couldn't shake the sensation that something was following us. I quickened my pace, urging Cole forward without a word. He shot me a look, a question in his eyes, but didn't hesitate. Our footsteps quickened, falling into sync, a steady, tense rhythm echoing off the damp walls of the alley.

As we reached the end of the street, a figure melted out of the shadows, blocking our way. My heart seized, every instinct screaming to run, but there was no place to go. Cole moved in front of me, his body tense, his posture protective.

The man before us—a stranger, cloaked in black, with a face that seemed to be all angles and shadows—smiled, a flash of white against the dark. "Fancy meeting you here," he drawled, voice thick with amusement, as if we'd just wandered into a casual conversation instead of a midnight ambush.

"Who are you?" I demanded, hoping my voice held more strength than I felt. "What do you want?"

His smile widened, and he took a step closer, his hands spread wide in a gesture that was anything but friendly. "Relax. I'm just a messenger, here to deliver a bit of friendly advice." His eyes glinted, a predatory gleam that sent a shiver up my spine. "Draven might have led you to think you're safe, but trust me, sweetheart, safety's a lie in this world. The sooner you understand that, the longer you'll survive."

I didn't flinch, though every part of me wanted to recoil from his gaze. "You think we don't know that already? That we're just stumbling around clueless?"

"Oh, I think you know enough," he replied, and his tone was almost disappointed, like he'd expected more from us. "But knowledge is only useful if it doesn't get you killed. And right now, you're far too useful to certain... interested parties." He shot a quick glance over his shoulder, a flicker of something that looked almost like caution. "Let's just say, there are people who'd like you both alive. For now."

I couldn't suppress the flicker of anger rising within me. "Is that supposed to make us feel better? That we're being kept around like some pets for you to toy with?"

"Not pets, darling," he said with a smirk that made my skin crawl. "Think of it as being given a head start. The game's only just beginning." His voice was calm, but his words carried a dark weight, like he was daring us to challenge him, to fight back and prove him wrong.

Cole took a step forward, his jaw tight. "We don't care about your games. Whatever you or Draven or anyone else wants from us, we're done playing by your rules."

The stranger chuckled, a soft, mirthless sound. "Oh, you think you're done? That's cute." His gaze shifted to me, sharp and assessing. "You might want to keep an eye on your friend here. Draven isn't known for his loyalty, but he does know how to pick the right tools for the job. And you, sweetheart, have become quite the valuable tool."

The implication of his words sent a chill down my spine. Draven had manipulated us, used us, but this—this was something darker, a threat wrapped in a sickly sweet warning. I swallowed, refusing to let fear show on my face. "If you're so sure about that, then maybe you should tell your boss we're not for sale."

He arched a brow, amused. "Oh, I don't work for Draven. Let's just say I'm... keeping an eye on my own interests. And right now, my interest is in making sure you don't get too comfortable."

"Consider us warned," Cole said, voice steady but laced with barely concealed anger. "Now, are we done here?"

The man's smile faded, replaced by a look of bored indifference. "For now," he said, tipping an imaginary hat before stepping back into the shadows. "Just remember, the only thing more dangerous than trusting the wrong people... is trusting no one at all." His voice echoed as he vanished into the darkness, leaving us alone in the alley with his words hanging heavy in the air.

Cole exhaled sharply, breaking the tense silence. "Well, that was... enlightening," he muttered, raking a hand through his hair.

I managed a wry smile, though my heart was pounding. "Enlightening isn't exactly the word I'd use."

We started moving again, our footsteps echoing in the empty street. Despite the stranger's warning, despite Draven's twisted games, a strange resolve had settled within me. I wasn't going to be anyone's pawn, not anymore. And as Cole walked beside me, his presence warm and solid, I knew he felt the same.

But as we rounded the corner, I noticed something—another shadow, moving too quickly, too purposefully to be mere coincidence. I tensed, pulling Cole to a halt, my eyes scanning the street.

"Did you see that?" I whispered, heart thudding as the shadow vanished behind a parked car.

He nodded, his grip tightening on my hand. "Yeah. I saw."

We exchanged a glance, a silent agreement passing between us. We could run, try to escape whatever danger was lurking in the dark. But something held us in place, a stubborn defiance that wouldn't let us back down.

And then, just as we thought the street was empty, a figure stepped out from behind the car—a figure I recognized all too well. Draven.

My pulse quickened, a mix of relief and anger boiling up inside me. "Were you following us?" I demanded, trying to keep my voice steady.

He didn't answer right away, his gaze flickering between us, unreadable as ever. "You've been making friends," he said, voice low, as if we'd done something wrong.

"That was your doing," I shot back, unwilling to let him twist this into something it wasn't. "If you hadn't left us in the dark, maybe we wouldn't have to make friends with strange men in alleys."

Draven's expression hardened, a shadow crossing his face. "You think this is a joke? That this little game you're playing won't get you killed?"

"We're done with your games, Draven," Cole said, his voice tight with anger. "Whatever you're hiding, we'll find it out ourselves."

For the first time, a crack appeared in Draven's calm facade. He stepped closer, his gaze sharp and piercing. "You have no idea what you're dealing with," he hissed, barely containing his frustration. "If you keep pushing, there won't be anything left to save."

A beat of silence passed, the weight of his words settling heavily between us. But before I could respond, a sudden, sharp noise shattered the quiet—a gunshot, piercing the night like a dagger.

Draven's eyes widened, and he spun around, a curse slipping from his lips. Cole grabbed my hand, pulling me down behind a parked car as another shot rang out, the sound echoing in the narrow street. My heart pounded in my chest, panic and adrenaline mixing in a dizzying rush.

And then, in the confusion, a dark figure emerged from the shadows, gun in hand, aimed straight at us.

Chapter 24: A Glimpse of Hope

The darkness around me felt thick enough to choke on, like the air itself was tainted by secrets and lies. Every sound, every shadow, whispered that we were running out of time. Cole's footsteps behind me were soft but steady, the one thing I could rely on as we moved closer to the Syndicate's vault. The corridors were narrow, barely lit by the dim, flickering lights overhead. It was as if they'd designed this place to swallow people whole, never to let them back out.

I glanced back at Cole, catching the briefest glimpse of his face. There was a quiet intensity there, a resolve that had been missing for a while. Maybe it was the knowledge that this was our final shot—or maybe he'd finally shaken off whatever had been haunting him for the past few weeks. Either way, we couldn't afford distractions now. Too many people were counting on us, though most of them would never even know our names.

"Keep moving," he whispered, his voice barely louder than a breath. "We're almost there."

I nodded, swallowing the fear that kept curling its way up my throat. Every step felt like I was tempting fate, daring it to snatch away this one sliver of hope we had left. Because that's all it was, really—a hope wrapped in the flimsy paper of a rumor passed down from a friend who was supposed to be dead. Still, it was enough to get us here, to the heart of the Syndicate's empire.

The relic, supposedly buried somewhere in the vault, was rumored to hold the power to dismantle the entire organization from the inside out. Or at the very least, cripple it long enough for others to pick up the pieces we'd leave behind. I'd stopped wondering a while ago if it was true or just another ghost story passed between the desperate, the hunted. At this point, I didn't need it to be real. I just needed it to be close enough to keep me moving forward.

The corridor opened into a larger chamber, with towering steel doors at the far end. Cold air blasted from the vents along the walls, carrying a faint metallic scent that made my nose wrinkle. Cole was at my side in an instant, his eyes darting around the space, cataloging every potential threat. A faint smirk played on his lips, like he was amused by the sheer audacity of our situation.

"Is it just me," he murmured, "or does this place give you the creeps too?"

I snorted, resisting the urge to elbow him in the ribs. "Glad to see you're taking this so seriously," I replied, a bit sharper than I intended. His eyes flashed to mine, something unreadable sparking in them.

"Just trying to lighten the mood," he replied, a touch defensively. "You know, like you always tell me to."

The tension crackled between us for a heartbeat longer, but I let it go, pushing forward. "Less talking, more finding."

His smirk faded, but he followed without another word. We moved in silence until we reached the vault doors. They loomed over us, massive and cold, seemingly impenetrable. But I'd learned early on that even the most secure doors have their weak spots. The Syndicate might be ruthless, but they were also arrogant. And that arrogance bred mistakes.

Pulling out a small device from my bag, I crouched near the base of the door, scanning for the security panel hidden beneath a layer of plating. Cole crouched beside me, his breath warm against my neck as he leaned in close to get a look. My heart thudded a little harder, a reaction that had nothing to do with the mission. It was stupid, and probably dangerous, but there was something about his presence that made the world feel just a fraction safer.

"See anything interesting down there?" His voice was barely a whisper, yet it held that maddening hint of a smile.

"Keep distracting me, and I'll make sure you're the one explaining to headquarters why we failed," I shot back, not looking up. I could feel him grin, though.

"Noted."

I found the panel, pried it open, and started working on the wires. The mechanism was a bit more sophisticated than I'd expected, with a tangle of circuits and coded locks that told me they really didn't want anyone getting through this door. But I wasn't about to let a few locks stop us. I'd been trained for worse.

"How much longer?" Cole's voice was sharper now, and I could feel his gaze flicking around the room, his tension mounting. We were on borrowed time, and he knew it.

"Almost there," I muttered, but even I could feel my nerves fraying. This wasn't a small-time operation we were up against, and the stakes were higher than they'd ever been. My hands were steady, but every fiber of my being was stretched taut, ready to snap.

Just as I finished, a sudden noise echoed through the room—a faint, metallic scrape. Cole's hand shot out, gripping my arm. He pulled me back into the shadows, his body pressed against mine as we waited, barely breathing. The sound grew closer, footsteps echoing against the walls. A guard, maybe two.

I held my breath, praying they wouldn't check the door panel, wouldn't notice the slight dent where I'd pried it open. Cole's hand was warm and solid, grounding me in that sliver of a moment when everything could go wrong.

The footsteps paused. Silence filled the space like a living thing, heavy and oppressive. Cole's grip tightened, and I could feel the thud of his heart against my shoulder. He wasn't as calm as he pretended to be, not in moments like these. But that just made him seem more real, somehow.

After what felt like an eternity, the footsteps continued down the hall, fading until we were alone again. Cole exhaled, and his hand slipped from my arm, leaving a strange ache in its absence. I bit my lip, half out of relief and half because I could still feel the imprint of his fingers on my skin.

"Let's move," he said, his voice barely above a murmur. He glanced at me, and for a fleeting second, there was something raw in his gaze, something unguarded.

Nodding, I stepped forward, pushing the door open with a steady hand. Beyond it lay darkness, vast and waiting. We stepped inside, side by side, the weight of the world pressing down on our shoulders. But in that moment, we had something more potent than fear, more lasting than courage: a shared purpose, a flicker of hope that maybe, just maybe, this would be enough to tear down the Syndicate for good.

The relic's chamber sprawled before us, dimly lit with pools of harsh white light casting deep shadows on the ancient walls. Rows of artifacts sat on shelves, each with a thick layer of dust, as if untouched for centuries. It felt like stepping into a time capsule, one where forgotten remnants of power waited, silent and dormant. The room smelled stale, laced with a metallic bite, a relic of its own that seemed to crawl up my nostrils and linger in the back of my throat.

Cole's face was half-shrouded in shadow as he scanned the shelves. "Do you ever get the sense," he whispered, "that they're just mocking us at this point?"

I glanced over, amused despite myself. "You mean like the way they thought they'd be clever by locking their most powerful assets right under our noses?"

"Exactly. Like hiding a snake in plain sight and then saying, 'Bet you can't find it.'" He rolled his eyes, then reached out, hesitating before touching one of the dust-coated objects. His hand hovered just inches above it, as though it might spring to life.

I shook my head. "Don't even think about it. The last thing we need is you accidentally triggering an ancient curse."

"Oh, come on." He shot me a wry smile, his voice dipped in mischief. "Where's your sense of adventure?"

"Probably where yours went last week when you 'accidentally' triggered that trip wire in the catacombs."

He held his hands up in mock surrender, though his smile remained. "Touché."

Despite the banter, our nerves were on edge, buzzing like a live wire. The Syndicate was known for its tricks, for burying threats and power together, daring anyone foolish enough to come too close. If the relic was here, it would be well-hidden, wrapped in layers of magic and deception designed to crush any last shred of hope we might have clung to. But we were beyond fear now, beyond hesitation. I could feel the weight of every decision pressing down on me, sharper than ever.

Our footsteps were muffled, tentative as we moved deeper into the chamber. The relic was supposed to be unmistakable, glowing with a strange light that pulsed with a heartbeat of its own, according to our source. But so far, the only thing glowing was a faded neon sign above the vault's entrance—an odd relic of the modern world shoved into this cavern of antiquities.

Cole finally stopped beside a stone pedestal in the center of the room, his gaze sharpening as he spotted a faint, pulsing glow beneath a thick layer of dust. I watched him lean closer, his fingers hovering over the glow like it might suddenly bite. When he turned to me, his expression was wary, a rare flicker of uncertainty I didn't often see.

"What do you think?" he asked, his voice quiet, steady.

"I think if it bites, it's your fault."

He rolled his eyes again but reached out, brushing away the dust with cautious, feather-light strokes. Beneath the grime, a crystalline object began to take shape, faintly illuminated from within, a soft, pulsing blue like a heartbeat under glass. The sight of it made my skin prickle, each pulse a silent warning.

"There it is," I murmured, almost to myself. "The one thing that could undo them."

Cole swallowed, his gaze never leaving the relic. "And we're supposed to believe they just left it here? Unprotected?"

"It's the Syndicate." My voice was harder than I intended. "They don't think anyone's capable of getting this far. It's all arrogance."

"Arrogance or confidence," he replied, fingers brushing over the edge of the relic. "Not much of a difference when you're sitting on a pile of stolen power."

The tension hummed between us, crackling like static. He glanced at me, and for a second, I saw something vulnerable there—a flash of fear, maybe even doubt. But he covered it quickly, his usual mask sliding back into place. I knew that look all too well, the one that screamed, I'm fine even when everything around us was crumbling.

"Let's do it," I said, keeping my voice steady. "Before they realize what we're up to."

Cole nodded, his hand hovering over the relic once more. Just as his fingers brushed its surface, a loud clang echoed through the chamber. We froze, eyes darting toward the door. Someone was here. Our presence had been detected, and every second we wasted was a step closer to being cornered.

"Guess we're not alone," Cole whispered, his tone laced with sarcasm.

"Seems like it," I replied, feeling the adrenaline surge through me. There was no turning back now.

The door to the chamber creaked open, spilling harsh light onto the stone floor. Shadows flickered, and then figures appeared—tall, imposing, and far too many for my liking. The Syndicate had sent their guards, and from the look of it, they weren't here to chat.

Cole shot me a sidelong glance, his mouth set in a grim line. "Ready?"

I nodded, tightening my grip on the dagger at my side. It wasn't much against a small army, but I'd always been one for long odds. Cole moved beside me, his hand reaching for the hilt of his own weapon, his eyes narrowing as he surveyed the approaching threat.

The guards moved slowly, deliberate in their approach. They knew we were trapped, cornered like animals in a cage. One of them, a tall, muscular man with a cruel smile, stepped forward, his gaze flicking between Cole and me.

"You two must be very brave," he sneered, "or very, very stupid."

"Funny," I shot back, keeping my voice light, mocking. "I was just thinking the same thing about you."

The guard's smile faltered, a spark of anger flaring in his eyes. Beside me, Cole chuckled, a low, dark sound that seemed to rile the man up even more.

"We don't have to make this hard," the guard continued, his voice a cold hiss. "Just hand over the relic, and I might consider letting you walk out of here alive."

I arched an eyebrow. "Oh, is that so? And here I thought the Syndicate didn't believe in mercy."

The guard's eyes narrowed. "Mercy is reserved for those who know when they're beaten."

"Then I guess we're out of luck." My voice was calm, defiant. Cole shot me a look, one that held equal parts admiration and exasperation, as if he was just realizing how far I was willing to go.

In a single, smooth motion, he reached down and grabbed the relic, holding it aloft as its glow intensified. The guards hesitated, their eyes widening as they took in the pulsating light. It was a gamble, one that could backfire spectacularly, but Cole didn't waver.

"Think fast," he muttered, his gaze fixed on the guards.

They lunged forward, but we were faster, slipping through their grasp as the light from the relic grew blinding. I barely had time to register what was happening before we were moving, dashing through the open doorway, the sound of shouts and footsteps close behind.

Cole glanced at me, his grin wild and reckless. "See? Not so cursed after all."

I rolled my eyes, fighting back a smile even as we ran. "Let's just get out of here before you jinx it."

Together, we sprinted down the corridor, the weight of the relic burning hot in Cole's hand, the hope of freedom pulling us forward through the dark.

The narrow hall twisted and turned, each step we took reverberating through the stone walls. Our breath echoed in the stillness, our hearts racing in sync as we moved deeper into the maze of corridors. Somewhere behind us, the Syndicate's guards were still pursuing, their shouts bouncing off the walls, disorienting, as though they were both close and miles away. I clutched my dagger tightly, the cold metal reassuring against my palm, while Cole's grip on the relic was just as fierce, his knuckles white as the glow from it continued to pulsate, filling the dark hall with a ghostly blue light.

"Left or right?" Cole's voice cut through the tension as we reached a fork in the corridor, his gaze darting between our two options.

"Your guess is as good as mine," I replied, though the left path seemed slightly darker, quieter. Instinctively, I veered that way, hoping my gut hadn't finally betrayed me. Cole followed close behind, his footsteps light, though I could feel his apprehension like a shadow at my back.

We darted down the narrow passage, our shoulders brushing rough stone walls as we twisted and turned through the winding corridor. The air grew colder, biting, as though we were descending into the very bones of the earth. Ahead, I spotted a faint glimmer—a sliver of an opening leading to a larger space. Relief mingled with trepidation. Open spaces meant fewer places to hide, but we had little choice.

As we spilled into the cavernous chamber, I froze, my heart stuttering in my chest. The room was massive, its ceiling arching high above us, studded with stalactites that dripped condensation onto the floor below. It looked like a cathedral of rock, a sacred place twisted into something dark and foreboding. And standing across from us, with a look of smug satisfaction, was someone I hadn't expected to see.

"Surprise," drawled a voice as smooth as silk, chilling in its familiarity. My stomach twisted as the figure stepped into the light, the Syndicate's symbol gleaming proudly on the pin affixed to her collar. Celia. Once, she'd been a friend, one of the few people I trusted in this line of work. Now, she was an agent of the very machine we were trying to destroy.

Cole's hand tightened around my wrist, his body taut beside me. "I thought she was—" he started, but I shook my head, silencing him.

"Dead?" Celia arched an eyebrow, a slow, mocking smile creeping onto her lips. "No. But that's a flattering assumption. I'm touched."

Her gaze settled on the relic in Cole's hand, her expression hardening, all trace of humor vanishing. "Hand it over. You know it doesn't belong to you."

My fingers tightened around my dagger as I glared at her, every nerve in my body screaming at me to run, yet somehow unable to move. "And it doesn't belong to the Syndicate, either."

"Really?" Her voice was deceptively light, but there was steel beneath it, a darkness I hadn't seen before. "You think this little game you're playing is going to change anything? You're nothing but a pair of ants trying to lift a boulder. All it takes is one step to crush you."

Beside me, Cole smirked, his eyes glinting with defiance. "Last I checked, ants are surprisingly resilient."

Celia's gaze flickered, and for a moment, I saw a shadow of something—maybe regret, maybe weariness. But it was gone in an instant, replaced by cold calculation. She stepped forward, her movements graceful, almost predatory, as if she were savoring each step. Her hand moved toward her waist, where a slim, gleaming blade rested, ready to draw at any moment.

"You have two choices," she continued, her tone casual as though we were discussing the weather. "Give me the relic, and I might be persuaded to let you walk away. Or keep it, and I'll have to make an example of you."

Cole's grip on my wrist tightened, a silent signal, and I knew he was thinking the same thing I was. We had no intention of walking away empty-handed, and Celia must have sensed it too because her smile turned icy, her fingers curling around her blade.

"You always were stubborn," she said, almost regretfully, her gaze lingering on me. "I used to admire that about you."

"You used to admire a lot of things," I replied, my voice steady despite the storm raging inside me. "But you made your choice."

"Just as you're about to make yours," she replied, her voice soft but sharp. And then, like a shadow dissolving into the night, she lunged.

The room exploded into motion. Cole pulled me to the side just as Celia's blade slashed through the space we'd occupied a second ago. My own blade was in my hand before I knew it, and I met her advance, our knives clashing with a sharp, metallic scrape that echoed through the cavern. She was quick, her movements fluid and calculated, like she'd rehearsed this moment a thousand times in her mind.

"Funny," she murmured as she parried my strike, her voice carrying a dangerous edge. "I remember when you could barely hold a dagger properly."

I gritted my teeth, pushing against her with everything I had. "Guess we both changed."

She laughed, a low, hollow sound that sent a chill down my spine. "Oh, I haven't changed as much as you'd think." She ducked, slipping past my guard and aiming for Cole, who deflected her blow with a swift, well-timed block.

While Celia was momentarily thrown off-balance, Cole shot me a look, a wordless question. Now? My pulse quickened as I nodded, and he lifted the relic, its glow intensifying, filling the cavern with blinding light. Celia stumbled back, shielding her eyes, hissing in irritation as the light seared through the shadows around her.

"Nice trick," she sneered, squinting against the glow, but there was a flicker of fear in her eyes. "But you're out of your depth."

"Oh, I think you're the one who underestimated us," I replied, meeting her gaze with a fierce smile.

But even as I said it, I could feel the toll the relic was taking on Cole. His face was pale, beads of sweat forming on his brow as he struggled to contain the artifact's power. The relic pulsed with a wild, erratic rhythm, as though it sensed the tension in the room, growing hotter, heavier in his grasp.

Celia straightened, her mouth curling into a cruel smile. "Careful. That much power can be... unpredictable."

As if on cue, the relic flared, releasing a pulse of energy that shot through the room, shuddering the walls and sending cracks snaking across the stone floor. I stumbled, catching myself just in time to see Celia lunge again, taking advantage of Cole's faltering grip.

Time seemed to slow as she closed in, her blade gleaming, her eyes locked onto Cole with deadly intent. I saw the resolve in her face, the brutal calculation, and knew that in that split second, she intended to end this. My heart pounded, every instinct screaming to act, to do something—anything—to stop her.

Just as her blade sliced through the air, I flung myself forward, throwing my body between her and Cole. There was a sharp, searing pain as her blade grazed my side, and I bit back a gasp, the world spinning as I staggered back, my hand clutching the wound.

Celia paused, her eyes widening in surprise as she saw the blood on her blade. For a brief moment, we locked eyes, a silent understanding passing between us, sharp and electric. She took a step back, her expression unreadable, but I saw the hesitation, the flicker of something uncertain.

In that instant, the relic's light flared again, brighter, fiercer than before, filling the cavern with a blinding white glow. And then, with a sound like shattering glass, the relic exploded, casting us all into a chaos of light, shadow, and searing heat.

Chapter 25: The Final Heist

The city lay sprawled beneath a shroud of velvet darkness, its skyline punctuated by the metallic glint of the Syndicate's headquarters. The skyscraper loomed like a malevolent titan, a testament to greed and power, its glass façade reflecting the moonlight in a dance of shimmering deceit. I could feel the pulse of the city, alive with secrets, its heartbeat thrumming in my ears as we made our way to the entrance. The air was thick with tension, the kind that wraps around your throat like a noose, constricting, suffocating. I adjusted the collar of my leather jacket, a thin shield against the chill creeping in from the night.

Beside me, Jake was a shadow clad in darkness, his brow furrowed in concentration. "You ready for this?" he whispered, his breath ghosting in the cool night air. I shot him a glance, taking in the way the streetlights caught the edge of his jaw, casting him in a soft glow that belied the danger ahead. He always knew how to make my heart race—whether it was from adrenaline or something more personal, I wasn't sure.

"Born ready," I replied, forcing a grin despite the nerves coiling in my stomach like a snake ready to strike. My heart was a relentless drum in my chest, echoing my resolve. We had come too far to turn back now, too deep into this tangled web of lies and deception. The weight of our mission bore down on me, the relic we sought a beacon of hope and the promise of freedom. But it was more than that. It was a chance to finally break the chains binding us to the Syndicate, the very chains that had haunted my dreams for far too long.

We slipped through the entrance, merging with the shadows that clung to the polished floors and opulent decor. The interior was a grotesque display of wealth—marble pillars soared high, and lavish chandeliers hung like crystal fruit, casting a false warmth over the cold, corporate atmosphere. I felt the hairs on my arms rise as we navigated the labyrinth of security measures. Each sensor and camera was a reminder of the danger that lay ahead, a countdown ticking down to our inevitable confrontation.

As we approached the vault, my breath caught in my throat. The door loomed large, a monolithic guardian protecting the relic within. It was surreal, the culmination of countless hours spent planning, plotting, and dreaming. "This is it," I breathed, my fingers brushing against the cool metal of the vault's surface. I glanced at Jake, who nodded, a flicker of determination lighting his eyes. Together, we were a force to be reckoned with.

With a deftness that belied my nervousness, I accessed the keypad, the numbers flashing under my fingertips. My heart raced, not just from the fear of discovery but from the thrill of being on the cusp of victory. "Come on, come on," I muttered under my breath, willing the door to yield to our intentions. The seconds dragged on, stretching into an eternity until finally, a soft beep resonated through the stillness. The vault creaked open, revealing the treasure that lay inside—our prize, the relic encased in glass, shimmering with an ethereal glow.

It was beautiful, a masterpiece of craftsmanship and mystery. I reached out, my fingers grazing the glass, feeling the pulse of energy radiating from it. But as I turned to share the moment with Jake, a sudden blaring alarm shattered the silence, its shrill wail piercing through the tranquility like a dagger. My stomach dropped. "What the—?"

"Run!" Jake shouted, urgency lacing his voice as the building erupted into chaos. Sirens blared, and lights flickered, illuminating the stark horror of our situation. I could hear the thundering footsteps of guards racing toward us, the sound echoing in my ears like a death knell. Panic surged through me as I snatched the relic from its pedestal, the weight of it heavy in my hands, a reminder of everything we stood to lose.

"Back the way we came!" I shouted, adrenaline fueling my movements as we sprinted down the corridor, the air thick with the scent of fear and desperation. The polished floors felt like ice beneath my feet, and every turn seemed to spiral deeper into the abyss. I could hear the guards behind us, their voices a cacophony of anger and urgency, and I felt the icy tendrils of dread creep up my spine.

We skidded to a halt in front of a stairwell, the only escape route leading us further into the depths of the building. "We'll have to take the stairs," I said, my voice barely a whisper as we plunged into the narrow passage. The steps echoed beneath us, a relentless reminder of the time slipping away. Each step felt like a countdown to our doom, the weight of destiny pressing down on us as we raced against the ticking clock of our survival.

"Do you really think we can get out of this?" Jake panted, glancing back, his expression a mixture of fear and determination.

I paused, breathless, the relic clutched tightly to my chest. "We don't have a choice. This is our last shot." I tried to sound convincing, though inside, doubt clawed at me like a feral beast. With the guards closing in, we burst through a door onto a rooftop, the night air rushing past us in a wild embrace.

The city sprawled below, a patchwork of lights and shadows, each flicker a reminder of the lives we were trying to escape. I turned to Jake, my heart racing, uncertainty gnawing at me. "What now?"

"Now we fly," he said, a wicked grin breaking through the tension as he pulled out a pair of gliders from his backpack. I stared at them, part disbelief, part exhilaration. "You didn't really think we'd just run away, did you?"

In that moment, as I strapped the glider to my back, I felt a thrill of possibility surge through me. This was madness, yet there was a beauty in the chaos. Together, we were more than just two people trapped in a web of lies. We were rebels on the cusp of rewriting our destinies. With one last glance at the chaos unfolding below, I took a leap of faith, plunging into the night, our escape etched in the stars above.

The rooftop offered a disorienting view, the sprawling cityscape beneath us shifting with the promise of danger and possibility. I felt the weight of the glider strapping against my back, its fabric taut and reassuring, as I stood on the precipice, adrenaline coursing through my veins. Jake's playful grin flickered like the streetlights below, the bravado in his eyes a stark contrast to the chaos we had just escaped. "Ready to make a splash?" he quipped, his voice buoyant against the night's gravity.

I arched an eyebrow, trying to suppress a laugh as I took a deep breath, scanning the horizon where skyscrapers clawed at the stars. "As long as it's not a belly flop into a dumpster, I think I'll manage." The laughter was a balm against the tension, a momentary reprieve from the turmoil swirling just behind us.

"Trust me, we'll soar like eagles," he replied, his confidence infectious. "At least, that's the plan. Don't think about the landing."

"Great, thanks for that pep talk." With one last look at the chaos erupting in the distance, I pushed off the edge, letting gravity take hold. The rush was immediate—a surge of air whipped past me, filling my lungs with the exhilarating taste of freedom. I felt alive, alive in a way that went beyond the thrill of the moment. This was defiance against everything that had kept me trapped for so long. I was not just running; I was reclaiming my life.

Jake followed closely, his glider cutting through the night like a blade. We glided over the city, the wind tugging at our hair and clothes, and I let out a whoop that echoed through the empty expanse, the sound of it a pure declaration of joy. Beneath us, the city pulsed with life, and for the first time, I felt like I belonged to something greater—a tapestry woven from the dreams of all who dared to defy.

As we soared, the adrenaline began to meld with a creeping sense of reality. I had thought escaping the vault would be the end of our troubles, but now, high above the city, the gravity of our actions pressed down on me like a storm cloud. "What's the plan once we land?" I called to Jake, my heart racing faster than our descent.

"Just a quick pit stop at my apartment. I've got some gear stashed there, and we can lay low until the heat dies down," he replied, scanning the skyline ahead, his eyes sharp and alert. "You know, maybe grab a pizza? I'm starving."

"Pizza after a heist? Is that your secret to success?" I teased, the banter a familiar rhythm, easing the tension creeping back into my chest.

"It's called motivation," he shot back with a wink, and I couldn't help but smile. In this absurd moment, it felt almost normal, like we were just two friends out for a late-night adventure rather than fugitives fleeing a crime scene.

As we approached Jake's apartment building, the glimmer of lights below softened, and the city felt less threatening, more like a partner in our escape. I tucked my legs under me and landed with a practiced grace, rolling into the shadows just as Jake followed suit. We both paused, our breaths mingling in the cool night air, eyes scanning for any sign of pursuit.

"Not bad for a couple of thieves," I said, brushing off my pants, trying to shake off the lingering thrill.

"Not bad at all." He smirked, a glint of mischief dancing in his eyes. "Now, let's grab that pizza before we end up back in the Syndicate's clutches."

The stairs creaked under our feet as we ascended, and the hallway smelled faintly of burnt popcorn and forgotten dreams. Jake fished his keys from his pocket, and I couldn't help but admire how effortlessly he moved, confidence radiating from him like a warm light. He opened the door to his apartment, and we stepped inside, the stark simplicity of the space a welcome change from the opulence of the Syndicate's lair.

"I may have neglected the cleaning," he said sheepishly, gesturing to the chaos of scattered clothes and the half-empty pizza box perched precariously on the coffee table. "But I promise it's not as bad as it looks."

I raised an eyebrow, surveying the room. "Oh, really? Because I'm pretty sure I saw a sock try to escape."

"Hey, that's a loyal sock! It's been through a lot." He chuckled, moving past me to the kitchen, the sound of the fridge door opening an anchor in the whirlwind of our night.

He pulled out a bottle of water and tossed it to me. "Here, hydrate. You're going to need your strength for the next part."

"Next part?" I echoed, the question laced with curiosity and a flicker of unease. "What do you mean by that?"

Jake leaned against the counter, a sly smile creeping onto his lips. "We're not just hiding out, you know. We have to figure out what to do with the relic."

The weight of the glass object nestled safely in my backpack pressed heavily against me, the thrill of the heist fading under the shadow of its implications. "You mean we can't just, I don't know, sell it and ride off into the sunset?"

"Not quite that simple," he said, his expression shifting to one of seriousness. "The Syndicate isn't going to let this go. They'll be hunting us down, and that relic... it's more than just a piece of history. It's valuable, and everyone knows it. We need to be smart."

My pulse quickened, thoughts racing faster than my breath. "So, what's the plan? Hand it over to the authorities?" I scoffed, the idea feeling as absurd as it was noble. "Because that's worked out so well in the past."

"I don't know yet," he admitted, running a hand through his hair, his frustration palpable. "But I do know we can't just toss it away or hope for the best. We need allies, people who can help us figure out what to do next. And I might know just the person."

The mention of allies stirred something deep within me. It was a step away from the solitary existence I had fought so hard to escape. "And who might that be?" I asked, my curiosity piqued.

He straightened, a spark igniting in his eyes. "A historian. She's been tracking artifacts for years, and she has the connections to get us out of this mess."

"Sounds risky," I said, crossing my arms, uncertainty threading through my words. "What if she's not on our side?"

"She will be," Jake replied, conviction coloring his tone. "She has her own reasons for wanting to keep this relic out of the Syndicate's hands."

I met his gaze, the flicker of hope mingling with the fear churning in my stomach. "Alright, then let's get in touch with her. But after that, can we please get pizza?"

His laughter echoed through the small apartment, a sound of relief that seemed to push back against the looming shadows. "Deal. Let's save the world first, then we'll feast."

With that, a plan began to form between us, a tentative alliance fortified by our shared history and the undeniable spark of adventure. The world outside may have been dangerous, but in that moment, together we felt invincible.

With the weight of the relic pressing against my back, I found myself pacing Jake's small living room, my mind racing faster than my heart. It was a stark space, dominated by mismatched furniture that spoke of hasty decisions and a life lived on the edge. My eyes darted around, landing on a stack of old books precariously teetering on a rickety shelf. They looked like the very tomes I'd imagined studying in some hallowed hall, not in the clutter of a fugitive's hideout.

"Okay, let's think this through," I said, forcing myself to focus. "You said you have a way to contact this historian?"

Jake leaned against the counter, arms crossed, his posture a blend of confidence and anxiety. "Yeah, her name's Eliza. She's a bit eccentric, but she knows her stuff. If anyone can help us figure out what to do with the relic, it's her."

"Eccentric how? Are we talking capes and crystal balls, or more like artfully disheveled and armed with obscure knowledge?" I asked, unable to resist the jab.

"More the latter, I assure you. Just trust me." His smile was reassuring, but beneath it lay a current of urgency that sent my pulse racing.

The air crackled with the tension of the unknown as I nodded, reluctantly agreeing. "Fine, let's get this over with. But if she tries to perform a seance or something, I'm out."

He pulled out his phone and thumbed through his contacts, pausing briefly as if considering the weight of the decision. "We need to be careful about how we approach her. She's paranoid about the Syndicate too. If they get wind of her involvement—"

"—we'll all be in hot water. Got it. Just... don't mention we're on the run," I interrupted, my voice steady despite the uncertainty gnawing at me. "Let's just present ourselves as two harmless souls looking for knowledge."

"Two harmless souls with a very dangerous artifact," he muttered, but the grin creeping onto his face belied any worry he might have felt.

With a few taps, he dialed Eliza, and the phone rang, each tone echoing my mounting anxiety. "She might not pick up," he said, as if trying to soothe me, but I could see the tension in his jaw.

"I just hope she's not in the middle of one of her archaeological digs or something."

"Knowing her, she's probably in her apartment surrounded by an army of ancient artifacts. Just go with the flow," he replied, a note of mischief returning to his voice.

After what felt like an eternity, the call connected. "Eliza? It's Jake," he said, his tone shifting from casual to serious in an instant. "I need your help."

"Jake?" Her voice crackled through the speaker, low and intrigued. "What have you gotten yourself into this time?"

"Let's just say it involves a rather significant artifact, and we're not in the safest of situations. Can we come over?"

A pause stretched between us, thick with implications. "You're not joking, are you? The Syndicate?"

"Not if we can help it," he replied, glancing at me, his expression unreadable. "We're in a bit of a tight spot. Please, Eliza."

"Fine," she finally relented, her voice taking on a brisk edge. "Just hurry. I can't protect you if you're too late."

With that, Jake ended the call, his shoulders relaxing slightly. "She's in," he announced, a hint of triumph lighting his features.

"Great," I replied, though the feeling was still tinged with apprehension. "Now, how do we get there without being caught? I don't fancy another escape route that involves soaring through the air like a human kite."

"I have a car. We'll go in the dead of night. Less traffic, and fewer eyes on us," he assured me, the determination evident in his voice. "Let's move."

The two of us rushed through the apartment, gathering what few belongings we had. I stuffed the relic securely into my bag, my fingers lingering over its surface, a reminder of the stakes at play. Together, we slipped out into the night, the chill of the air wrapping around us like an unwelcome embrace. The streets felt different now, each shadow a potential threat, each sound amplified in the stillness of the night.

Jake led the way to a sleek, unassuming car parked a few blocks away. As we settled into the vehicle, the world outside blurred into a kaleidoscope of lights and shadows. "You sure this is going to work?"

I asked, glancing sideways at him, anxiety creeping back into my mind.

"Just keep your head down, and don't draw attention. We'll be fine," he said, starting the engine, the soft rumble providing a strange comfort amidst the chaos.

As we drove through the darkened streets, the city felt alive, each block pulsating with stories untold. I stole glances at Jake, his expression focused and determined, yet I could sense the undercurrent of fear swirling beneath the surface. It mirrored my own, an unspoken agreement that we were venturing into the unknown, our fates intertwined in a precarious dance.

"Do you think Eliza will know what to do?" I asked, breaking the silence that had settled between us like a fog.

"She better," Jake replied, his eyes fixed on the road ahead. "If anyone can help us navigate this mess, it's her."

"Do you trust her?"

The question hung in the air, heavy with implications. Jake hesitated before answering, a flicker of doubt crossing his features. "I trust her knowledge. People, though? That's another story."

Before I could respond, a flash of headlights blazed behind us, and I turned, my stomach dropping as I recognized the unmistakable shape of a police vehicle. "Jake," I whispered, panic lacing my voice. "They're onto us!"

He cursed under his breath, his grip tightening on the wheel. "Stay calm. Just act natural. If they pull us over, we play it cool."

"Right, because I'm the poster child for cool under pressure," I muttered, my heart racing as the car surged closer, lights flashing like a beacon of doom.

With the siren blaring, Jake sped up, navigating the streets with a mix of skill and desperation. "What now?" I asked, my voice trembling.

"Head for the alley! I'll lose them there." He swerved sharply, tires screeching as we hurtled into a narrow passage, the world outside blurring into a tapestry of color.

The alley was dark, littered with refuse and shadows. Jake took the sharp corners expertly, but I could hear the police car's sirens closing in, the sound an ominous reminder of the precarious line we were walking.

"We're going to need a miracle," I said, my voice barely above a whisper.

"Just hold on," he said, a fierce determination lighting his eyes as he turned sharply into another alleyway, the car bouncing slightly over the uneven pavement. I clutched the edge of my seat, the tension thick enough to slice through.

Suddenly, the headlights behind us surged, illuminating our path. "They're right on us!" I yelled, the urgency mounting as panic threatened to swallow me whole.

"Almost there!" Jake replied, his expression a blend of focus and fear. Just as I felt the walls closing in, a loud crash reverberated through the night, and the police car veered off course, momentarily losing its grip on the chase.

"What was that?" I gasped, glancing back just in time to see another vehicle, its hood crumpled, collide with the police cruiser, sending it spinning.

"Guess we found our miracle," Jake said, a hint of disbelief creeping into his tone.

As we shot out of the alley, I looked back at the chaos behind us, the surreal scene echoing my racing heart. "Let's just hope it lasts long enough to get us to Eliza," I breathed.

But the moment of relief was short-lived. A second police vehicle appeared from around the corner, lights flashing ominously as it bore down on us. "Jake!" I shouted, fear clawing at my throat.

"We have to get to her now," he said, his voice taut with determination. "Just hold on tight!"

As we sped away, the sirens wailing behind us, the world seemed to contract, a whirlwind of shadows and noise closing in. I felt the weight of the relic digging into my back, a reminder that we were not just running from the law—we were running toward an uncertain future, one that felt increasingly precarious.

The city blurred past us, each moment stretching into the next, until it felt as if time itself had begun to unravel. Then, without warning, Jake slammed on the brakes. The car skidded to a halt just outside Eliza's building, the tires screeching against the pavement.

"Out! Now!" he commanded, throwing the door open as I scrambled to unbuckle my seatbelt.

Together, we bolted toward the entrance, our hearts racing with each step. But as we reached the door, the sound of approaching sirens pierced the air once more, and I turned to see shadows closing in, figures emerging from the darkness.

"Jake, they're coming!" I cried, my pulse pounding in my ears.

"Get inside!" he shouted, pushing me ahead as he turned back, ready to confront whatever was about to come.

Just as I reached for the door

Chapter 26: The Phantom Unmasked

Adrenaline surged through me as we bolted from the Syndicate's headquarters, the air thick with the stench of burnt wires and desperation. Each footfall echoed against the concrete walls, a relentless reminder of the chaos we had just escaped. Cole was by my side, his presence a sturdy anchor amidst the swirling storm of uncertainty. He moved with a purpose, every muscle in his body coiled and ready, as if he could sense the impending confrontation before it even materialized.

The moment we turned the corner, however, our path was abruptly obstructed. There he stood—the Phantom—his silhouette framed by the flickering light of a malfunctioning streetlamp. Shadows danced around him, cloaking his features in an ominous haze, but his posture was unmistakably imposing. My heart raced, a frantic drum echoing in my chest as I exchanged a glance with Cole. There was no backing down now.

"Get back!" Cole shouted, his voice slicing through the tension like a knife. He stepped forward, defiant, his eyes ablaze with a mixture of fear and fury. I wanted to reach out, to hold him back, but the force of his determination was infectious, urging me to stand my ground.

The Phantom shifted, a predator sizing up his prey. His voice was low and menacing, dripping with a calm that sent chills racing down my spine. "You think you can escape me so easily?"

Every instinct screamed at me to run, but I couldn't move. I was paralyzed, caught in the web of our shared past and the darkness that loomed before us. The moon hung high, casting a silvery glow over the scene, illuminating the edges of his mask. It was a grotesque and beautiful piece, a fusion of art and menace that mirrored the twisted games he played.

As the air thickened with tension, Cole's jaw clenched. "You're just a coward hiding behind that mask," he shot back, each word laced with contempt. "What are you afraid of?"

The Phantom laughed, a chilling sound that ricocheted off the walls. "Fear? No, my dear Cole. I'm not afraid. I'm simply... unmasked."

With that, he lunged forward, a blur of black fabric and lethal intent. Time slowed as Cole braced himself, his hands curling into fists, ready to counter whatever this monster had in store. The impact was electric, a collision of wills that sent shockwaves through the air. I was rooted to the spot, watching as they grappled, each movement a lethal dance of power and resolve.

Then, in a flurry of motion, the Phantom's mask shattered against the ground, a cascade of pieces spilling like shards of a broken dream. The sound reverberated in my ears, and as the dust settled, the face that emerged was one I never expected to see.

Draven.

Recognition crashed over me like a tidal wave, dragging me under. My breath caught in my throat as disbelief transformed into a swirling vortex of anger and betrayal. Draven had been a beacon of hope, a guide through the shadows that had once enveloped our lives. Yet here he was, revealing the twisted truth beneath that carefully crafted facade.

"Draven?" I breathed, the name tasting bitter on my tongue. "You... you were behind all of this?"

He looked at me, a mixture of regret and resolve dancing in his stormy gray eyes. "I didn't want it to come to this, but you left me no choice."

My heart shattered at his words, each syllable a reminder of the trust I had so willingly placed in him. "You deceived us! You played with our lives!" The accusation hung heavy in the air, my voice breaking as the weight of betrayal bore down on me.

Cole and Draven were locked in combat, each trying to overpower the other, but the sight of the man I once admired made my head spin. Memories flooded my mind: shared laughter over late-night strategizing, the warmth of his encouragement as we navigated the dark waters of the Syndicate's threat. The betrayal cut deeper than any physical blow.

"I did it for the greater good!" Draven shouted, dodging a punch from Cole that nearly connected. "I needed to protect what remains of our world. Sometimes you have to make hard choices."

"Hard choices?" I spat, stepping forward, fueled by rage and disbelief. "You think this is protection? You think turning against us will save anyone?"

For a moment, the fight paused, and I felt the weight of his gaze settle on me, piercing and unyielding. "You don't understand," he said, his voice softer now, almost pleading. "I had to play both sides. The Syndicate wouldn't stop until they had complete control. I thought I could undermine them from within."

"So you chose to betray your allies? You thought we wouldn't find out?" My heart raced, the ache of betrayal morphing into something sharper, more painful.

Cole seized the moment of distraction to land a solid hit against Draven, sending him staggering back. "Enough!" he barked, his voice an explosive mix of fury and desperation.

In the midst of the chaos, I felt a flicker of hope—a fleeting chance to reason with him, to pull back the layers of his deception. "Draven, we can work together. We can still stop the Syndicate! There's time!"

But as he staggered to his feet, brushing off the remnants of his shattered mask, I could see the determination etched across his features. "It's too late for that," he murmured, almost to himself. "You'll never understand the sacrifices I had to make."

With that final proclamation, he turned on his heel, vanishing into the depths of the night, the very shadows that had once enveloped him swallowing him whole. My heart plummeted, the weight of his betrayal lingering in the air like a specter.

I stood there, trembling with unresolved emotions, staring into the darkness he had slipped into. Cole's breath was heavy beside me, his presence grounding, yet the silence that followed felt suffocating. The world had shifted around us, and we were left grappling with the enormity of the truth and the scars left in Draven's wake.

The darkness closed in around us as I tried to process the betrayal, my heart thundering like a war drum in my chest. The alleyway, once a lifeline of escape, now felt like a confining trap. Cole stood beside me, his fists still clenched, the remnants of adrenaline coursing through his veins. We had faced danger before, but this was different—this was personal. The weight of Draven's revelation hung heavily in the air, each second stretching like an eternity, and my mind raced to piece together what had just happened.

"Are you okay?" Cole's voice sliced through my thoughts, tinged with concern. His eyes searched mine, and I felt an inexplicable urge to fall into his embrace, to find solace in his unwavering strength. Instead, I shook my head, the motion accompanied by a surge of frustration.

"Do I look okay?" I snapped, perhaps a bit too sharply. "We just discovered that our ally was working for the enemy. He turned on us, Cole!" The words tumbled out, fueled by the raw mix of anger and hurt that threatened to consume me.

Cole stepped closer, his brow furrowed. "I know. I just... I wanted to make sure you were all right."

"I'm not all right! I'm... I'm reeling," I admitted, my voice wavering. "Draven was supposed to be on our side. I can't believe he betrayed us like this."

"People do what they think is necessary," he said softly, his gaze unwavering. "Sometimes that means making choices we can't understand."

The bitterness in my chest twisted painfully as I considered his words. "But why? What could he possibly gain from this?" My mind flooded with memories—Draven's encouragement, his laughter, the way he made me feel like I could conquer the world. It was all a façade, a beautifully crafted mask that hid a heart of betrayal. "I thought we had a shared mission, a common goal."

Cole's expression hardened. "Clearly, he had his own agenda. But we can't dwell on him now. We need to regroup and figure out our next move."

"Regroup?" I echoed, a laugh bursting forth that was devoid of humor. "After that? How do we trust anyone again?"

"Trust is a tricky thing," he admitted, glancing back down the alley where Draven had vanished. "It's built over time, but it can be destroyed in an instant. Right now, we need to focus on what's ahead. We're still in danger."

I took a deep breath, forcing myself to regain some semblance of composure. Cole was right; dwelling on the past wouldn't help us now. I could feel the tremors of uncertainty creeping back into my bones, but I pushed them aside. "Let's get out of here then," I said, my voice steadier.

As we navigated through the labyrinth of narrow streets, the city around us felt strangely alive, the night pulsating with a rhythm of its own. Streetlights flickered overhead, casting shadows that seemed to dance in time with our hurried steps. Each corner we turned heightened my senses, and every distant sound made me jump. I was acutely aware that Draven—or whatever remnants of him existed now—was out there, possibly orchestrating something even more sinister than before.

"Where do we go?" I asked, my breath hitching as we paused at a crossroad.

"There's an old safe house a few blocks away," Cole replied, glancing around as if checking for unseen threats. "It's off the grid—should give us a moment to breathe and figure out our next steps."

I nodded, grateful for the plan, yet anxiety coiled in my stomach. We hadn't had time to strategize. I couldn't shake the feeling that we were running blind. "What if Draven has already anticipated our moves? What if he's waiting for us?"

Cole met my gaze, his determination flaring. "Then we'll be ready for him. We've faced worse odds."

His conviction sparked something within me, a flicker of hope against the oppressive weight of despair. Together, we pushed forward, the shadows of the city swallowing us whole as we sprinted toward the safe house, our footsteps muffled against the damp pavement.

As we reached the safe house, its unassuming façade blended seamlessly with the surroundings. I marveled at how such a place could exist in the heart of the city, a sanctuary hidden in plain sight. Cole nudged open the door, revealing a dimly lit interior filled with the scent of aged wood and something metallic—perhaps a hint of memories left behind by those who sought refuge here before us.

Once inside, I let out a breath I hadn't realized I was holding. The atmosphere was heavy, and the silence felt almost tangible. Cole moved to the window, peering through the grimy glass as he surveyed the street outside. I took a moment to explore, my fingers brushing against the worn furniture, relics of a past filled with uncertainty and secretive dealings.

"Looks clear for now," Cole called over his shoulder. "But we can't let our guard down."

"Right," I said, attempting to sound resolute, though doubt gnawed at me. "We need to figure out what Draven's next move might be. If he's still working with the Syndicate, he won't stop until he gets what he wants."

Cole nodded, a pensive look crossing his face. "We can't underestimate him. He knows us better than we know ourselves at this point. We need to think outside the box."

"What do you have in mind?" I asked, leaning against the wall, desperate for direction.

He turned, an idea sparking in his eyes. "What if we draw him out? Make him think we're vulnerable?"

I raised an eyebrow, intrigued. "You mean set a trap? But what if it backfires? He could come for us with everything he has."

"Then we'll be ready," he countered, his confidence steadying my nerves. "We can use what we know about him, play on his emotions. Make him think he has the upper hand."

A plan began to crystallize in my mind, but it came with risks. "And if he doesn't take the bait? What if he decides to cut his losses and go after someone else?"

"We'll have to be vigilant. But we can't let fear dictate our actions. We're stronger together, and we know how he thinks."

As we brainstormed, the shadows around us felt less threatening, the air crackling with the possibility of reclaiming our lives. There was still so much uncertainty ahead, but in that moment, I felt a renewed sense of purpose, ignited by the spark of rebellion against the betrayal that had threatened to engulf us. We would not be victims; we would be fighters, ready to reclaim what was ours.

The tension hung in the air like a thick fog, a palpable reminder of the stakes we faced. I paced the small confines of the safe house, every creak of the floorboards sending prickles of anxiety skittering down my spine. Cole was crouched by the window, his silhouette framed against the flickering light outside. Shadows danced across his face, and I could see the gears turning in his mind, contemplating our next move.

"Do you think he'll come?" I asked, the words slipping from my lips before I could stop them. My voice was barely a whisper, a reflection of the dread curling in my stomach.

Cole straightened, turning to face me, the determination etched on his features providing a brief respite from my spiraling thoughts. "If he wants to finish what he started, he will. We have to be prepared."

Prepared. The word echoed in my mind, but how does one prepare for the unpredictable nature of betrayal? Draven was no longer just a name associated with trust and camaraderie; he had become an enigma, a shadow lurking in the recesses of my mind.

"What are you thinking?" I asked, pushing away the looming uncertainty that threatened to overtake me.

He stepped closer, his intensity almost magnetic. "We need to set up a decoy—something to lure him in. He'll want to see if we're really as vulnerable as we seem."

I tilted my head, my heart racing at the audacity of his plan. "A decoy? You mean, like make it look like we're hiding somewhere else?"

"Exactly. We can use the old warehouse down by the docks as bait," Cole said, his eyes gleaming with a mix of excitement and strategy. "It's isolated, and we can rig it to keep an eye on everything."

I crossed my arms, the notion swirling in my mind like a tempest. "That's risky. What if he realizes it's a trap? What if he brings backup?"

Cole stepped even closer, his voice low, almost conspiratorial. "That's why we're going to have a few surprises of our own. We can't just sit here waiting for him to make the next move. We have to take control."

As his words washed over me, I felt a flicker of hope ignite within, battling against the darkness of betrayal that clung to me like a second skin. "All right," I said, my voice stronger. "Let's do it. We'll make him wish he'd never come after us."

With newfound resolve, we set to work. The sun dipped below the horizon, painting the sky in hues of orange and purple, and the shadows lengthened around us. We gathered what supplies we could find—old crates, rope, anything that could help us craft our plan into something tangible. The air was thick with determination, a sense of purpose driving us forward despite the lurking danger.

As we prepared the warehouse, I couldn't shake the feeling that we were racing against time. Each creak of the floorboards made me jump, and I caught myself glancing toward the door, half-expecting Draven to come bursting through.

"I'll check the perimeter," Cole said, breaking my concentration. "Make sure we're not being watched."

I nodded, a mix of gratitude and unease swirling inside me as he slipped into the gathering darkness. Alone in the dim light, I took a moment to breathe, reminding myself that this was our chance. We were no longer merely pieces on a chessboard; we were players, strategizing to outmaneuver the very forces that sought to tear us apart.

Moments turned into what felt like hours, my thoughts swirling around the possibilities of what might happen next. The warehouse loomed ahead, shadows pooling in the corners, every sound magnified in the silence. I was lost in my thoughts when the door creaked open, and Cole returned, his expression serious.

"It's quiet. Too quiet, actually," he said, his brow furrowed. "We need to move. We can't afford to let our guard down."

Together, we slipped into the night, the moon casting a silvery glow over the deserted streets as we made our way toward the warehouse. Each step echoed in the stillness, and the air felt charged, as if the world was holding its breath, waiting for something to break the tension.

As we approached the warehouse, I caught a glimpse of movement out of the corner of my eye—a figure darting between the shadows, quick and fluid. My heart raced. "Did you see that?"

Cole nodded, his expression hardening. "Stay close."

We moved cautiously, each footfall deliberate, each breath a silent prayer. The heavy metal door of the warehouse loomed before us, and Cole pushed it open with a slight creak. The interior was dim, illuminated only by the slivers of moonlight filtering through broken windows.

"This is it," he murmured, scanning the area. "Let's set up."

We hurried to arrange our makeshift defenses, using the crates to create barriers and rigging some old fishing nets as traps. My heart raced with every creak of wood and rustle of the wind, and I felt the tension building like a coiled spring.

Just as we finished, a sound sliced through the silence—the unmistakable click of footsteps approaching. Cole tensed, his eyes narrowing. "Get behind the crates," he whispered urgently.

I nodded, crouching low as I hid behind a stack of crates. The shadows grew thicker as the figure drew closer, each footfall echoing louder in the stillness.

Then, suddenly, a familiar voice rang out, filled with venom and amusement. "Well, well, what do we have here?"

Draven.

My breath caught in my throat as I peeked through the narrow gap in the crates. There he stood, an image of confidence, illuminated by the moonlight streaming through the shattered windows. His expression was a mask of mischief, as if he enjoyed the game we were playing. "I expected a little more from you two," he taunted, his voice smooth as silk.

"Draven," Cole hissed, emerging from his hiding place, anger shimmering beneath the surface. "You've got a lot of nerve showing your face here."

"Oh, but this is where the fun begins," he replied, a sly smile curving his lips. "I have something you might find interesting."

Before I could process his words, the warehouse was suddenly flooded with light, and armed figures appeared behind him, their silhouettes sharp against the brightness. My heart dropped as realization hit me—the trap we had set was now ensnaring us.

"Welcome to my little party," Draven said, the mirth in his voice a chilling contrast to the danger encroaching around us. "I hope you brought your dancing shoes."

Cole's expression shifted from anger to urgency. "We need to get out of here—now!"

But before we could react, Draven raised a hand, and the shadows around us seemed to come alive, closing in like a tightening noose. My pulse quickened as I glanced at Cole, whose eyes were filled with fierce determination.

"On three," he whispered, but before he could finish counting, the air crackled with tension, and the figures began to advance.

My heart raced, pounding like a war drum, and I could almost hear the countdown in my head: one, two, three...

Chapter 27: The Last Stand

The air hung thick with the scent of damp earth and decay, a lingering reminder of the city's forgotten past. Shadows flickered along the walls of the tunnel as we gathered, a ragtag assembly of rebels who had chosen to defy the encroaching darkness of the Syndicate. The low hum of whispered fears and half-formed plans echoed in the cavernous space, amplifying the tension that gripped us all. I stood among them, my heart racing, acutely aware that our fragile alliance might just shatter under the weight of what lay ahead.

Cole's presence anchored me, his hand warm and steady in mine. He stood beside me, tall and resolute, the kind of man who could silence a room with a single glance. His dark hair fell messily across his forehead, and those piercing blue eyes, once filled with shadows of doubt, now burned with a fierce determination. I admired the way he held himself, a quiet strength radiating from him as he addressed the group, his voice steady and clear, cutting through the nervous murmurs.

"We've faced worse odds before," he said, a slight smirk playing at the corners of his lips, as if he were sharing a private joke. "Remember the time we snuck past a dozen guards to rescue Clara from that hellhole? This is just another day at the office, right?" Laughter rippled through the crowd, tension easing for a fleeting moment, and I couldn't help but smile back at him. Cole had a way of lightening the darkest moments, weaving threads of hope where despair threatened to take hold.

As we surveyed our makeshift war room—a cavern draped in flickering lanterns that cast dancing shadows on the stone walls—I felt a sense of belonging, a kinship with these warriors who had braved their fears for the sake of something greater than themselves. Each person present had a story etched into their features, scars that whispered tales of loss and survival. I thought of Clara, the fierce redhead who had once been our enemy, now a loyal ally with a penchant for sarcasm that rivaled even my own. She shot me a wink from across the room, her confidence radiating like sunlight breaking through the clouds, and I felt a spark of hope igniting within me.

The moment of levity didn't last long; soon, our faces turned serious again as Cole laid out our plan. His voice dropped to a low rumble, conveying the gravity of our mission. "The Syndicate has been wounded, but they're still dangerous. We'll hit them hard and fast, taking the fight to their doorstep. We know their routes; we know their weaknesses. It's time we remind them that we're not afraid."

As he spoke, I watched the determination etch itself deeper into the faces of our allies, the flickering lantern light catching the resolute glint in their eyes. There was something intoxicating about the possibility of finally breaking free from the Syndicate's stranglehold, a dream that had once felt distant but now loomed large, almost tangible. My heart raced with a mix of fear and exhilaration.

We moved through the tunnels, adrenaline thrumming through my veins. The sounds of our footsteps echoed, a heartbeat pulsing through the stone corridors as we navigated the labyrinthine passageways. With each step, I could feel the weight of our purpose, a collective hope binding us together. I clutched Cole's hand tighter, the warmth of his skin a reassuring balm against the chill of uncertainty that crept in.

As we neared the Syndicate's stronghold, the atmosphere shifted. The air grew thick, heavy with an unseen presence. I could sense the danger lurking just beyond the reach of our flickering lanterns, an ominous shadow waiting to strike. The collective breath of our group seemed to hold, a momentary pause as we stood at the threshold of a confrontation that could change everything.

"We have to be ready for anything," I whispered to Cole, a tremor of doubt creeping into my voice. "They won't go down without a fight."

His gaze met mine, fierce and unwavering. "And we won't let them take us down, either," he assured me, his voice firm. "We're stronger together."

The words hung in the air, a promise and a challenge all at once. With one last shared glance, we surged forward, our hearts pounding in unison as we burst into the Syndicate's lair. The world shifted in an instant—the dim light from our lanterns revealed a chaotic scene. Shadows danced violently on the walls, and the sharp crack of fists meeting flesh echoed through the space.

I found myself swept into the whirlwind of battle, adrenaline coursing through my veins like fire. I moved beside Cole, our movements instinctive, a practiced rhythm born of countless skirmishes. Each strike felt powerful, fueled by the knowledge that we were fighting not just for ourselves, but for everyone who had suffered under the Syndicate's iron grip. With every punch, every kick, I could feel the tide shifting, the balance of power tilting in our favor.

But in the throes of chaos, a sharp whistle sliced through the din, an unmistakable signal. My heart dropped as I recognized the sound, the icy realization dawning upon me that this battle was far from over. The Syndicate had one final trick up their sleeve, and we were about to be drawn into a web far more tangled than we had anticipated. As the chaos erupted around us, I tightened my grip on Cole's hand, determined to face whatever came next, side by side.

In the heart of the city's forgotten underbelly, the air was thick with the scent of dust and unfulfilled dreams. Shadows clung to the crumbling walls like memories too painful to shake off, remnants of a time when power was unchallenged and the Syndicate ruled with an iron fist. We gathered in the dim light, our ragtag team of allies standing shoulder to shoulder, each face a portrait of resolve and trepidation. I looked at Cole, his jaw set, eyes gleaming with determination, and felt a flicker of hope ignite within me, battling against the dread that accompanied such a monumental task.

"Ready to play hero?" he teased, a smirk dancing on his lips, the flicker of charm never fading even in the direst circumstances. I couldn't help but laugh, the sound echoing softly in the cavernous space, its resonance a reminder that even in darkness, light can find a way to slip through.

"Only if you promise to keep up," I shot back, my heart racing with a mix of adrenaline and affection. We had fought our way through adversity together, and now, as the stakes reached their peak, I knew that this was our moment to reclaim not just the city but a piece of ourselves that had been lost along the way.

The tunnel twisted ahead, a serpentine path leading us into the unknown. Each step felt like a countdown, the very walls seeming to pulse with anticipation. Whispers of the Syndicate's remnants filled my ears—a cacophony of fear, greed, and desperation. They had underestimated us, had thought their legacy invincible, but we were determined to prove them wrong. As we moved deeper, the sound of our boots against the cold concrete became a rallying cry, an anthem for the resistance we had built.

Suddenly, we stumbled upon a chamber, its entrance flanked by rusted metal beams, remnants of a time long past. The flickering lights overhead revealed a scene that was both harrowing and exhilarating. Members of the Syndicate were gathered, their demeanor a mix of bravado and anxiety, clinging to their waning power as if it were a life raft. I caught Cole's gaze, and in that shared look, an unspoken agreement passed between us. We would not falter.

"Time to crash their party," he whispered, drawing me close as the first strike erupted like a thunderclap. We charged in, a whirlwind of fury and purpose, and chaos erupted in an instant. Our allies flanked us, a mosaic of strength and resilience, each of us an integral part of the tapestry that would ultimately unravel the Syndicate's hold.

The clash of bodies and shouts echoed in the chamber, the atmosphere electric with the thrill of the fight. I found myself moving instinctively, every muscle in sync with Cole's as we maneuvered through the chaos. I felt a strange comfort in the rhythm we had developed—his hand always within reach, guiding me, protecting me, and igniting the fire that surged within my veins.

"Watch your left!" Cole shouted, his voice slicing through the din. I barely had time to react, spinning around just in time to block a blow aimed at my side. The impact jarred me, but I recovered quickly, countering with a swift kick that sent my attacker sprawling. The taste of victory mingled with the adrenaline coursing through my body, a potent reminder of what we were fighting for.

In the fray, a familiar figure emerged from the shadows—Gideon, the Syndicate's second-in-command, his eyes dark with malice. I could feel the air thicken with animosity, the world narrowing down to just the two of us. "You think you can win?" he sneered, the arrogance in his voice almost palpable. "You're nothing without your precious Syndicate."

"Funny, I was thinking the same about you," I retorted, feeling a surge of confidence. With each word, I could feel the tide shifting, not just in the battle but within myself. This was my moment, the culmination of every hardship, every betrayal, and every ounce of doubt that had threatened to consume me.

As we exchanged blows, the fight became a blur of movement and strategy. Cole was by my side, our partnership fluid, a dance of instinct and trust. I could see the Syndicate's facade crumbling around us, their numbers dwindling, their bravado fading into desperation. Yet, amid the chaos, a nagging thought pulled at my mind—what if this wasn't the end? What if they had a contingency plan, a last-ditch effort to cling to power even as the walls closed in on them?

With that thought swirling like a storm cloud, I plunged deeper into the fray, determined to put an end to this nightmare. We fought relentlessly, the room echoing with cries of defiance and pain. I glanced at Cole, and in that moment, the intensity of our shared purpose flared. We weren't just fighting for ourselves; we were fighting for the city, for the people who had been oppressed for too long. We were reclaiming our futures, one blow at a time.

Suddenly, a loud explosion reverberated through the tunnels, shaking the ground beneath us. The lights flickered and went out, plunging us into darkness, save for the distant glow of fires that had erupted amidst the chaos. The air filled with the acrid scent of smoke, a reminder that this battle was far from over.

"Stick together!" I shouted, my heart racing as I felt the chaos around us shift again. The darkness was oppressive, but it was in these moments that we truly shone. I could hear the clattering of weapons and the muffled curses of Syndicate members struggling to regroup. We would use this confusion to our advantage, pushing forward with renewed vigor.

As we fought through the smoke and chaos, each movement felt more purposeful, a concerted effort to dismantle everything they had built. We were on the brink of something monumental, a final stand that would reshape not just our destinies but the very fabric of the city itself.

The darkness enveloped us like a thick fog, the kind that clung to your skin and made every breath feel heavy with anticipation. Smoke swirled around, twisting into ghostly shapes that danced in the flickering light of distant flames. Each shadow felt like a reminder of what we were fighting against, a chilling echo of the Syndicate's tyranny that had suffocated the city for far too long. I could barely see Cole beside me, but I felt his presence like a beacon, steady and unwavering, urging me forward even as uncertainty loomed.

"Is it just me, or is this starting to feel like one of those horror movies?" I quipped, my voice strained but laced with defiance. A chuckle escaped him, the sound breaking through the tension like a well-timed punchline.

"Let's just hope there aren't any jump scares waiting for us," he replied, his tone light but his eyes scanning the darkness, alert to every sound. It was this mix of humor and caution that kept us grounded, reminding me that we weren't just facing our fears; we were facing them together.

Suddenly, the air shifted, a tension thick enough to slice. A low rumble echoed through the tunnels, and I could feel the vibrations in my bones. "What was that?" I asked, my heart racing. Cole's expression hardened, his instincts kicking into high gear.

"Stay close," he murmured, and I tightened my grip on his hand, feeling the strength and warmth of him grounding me amid the chaos. We moved deeper into the labyrinth, the walls closing in as if the very earth was conspiring against us.

The sounds of conflict reverberated ahead, a chaotic symphony of shouts and clashes that intensified the closer we got. I couldn't shake the feeling that we were on the precipice of something monumental. With every step, I recalled the faces of those who had suffered at the hands of the Syndicate—their hopes shattered and futures dimmed. We couldn't allow their sacrifices to be in vain.

We rounded a corner, and suddenly, the corridor opened into a vast chamber illuminated by the harsh light of makeshift torches. The Syndicate's remnants were gathered, their expressions a blend of shock and fury. Gideon stood at the center, his dark silhouette a stark contrast against the flames. The flicker of the fire danced in his eyes, and a sly smile spread across his face as he caught sight of us.

"Ah, the fearless duo," he drawled, his voice smooth yet laced with malice. "You're too late. The Syndicate will not be defeated today."

"Oh, really?" I shot back, my voice steadier than I felt. "Looks to me like you're outnumbered and outmatched." Behind us, our allies emerged from the shadows, a fierce band of warriors united by a common purpose.

Gideon's smile faltered for a heartbeat, but he quickly recovered, his confidence returning like a well-rehearsed play. "Numbers don't dictate power. It's the will to use it that counts." With a swift motion, he raised his hand, and the air crackled with tension.

"Let's find out what that will amounts to, shall we?" Cole challenged, stepping forward, and I felt an electric thrill run through me. It was now or never, the moment where everything we had fought for would either flourish or crumble.

In a split second, the chamber erupted into chaos. Cole and I surged forward, our movements instinctive, honed by countless battles fought side by side. The clamor of our allies clashing with Syndicate members filled the air as we darted through the fray, our focus razor-sharp. Every punch, every kick, was fueled by our shared resolve and the desperate desire to reclaim our lives from the clutches of fear.

Amid the frenzy, I locked eyes with Gideon, and a silent challenge passed between us. I could feel the fire within me igniting, the passion to protect what we had built and the people we loved. It was a volatile cocktail of fear and courage that propelled me forward.

"Remember the faces, Gideon," I called out as I sidestepped an incoming blow, "they won't forget your betrayal." He responded with a snarl, but I could see the flicker of doubt in his eyes. He had underestimated not only our strength but the collective will of everyone who had been hurt by the Syndicate's greed.

The fight escalated, our allies pushing back against the remnants of the Syndicate, and for a moment, it felt like the tide had turned. But just as hope began to take root, I sensed a shift in the atmosphere, a chilling sensation creeping down my spine. A group of Syndicate enforcers emerged from a side corridor, their faces twisted in rage, brandishing weapons that glinted ominously in the torchlight.

"Cole!" I shouted, my heart pounding as I saw them barreling toward us. He turned, his expression morphing from determination to alarm as we realized we were outnumbered yet again.

"Get back!" he yelled, but it was too late. They were upon us, and I felt the world tilt on its axis as the chaos erupted anew. I ducked and weaved, fighting tooth and nail, but the sheer force of the Syndicate's renewed strength pressed down on us.

In the melee, I lost sight of Cole, the darkness swallowing him whole as I was forced to fend off two attackers at once. Panic surged within me, but I pushed it aside, focusing on the fight. I couldn't allow fear to paralyze me. I couldn't let anything happen to him.

But just as I managed to throw one opponent off balance, I heard a chilling shout echoing through the chamber—a voice I recognized too well. "You think you can defeat us? This city is ours!" It was Gideon, his voice dripping with venomous confidence, and I felt a swell of dread.

"Cole!" I screamed, desperation clawing at my throat as I fought harder, my vision narrowing. The stakes were climbing higher, and I could feel the weight of every life we were fighting for resting on my shoulders.

In that moment, a loud crash erupted from the back of the chamber, and I turned just in time to see the structure begin to crumble, debris raining down around us. The realization hit like a slap to the face—this wasn't just a fight for our freedom; it was also a race against time. We had to escape, had to survive.

But the chaotic swirl of bodies made it impossible to see. I frantically searched for Cole amidst the turmoil, my heart racing as the ground shook beneath us. It was becoming clearer with every passing second: we were running out of time.

And then, in a split second that felt like an eternity, everything shifted. A loud boom echoed through the chamber, and I could see Gideon's triumphant expression morph into one of sheer panic. The ceiling above him began to buckle, the walls groaning in protest.

"Cole!" I shouted again, my voice hoarse as I strained to push through the throng of bodies. But as I took a step forward, a loud crash reverberated, and the ground trembled violently beneath my feet.

In that moment of chaos, I felt the ground give way, and before I could react, I was engulfed in darkness, the world collapsing around me as I was pulled into the unknown.

Chapter 28: Beyond the Darkness

The alley, once a narrow chasm of brick and despair, now glows softly under the streetlamps, their light refracted by the residual rain on the cobblestones. I can almost hear the echoes of our earlier selves—the sharp breaths, the hesitant laughter, the desperate exchanges. This space, once a battleground of animosity, has transformed into a sacred ground, a threshold between what was and what could be. I lean against the damp wall, my heart racing not with fear, but with the warmth of an unfamiliar hope.

Cole stands close, his presence a steady anchor in the shifting currents of my thoughts. His dark hair, slicked back from the rain, glistens under the streetlight, and I find myself momentarily lost in the depths of his stormy eyes. They've always held a certain intensity, a flicker of something raw and untamed. But now, they reveal a softness, a vulnerability that pulls me in. The remnants of the battle still cling to us like ghosts, and I can't shake the feeling that we are not just two survivors, but two souls intertwined by fate.

"I never thought we'd end up back here," he says, his voice low and gravelly, the hint of a smile playing at the corners of his lips. "You used to look so terrified."

I huff a laugh, the sound breaking the weight of the moment. "And you looked like you'd just walked out of a noir film, all brooding and mysterious."

He chuckles, the sound rich and infectious, reverberating in the quiet alley. "I suppose we both have our roles to play. The terrified damsel and the dark hero."

"Damsel?" I arch an eyebrow, pretending to be offended. "I'd hardly call myself that. I've fought harder than most."

"True," he concedes, his grin widening. "More like a fierce warrior princess. But even warriors need a moment to breathe."

His gaze drifts past me, and for a moment, we're both lost in the memories of the past few weeks—of the bloodshed, the losses, the betrayals. Each moment we shared felt like a page torn from a book filled with chaos, but this moment is different. There's an air of tranquility surrounding us, almost like the city itself has decided to exhale.

"Do you think it's over?" I ask, my voice barely above a whisper, the vulnerability in my question hanging between us like a fragile thread.

He turns to me, his expression serious. "I want to believe it is. But the scars run deep. There will always be those who crave power, those who feed off chaos. We need to be ready."

"Ready?" I echo, feeling a mix of determination and dread. "For what? More battles? More blood?"

"No," he replies firmly, stepping closer. "For rebuilding. For living. We can't let fear dictate our future. We've fought too hard for that."

As he speaks, I feel a shift within me. It's as though his words unlock something I've kept buried—an unyielding desire not just for survival, but for life, for love. I can't remember the last time I allowed myself to dream, to hope. The chaos has consumed me for so long, but standing here, with Cole, I feel a flicker of something brighter.

The air grows still, charged with unspoken tension, and I can see the moment his resolve solidifies. It's in the way his eyes darken, the way his posture shifts. "Lena, I—"

Before he can finish, a sudden sound interrupts us, a distant rumble echoing through the alley. It startles me, my heart jumping into my throat. "What was that?"

Cole's expression hardens, the playful warmth dissipating as he scans the shadows. "I don't know, but we should—"

A figure emerges from the darkness, moving with a swift, menacing grace. My pulse quickens as recognition floods through me. It's a silhouette I've seen before—one that embodies the very chaos we've been fighting against. The shadows twist and meld, revealing a face I thought I'd never see again, a haunting reminder of betrayal and broken trust.

"Back for round two?" I spit, my voice steady despite the surge of fear within.

The figure chuckles, a low, dark sound that reverberates through the alley. "Oh, dear Lena. You really think it's that simple? You've only just begun to scratch the surface of what's coming."

Cole steps in front of me, a protective barrier, his stance tense. "Get out of here. You don't belong in this place anymore."

The figure tilts their head, amusement dancing in their eyes. "And what will you do if I refuse? You think you've won? You're merely pawns in a game much larger than you can comprehend."

My heart races as I glance at Cole, his jaw clenched, the tension between us palpable. "We're not pawns. We're players now," I reply, my voice laced with defiance.

The figure smirks, the shadows shifting around them like living creatures. "Then let the game begin."

In that moment, everything shifts. The air thickens with anticipation, a storm brewing on the horizon. Cole and I exchange a glance, an unspoken agreement passing between us. We've come too far to turn back now. Whatever darkness looms ahead, we will face it together, unyielding and fierce. The alley may have changed, but so have we.

The figure before us shifts in the dim light, the very air around it trembling with an electric intensity that sends a shiver down my spine. My heart thuds in my chest, a drumbeat of both fear and exhilaration, as I stand shoulder to shoulder with Cole, our resolve hardening like steel. The shadows behind the figure seem to pulse, a dark halo that amplifies the menace emanating from their presence. I brace myself, the moment stretching like a taut wire ready to snap.

"Don't think for a moment you've won," the figure taunts, their voice smooth and dripping with disdain. "You may have survived the last skirmish, but this is far from over. The real game is just beginning."

"Game?" I retort, letting the challenge boil over. "You're the one playing with fire, and this time, it's going to burn you."

Cole shifts slightly, his eyes narrowed, assessing the threat. I can feel the tension radiating off him, and it anchors me in this swirling chaos. Whatever power this figure thinks they wield, they have no idea who they're dealing with now.

"Oh, how delightfully naive," the figure replies, smirking. "You've become quite the little warrior, haven't you? But you're still too wrapped up in your emotions to see the bigger picture. Tell me, what happens when the next wave hits? Will you fight then, or will you cower behind your precious little hero?"

"Cowering is not on my agenda," I shoot back, feeling a rush of defiance bubble up. "You clearly underestimate what we're capable of. You think shadows and threats can intimidate us? We've faced worse and lived to tell the tale."

The figure's smile falters for just a heartbeat, and in that moment, I know we've struck a nerve. "Words can only do so much," they say, voice low, eyes glimmering with dark intent. "But actions, dear Lena, actions speak louder. I'll enjoy watching your little rebellion crumble when it realizes it's fighting against its own."

I share a glance with Cole, a silent communication that speaks volumes. This was not just a battle of physical strength but of wills, and we were not about to back down. "If you think we'll just stand aside and let you wreak havoc, you clearly don't know us at all," Cole says, stepping forward, his presence formidable.

With a flick of their wrist, the figure vanishes into the shadows, leaving behind a chilling silence that envelops us. I feel a shudder course through me, the weight of their words pressing down like a dense fog. "We need to get out of here," I say, breaking the stillness.

Cole nods, his expression serious as he scans the alley, alert and vigilant. "Let's find somewhere safe to regroup. We need to plan our next move."

As we navigate through the alley, the city's pulse seems to mirror my own. I can hear the distant hum of traffic, the soft murmur of nightlife beginning to stir, a stark contrast to the turmoil that churns within me. We emerge onto a bustling street, the neon lights shimmering against the damp pavement, but I feel oddly detached from it all, like a spectator in a world that has moved on while I remain anchored in uncertainty.

"Where to now?" Cole asks, glancing down at me. His dark eyes are searching, full of an intensity that both unnerves and comforts me. I can't tell if he's more concerned about our safety or the future of our burgeoning connection.

"There's a café a few blocks away," I suggest, remembering a place that used to be a sanctuary for me during darker times. "They'll have a back room we can use. It'll give us a chance to think."

"Lead the way," he says, and there's a warmth in his tone that makes the knot in my stomach loosen ever so slightly.

We weave through the crowd, the city alive around us, and yet the undercurrent of tension lingers like an uninvited guest. The café is just as I remember it—cozy, with the rich scent of coffee and baked goods wafting through the air. The barista, a friendly face with a warm smile, waves as we slip inside.

"Busy night?" I ask, the familiar atmosphere bringing a semblance of normalcy to my frayed nerves.

"You could say that. It's one of those nights when everyone needs a little caffeine boost," she replies cheerily, before turning her attention to the next customer.

Cole and I find a small table in the back corner, and the moment we sit, the noise of the café fades into a gentle hum. I pull my hair back, the weight of the encounter still heavy in my mind. "What do you think they meant?" I ask, my voice barely a whisper amidst the clinking of cups and the soft chatter.

Cole leans forward, his brow furrowed in thought. "I think they're trying to play mind games with us. They're banking on our fear and uncertainty. But we can't let that happen. We need to gather our allies, rally everyone to our cause. If they think we're fractured, we'll prove them wrong."

I nod, the fire of determination sparking within me. "We can't give them the satisfaction of seeing us crumble. There's strength in unity, and we've built something worth fighting for."

He reaches across the table, taking my hand in his. The warmth of his touch ignites a flame of hope within me, a reminder that we're in this together. "No matter what comes next, I've got your back. You're not alone in this fight."

The sincerity in his voice sends a rush of warmth through me, and for a fleeting moment, the chaos outside this café fades into the background. "And I've got yours," I reply, my voice steady. "We'll face whatever this is head-on. Together."

As we sit in the comforting glow of the café, plotting our next steps, the shadows that once loomed over us seem a little less menacing, a little more like a challenge we can conquer. Whatever awaits us beyond these walls, I feel the weight of our shared journey solidifying into something unbreakable. There is power in partnership, and together, we can light a path through the darkness.

The café buzzes with life, the aroma of freshly brewed coffee wrapping around us like a warm embrace. I take a moment to soak it all in—the laughter of friends catching up, the clinking of spoons against porcelain, the comforting murmur of conversations blending together. Yet, underneath this layer of normalcy, a tension simmers, a reminder of the shadows that linger just outside the door.

Cole leans back, his gaze fixed on the half-finished latte in front of him. "What's our next move, strategist?" His tone is light, but there's an edge to it that hints at the seriousness of our situation.

I pick at the napkin on the table, my mind racing. "We need to gather everyone. The people who fought with us, those who believe in what we're trying to build. If we're going to stand against this figure—whoever they are—we can't do it alone."

"Right. A united front," he muses, his fingers drumming lightly against the table. "But we also need to be cautious. There's no telling how far they're willing to go to break us apart."

His words hang in the air, a stark reminder of the fragility of our alliance. I watch him as he wrestles with his thoughts, and I can see the shadows of doubt flickering in his eyes. It makes me want to reach out and assure him that we're stronger than the fear that looms over us. "We'll be careful. We've survived this long, haven't we? We've faced worse."

He meets my gaze, and for a moment, the storm in his eyes softens. "Yeah, I suppose we have. It's just... I don't want to lose you, Lena. Not now, not after everything."

My heart tugs at his words, the weight of his vulnerability settling in the space between us. "You won't lose me. We're in this together, remember? That's the point." I give him a smile that I hope conveys my determination, but I can feel the undercurrents of fear swirling just beneath the surface.

The door swings open, and a gust of wind sweeps through the café, carrying with it a flurry of leaves and a chill that bites at my skin. My gaze shifts to the entrance, where a group of familiar faces steps inside—our allies. Their eyes dart around, assessing the situation, but relief washes over them when they spot us.

"Lena! Cole!" Jace, a tall, broad-shouldered man with a perpetually scruffy beard, strides forward, his expression a mix of concern and determination. "We heard about the confrontation. Are you two okay?"

"We're fine," Cole assures, though I can sense the tension in his posture. "But we need to talk. Things just got a lot more complicated."

The rest of our group—Eva, a sharp-witted woman with an infectious laugh, and Marco, whose easy smile belies his strategic mind—join us at the table. The café's atmosphere shifts from casual chatter to a hushed urgency as we begin to discuss our next steps.

Jace leans in, his voice low. "The word is spreading that someone is trying to destabilize our operations. We can't let them tear apart what we've built. We need to hit back before they come for us."

"Agreed," I reply, feeling the adrenaline surge through me. "But we have to be smart about it. We need to find out who's pulling the strings. This isn't just some random act; it feels personal."

"Personal? With our luck, it's probably a grudge match," Marco quips, trying to lighten the mood, but the tension in the air remains thick.

"Or a power play," Eva interjects, her expression serious. "We need to gather more information. If we can find out who's behind this, we can counter their moves."

"Let's split up," Cole suggests, his tone commanding. "Jace and Eva, you can check in with our contacts. See if anyone has seen or heard anything unusual. Marco and I will hit the streets and try to gather intel on that figure from the alley. We need to know what we're dealing with."

"What about you?" Jace asks, his brow furrowing.

"I'm going to stay with Lena," Cole replies firmly, his gaze locked onto mine. "We're stronger together."

The decision settles around us like a blanket, both comforting and stifling. There's a part of me that feels safe with Cole by my side, yet the thought of facing the unknown again sends a shiver down my spine. I can't let fear dictate my actions, especially now that we're this close to uncovering the truth.

As our group begins to disperse, a sense of urgency pulses through me. "Wait," I call out, and everyone pauses, turning to look at me. "If we're going to do this, we need to be ready for anything. Trust each other, and communicate. We can't afford any slip-ups."

They nod, and I feel a flicker of pride for what we've become—a team, a family forged in the fires of adversity. The air buzzes with the weight of our shared commitment as they move toward the door.

Cole's hand finds mine, his grip reassuring. "We'll get through this, Lena. We've come too far to back down now."

"Yeah," I reply, squeezing his hand. "And whatever happens, we'll face it together."

The moment stretches, charged with unspoken promises. I'm struck by how far we've come, but also how close the danger feels. As the last of our allies slip out into the night, a sudden crash echoes from the back of the café, reverberating through the room like a thunderclap.

"What was that?" I gasp, adrenaline spiking through my veins.

Cole's expression shifts instantly, all humor gone as he scans the room. "Stay close," he murmurs, and the protective instinct in his voice sends a thrill of anticipation coursing through me.

We move toward the sound, a mix of apprehension and resolve propelling us forward. The café feels smaller, the walls closing in as we approach the source of the disturbance. The door to the back room swings open, and the light flickers ominously, casting eerie shadows on the walls.

Then, out of the darkness, a figure lunges toward us—a silhouette framed by chaos. My heart drops as I recognize the face, twisted with malice, a smirk playing on their lips.

"You thought you could hide from me?" they hiss, the challenge hanging thick in the air.

In that moment, time freezes, and every instinct screams for me to run. The figure steps closer, and my breath catches, a sense of dread settling in my stomach. We are not done yet, not by a long shot, and the stakes have just been raised.

Chapter 29: A New Dawn

The sun unfurls its golden tendrils, stretching languorously over the city, illuminating the streets that pulse with the rhythm of a new day. I squeeze Cole's hand, the warmth of his grip anchoring me to the moment. The world is waking up, and so are we, shaking off the remnants of the past like dust from our shoulders. Each step we take feels imbued with promise, the air rich with the scent of blooming jasmine mingling with the distant hum of city life.

Our footsteps echo softly on the cobblestone path, a melody of liberation. The weight of the Syndicate's grip has finally slipped away, replaced by the exhilarating thrill of uncharted territory. I glance sideways at Cole, who walks with an easy confidence, his dark hair tousled in a way that makes him look both fierce and boyishly charming. There's something undeniably magnetic about him this morning—maybe it's the sunlight catching the glints in his eyes, or perhaps it's the way he smiles as if the weight of the world has been lifted from his shoulders too.

"Look," I say, breaking the comfortable silence. I gesture toward a small café on the corner, its patio draped in vibrant flowers, their colors popping against the brick façade. "What do you think? Coffee to go with our new beginnings?"

His eyes spark with mischief. "Only if we can add pastries to that agenda. I have a feeling the universe owes us a few indulgences."

I laugh, the sound light and freeing, a sharp contrast to the muffled echoes of my past. As we approach the café, the barista greets us with a wide smile, her apron dusted with flour, and I can almost taste the cinnamon rolls baking behind her. The scent wraps around us, and for a moment, I let myself bask in the ordinary joys of life—fluffy pastries, rich coffee, and the fluttering of butterflies in my stomach that have little to do with nerves and everything to do with possibility.

With our steaming cups in hand, we find a table outside under the bright morning sun, where laughter and chatter fill the air like a comforting blanket. I take a sip, the coffee smooth and bold, a perfect companion to the buttery croissant that flakily crumbles at my touch. "You know," I begin, savoring the moment, "I never imagined we'd be here, enjoying something as simple as breakfast. It feels... surreal."

Cole leans back, his expression thoughtful as he watches the passersby. "Life can be funny that way. One minute you're dodging bullets, and the next, you're debating the merits of croissants versus danishes." He takes a deliberate sip of his coffee, smirking. "But let's be real, nothing beats a good croissant."

There's a teasing glimmer in his eyes that I can't help but mirror. "You just want to justify the calories. You know they're practically illegal in some circles."

"Maybe in the circles we used to run in," he says, leaning in closer, his voice low and conspiratorial. "But here? Here, we can be gluttons without fear. It's practically our right."

I can feel my cheeks warm under the sun and the thrill of sharing such a light-hearted moment with him. "Okay then, let's live on the edge. One croissant and one danish each. Just for research purposes."

As we dig into our treats, I'm struck by how different this feels—how light and uncomplicated it is. Cole and I slip into easy banter, each playful jab layered with the warmth of familiarity. The heavy memories of our shared past begin to dissolve, replaced by this new, more innocent intimacy.

But the comfort doesn't last. As I take a bite of the danish, a shadow passes over our table. I look up to find a figure standing there, tall and cloaked in a leather jacket that glints with hidden menace in the sunlight. My heart races, and I instinctively reach for Cole's hand, but before I can squeeze it in reassurance, the figure speaks.

"Nice to see you both enjoying the finer things in life," he says, his voice smooth, like the sharp edge of a knife. My breath catches in my throat as I recognize him—Derek, a remnant from the Syndicate's days, someone I never expected to see again.

Cole's expression hardens, a protective instinct flaring to life. "What do you want, Derek?"

Derek smirks, the corners of his mouth curling in a way that sends a chill down my spine. "Oh, just checking in on my favorite fugitives. You see, the Syndicate doesn't just disappear. We have a way of resurfacing, and I've got some news that might interest you."

The bustling café fades into the background, the laughter and chatter silenced by the tension that suddenly envelops our little table. I glance at Cole, whose jaw is clenched, his demeanor shifting from playful to vigilant in the blink of an eye.

"Whatever you think you have, we're done with the Syndicate," Cole replies, his voice steady, but I can hear the undercurrent of tension laced within it. "Whatever you're selling, we're not buying."

Derek leans in, his eyes glinting with an unsettling mix of amusement and something darker. "Oh, I think you'll want to hear me out. You see, there are forces at play, and your little fairy tale isn't quite over yet. Not by a long shot."

The words hang heavy in the air, and the aroma of coffee and pastries feels like a cruel joke against the gravity of the situation. I can't help but wonder if we've truly escaped or if we've merely traded one cage for another.

As Derek continues to speak, detailing the threats that loom in the shadows, my heart races, not just with fear but with an unyielding resolve. I look at Cole, and I know then that whatever challenges await us, we will face them together. The dawn might be beautiful, but we are still in the midst of a storm, and I refuse to let the past dictate our future any longer.

Derek's presence looms larger than life, and as he leans closer, I can almost taste the tension in the air—a metallic tang that stirs the memories of battles fought and the scars that still mar my heart. His eyes, dark and calculating, flicker between Cole and me, searching for any sign of weakness. I feel a surge of defiance rising within me, fueled by the knowledge that I am no longer the same girl who was haunted by fear.

"You think you can just stroll back into our lives and threaten us?" I manage, my voice steady despite the tremor of adrenaline coursing through me. "You have no power here anymore."

Derek chuckles softly, a sound devoid of genuine amusement. "Ah, but that's where you're mistaken. The Syndicate is far from gone. You may have escaped my grasp, but the real question is—can you escape what's coming for you?"

Cole's grip tightens around my hand, a subtle reminder that I'm not alone in this. "We're not interested in your mind games, Derek. Whatever you think you know, you're wrong."

But Derek shakes his head, his smile transforming into something more sinister. "You're playing with fire, Cole. And you know what they say about fire—it can warm your heart or burn your world to ashes. I'd hate for you to find out the hard way."

I swallow hard, my stomach twisting into knots. The world around us seems to blur as Derek's words sink in, and I suddenly feel like a character in a story I didn't choose. The bustling café fades into a muted backdrop, patrons oblivious to the storm brewing at our table.

"What do you want?" I ask, forcing the words out with more bravado than I feel. "If you're here to make threats, you can save your breath."

Derek leans back, feigning nonchalance, but I can see the flicker of amusement in his eyes. "Oh, I'm not here to make threats. I'm here to offer you a deal."

"A deal?" Cole's voice drips with skepticism, and I can see his mind racing through the implications. "You think we'd ever trust you?"

"Trust is a tricky business," Derek replies, his tone casual, like we're discussing the weather rather than our very lives. "But you might not have a choice. The Syndicate is expanding, and you two are still on our radar. I can help you—if you're willing to listen."

A knot of unease curls in my stomach. "And what do you want in return?"

Derek's smile sharpens, revealing a glimmer of the predator beneath the surface. "Just your cooperation. You could be valuable assets to us. After all, you've been through the fire. You know how it works. With the right resources, you could help us expand even further."

"Thanks, but no thanks," Cole says, his voice firm. "We've already paid our dues. We're done playing your games."

Derek's demeanor shifts, the casual air replaced by something more menacing. "You think you can just walk away? I've seen your weaknesses, and believe me, they won't stay hidden for long. You may be enjoying your little coffee date, but shadows linger, waiting to pounce."

With that, he straightens up and takes a step back, hands tucked into the pockets of his jacket. "You have until the end of the week to reconsider my offer. I'd hate for something unfortunate to happen before then."

And just like that, he turns on his heel and strides away, leaving us in a whirlwind of unease. The café returns to its normal buzz, laughter and clinking cups filling the space, but our world has shifted.

I look at Cole, who is visibly tense, his jaw clenched. "What now?" I ask, my voice barely above a whisper.

"Now," he replies, his eyes darkening with determination, "we prepare. We need to gather information, figure out what Derek knows and how much trouble we're really in."

"Great," I say, trying to inject a note of humor into the heavy atmosphere. "I thought we were done with secrets and shadows. Apparently, I was mistaken."

Cole shoots me a look that almost softens the edges of his worry. "Trust me, I'd rather be enjoying pastries with you, but it seems like we have to face the reality of our situation."

As we leave the café, the vibrant world outside feels tainted. The flowers in their pots seem to droop under the weight of our new reality, and the sun, which had moments ago bathed us in warmth, now feels harsh and unforgiving.

We stroll in silence, the streets alive with activity, but I can only focus on the rapid beating of my heart and the dark shadow of Derek's words echoing in my mind. "We need a plan," I finally say, breaking the heavy quiet.

Cole nods, his brow furrowed. "Let's head back to the apartment. We can go through our resources and see what we can dig up about Derek and the Syndicate's recent activities."

As we make our way through the familiar streets, a sense of urgency propels us forward. I replay our conversation with Derek in my mind, piecing together the clues he had dropped like breadcrumbs, each one leading us deeper into a forest of uncertainty.

"Do you really think we're still on their radar?" I ask, glancing sideways at Cole. "I mean, after everything, I thought we'd managed to slip away."

He pauses, his expression thoughtful. "The Syndicate doesn't let go easily. If Derek is involved, he likely knows more than we realize. We can't underestimate what they're capable of, especially if they think we have something they want."

We arrive at our apartment, the door creaking open to reveal the sanctuary we've crafted together, filled with remnants of laughter and stolen moments. But the atmosphere feels charged now, like a storm on the horizon, threatening to upend our fragile peace.

As we settle in, Cole pulls out his laptop, the glow of the screen illuminating his face in the dim light. "Let's see what we can find out. If Derek thinks we're a threat, it means we still hold some power. We just need to figure out how to wield it."

"Or we could just binge-watch a terrible reality show and pretend none of this is happening," I suggest with a smirk, trying to lighten the mood.

Cole chuckles, shaking his head. "If only that were an option. But I'll settle for a strategy session over popcorn if it keeps us one step ahead."

With a renewed sense of purpose, we dive into the task, unraveling the threads of the past and piecing together our next moves. The shadows may still linger, but as we face this new challenge, I find strength in knowing that whatever comes our way, we will face it together—no longer bound by the chains of our past, but free to forge our own path forward.

The late afternoon light spills into our apartment, casting long shadows that dance across the floor as Cole and I sift through our scattered notes and digital leads. A motley collection of memories and half-formed strategies lies before us, remnants of our past conquests mingling with the chilling reminder that we may not be as free as we hoped.

"Okay, let's recap," Cole says, tapping away on the laptop, his brow furrowed with concentration. "We've got Derek, who clearly thinks he can manipulate us, and the Syndicate, which is still lurking in the background. But what we need is a solid plan—something proactive instead of reactive."

I lean back in my chair, allowing my thoughts to roam. "Right, but what do we even know about Derek's current connections? We need intel on who he's working with, and if there's any indication of a larger agenda."

"Not to mention why he thinks we're still worth pursuing," Cole adds, his fingers flying over the keyboard. "I mean, we're not exactly the prize he thinks we are."

"Speak for yourself," I retort playfully, unable to resist a jab at his seriousness. "I mean, have you seen my pastry skills? I could totally be a prize worth chasing."

He shoots me a sideways glance, his lips twitching at the corners. "Oh, please, the only prize here is the cozy life we've carved out for ourselves. And I'm not giving that up without a fight."

A comfortable silence falls between us as we dive into research, the faint hum of the laptop filling the space. The air, once thick with tension, now crackles with determination. Every piece of information we gather becomes a stepping stone, a way to dismantle the barriers that threaten our newfound peace.

Hours pass as we delve deeper into the underbelly of the Syndicate, poring over reports of their recent activities, searching for clues that could reveal their plans. I pull up a list of names connected to Derek, my heart racing at the realization that these people could be as dangerous as he is.

"Look at this," I say, pointing to a name that sends a shiver down my spine. "This guy, Viktor Marlowe, he was known for his ruthless tactics in the past. If Derek's trying to pull him into the mix, we need to tread carefully."

Cole leans closer, scanning the details. "Marlowe has a reputation for leaving destruction in his wake. If he's aligned with Derek, it's a whole new level of trouble. We need to find a way to sever that connection."

A sudden noise interrupts our focus—a soft but persistent thump against the door, breaking the stillness of our sanctuary. We exchange wary glances, the playful atmosphere shattering like glass.

"Did you order something?" Cole asks, his voice low, as if speaking too loudly might summon the source of the noise.

"Nope. Unless someone is delivering a bouquet of trouble, I think we should stay quiet." I inch closer to the door, my heart racing as I peer through the peephole. All I see is the blurry outline of a figure shifting impatiently outside.

"Who is it?" Cole whispers, rising from his chair, tension radiating from his body.

"I can't tell. But I think we should be ready for anything," I reply, moving to the side to let him take a look.

Cole glances through the peephole and goes pale. "It's not good. I think it's the last person we want to see right now."

"What do you mean?" My stomach drops as dread settles in. "Who is it?"

"Derek." His voice is barely above a whisper, but it cuts through the air like ice.

"Great," I deadpan, frustration boiling beneath my surface. "What is this, a surprise party? I didn't get the memo."

"Let's just stay quiet and see what he wants," Cole suggests, moving stealthily to the side of the door, his body tense and ready for whatever might come next.

The knocking grows more insistent, each thud resonating like a drumroll heralding something ominous. "Open up!" Derek's voice carries through the door, cool and commanding. "I know you're in there."

"What do we do?" I whisper, the urgency of the moment making my pulse quicken.

Cole's eyes flash with determination. "We're not letting him in. We need to think this through. If we can just—"

Before he can finish, the door rattles violently under the weight of Derek's relentless pounding. "I'm not leaving until we talk. I've got something you'll want to hear."

I exchange a glance with Cole, fear and defiance swirling in my chest. "We can't trust him, but we can't ignore him either."

"Let me handle this," Cole murmurs, moving to the door and gripping the knob. "Whatever he wants, we'll turn it against him."

As he hesitates for just a moment, I can see the gears in his mind turning. "Remember, he's dangerous," I say urgently. "Don't let him in, no matter what."

With a firm nod, he opens the door just a crack, peering out with a fierce expression. "What do you want, Derek?"

The sight that greets us sends my heart racing. Derek stands there, eyes glinting with a mix of annoyance and intrigue. Behind him, however, stands another figure, a tall silhouette with an unmistakable aura of danger.

"I'm here to offer you that deal I mentioned," Derek says smoothly, but it's the figure behind him that sends a jolt of recognition through me. It's Viktor Marlowe, his presence dark and foreboding, a shadow that threatens to swallow the light.

"Now, let's talk," Derek continues, his voice low and dangerous. "You really don't want to turn me down. Trust me, I come bearing gifts."

The door is only a few inches ajar, but I can feel the weight of their intentions pressing in, as suffocating as a fog creeping through the night. The air feels electric with the tension of impending choices and unspoken threats.

With every fiber of my being, I want to slam the door and shut them out, but I know that the battle has just begun. I take a step back, heart pounding, caught between the urge to flee and the instinct to stand my ground.

"Cole," I whisper urgently, as the door creaks wider, inviting chaos into our lives once more. "We need a plan—and fast."

And as Derek's smile widens, a predatory gleam in his eyes, I know this moment is only the beginning of a confrontation that could change everything.